D1310986

Praise for Geraldine Brooks and *People of the Book*

"Geraldine Brooks' novel *People of the Book* arrives with high expectations. Booksellers are comparing it to *The Da Vinci Code* and calling it the first literary hit of 2008. Does Brooks deliver? Yes, and with less flash and more substance than *Da Vinci*. . . . If Brooks becomes the new patron saint of booksellers, she deserves it. The stories of the Sarajevo Haggadah, both factual and fictional, are stirring testaments to the people of many faiths who risked all to save this priceless work." —*USA Today*

"Complex and moving." —*The New Yorker*

"In *People of the Book* [Brooks] has constructed a marvelously intertwined narrative, with one strand tied to the contemporary world and the other leading us back into European history, into wars and inquisitions and family tragedies, all of this making up a vividly narrated, powerfully emotional quest." —*The Dallas Morning News*

"[Brooks] has accomplished something remarkable, fashioning a story that is compelling and eminently readable, even as she maintains high intentions and an earnest purpose." —*The New York Sun*

"Deep into Geraldine Brooks' exhilarating new novel—a book that may well set the standard by which 2008 fiction will be measured—there's an intriguing aside about how something can captivate us and we 'fall down a rabbit hole and the rest of the world disappears.' *People of the Book,* which treats six centuries of Jewish and world experience, has that effect. . . . Brooks' novel meticulously, lovingly amalgamates mystery and history with the personal story of its heroine, rare-book expert and conservator Hanna Heath. . . . Vibrant." —*Houston Chronicle*

"Have you ever picked up a book at a used book store and had a receipt fall out, discovered a phone number scribbled on a note stuffed into the spine, or read an endearing inscription to someone who no longer valued the sentiment? Did it make you wonder about the lives of those who had palmed those pages before you? *People of the Book* capitalizes on that kind of intrigue." —*Chicago Sun-Times*

"Like her fictional heroine, Brooks demonstrates her own imaginative power by dreaming up five centuries' worth of characters, all connected to the mystery and beauty of the Sarajevo Haggadah."

—*The Atlanta Journal-Constitution*

"Remarkable . . . *People of the Book* is well researched, extremely well written, and full of surprises. It is at once literary and a page-turner. The biggest problem I had was to temper my enthusiasm. I didn't want to sound too effusive. But I can't help myself; this is simply one of the best books I've read in I don't know how long." —*Milwaukee Journal Sentinel*

"Geraldine Brooks' third novel has the same powerful appeal as her bestsellers *Year of Wonders* and the Pulitzer Prize–winning *March*. . . . *People of the Book* shows the author's gift for entering difficult, pivotal times in history with a story so psychologically intimate and sensual that we feel we're there." —*More*

"A multilayered novel that shifts across centuries and continents. . . . In *People of the Book*, Brooks tosses out the tongs, grabs onto her plot, and doesn't let go." —*TimeOut New York*

"A sprawling historical work—based on an ancient Hebrew text—that is richly imagined and at times almost unbearably exciting. . . . An ambitious book, a pleasure to read, and wholly successful in its attempt to give a sense of how miraculous, unlikely and ultimately binding the history of objects can be." —*Star Tribune* (Minneapolis)

"*People of the Book* is an ambitious effort filled with many fascinating historical details, characters, and stories, and it's capable of casting a spell for many pages at a time." —*Rocky Mountain News*

"Brooks skillfully sets the stage for everything that follows her information-packed yet highly readable opening chapter." —*Chicago Tribune*

"Dazzling new novel . . . these narratives show Brooks' writing at her very best. . . . Her gift for storytelling, happily, is timeless."

—*Publishers Weekly*

PENGUIN BOOKS

PEOPLE OF THE BOOK

Geraldine Brooks is the Pulitzer Prize–winning author of *March* and *Year of Wonders* and the nonfiction works *Nine Parts of Desire* and *Foreign Correspondence*. Previously, Brooks was a correspondent for *The Wall Street Journal* in Bosnia, Somalia, and the Middle East. Born and raised in Australia, she lives on Martha's Vineyard with her husband Tony Horwitz, their son Nathaniel, and three dogs.

Geraldine Brooks

PEOPLE

of the

BOOK

A Novel

Penguin Books

PENGUIN BOOKS

Published by the Penguin Group

Penguin Group (USA) Inc., 375 Hudson Street, New York, New York 10014, U.S.A.

Penguin Group (Canada), 90 Eglinton Avenue East, Suite 700, Toronto,
Ontario, Canada M4P 2Y3 (a division of Pearson Penguin Canada Inc.)

Penguin Books Ltd, 80 Strand, London WC2R 0RL, England

Penguin Ireland, 25 St Stephen's Green, Dublin 2, Ireland (a division of Penguin Books Ltd)

Penguin Group (Australia), 250 Camberwell Road, Camberwell,
Victoria 3124, Australia (a division of Pearson Australia Group Pty Ltd)

Penguin Books India Pvt Ltd, 11 Community Centre, Panchsheel Park, New Delhi – 110 017, India

Penguin Group (NZ), 67 Apollo Drive, Rosedale, North Shore 0632,
New Zealand (a division of Pearson New Zealand Ltd)

Penguin Books (South Africa) (Pty) Ltd, 24 Sturdee Avenue,
Rosebank, Johannesburg 2196, South Africa

Penguin Books Ltd, Registered Offices:
80 Strand, London WC2R 0RL, England

First published in the United States of America by Viking Penguin,
a member of Penguin Group (USA) Inc. 2008
Published in Penguin Books 2008

19   20

PUBLISHER'S NOTE

This is a fictional work inspired by real events. While some of the facts are true to the history
of the Hebrew codex known as the Sarajevo Haggadah, most of the plot and all of the characters
are fictitious. The known facts relating to the haggadah are related in the Afterword.

ISBN 978-0-670-01821-5 (hc.)
ISBN 978-0-14-311500-7 (pbk.)
CIP data available

Printed in the United States of America
Set in Dante
Designed by Francesca Belanger
Map and decorative art by Laura Hartman Maestro
Hebrew calligraphy on page 221 generously provided by Jay S. Greenspan

For the librarians

There, where one burns books,
one in the end burns men.

—Heinrich Heine

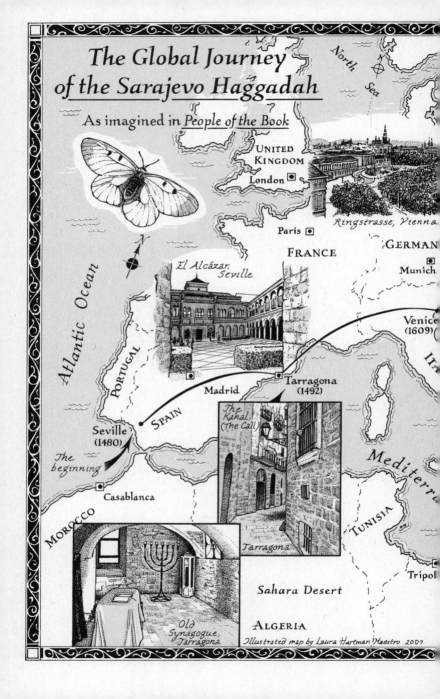

The Global Journey of the Sarajevo Haggadah

As imagined in *People of the Book*

North Sea

UNITED KINGDOM

London

Ringstrasse, Vienna

Paris

FRANCE

GERMAN

Munich

El Alcázar, Seville

Atlantic Ocean

Venice (1609)

ITA

PORTUGAL

Madrid

Tarragona (1492)

SPAIN

The Kahal, (The Call)

Seville (1480)

The beginning

Casablanca

Mediterr

MOROCCO

Tarragona

TUNISIA

Old Synagogue, Tarragona

Sahara Desert

Tripol

ALGERIA

Illustrated map by Laura Hartman Maestro 2007

Hanna

Sarajevo, Spring 1996

I

I MIGHT AS WELL SAY, right from the jump: it wasn't my usual kind of job.

I like to work alone, in my own clean, silent, well-lit laboratory, where the climate is controlled and everything I need is right at hand. It's true that I have developed a reputation as someone who can work effectively out of the lab, when I have to, when the museums don't want to pay the travel insurance on a piece, or when private collectors don't want anyone to know exactly what it is that they own. It's also true that I've flown halfway around the world, to do an interesting job. But never to a place like this: the boardroom of a bank in the middle of a city where they just stopped shooting at each other five minutes ago.

For one thing, there are no guards hovering over me at my lab at home. I mean, the museum has a few quiet security professionals cruising around, but none of them would ever dream of intruding on my work space. Not like the crew here. Six of them. Two were bank security guards, two were Bosnian police, here to keep an eye on the bank security, and the other two were United Nations peacekeepers, here to keep an eye on the Bosnian police. All having loud conversations in Bosnian or Danish over their crackly radio handsets. As if that wasn't enough of a crowd, there was also the official UN observer, Hamish Sajjan. My first Scottish Sikh, very dapper in Harris tweed and an indigo turban. Only in the UN. I'd had to ask him to point out to the Bosnians that smoking wasn't going to be happening in a room that would shortly contain a fifteenth-century manuscript. Since then, they'd been even more fidgety.

I was starting to get fidgety myself. We'd been waiting for almost two hours. I'd filled the time as best I could. The guards had helped me reposition the big conference table nearer to the window, to take advantage of the light. I'd assembled the stereo microscope and laid out my tools: documentation cameras, probes, and scalpels. The beaker of gelatin was softening on its warming pad, and the wheat paste, linen threads, gold leaf were laid out ready, along with some glassine envelopes in case I was lucky enough to find any debris in the binding—it's amazing what you can learn about a book by studying the chemistry of a bread crumb. There were samples of various calfskins, rolls of handmade papers in different tones and textures, and foam forms positioned in a cradle, ready to receive the book. If they ever brought the book.

"Any idea how much longer we're going to have to wait?" I asked Sajjan. He shrugged.

"I think there is a delay with the representative from the National Museum. Since the book is the property of the museum, the bank cannot remove it from the vault unless he is present."

Restless, I walked to the windows. We were on the top floor of the bank, an Austro-Hungarian wedding cake of a building whose stuccoed facade was speckled with mortar pockmarks just like every other structure in the city. When I put my hand on the glass, the cold seeped through. It was supposed to be spring; down in the small garden by the bank's entrance, the crocuses were blooming. But it had snowed earlier that morning, and the bowl of each small flower brimmed with a foam of snowflakes, like tiny cups of cappuccino. At least the snow made the light in the room even and bright. Perfect working light, if only I could get to work.

Simply to be doing something, I unrolled some of my papers— French-milled linen. I ran a metal ruler over each sheet, working it flat. The sound of the metal edge traveling across the large sheet was like the sound of the surf I can hear from my flat at home in Sydney.

I noticed that my hands were shaking. Not a good thing in my line of work.

My hands are not what you'd call one of my better features. Chapped, wattled across the back, they don't look like they belong on my wrists, which I am happy to report are slender and smooth like the rest of me. Charwoman's hands, my mother called them, the last time we argued. After that, when I had to meet her at the Cosmopolitan for coffee—brief, correct, the pair of us brittle as icicles—I wore a pair of gloves from the Salvos as a sort of piss-take. Of course, the Cosmopolitan is probably the only place in Sydney where someone might miss the irony in that gesture. My mother did. She said something about getting me a hat to match.

In the bright snow light, my hands looked even worse than usual, all ruddy and peeling from scouring the fat off cow gut with a pumice stone. When you live in Sydney, it's not the simplest thing in the world to get a meter of calf's intestine. Ever since they moved the abattoir out of Homebush and started to spruce the place up for the 2000 Olympics, you have to drive, basically, to woop woop, and then when you finally get there, there's so much security in place because of the animal libbers you can barely get in the gate. It's not that I blame them for thinking I was a bit sketchy. It's hard to grasp right off the bat why someone might *need* a meter of calf's appendix. But if you are going to work with five-hundred-year-old materials, you have to know how they were made five hundred years ago. That's what my teacher, Werner Heinrich, believed. He said you could read about grinding pigments and mixing gesso all you like, but the only way to understand is to actually do it. If I wanted to know what words like *cutch* and *schoder* really described, I had to make gold leaf myself: beat it and fold it and beat it again, on something it won't stick to, like the soft ground of scoured calf intestine. Eventually, you'll have a little packet of leaves each less than a thousandth of a millimeter thick. And you'll also have horrible-looking hands.

I made a fist, trying to smooth out the old-lady wattle skin. Also to see if I could stop the trembling. I'd been nervous ever since I changed planes in Vienna the day before. I travel a lot; you basically have to, if you live in Australia and want a piece of the most interesting projects in my field, which is the conservation of medieval manuscripts. But I don't generally go to places that are datelines in war correspondents' dispatches. I know there are people who go in for that sort of thing and write great books about it, and I suppose they have some kind of "It can't happen to me" optimism that makes it possible for them. Me, I'm a complete pessimist. If there's a sniper somewhere in the country I'm visiting, I fully expect to be the one in his crosshairs.

Even before the plane landed, you could see the war. As we broke through the gray swag of cloud that seems to be the permanent condition of the European sky, the little russet-tiled houses hugging the Adriatic looked familiar at first, just like the view I'm used to, down over the red rooftops of Sydney to the deep blue arc of Bondi Beach. But in this view, half the houses weren't there anymore. They were just jagged bits of masonry, sticking up in ragged rows like rotting teeth.

There was turbulence as we went over the mountains. I couldn't bring myself to look as we crossed into Bosnia so I pulled down the window shade. The young bloke next to me—aid worker, I guessed, from the Cambodian scarf and the gaunt malarial look of him—obviously wanted to look out, but I ignored his body language and tried to distract him with a question.

"So, what brings you here?"

"Mine clearance."

I was tempted to say something really borderline like, "Business booming?" but managed, uncharacteristically, to restrain myself. And then we landed, and he was up, with every single other person in the plane, jostling in the aisle, ferreting around in the overhead bins. He shouldered an immense rucksack and then proceeded to almost break the nose of the man crowding the aisle behind him. The lethal backpacker ninety-degree turn. You see it on the bus at Bondi all the time.

The cabin door finally opened, and the passengers oozed forward as if they were glued together. I was the only one still seated. I felt as if I'd swallowed a stone that was pinning me to my spot.

"Dr. Heath?" The flight attendant was hovering in the emptied aisle.

I was about to say, "No, that's my mother," when I realized she meant me. In Australia only prats flaunt their PhDs. I certainly hadn't checked in as anything other than Ms.

"Your United Nations escort is waiting on the tarmac." That explained it. I'd already noticed, in the run-up to accepting this gig, that the UN liked to give everyone the flashiest possible handle.

"Escort?" I repeated stupidly. "Tarmac?" They'd said I'd be met, but I thought that meant a bored taxi driver holding a sign with my name misspelled. The flight attendant gave me one of those big, perfect, German smiles. She leaned across me and flung up the drawn shade. I looked out. Three huge, armor-plated, tinted-window vans, the kind they drive the American president around in, stood idling by the plane's wingtip. What should have been a reassuring sight only made the stone in my gut a ton heavier. Beyond them, in long grass posted with mine-warning signs in various languages, I could see the rusting hulk of a huge cargo plane that must have missed the runway during some earlier unpleasantness. I looked back at Fräulein Smiley-Face.

"I thought the cease-fire was being observed," I said.

"It is," she said brightly. "Most days. Do you need any assistance with your hand luggage?"

I shook my head, and bent to tug out the heavy case wedged tightly under the seat in front of me. Generally, airlines don't like collections of sharp metal things on board, but the Germans are great respecters of trades, and the check-in clerk understood when I explained how I hate to check my tools in case they end up touring Europe without me while I sit on my rear end unable to do my work.

I love my work. That's the thing. That's why, despite being a world-class coward, I agreed to take this job. To be honest, it never occurred to me not to take it. You don't say no to the chance to work on one of the rarest and most mysterious volumes in the world.

The call had come at 2:00 a.m., as so many calls do when you live in Sydney. It drives me spare sometimes, the way the smartest people—museum directors who run internationally renowned institutions or CEOs who can tell you to the cent what the Hang Seng was at on any given day—can't retain the simple fact that Sydney is generally nine hours ahead of London and fourteen hours ahead of New York. Amitai Yomtov is a brilliant man. Probably the most brilliant in the field. But could he figure the time difference between Jerusalem and Sydney?

"Shalom, Channa," he said, his thick sabra accent putting a guttural *ch* sound into my name as usual. "I'm not waking you?"

"No, Amitai," I said. "I'm always up at two a.m.; best part of the day."

"Ah, well, sorry, but I think you might be interested to know that the Sarajevo Haggadah has turned up."

"No!" I said, suddenly wide awake. "That's, um, great news." And it was, but it was great news I could easily have read in an e-mail at a civilized hour. I couldn't imagine why Amitai had felt it necessary to call me.

Amitai, like most sabras, was a pretty contained character, but this news had made him ebullient. "I always knew that book was a survivor. I knew it would outlast the bombs."

The Sarajevo Haggadah, created in medieval Spain, was a famous rarity, a lavishly illuminated Hebrew manuscript made at a time when Jewish belief was firmly against illustrations of any kind. It was thought that the commandment in Exodus "Thou shalt not make unto thee any graven image or likeness of any thing" had suppressed figurative art by medieval Jews. When the book came to light in Sarajevo in 1894, its pages of painted miniatures had turned this idea on its head and caused art history texts to be rewritten.

At the beginning of the Sarajevo siege in 1992, when the museums and libraries became targets in the fighting, the codex had gone missing. The Bosnian Muslim government had sold it to buy arms, one rumor said. No, Mossad agents had smuggled it out through a tunnel under the Sarajevo airport. I never believed either scenario. I thought that the beautiful book had probably been part of the blizzard of burning pages—Ottoman land deeds, ancient Korans, Slavic scrolls—that had fallen in a warm snow upon the city after the flames of phosphorous bombs.

"But, Amitai, where's it been the past four years? How did it turn up?"

"You know it's Pesach, right?"

As a matter of fact I did; I was still nursing the ragged end of a red wine hangover from the raucous and highly unorthodox Passover picnic that one of my mates had hosted on the beach. The name for the ritual meal in Hebrew is *seder,* which means order; this had been one of the more *dis*orderly nights in my recent history.

"Well, last night the Jewish community in Sarajevo had their seder, and in the middle of it—very dramatic—they brought out the haggadah. The head of the community made a speech saying that the survival of the book was a symbol of the survival of Sarajevo's multiethnic ideal. And do you know who saved it? His name is Ozren Karaman, head of the museum library. Went in under intense shelling." Amitai's voice suddenly seemed a bit husky. "Can you imagine, Channa? A Muslim, risking his neck to save a Jewish book."

It wasn't like Amitai to be impressed by tales of derring-do. An indiscreet colleague had once let drop that Amitai's compulsory army service had been in a commando squad so supersecret that Israelis refer to it only as "the unit." Even though that was long in his past when I first met him, I'd been struck by his physique, and by his manner. He had the dense muscle of a weight lifter and a kind of hypervigilance. He'd look right at you when he was talking to you, but the rest of the time his eyes seemed to be scanning the surroundings, aware of everything. He'd seemed genuinely pissed off when

I'd asked him about the unit. "I never confirmed this to you," he'd snapped. But I thought it was pretty amazing. You certainly don't meet that many ex-commandos in book conservation.

"So what did this old bloke do with the book once he had it?" I asked.

"He put it in a safe-deposit box in the vault of the central bank. You can imagine what that's done to the parchment. . . . No one in Sarajevo's had any heat through at least the last two winters . . . and some metal cash box . . . metal, of all things . . . it's back there now. . . . I can't bear to think about it. Anyway, the UN wants some-one to inspect its condition. They're going to pay for any necessary stabilization work—they want to exhibit it as soon as possible, to raise the city's morale, you know. So I saw your name on the pro-gram for next month's conference at the Tate, and I thought that, while you are coming to this side of the world, maybe you could fit this job in?"

"Me?" My voice actually squeaked. I don't go in for false modesty: I'm great at what I do. But for a job like this, a once-in-a-lifetime ca-reer maker, there were at least a dozen people with more years on the clock and better connections in Europe. "Why not you?" I asked.

Amitai knew more about the Sarajevo Haggadah than anybody alive; he'd written monographs on it. I knew he would have loved this chance to handle the actual codex. He gave a deep sigh. "The Serbs have spent the past three years insisting that the Bosnians are fanatical Muslims, and finally, maybe, a few Bosnians have started to believe them. Seems the Saudis are big donors there now, and there was opposition to giving the job to an Israeli."

"Oh, Amitai, I'm sorry. . . ."

"It's all right, Channa. I'm in good company. They didn't want a German either. Of course, I suggested Werner first—no offense. . . ." Since Herr Doktor Doktor Werner Maria Heinrich was not only my teacher, but also, after Amitai himself, the leading Hebrew manu-scripts specialist in the world, I was hardly likely to take any. But

Amitai explained that the Bosnians were still carrying a grudge against Germany for setting off the war in the first place, by recognizing Slovenia and Croatia. "And the UN doesn't want an American because the U.S. Congress is always bad-mouthing UNESCO. So I thought you would be good, because who has any strong opinions about Australians? Also I told them that your technical skills are not bad."

"Thanks for that ringing endorsement," I said. And then, more sincerely, "Amitai, I'll never forget this. Thank you, really."

"You can repay me by making good documentation of the book, so at least we can print a beautiful facsimile. You'll send me the pictures you make, yes, and a draft of your report, as soon as you can?"

His voice sounded so wistful I felt guilty about my own elation. But there was one question I had to ask him.

"Amitai, are there any issues of authenticity? You know the rumors, during the war . . ."

"No, we have no concerns there. The librarian Karaman and his ~~d~~ess, the director of the museum, have authenticated it beyond ~~doub~~ Your job is merely technical at this point."

~~Te~~chnical. We'll see about that, I thought to myself. A lot of what ~~I do i~~s technical; science and craftsmanship that anyone with decent intelligence and good fine-motor skills can be taught to do. But there is something else, too. It has to do with an intuition about the past. By linking research and imagination, sometimes I can think myself into the heads of the people who made the book. I can figure out who they were, or how they worked. That's how I add my few grains to the sandbox of human knowledge. It's what I love best about what I do. And there were so many questions about the Sarajevo Haggadah. If I could answer just one of them . . .

I couldn't get back to sleep, so I threw on my sweats and went out, through the nighttime streets still faintly sour with the mingled stink of spewed beer and deep-fryer fat, down to the beach, where the air blows, clean and briny, over half a planet's worth of uninterrupted ocean. Because it was autumn, and a midweek night, there was hardly anyone around. Just a few drunks, slumped by the wall of the surf club, and a pair of lovers, entwined on a beach towel. No one to notice me. I started walking along the edge of the foam, luminous against the lacquered darkness of the sand. Before I knew it, I was running and skipping, dodging the breakers like a child.

That was a week ago. In the days following, that feeling of exhilaration had been gradually buried under visa applications, reissued airline tickets, UN red tape, and a thick dollop of nerves. As I staggered down the stairs from the plane to the tarmac under the weight of my case, I had to keep reminding myself that this was exactly the kind of assignment I lived for.

I had barely a second to take in the mountains, rising all around us like the rim of a giant bowl, and then a blue-helmeted soldier— tall and Scandinavian-looking—leaped from the middle vehicle and seized my bag, hurling it into the rear of the van.

"Steady!" I said. "There's delicate equipment in there!" The soldier's only reply was to grab me by the arm and propel me into the backseat, slamming the door and jumping in front alongside the driver. The automatic locks clicked down with a definitive *thunk* the driver gunned the engine.

"Well, this is a first for me," I said, trying for some wan levity. "Book conservators don't usually have much call to travel in armored cars." There was no response from the soldier or the thin, drawn civilian hunched over the wheel of the immense vehicle, his head pulled into his shoulders like a tortoise. Through the tinted glass the devastated city passed in a blur of shrapnel-splashed buildings. The vans drove fast, swerving around cavernous potholes made by mortar shells and bumping over bitumen shredded by the tracks of armored vehicles. There wasn't much traffic. Most people were on foot; gaunt, exhausted-looking people, coats pulled tight against the chill of a spring that hadn't quite arrived. We passed an apartment block that looked like the dollhouse I'd had as a girl, where the entire front wall lifted off to reveal the rooms within. In this block, the wall had been peeled away by an explosion. But like my dollhouse, the exposed rooms were furnished. As we sped by, I realized that people were somehow still living there, their only protection a few sheets of plastic billowing in the wind. But they'd done their laundry. It flapped from lines strung between the twisted spikes of reinforcing bars that protruded from the shattered concrete.

I thought they'd take me straight to see the book. Instead, the day was consumed by endless, tedious meetings, first with every UN official who'd ever had a thought about a cultural matter, then with the director of the Bosnian museum, then with a bunch of government officials. I doubt I'd have gotten much sleep anyway, given the anticipation of starting work, but the dozen or so cups of strong Turkish coffee I'd been served in the course of the day hadn't helped. Maybe that's why my hands were still shaking.

There was a burst of static from the police radios. Suddenly all the people were up on their feet: the police, the guards, Sajjan. The bank official shot the door bolts and a whole lot more guards entered in a sort of flying wedge. At the center was a thin young man in faded blue jeans. The slacker from the museum, probably, who'd kept us all waiting. But I didn't have time to be irritated with him, because he was cradling a metal box. When he set it down on the bench I saw it was sealed in several places with stamped wax and adhesive papers. I passed him my scalpel. He broke the seals and eased open the lid. He unwrapped several sheets of silk paper. And then he handed me the book.

II

As many times as I've worked on rare, beautiful things, that first touch is always a strange and powerful sensation. It's a combination between brushing a live wire and stroking the back of a newborn baby's head.

No conservator had handled this manuscript for a century. I had the forms positioned, ready. I hesitated for just a second—a Hebrew book, therefore spine to the right—and laid it in the cradling foam.

Until you opened it, the book was nothing that an untrained eye would look twice at. It was small, for one thing, convenient for use at the Passover dinner table. Its binding was of an ordinary nineteenth-century style, soiled and scuffed. A codex as gorgeously illustrated as this one would originally have had an elaborate binding. You don't make filet mignon then serve it on a paper plate. The binder might have used gold leaf or silver tooling, maybe inlays of ivory or pearl shell. But this book had probably been rebound many times in its long life. The only one we knew about for sure, because it had been documented, was the last time, in Vienna in the 1890s. Unfortunately, the book had been terribly mishandled in that instance. The Austrian binder had cropped the parchment heavily and discarded the old binding—something no one, especially not a professional working for a major museum—would ever do anymore. It was impossible to say what information might have been lost at that time. He had re-bound the parchments in simple cardboard covers with an inappro-priate Turkish printed floral paper decoration, now faded and discolored. Only the corners and spine were calfskin, and this was dark brown and flaking away, exposing the edge of the gray board beneath.

I ran my middle finger lightly along the cracked corners. These I would consolidate over the coming days. As my finger followed the edges of the board, I noticed something unexpected. The binder had made a pair of channels and a set of small holes in the board edge to accept a pair of clasps. It was usual for books of parchment to have clasps, to hold the pages flat. Yet there were no clasps on this binding. I made a note to myself to investigate this.

Moving the forms to support the spine, I opened the cover and leaned close to examine the torn endpapers. I would mend these with wheat paste and shreds of matching linen paper. I could see at once that the linen cords the Viennese binder had used were frayed, barely holding. That meant I would have to take the quires apart and restitch them. Then I breathed deeply and turned the page to the parchment of the manuscript itself. This was what mattered; this was what would disclose what four hard years had done to a survivor of five centuries.

The snow light flared on brightness. Blue: intense as a midsummer sky, obtained from grinding precious lapis lazuli carried by camel caravan all the way from the mountains of Afghanistan. White: pure, creamy, opaque. Less glamorous, more complicated than the blue. At that time it would still have been made according to the method discovered by ancient Egyptians. You cover lead bars with the dregs of old wine and seal them up in a shed full of animal dung. I'd done it once, in my mother's greenhouse in Bellevue Hill. She'd had a load of manure delivered, and I couldn't resist. The acid in the vinegary wine converts lead to its acetate, which in turn combines with the carbon dioxide released by the dung to make basic white lead carbonate, $PbCO_3$. My mother pitched a fit about it, of course. Said she couldn't stand to go near her bloody prize orchids for weeks.

I turned a page. More dazzle. The illuminations were beautiful, but I didn't allow myself to look at them as art. Not yet. First I had to understand them as chemicals. There was yellow, made of saffron. That beautiful autumn flower, *Crocus sativus Linnaeus,* each with just three tiny precious stigmas, had been a prized luxury then and remained one, still. Even if we now know that the rich color comes from a carotene, crocin, with a molecular structure of 44 carbon, 64 hydrogen, and 24 oxygen, we still haven't synthesized a substitute as complex and as beautiful. There was malachite green, and red; the intense red known as worm scarlet—*tola'at shani* in Hebrew— extracted from tree-dwelling insects, crushed up and boiled in lye. Later, when alchemists learned how to make a similar red from sulfur and mercury, they still named the color "little worm"—*vermiculum.* Some things don't change: we call it vermilion even today.

Change. That's the enemy. Books do best when temperature, humidity, the whole environment, stay the same. You could hardly get more dramatic changes than this book had been through: moved under extreme difficulties and without preparation or precaution, exposed to wild swings of temperature. I'd been worried that the parchment might have shrunk, the pigments cracked and lifted. But the colors had held fast, as pure and as vivid as the day the paint was applied. Unlike the leaf on the spine, which had flaked away, the burnished gold of the illuminations was fresh and blazing. The gilder of five hundred years ago had definitely had a better grasp of his trade than the more modern Viennese bookbinder. There was silver leaf also. This had oxidized and turned dark gray, as you would expect.

"Will you be replacing that?" It was the thin young man from the museum. He was pointing at a distinct area of tarnish. He was standing too close. Because parchment is flesh, human bacteria can degrade it. I moved my shoulder so that he had to withdraw his hand and take a step backward.

"No," I said. "Absolutely not." I did not look up.

"But you're a restorer; I thought . . ."

"Conservator," I corrected. The last thing I wanted right then was a long discussion on the philosophy of book conservation. "Look," I said, "you're here; I'm instructed that you have to be here, but I'd appreciate it if you didn't interrupt my work."

"I understand," he said, his voice gentle after my abrasiveness. "But you must also understand: I am the *kustos,* the book is in my care."

Kustos. It took a minute to sink in. I turned then, and stared at him. "*You* can't be Ozren Karaman? The one who saved the book?"

The UN rep, Sajjan, sprang up, all apologies. "I am sorry, I should have made the introduction. But you were so anxious to get to work. I— Dr. Hanna Heath, please may I present Dr. Ozren Karaman, chief librarian of the National Museum and professor of librarianship at the National University of Bosnia."

"I— Sorry, that was rude of me," I said. "I expected that you'd be much older, to be chief curator of such a major collection." I also didn't expect a person in that position to look quite so disheveled. He was wearing a scuffed leather jacket over a crumpled white T-shirt.

His jeans were frayed. His hair—wild, curly, neither combed nor cut—flopped over a pair of glasses that were mended in the middle with a bit of duct tape.

He raised an eyebrow. "You yourself, of course, being so very advanced in years, would have every reason to think that." He kept a perfectly straight face as he said this. I guessed he was about thirty, like me. "But I would be very pleased, Dr. Heath, if you could spare a moment to say what you have in mind to do." He shot Sajjan a glance as he said this, and in it I could read a volume. The UN thought it was doing Bosnia a favor, funding the work so that the haggadah could be properly displayed. But when it comes to national treasures, no one wants outsiders calling the shots. Ozren Karaman clearly felt he'd been sidelined. The last thing I wanted was to get involved in any of that. I was here to care for a book, not some librarian's bruised ego. Still, he had a right to know why the UN had chosen someone like me.

"I can't say exactly the extent of my work till I've thoroughly inspected the manuscript, but here's the thing: no one hires me looking for chemical cleanups or heavy restorations. I've written too many papers knocking that approach. To restore a book to the way it was when it was made is to lack respect for its history. I think you have to accept a book as you receive it from past generations, and to a certain extent damage and wear reflect that history. The way I see it, my job is to make it stable enough to allow safe handling and study, repairing only where absolutely necessary. This, here," I said, pointing to a page where a russet stain bloomed over the fiery Hebrew calligraphy, "I can take a microscopic sample of those fibers, and we can analyze them, and maybe learn what made that stain— wine would be my first guess. But a full analysis might provide clues as to where the book was at the time it happened. And if we can't tell now, then in fifty, a hundred years, when lab techniques have advanced, my counterpart in the future will be able to. But if I chemically erased that stain—that so-called damage—we'd lose the chance at that knowledge forever." I took a deep breath.

Ozren Karaman was looking at me with a bemused expression. I suddenly felt embarrassed. "Sorry, you know all that, of course. But it's a bit of an obsession with me, and once I get started . . ." I was only digging a deeper hole, so I stopped. "The thing is, they've given me only a week's access to the book, so I really need every minute. I'd like to get started. . . . I'll have it till six this evening, yes?"

"No, not quite. I'll need to take it about ten minutes before the hour, to get it secured before the bank guards change shifts."

"All right," I said, drawing my chair in close. I inclined my head to the other end of the long table where the security detachment sat. "Any chance we could get rid of a few of them?"

He shook his uncombed head. "I'm afraid we'll all be staying."

I couldn't help the sigh that escaped me. My work has to do with objects, not people. I like matter, fiber, the nature of the varied stuffs that go to make a book. I know the flesh and fabrics of pages, the bright earths and lethal toxins of ancient pigments. Wheat paste—I can bore the pants off anyone about wheat paste. I spent six months in Japan, learning how to mix it for just the necessary amount of tension.

Parchment, especially, I love. So durable it can last for centuries, so fragile it can be destroyed in a careless instant. One of the reasons, I'm sure, that I got this job was because I have written so many journal articles on parchment. I could tell, just from the size and scatter of the pore holes, that the parchments in front of me had been made from the skin of a now-extinct breed of thick-haired Spanish mountain sheep. You can date manuscripts from the kingdoms of Aragon and Castile to within a hundred years or so if you know when that particular breed was all the go with the local parchment makers.

Parchment is leather, essentially, but it looks and feels different because the dermal fibers in the skin have been reorganized by stretching. Wet it, and the fibers revert to their original, three-dimensional network. I had worried about condensation within the metal box, or exposure to the elements during transport. But there was very little sign of either. There were some pages that showed signs of older water damage, but under the microscope I saw a rime of cube-shaped crystals that I recognized: NaCl, also known as plain old table salt. The water that had damaged this book was probably the saltwater used at the seder table to represent the tears of the slaves in Egypt.

Of course, a book is more than the sum of its materials. It is an artifact of the human mind and hand. The gold beaters, the stone grinders, the scribes, the binders, those are the people I feel most comfortable with. Sometimes, in the quiet, these people speak to me. They let me see what their intentions were, and it helps me do my work. I worried that the *kustos,* with his well-meaning scrutiny, or the cops, with the low chatter of their radios, would keep my friendly ghosts at bay. And I needed their help. There were so many questions.

For a start, most books like this, rich in such expensive pigments, had been made for palaces or cathedrals. But a haggadah is used only at home. The word is from the Hebrew root *ngd,* "to tell," and it comes from the biblical command that instructs parents to tell their children the story of the Exodus. This "telling" varies widely, and over the centuries each Jewish community has developed its own variations on this home-based celebration.

But no one knew why this haggadah was illustrated with numerous miniature paintings, at a time when most Jews considered figurative art a violation of the commandments. It was unlikely that a Jew would have been in a position to learn the skilled painting techniques evinced here. The style was not unlike the work of Christian illuminators. And yet, most of the miniatures illustrated biblical scenes as interpreted in the Midrash, or Jewish biblical exegesis.

I turned the parchment and suddenly found myself gazing at the illustration that had provoked more scholarly speculation than all the others. It was a domestic scene. A family of Jews—Spanish, by their dress—sits at a Passover meal. We see the ritual foods, the matzoh to commemorate the unleavened bread that the Hebrews baked in haste on the night before they fled Egypt, a shank bone to remember the lamb's blood on the doorposts that had caused the angel of death to "pass over" Jewish homes. The father, reclining as per custom, to show that he is a free man and not a slave, sips wine from a golden goblet as his small son, beside him, raises a cup. The mother sits serenely in the fine gown and jeweled headdress of the day. Probably the scene is a portrait of the family who commissioned this particular haggadah. But there is another woman at the table, ebony-skinned and saffron-robed, holding a piece of matzoh. Too finely dressed to be a servant, and fully participating in the Jewish rite, the identity of that African woman in saffron has perplexed the book's scholars for a century.

Slowly, deliberately, I examined and made notes on the condition of each page. Each time I turned a parchment, I checked and adjusted the position of the supporting forms. Never stress the book—the conservator's chief commandment. But the people who had owned this book had known unbearable stress: pogrom, Inquisition, exile, genocide, war.

As I reached the end of the Hebrew text, I came to a line of script in another language, another hand. *Revisto per mi. Gio. Domenico Vistorini, 1609.* The Latin, written in the Venetian style, translated as "Surveyed by me." Were it not for those three words, placed there by an official censor of the pope's Inquisition, this book might have been destroyed that year in Venice, and would never have crossed the Adriatic to the Balkans.

"Why did you save it, Giovanni?"

I looked up, frowning. It was Dr. Karaman, the librarian. He gave a tiny, apologetic shrug. Probably he thought I was irritated at the interruption, but actually I was surprised that he had voiced the very question in my mind. No one knew the answer; any more than they knew how or why—or even when—the book had come to this city. A bill of sale from 1894 stated that someone named Kohen had sold it to the library. But no one had thought to question the seller. And since World War II, when two-thirds of the Jews in Sarajevo were slaughtered and the city's Jewish quarter ransacked, there had been no Kohens left in the city to ask. A Muslim librarian had saved the book from the Nazis then, too, but the details of how he'd done it were sparse and conflicting.

When I had completed the notes on my initial examination, I set up an eight-by-ten camera and worked through again from the beginning, photographing every page so as to make an accurate record of the book's condition before any conservation work was attempted. When I was done with the conservation work and before I re-bound the pages, I would photograph each page again. I would send the negatives to Amitai in Jerusalem. He would direct the making of a set of high-grade prints for the world's museums and the printing of a facsimile edition that ordinary people everywhere would be able to enjoy. Normally, a specialist would do those photos, but the UN didn't want to jump through the hoops of finding another expert that passed muster with all the city's constituencies, so I'd agreed to do it.

I flexed my shoulders and reached for my scalpel. Then I sat, my chin resting on one hand, the other poised over the binding. Always a moment of self-doubt, at the instant before you begin. The light glinted on the bright steel, and made me think of my mother. If she hesitated like this, the patient would bleed out on the table. But my mother, the first woman to chair a department of neurosurgery in the history of Australia, was a stranger to self-doubt. She hadn't doubted her right to flout every convention of her era, bearing a child without troubling to take a husband, or even naming a father. To this day, I have no idea who he was. Someone she loved? Someone she used? The latter, more likely. She thought she was going to raise me in her own image. What a joke. She's fair and perpetually tennis-tanned; I'm dark and pale as a Goth. She has champagne tastes. I prefer beer straight out of the tinnie.

I realized a long time ago that she would never respect me for choosing to be a repairer of books rather than bodies. For her, my double-honors degrees in chemistry and ancient Near Eastern languages might as well have been used Kleenex. A masters in chemistry and a PhD in fine art conservation didn't cut it, either.

"Kindergarten work," she calls it, my papers and pigments and pastes. "You'd be through your internship by now," she said when I got back from Japan. "At your age I was chief resident" was all I got when I came home from Harvard.

Sometimes, I feel like a figure in one of the Persian miniatures I conserve, a tiny person forever watched by immobile faces, staring down from high galleries or spying from behind lattice screens. But in my case, the faces are always just that one face, my mother's, with her pursed mouth and disapproving glare.

And here I am, thirty years old, and still she can get between me and my work. That feeling, of her impatient, disapproving scrutiny, finally stirred me. I slipped the scalpel under the thread, and the codex eased apart into its precious folios. I lifted the first one. A tiny speck of something fluttered from the binding. Carefully, with a sable brush, I moved it onto a slide and passed it under the microscope. Eureka. It was a tiny fragment of insect wing, translucent, veined. We live in a world of arthropods, and maybe the wing came from a common insect and wouldn't tell us anything. But maybe it was a rarity, with a limited geographic range. Or maybe it was from a species now extinct. Either would add knowledge to the history of the book. I placed it in a glassine envelope and labeled it with a note of its position.

A few years ago, a tiny sliver of quill paring I'd found in a binding had caused a complete uproar. The work was a very beautiful little set of suffrages, short prayers to individual saints, supposedly part of a lost Book of Hours. It was owned by an influential French collector who had charmed the Getty into considering paying an absolute fortune for it. The collector had provenance documents going way back, attributing it to the Bedford Master who had painted in Paris around 1425. But something about it didn't sit just right with me.

Generally, a quill paring won't tell you much. You don't need an exotic feather to make a quill. Any good strong flight feather from any robust bird can be made into a serviceable pen. It always makes me laugh when I see actors in period movies scribbling away with flamboyant ostrich feathers. For one thing, there weren't a whole lot of ostriches marching around in medieval Europe. And for another, scribes always trimmed the feather down to something that looked pretty much like a stick, so the fluffy bits didn't get in their way while they were working. But I insisted on checking out the paring with an ornithologist, and what do you know? The paring came from a Muscovy duck feather. Muscovys are common everywhere these days, but in the 1400s they were still pretty much confined to Mexico and Brazil. They weren't introduced to Europe until the early 1600s. Turned out the French "collector" had been faking manuscripts for years.

As I gently lifted off the haggadah's second folio, I drew out the frayed thread holding it, and noticed that a fine white hair, about a centimeter long, had become trapped in the thread fiber. Checking under magnification, I could see that the hair had left a very slight indentation near the binding, on the page that depicted the Spanish family seder. Gently, with surgical tweezers, I disentangled it and placed it in its own envelope.

I needn't have worried about the people in the room being a distraction. I didn't even notice they were there. People came and went, and I didn't raise my head. It was only when the light began to fade that I realized I'd worked right through the day without a break. I suddenly felt stiff from tension, and ravenously hungry. I stood, and Karaman was immediately there, his dreadful metal box ready. I laid the book with its separated folios carefully inside.

"We absolutely have to change this right away," I said. "Metal is the worst thing for transmitting variations in heat and cold." I placed a sheet of glass on top and weighed it with little velvet sandbags to keep the parchments flat. Ozren fiddled with his wax, stamps, and strings while I cleaned and organized my tools. "How do you find our treasure?" he said, inclining his head toward the book.

"Remarkable for its age," I said. "There's no apparent recent damage from inappropriate handling. I'm going to do some tests on a few microscopic samples to see what they'll tell us. Otherwise, it's just a matter of stabilization, and repair of the binding. As you know, it's a late-nineteenth-century binding, and about as physically and mechanically tired as you'd expect."

Karaman leaned down hard on the box, pressing the library's stamp into the wax. Then he stood aside while a bank official did the same with the bank's stamp. The elaborate weave of strings and wax seals meant that any unauthorized access to the contents of the box would be instantly apparent.

"I'd heard that you are Australian," Karaman said. I suppressed a sigh. I was still transported by my day's work and not in the mood for small talk. "It seems a strange occupation for a person from such a young country, looking after other people's ancient treasures." I didn't say anything. Then he added: "I suppose you were hungry for some culture, growing up there?"

Because I had been rude before, I made an effort now. A slight effort. That young country–cultural desert stuff gets very old. Australia happens to have the longest continuous artistic tradition in the world—Aboriginal people were making sophisticated art on the walls of their dwellings thirty thousand years before the people in Lascaux chewed the end off their first paintbrush. But I decided to spare him the full lecture. "Well," I said, "you should consider that immigration has made us the most ethnically diverse country in the world. Australians' roots run very deep and wide. That gives us a stake in all the world's cultural heritage. Even yours." I didn't add that when I was growing up, the Yugoslavs were famous as the only migrant group who'd managed to import their Old World grievances. Everyone else soon succumbed to a kind of sunstruck apathy, but Serbs and Croats were forever going at it, bombing each other's soccer clubs, stoushing with each other even in end-of-the-earth outback shitholes like Coober Pedy.

He received the barb with good grace, smiling at me over the box. He had a very nice smile, I have to say. His mouth sort of turned down and up at the same time, like a Charles Schulz drawing.

The guards stood to escort Karaman and the book. I followed

down the long, ornate corridors until they descended the marble staircase to the vaults. I was waiting for someone to unlock the main doors when Karaman turned back and called after me.

"Perhaps I could invite you to dinner? I know a place in the Old City. It just reopened last month. To be quite frank and sincere, I cannot guarantee the food, but at least it will be Bosnian."

I was about to say no. It's just a reflex with me. And then I thought, why not? Better than some bland, room-service mystery meat in my bleak little hotel room. I told myself that it was legitimate research. Ozren Karaman's rescue had made him part of the history of the book, and I wanted to know more about that.

I waited for him at the top of the stairs, listening to the pneumatic swish of the vault and then the clang of the metal bars that enclosed it. The sound was final and reassuring. The book, at least, would be safe for the night.

III

WE STEPPED OUT into the dark city streets, and I shivered. Most of the snow had disappeared during the day, but now the temperature was dropping again, and heavy clouds hid the moon. There were no streetlights working. When I realized that Karaman proposed to walk to the Old City, the feeling of a stone in the gut returned.

"Are you sure that's, you know, OK? Why don't we have my UN escort drive us?"

He made a slight face, as if he smelled something unappetizing. "Those oversized tanks they drive will not fit in the narrow ways of the Baščaršija," he said. "And there has been no sniping for over a week now."

Great. Tremendous. I let him handle the argy-bargy with the UN Vikings, hoping he wouldn't be able to convince them to let me go on without an escort. Unfortunately, he was a pretty persuasive fellow—stubborn, anyway—and finally we set off on foot. He had a long-legged stride, and I had to quicken my pace to keep up with him. As we walked, he delivered a kind of countertourism monologue—a guide-from-hell kind of a thing—describing the city's various shattered structures. "That is the Presidency Building, neo-Renaissance style and the Serbs' favorite target." A few blocks farther: "That is the ruins of the Olympic Museum. That was once the post office. This is the cathedral. Neo-Gothic. They had midnight Mass there last Christmas, but they held it at noon because, of course, no one went out at night at that time unless they were suicidal. On its left you see the synagogue and the mosque. On the right the Orthodox church. All the places where none of us go to worship, situated within a very convenient hundred meters of one another."

I tried to imagine how I would feel if Sydney were suddenly scarred like this, the landmarks of my childhood damaged or destroyed. Waking up one day and finding that the people in North Sydney had set up barricades on the Harbour Bridge and started shelling the Opera House.

"I suppose it's still a bit of a luxury to walk in the city," I said, "after four years of running from snipers." He was walking a little bit ahead of me. He stopped suddenly.

"Yes," he said. "Quite." Somehow he poured a whole bucket of sarcasm into that terse reply.

The wide avenues of Austro-Hungarian Sarajevo had gradually given way to the narrow, cobbled footpaths of the Ottoman town, where you could stretch out your arms and almost touch buildings on opposite sides of the way. The buildings were small scale, as if built for halflings, and pressed together so tightly that they reminded me of tipsy friends, holding each other upright on the way home from the pub. Large parts of this area had been out of range of the Serb guns, so the damage here was much less evident than in the modern city. From a minaret, the *khoja* called the faithful to *aksham,* the evening prayer. It was a sound I associated with hot places— Cairo, Damascus—not a place where frost crunched underfoot and pockets of unmelted snow gathered in the crotch between the mosque's dome and its stone palisade. I had to remind myself that Islam had once swept north as far as the gates of Vienna; that when the haggadah had been made, the Muslims' vast empire was the bright light of the Dark Ages, the one place where science and poetry still flourished, where Jews, tortured and killed by Christians, could find a measure of peace.

The *khoja* of this small mosque was an old man, but his voice carried, unwavering and beautiful on the cold night air. Only a handful of other old men answered; shuffling across the cobbled courtyard, dutifully washing their hands and faces in the icy water of the fountain. I stopped for a moment to watch them. Karaman was ahead of me, but he turned back, and followed my gaze. "There they are," he said. "The fierce Muslim terrorists of the Serb imagination."

The restaurant he had chosen was warm and noisy and full of delicious aromas of grilling meat. A photograph by the door showed the proprietor, in military fatigues, brandishing an immense bazooka. I ordered a plate of *cevapcici*. He ordered a salad of shaved cabbage and a dish of yogurt.

"That's a bit austere," I said.

He smiled. "I've been a vegetarian since I was a child. That was useful, during the siege, since there wasn't any meat. Of course, the only greens you could get most of the time were grass clippings. Grass soup, that became my specialty." He ordered two beers. "Beer, you could get, even during the siege. The brewery was one thing in the city that never closed down."

"Aussies would approve of that," I said.

"I was thinking about what you said earlier, about the people from this country who migrated to Australia. Actually, we had quite a few Australians visiting the museum library, just before the war."

"Oh?" I said absently, sucking on my beer, which was, I have to say, a little soapy.

"Well dressed, speaking terrible Bosnian. Same peoples came

from the United States as well. We averaged about five a day, looking up their family history. At the library we gave them a nickname, after that black man in the American TV show—Kinta Kunte."

"Kunta Kinte," I corrected.

"Yes, him: we called them the Kunta Kintes because they were searching for their roots. They wanted to look at the official gazettes, 1941 to '45. Never looking for Partisans in their family tree. They didn't want to be descendants of leftists. Always it was the nationalist fanatics—Chetniks, Ustashe, the killers of the Second World War. Imagine wanting to be related to such people. I wish I'd known then that they were the storm crows. But we didn't want to believe that such madness could ever come here."

"I've always kind of admired Sarajevans for being so surprised by the war," I said. It had seemed the rational response to me. Who wouldn't be in a state of denial when your next-door neighbor suddenly starts shooting at you, casually and without remorse, like you're some kind of unwanted introduced species, the way the farmers at home eradicate rabbits.

"It's true," he said. "Years ago, we watched Lebanon fall apart and said, 'That's the Middle East, they're primitive over there.' Then we saw Dubrovnik in flames, and we said, 'We're different in Sarajevo.' That's what we all thought. How could you possibly have an ethnic war here, in this city, when every second person is the product of a mixed marriage? How to have a religious war in a city where no one ever goes to church? For me, the mosque, it's like a museum, quaint thing to do with grandparents. Picturesque, you know. Once a year, maybe, we'd go and see the *zikr,* when the dervishes dance, and it was like theater—like, what do you call it? A pantomime. My best friend, Danilo, he's a Jew, and he's not even circumcised. There was no *mohel* here after the war; you had to go to the local barber. Anyway, our parents were all leftists, they thought such things were primitive. . . ." He trailed off, downing his beer in a couple of swallows and ordering two more.

"I wanted to ask you about the day you saved the haggadah."

He grimaced and looked down at his hands, which were spread out on the speckled Laminex of the café table. His fingers were long and delicate. Funny how I hadn't noticed that earlier, when I'd been rude to him and worried he might lay an unauthorized paw on my precious parchment.

"You have to understand. It is as I was just saying. We did not believe in the war. Our leader had said, 'It takes two sides to have a war, and we will not fight.' Not here, not in our precious Sarajevo, our idealistic Olympic city. We were too intelligent, too cynical for war. Of course, you don't have to be stupid and primitive to die a stupid, primitive death. We know that now. But then, those first few days, we all did things that were a little crazy. Kids, teenagers, they went off to demonstrate against the war, with posters and music, as if they were going to a picnic. Even after the snipers shot a dozen of them, we still didn't get it. We expected that the international community would put a stop to it. I believed that. I was worried about getting through a few days, that's all, while the world—how do you say?— got its act together."

He was speaking so quietly I could barely hear him over the buzz of laughter that filled the restaurant. "I was *kustos;* the museum was being shelled. We were not prepared for it. Everything there was exposed. There were two kilometers of books in the museum, and the museum was just twenty meters from the Chetnik guns. I was thinking that one phosphorous bomb could burn the whole thing down, or that these . . . these . . . the Bosnian word *papci,* I can't translate it." He curled his hand into a fist and walked it across the table. "What do you call the foot part of an animal? A cow or a horse?"

"A hoof?" I said.

"Yes, that's it. We called the enemy 'hoofs'—something from the barnyard. I thought, if they got into the museum, they would trample the place looking for gold, and destroy things whose value they were too ignorant even to guess at. Somehow, I made my way to the police station. Most of the police had gone to defend the city as best they could. The desk officer said, 'Who wants to put his head on the block to save some old things?' But when he realized that I was going anyway, alone, he rounded up two 'volunteers' to help me. He said he couldn't have people saying that a dusty librarian has more guts than the police."

Some larger things they had moved to inner rooms. Smaller valuable items they had hidden away where looters might not look, like the janitor's supply room. Ozren's long hands fanned the air as he described the artifacts he had saved—the skeletons of Bosnia's ancient kings and queens, the rare natural history specimens. "And then I tried to find the haggadah." In the 1950s a museum staffer had been implicated in a plot to steal the haggadah, so ever since then, the museum's director was the only one who was allowed to know the combination for the safe where it was kept. But the director lived across the river, where the fighting was most intense. Ozren knew he would never make it to the museum.

Ozren continued speaking quietly, in short, undramatic sentences. No light. A fractured pipe. Rising water. Shells hitting the walls. It was left for me to fill in the blanks. I'd been in enough museum basements to imagine how it was; how every shell burst that shook the building must have sent a rain of plaster falling over the precious things, and over him, too, into his eyes as he crouched in the dark, hands shaking, striking match after match to see what he was doing. Waiting for a lull in the bombing so that he could hear the fall of the tumblers as he tried one combination and then another. Then not being able to hear anyway, because the beating of the blood in his head was so loud.

"How on earth did you ever manage to crack it?"

He raised his hands, palms up. "It was an old safe, not very sophisticated. . . ."

"But still, the odds . . ."

"I am not, as I told you, a religious man, but if I did believe in miracles . . . the fact I got to that book, in those conditions . . ."

"The miracle," I said, "was that you—"

He didn't let me finish. "Please," he interrupted, wrinkling his face with distaste. "Don't make me out to be a hero. I don't feel like one. Frankly, I feel like shit, because of all the books I couldn't save. . . ." He looked away.

I think that's what got me, that look. That reticence. Maybe because I'm the opposite of brave, I've always been a bit suspicious of heroes. I'm inclined to think they lack imagination, or there's no way they could do the madly daring things they do. But this was a guy who got choked up over lost books, and who had to be dragged through an account of what he'd done. I was starting to think I liked him quite a bit.

The food arrived then, juicy little patties of meat, peppery and thyme-scented. I was ravenous. I fell on the plate, scooping up the meat with rounds of hot, soft Turkish bread. I was so intent on the food that it took me a while to realize that Ozren wasn't eating, just staring at me. He had green eyes, a deep, mossy green, flecked with glints of copper and bronze.

"I'm sorry," I said. "I shouldn't have asked you about all that. I've put you off your food."

He grinned—that attractive, crooked grin. "It's not that."

"What's up, then?"

"Well, when I watched you working today, your face was so still and serene, you reminded me of a Madonna in the icons of the Orthodox. It's just quite amusing to me, a heavenly face with such an earthy appetite."

I can't bear that I still blush like a schoolgirl. I could feel the blood rising, so I tried to pretend that no compliment was intended. "And that's one way of pointing out that I eat like a pig," I said with a laugh.

He reached over then and wiped a smear of grease off my cheek. I stopped laughing. I reached for his hand before he could withdraw it, and turned it over in my own. It was a scholar's hand, to be sure, with clean, well-kept nails. But there were calluses as well. I suppose even scholars had to chop wood, if they could find any, during the siege. The tips of his fingers glistened with the lamb grease from my cheek. I brought them to my lips and licked them, slowly, one by one. His green eyes regarded me, asking a question anyone could understand.

His apartment was close by, an attic above a pastry shop on a crossroads called Sweet Corner. The door to the shop was steamy, and a wall of warmth hit us as we entered. The proprietor raised a floury hand in greeting. Ozren waved in reply and then steered me through the crowded café to the attic stairs. The scent of crisp pastry and burned sugar followed us.

Ozren could just stand up under the swooping eaves of the attic. The ends of his unruly curls brushed the lowest beams. He turned to take my jacket, and as he did so, touched my throat, lightly. He ran his middle finger over the tiny arc of bone at the back of my neck, where my hair lifted and swirled into a twist. He traced the line of bone along my shoulder and then down, over my sweater. When he reached my hips, he slid his hands under the cashmere and eased it up, over my head. The wool caught on my hair clip. The clip rattled as it hit the floor and the twist of hair unfurled over my bare shoulders. I shivered, and he wrapped his arms around me.

Later, we lay in a tangle of sheet and clothing. He lived like a student, his bed a thin mattress pushed up against the wall, piles of books and newspapers pushed carelessly into corners. He was as spare as a racehorse, all long bone and lean muscle. Not a gram of fat on him. He fingered a strand of my hair. "So straight. Like a Japanese," he said.

"Expert, are you?" I teased. He grinned and got up and poured two little glasses of fiery *rakija*. He hadn't turned on the light when we'd come in, but now he lit a pair of candles. As the flame steadied, I could see that the far wall of the attic was filled by a large figurative painting, a portrait of a woman and an infant, in a thick, urgent impasto. The baby was partly hidden by the curve of the woman's body, which seemed to shelter it in a protective arc. The woman was turning away from us and toward the child, but she looked back at the artist—at us—with a steady, appraising gaze, beautiful and grave.

"It's a wonderful painting," I said.

"Yes, my friend Danilo—the one I told you about—he painted it."

"Who is she?"

He frowned, and sighed. Then he raised his glass in a kind of toast.

"My wife."

IV

WHEN YOU HAVE WORKED WELL, there should be no sign that you have worked at all.

Werner Heinrich, my instructor, taught me that. "Never mistake yourself for an artist, Miss Heath. You must be always behind your object."

At the end of a week, there probably weren't ten people in the world who could have told for sure that I'd taken this book apart and put it back together. The next thing I had to do was pay visits on a few old friends who'd be able to tell me what, if anything, the tiny samples I'd extracted from the codex meant. The UN had asked me to contribute an essay that would be included in the catalog when the book went on exhibition. I'm not ambitious in the traditional sense. I don't want a big house or a big bank account; I don't give a rat's about those things. I don't want to be the boss of anything or manage anyone but myself. But I do take a lot of pleasure in surprising my stuffy old colleagues by publishing something they don't know. I just love to move the ball forward, even if it's only a millimeter, in the great human quest to figure it all out.

I stood away from the table, and stretched. "So, my *kustos,* I think that I can return the haggadah now to your care."

Ozren did not smile, or even look at me, but just rose and went to get the new box he'd had made to my specifications, a properly designed archival container that would hold the book safely while the UN finished the work on a climate-controlled exhibition room at the museum. It was to be a shrine to the survival of Sarajevo's multiethnic heritage. The haggadah would have pride of place, but all around the walls would be Islamic manuscripts and Orthodox icons that would show how the people and their arts had grown from the same roots, influencing and inspiring one another.

As Ozren took the book, I laid a hand on his hand. "They've invited me back for the opening. I'm supposed to be giving a paper at the Tate the week before. If I flew here from London, would I see you then?"

He moved so that my hand fell away from his. "At the ceremony, yes."

"And after?"

He shrugged.

We'd spent three nights together at Sweet Corner, but he hadn't said a single word about the wife who gazed at us from the painting. Then, on the fourth night, I'd woken up a little before dawn, because the pastry chef was clumping around, firing his bread ovens. I'd rolled over and found Ozren wide awake, staring at the painting. He had a haggard look, very sad. I touched his face lightly.

"Tell me," I said.

He turned and looked at me, taking my face in his hands. Then he got up off the mattress and pulled on his jeans, throwing my clothes from the night before over to me. When we were dressed, I followed him downstairs. He talked to the pastry chef for a few minutes, and the guy tossed him a set of car keys.

We found the battered old Citroën at the end of the narrow alley. We drove in silence out of town, up into the mountains. It was beautiful up there; the first rays of the sun turned the snow golden and pink and tangerine. A powerful wind tossed the pine boughs around, and the smell brought incongruous memories: the resinous tang of Christmas trees, the scent of their sap so strong on the heat-wave December days of Sydney's midsummer.

"This is Mount Trebevic," he said at last. "It was the bobsled run during the winter Olympics, before the Serbs moved in with their high-powered rifles and their telescopic sights and turned it into a sniper pit." He put out a hand to grab me as I moved toward the pit. "There are land mines everywhere up here, still. You have to keep to the roadway."

From where we stood, there was a perfect view down into the city. They'd taken aim at her from here, as she stood holding her infant son in a UN water line. The first bullet had severed her femoral artery. She had crawled, dragging the baby, to the nearest wall and thrown her body across her son. No one dared to help her, not the UN soldiers, who stood by as she bled to death, or the terrified civilians who scattered, wailing, for whatever poor hiding places they could find.

"The heroic people of Sarajevo." Ozren's voice was tired and bitter, his words hard to hear as he spat them out into the teeth of the wind. "That's what CNN was always calling us. But most of us weren't so heroic, believe me. When the shooting started, we'd run just as fast as the next person."

Aida, wounded, bleeding, had been an irresistible target for the Mount Igman murderer. The second shot pierced her shoulder and hit bone. The bullet shredded, so only a small fragment of metal passed through her and into the baby's skull. The baby's name was Alia. Ozren said it in a whisper, like a sigh.

The *initial insult*—that's the technical neurosurgical term. When I was a teenager, I'd overhear my mother, on the phone, taking the calls that often came as a welcome interruption to our dinner table arguments. It would be some nervous young resident in the emergency room. I'd always thought "insult" was a pretty apt term for something like being shot in the head or whacked across the skull with a bit of two-by-four. Hard to get more insulting than that. In Alia's case, the initial insult had been compounded by the fact that Sarajevo had no neurosurgeon, let alone a pediatric specialist. The general surgeon had done his best, but there'd been swelling and infection—a "secondary insult"—and the little boy had lapsed into a coma. By the time a neurosurgeon got to the city, months later, he'd declared that nothing further could be done.

When we came down from the mountain, Ozren asked if I wanted to go to the hospital, to see his boy. I didn't. I hate hospitals. Always have. Sometimes, on weekends, when the housekeeper had the day off, my mother would drag me with her on rounds. The bright lights, the sludge green walls, the noise of metal on metal, the sheer bloody misery hanging over the halls like a shroud—I hated the lot of it. The coward in me has total control of my imagination in hospitals. I see myself in every bed: in the traction device or unconscious on the gurney, oozing blood into drainage bags, hooked up to urinary catheters. Every face is my own face. It's like those kids' flip books where you keep the same head but keep changing the bodies. Pathetic, I know. Can't help it, though. And Mum wondered why I didn't want to be a doctor.

But Ozren was looking at me with this expression, like a really gentle dog, head tilted, expecting kindness. I couldn't say no. He told me then that he went every day, before work. I hadn't realized. The past few mornings, he'd walked me back to my hotel so I could shower—if there was any running water—and change my clothes. I hadn't known that he'd gone to the hospital after that, to spend an hour with his son.

I tried not to look right or left, into the wards, as we walked down the hall. And then we were in Alia's room, and there was nowhere to look but at him. A sweet, still face, slightly swollen from the fluids they pumped into him to keep him alive. A tiny body threaded with plastic tubes. The sound of the monitors, measuring out the minutes of his limited little life. Ozren had told me his wife had died a year ago, so Alia couldn't have been more than three years old. It was hard to tell. His underdeveloped body could have belonged to a younger infant, but the expressions that passed across his face seemed to register emotions of someone very old. Ozren brushed the brown hair off the small brow, sat down on the bed, and whispered softly in Bosnian, gently flexed and straightened the rigid little hands.

"Ozren," I said quietly. "Have you considered getting another opinion? I could take his scans with me and—"

"No," he said, cutting me off midsentence.

"But why not? Doctors are only people, they make mistakes." I can't count the times I heard my mother dismiss the views of a supposedly eminent colleague: "Him! I wouldn't go to him for an ingrown toenail!" But Ozren just shrugged and didn't answer me.

"Have you got MRI scans, or just CTs? MRIs show a lot more, they—"

"Hanna, shut up, please. I said no."

"That's funny," I said. "I never would've picked you as a believer in that bullshit, *insha'Allah,* fatalist mentality."

He got up off the bed and took a step toward me, grabbing my face between his hands and bringing his own face so close to mine that his angry features blurred.

"You," he said, his voice a low, contained whisper. "You are the one who is consumed by bullshit."

His sudden ferocity scared me. I pulled away.

"You," he continued, grabbing my wrist. "All of you, from the safe world, with your air bags and your tamper-proof packaging and your fat-free diets. You are the superstitious ones. You convince yourself you can cheat death, and you are absolutely offended when you learn that you can't. You sat in your nice little flat all through our war and watched us, bleeding all over the TV news. And you thought, 'How awful!' and then you got up and made yourself another cup of gourmet coffee." I flinched when he said that. It was a pretty accurate description. But he wasn't done. He was so angry he was actually spitting.

"Bad things happen. Some very bad things happened to me. And I'm no different from a thousand other fathers in this city who have kids who suffer. I live with it. Not every story has a happy ending. Grow *up*, Hanna, and accept that."

He flung my wrist away. I was shaking. I wanted to get away, to get out of there. He turned back to Alia and sat down again on the bed, facing away from me. I pushed past him on the way to the door, and saw that he had a kids' book, in Bosnian, in his hands. From the familiar illustrations, I could tell it was a translation of *Winnie-the-Pooh*. He put the book down and rubbed his palms over his face. He looked up at me, his expression drained. "I read to him. Every day. It is not possible for a childhood to pass by without these stories." He turned to a page he'd bookmarked. I had my hand on the door, but the sound of his voice held me. Every now and then, he'd look up and talk to Alia. Maybe he was explaining the meaning of a hard word, or sharing some fine point of Milne's English humor. I'd never seen anything so tender between a father and his child.

And I knew I couldn't bear to see it again. That night after work Ozren started to apologize for his outburst. I wasn't sure if it was going to be a prelude to another invitation to spend the night, but I didn't let him get that far. I made some lame excuse as to why I had to go back to my hotel room. Same thing the next night. By the third night he stopped asking. And anyway, by then it was time for me to go.

I was once told, by a very handsome and very hurt botanist, that my attitude to sex was like something he'd read about in a sociology textbook about the 1960s. He said I acted like the book's description of a prefeminist male, acquiring partners for casual sex and then dumping them as soon as any emotional entanglement was required. He hypothesized that because I didn't have a father and because my mother was emotionally unavailable, no one had modeled a healthy, caring, reciprocal relationship in my life.

I told him if I wanted to hear psychobabble, I could visit a shrink cheap on Medibank. I'm not casual about sex, far from it. I'm actually very picky. I prefer the fit few to the mediocre masses. But I'm not big on wringing out other people's soggy hankies, and if I wanted a partner, I'd join a law firm. If I do choose to be with someone, I want it to stay light and fun. It gives me no pleasure, none at all, to hurt people's feelings, especially not tragic cases like Ozren, who is clearly a spectacular human being, brave and intelligent and all the rest of it. Even handsome, if you can cope with the unkempt thing. I felt bad about the botanist, too. But he'd started talking about bushwalking with kids in the backpack. I had to let him go. I wasn't even twenty-five at the time. Kids are definitely a midlife luxury, in my opinion.

As for my dysfunctional so-called family, it's true that I've inherited a core belief, to wit: don't rely on some other sod for your emotional sustenance. Find something absorbing to do—something so absorbing that you don't have time to dwell on the woe-is-me stuff. My mother loves her work, I love mine. So the fact that we don't love each other . . . well, I hardly ever think about it.

When Ozren was done with his seals and strings, I walked with him down the stairs of the bank building for what would be the last time. If I came back to Sarajevo for the opening, the book would be where it belonged, in its nice, new, state-of-the-art, securely guarded display space at the museum. I waited for Ozren to put the book in the vault, but when he came back up, he was in conversation in Bosnian with the guards, and he did not turn.

The guard unlocked the front door for him.

"Good night," I said. "Good-bye. Thank you."

He had his hand on the ornate silver door pull. He looked back at me and nodded curtly. Then he pushed the door open and walked out into the dark. I went back upstairs, alone, to pack up my tools.

I had my glassine envelopes with the bit of insect's wing and the single white hair from the binding, and tiny samples, each no bigger than the full stop at the end of a sentence, that I'd lifted on scalpel tip from the pages that were stained. I placed these things carefully in my document case. Then I paged through my notebook to make sure I hadn't forgotten anything. I skimmed the notes I'd made the first day, when I'd dismantled the binding. I saw the memo I'd scrib-

bled about the channels in the board edges and my query to myself
about missing clasps.

To get to London from Sarajevo, you had to change planes in
Vienna. I was planning to use that necessary stopover to accomplish
two things. I had an old acquaintance—an entomologist—who was
a researcher and curator at the Naturhistorisches Museum there. She
could help me identify the insect fragment. I also wanted to visit my
old teacher, Werner Heinrich. He was a dear man, kind and courtly,
sort of like the grandfather I'd never had. I knew he'd be keen to hear
about my work on the haggadah, and I also wanted to get his advice.
Maybe his influence would allow me to break through Viennese for-
malities at the museum where the rebinding had been done in 1894.
If he could get me access to the archives, it was just possible I'd find
some old records about the condition of the book when it arrived at
the museum. I put the notebook in my case. Last of all, I slipped in
the large manila envelope from the hospital.

I'd forged the request in my mother's name and made the word-
ing ambiguous: ". . . asked to consult at the request of a colleague of
Dr. Karaman in the case of his son. . . ." They knew her name, even
here. She'd coauthored a text on aneurysms that was the standard
reference in the field. Not that I was in the habit of asking her for
favors. But she'd said she was heading to Boston to give a paper at the
American neurosurgeons' annual gabfest, and I had a client in Boston,
a bezillionaire and a major manuscripts collector, who'd been after
me to look at a codex he was thinking of buying from a Houghton
Library deaccessioning sale.

Australians in general are pretty casual about traveling. If you
grow up there, you basically get trained in long-haul flights—fifteen
hours, twenty-four—it's what we're used to. For us, eight hours
across the Atlantic seems like a doddle. He'd offered to pay for a first-
class ticket, and I don't usually get to sit in the pointy end. I figured I
could cram in the appraisal, pick up a nice fee, and be back in London
in time to deliver my paper at the Tate. Usually I would have arranged my itinerary so that Mum and I would just miss each other.

There'd be a brief telephone call: "What a pity!" "Yes, can you believe it?" Each outdoing the other in insincerity. The night before, when I'd suggested we actually meet up in Boston, there'd been a minute of dead air on the phone, the crackle of Sarajevo-to-Sydney static. Then, in an affectless voice: "How nice. I'll try to find a time."

I didn't ask myself why exactly I was subjecting myself to this. Why I was butting in, invading a man's privacy, flouting his wishes, which could not have been expressed more clearly. I suppose the answer was that if something can be known, I can't stand not knowing it. In that way, Alia's brain scans were just like the bits of fiber in my glassine envelopes, messages in a code that expert eyes might just be able to read for me.

V

VIENNA SEEMED to be doing rather well off the fall of communism. The whole of the city was getting a makeover, like a wealthy matron going under the knife. As my taxi merged with the traffic on the Ringstrasse, I saw construction cranes everywhere, bowing over the city's wedding cake skyline. Light flared off the freshly gilded Hofburg friezes, and sandblasters had flushed the soot off dozens of neo-Renaissance facades, revealing the warm cream stone that had been obscured by centuries of grime. Western capitalists evidently wanted spruced-up headquarters for all their new joint ventures with neighboring countries like Hungary and the Czech Republic. And now they had cheap laborers from the east to do the work.

When I'd been in Vienna in the early 1980s on a traveling scholarship, it had been a gray, grimy place. Every building was filthy, although I didn't realize that at the time. I thought they were all meant to be black. I'd found it a depressing place and a bit creepy. Vienna's location, teetering at the far edge of Western Europe, had made it a Cold War listening post. The stout matrons and the loden-clad gents with their bourgeois solidity existed in an atmosphere that always seemed a little stirred, a little charged, like the air after lightning. But I had liked the gilded rococo *Kaffeehäuser* and the music, which was everywhere—the city's pulse and its heartbeat. The joke was that anyone in Vienna who wasn't carrying a musical instrument was either a pianist, a harpist, or a foreign spy.

One didn't think of the city as a hub of science, and yet it had its share of high-tech businesses and innovative labs. My old mate Amalie Sutter, the entomologist, headed one of them. I'd met Amalie years earlier, when she was a postdoc, living about as far as you could get from gilded rococo cafés. I came across her on the side of a mountain in remote northern Queensland. She lived in an upended, corrugated-iron water tank. I was backpacking at the time. I dropped out of my expensive, elitist girl's school at sixteen, which was the first possible moment I could get free of it. I'd tried to get them to expel me earlier, but they were too scared of Mum to go for it, no matter what outrages against decorum I managed to devise. I walked out of our palatial home and joined that shifting band—the healthy Scandinavian kids on working holidays, the surfie dropouts, and the gaunt druggies—drifting north to Byron Bay and then on up the coast, past Cairns, past Cooktown, until the road ran out.

I'd traveled almost two thousand clicks to get away from my mother, and I ended up finding someone who was, in some ways, exactly like her. Or like she might have been in a parallel universe. Amalie was my mother stripped of social pretensions and material ambition. But she was just as driven by what she did, which was to study how a certain species of butterfly relied on ants to keep its caterpillars safe from predators. She let me stay in her water tank and taught me all about compostable toilets and solar showers. Even though I didn't realize it at the time, I now think those weeks on the mountain, watching the way she looked at the world with this close, passionate *attention*, the way she busted her butt just for the chance to find out something new about how the world worked, were what turned me around and headed me back to Sydney, to start my real life.

Years later, when I came to Vienna and apprenticed myself to Werner Heinrich, I ran into her again. Werner had asked me to investigate the DNA of a book louse he'd extracted from a binding, and someone said the DNA lab over at the Naturhistorisches Museum was the best in the city. At the time I thought that seemed odd. The museum was a fantastic antique of a place, full of moth-eaten stuffed animals and nineteenth-century gentlemen's rock collections. I loved to wander around in there because you never knew what you'd find. It was like a cabinet of curiosities. There was a rumor, though I'd never confirmed it, that they even had the severed head of the Turkish vizier who'd lost the siege of Vienna in 1623. Supposedly, they kept him in the basement.

But Amalie Sutter's lab was a state-of-the-art facility for the research of evolutionary biology. I remembered the rather bizarre directions to her office: take the elevator to the third floor, follow the skeleton of the *diplodocus,* and when you reach the jawbone, her door is on the left. An assistant told me she was in the collections room and walked me down the corridor. I opened the door to a pungent blast of mothball odor. There was Amalie, pretty much as I'd left her, poring over a drawer full of silvery blue shimmer.

She was pleased to see me, but even more pleased to see my specimen. "I thought you were bringing me another book louse." Last time, she'd had to grind it up to extract the DNA, amplify it, and then wait days to do an analysis. "But this," she said, holding the envelope carefully. "This, if I'm not much mistaken, is going to be a lot easier. I think what you've got here is an old friend of mine."

"A moth?"

"No, not a moth."

"It can't be part of a *butterfly?*" Bits of butterfly don't generally wind up in books. Moths do, because they come indoors, where books are kept. But butterflies are outdoor creatures.

"I think it might be." She stood and closed the collection cabinet. We walked back to her office, where she scanned the floor-to-ceiling bookshelves, then hauled down a huge tome on wing veination. She pushed open a tall door that had a life-size picture of her as a graduate student, in the Malaysian rain forest, brandishing a four-meter butterfly net. It was remarkable how little she'd aged since then. I think her absolute enthusiasm for her work acted on her like some kind of preservative. On the other side of the door was a gleaming lab, with postdocs wielding pipettes and peering at DNA graphs on computer monitors. She gently lifted my little bit of wing onto a slide and placed it under a powerful microscope.

"Hello, lovely," she said. "It *is* you." She looked up and beamed at me. She hadn't even glanced at the veination diagrams. "*Parnassius mnemosyne leonhardiana*. Common throughout Europe."

Damn. My heart sank, and my face must have shown it. No new information there. Amalie's smile widened. "Not much help?" She beckoned me to follow her back down the corridor to the room filled with collection cabinets. She stopped in front of one and opened the tall metal door with a clang. She slid out a wooden drawer. Rows of *Parnassius* butterflies hovered in their perpetual stasis, afloat forever above their carefully lettered names.

The butterflies were lovely in a subtle, muted way. They had creamy white forewings, splashed with black dots. The rear wings were almost translucent, like lead glass, divided into panes by the distinct tracery of black veins. "Not the flashiest butterfly in the world by any means," said Amalie. "But collectors love them. Perhaps because you have to climb a mountain to get one." She closed the drawer and turned to me. "Common throughout Europe, yes. But confined to high alpine systems, generally around two thousand meters. The caterpillars of the *Parnassius* feed only on an alpine variety of larkspur that grows in steep, stony environments. Your manuscript, Hanna, dear. Has it been on a trip to the Alps?"

An Insect's Wing

Sarajevo, 1940

Here lies the grave. Stay, for a while,
when the forest listens.
Take off your caps! Here rests the flower
of a people that knows how to die.

—Inscription, World War II memorial, Bosnia

THE WIND BLEW ACROSS the Miljacka River, hard as a slap. Lola's thin coat was no protection. She ran across the narrow bridge, her hands thrust deep in her pockets. On the other side of the river, a set of rough-hewn stone stairs rose abruptly, leading to a warren of narrow lanes lined with shabby apartment buildings. Lola took the stairs two at a time and turned in to the second alleyway, sheltered at last from the bitter gusts.

It was not yet midnight, so the outer door to her building hadn't been locked. Inside, it was not much warmer than on the street. She steadied herself and took a moment to catch her breath. A heavy smell of boiled cabbage and fresh cat piss hung over the foyer. Lola crept up the stairs and gently turned the latch on her family's apartment. Although her right hand reached up instinctively to touch the mezuzah on the doorjamb before she slipped inside, Lola could not have said why. She took off her coat, unlaced her boots, and carried them as she tiptoed past the sleeping forms of her mother and father. The apartment was one room, with a dividing curtain the only privacy.

Her little sister was just a bulge beneath the quilt. Lola lifted the coverlet and slid in beside her. Dora was curled up like a small animal, radiating welcome heat. Lola reached for the warmth of her sister's back. The child protested in her sleep, uttering a tiny cry and pulling away. She tucked her icy hands into her own armpits. Despite the cold, her face was still flushed, her brow still damp from the dancing, and if her father woke, he might notice that.

Lola loved the dancing. That was what had lured her to the Young Guardians meetings. She liked the hiking, too; the long, hard walks in the mountains to a hanging lake or the ruins of an ancient fortress. The rest of it, she didn't care much for. The endless discussions of politics bored her. And the Hebrew—she didn't even enjoy reading in her own language, much less struggling to decode the strange black squiggles that Mordechai was always trying to get her to remember.

She thought about his arm across her shoulder in the circle. She could still feel the pleasant weight of it, muscular from farm labor. When he'd rolled up his sleeves, his forearm had been brown and hard as a hazelnut. Even though she didn't know the steps, it was easy to follow the dance with him beside her, smiling encouragement. A Sarajevan—even a poor one like Lola—would never give a second glance to a Bosnian peasant. Never mind if the farmer was quite well-off, a city person felt superior. But Mordechai was another thing entirely. He'd grown up in Travnik, which, while not Sarajevo, was a fine town nevertheless. He was educated; he'd attended the gymnasium. Yet two years earlier, at the age of seventeen, he'd gone off on a boat to Palestine to work on a farm. And not a prosperous farm either, by his description. A dried-out, barren piece of dust where you had to break your back to raise a crop. And for no profit, just the food in your mouth and the work clothes on your back. Worse than a peasant, really. Yet when he talked about it, it was as if there was no more fascinating or noble profession in the world than digging irrigation ditches and harvesting dates.

Lola loved listening to Mordechai when he talked about all the practical things a pioneer had to know, like how to treat a scorpion bite or stanch a bad cut; how to site a sanitary latrine or improvise a shelter. Lola knew she would never leave home to pioneer in Palestine, but she liked to think about the kind of adventurous life that might demand such skills. And she liked to think about Mordechai. The way he spoke reminded her of the old Ladino songs her grandfather had sung to her when she was a little girl. He had a seed stand at the open-air market, and Lola's mother would sometimes leave her there with him while she worked. Grandfather was full of tales of knights and hidalgos, and poems from a magic place called Sepharad, where he said their ancestors had lived long ago. Mordechai spoke about his new land as if it were Sepharad. He told the group that he couldn't wait to get back there, to Eretz Israel. "I am jealous of every sunrise I am not there to see the white stones of the Jordan Valley turn to gold."

Lola didn't speak up in the group discussions. She felt stupid compared to the others. Many of them were Svabo Jijos, Yiddish-speaking Jews, who had come to the city with the Austrian occupation in the late nineteenth century. Ladino-speaking families like Lola's had been in the city since 1565, when Sarajevo was part of the Ottoman empire, and the Muslim sultan had offered refuge from Christian persecution. Most of those who came had been wandering since the expulsion from Spain in 1492, unable to find a permanent home. They had found peace in Sarajevo, and acceptance, but only a few families had really prospered. Most remained small-time merchants like her grandfather, or artisans with simple skills. The Svabo Jijos were more educated, more European in their outlook. Very soon they had much better jobs and were blending with the highest ranks of Sarajevan society. Their children went to the gymnasium and even sometimes to the university. At the Young Guardians, they were the natural leaders.

One was the daughter of a city councilor, one the son of the pharmacist, a widower, for whom Lola's mother did laundry. Another girl's father was a bookkeeper at the finance ministry, where Lola's father worked as a janitor. But Mordechai treated everyone as an equal, so gradually she gathered enough courage to ask a question.

"But Mordechai," she'd asked shyly, "aren't you glad to be home in your own country, speaking your own language, not having to work so hard?"

Mordechai had turned to her with a smile. "This isn't my home," he said gently. "And it isn't yours, either. The only true home for Jews is Eretz Israel. And that's why I'm here, to tell you all about the life you could have, to prepare you, and to bring you back with me, to build our Jewish homeland."

He raised his arms, as if including her in a communal embrace. "'If you will it, it is no dream.'" He paused, letting the words hang in the air. "A great man said that, and I believe it. What about you, Lola, will you act your dreams, and make them real?" She blushed, unused to the attention, and Mordechai smiled kindly. Then he spread his hands to include the whole group. "But think of this. What do you will? Is it to do the pigeon dance, scratching around for the crumbs of others, or will you be desert hawks, and soar to your own destiny?"

Isak, the pharmacist's son, was a slight, studious boy with pencil-thin limbs. Lola's mother often opined that for all his learning, the pharmacist didn't have the first idea about how to properly feed a growing child. But of all the young people in the hall, Isak alone fidgeted impatiently during Mordechai's rhetorical flight. Mordechai noticed and turned the full force of his warmth upon him. "What is it, Isak? Do you have a view to share with us?"

Isak pushed his wire-rimmed glasses up the bridge of his nose. "Maybe what you say is true for Jews in Germany. We all hear troubling news from there. But not here. Anti-Semitism has never been part of our lives in Sarajevo. Look where the synagogue is: between the mosque and the Orthodox church. I'm sorry, but Palestine is the Arabs' home, not yours. Certainly not mine. We are Europeans. Why turn our backs on a country that has offered us prosperity and education, in order to become a peasant among people who don't want us?"

"So, you are happy to be a pigeon?" Mordechai said this with a smile, but his intention to belittle Isak was clear, even to Lola. Isak pinched the bridge of his nose and scratched his head.

"Maybe so. But at least the pigeon does no harm. The hawk lives at the expense of the other creatures that dwell in the desert."

Lola had listened to the two of them argue until her head ached. She had no idea who was right. She turned over on the thin mattress and tried to quiet her mind. She had to get to sleep, otherwise she'd nod off over her tasks the next day, and her father would want to know why. Lola worked in the laundry with her mother, Rashela. If she was tired, it was a chore to walk the streets of the city with her heavy baskets, delivering fresh starched linens and picking up soiled clothes. The warm, moist steam would make her drowsy when she was supposed to be tending the copper. Her mother would find her, slumped in a corner, as the water cooled and a greasy scum congealed on the surface.

Lujo, her father, was not a harsh man, but he was a strict and practical one. At first, he had allowed her to go to the Young Guardians, Hashomer Haza'ir in Hebrew, after her work was done. His friend Mosa, the custodian at the Jewish community center, had spoken in favor of the group, saying it was a harmless and wholesome youth organization, like the Gentiles' Scouts. But then Lola had fallen asleep and let the fire that heated the copper go out. Her mother had scolded, and her father had asked why. When he learned that there was a dance, the hora, which boys and girls did together, he'd banned her from attending any more meetings. "You are only fifteen, daughter. When you are a little older, we will find a nice fiancé to partner with you, and then you may dance."

She had pleaded, saying she would sit down during the dances. "There are things I can learn there," she said.

"Things!" said Lujo contemptuously. "Things that will help you earn bread for your family? No? I did not think so. Wild ideas. Communistic ideas, from what I have heard. Ideas that are banned in our country and will get you into trouble you don't need. And a dead language that no one speaks, save for a handful of old men in the synagogue. Really, I don't know what Mosa was thinking. I will look to your honor, even if others forget the value of these things. Hiking, on Sunday, I don't mind it, if your mother has no chores for you. But from now on you spend your evenings at home."

From then on, in fact, Lola had begun to lead an exhausting double life. Hashomer met two nights a week. On those nights, she went to bed early, with her little sister. Sometimes, when she had worked very hard, it took an immense effort of will to keep herself awake, listening to the gentle, even breathing of Dora's little body next to her. But mostly her anticipation made it easy to feign sleep until her parents' snores told her it was safe to leave. Then she would creep out, scrambling into her clothes on the landing and hoping no neighbors came out of their doors to notice.

On the evening that Mordechai told the group he was leaving, Lola at first did not understand him. "I am going home," he said. Lola thought he meant Travnik. Then she realized he was taking a freighter back to Palestine, and that she would never see him again. He invited everyone to come to the train station on the day of his departure, to see him off. Then he announced that Avram, an apprentice printer, had decided to go with him.

"He is the first. I hope many of you will follow." He glanced at Lola, and it seemed to her that his gaze lingered. "Whenever you come home, we will be there to welcome you."

The day that Mordecai and Avram were to leave, Lola longed to go to the train station, but her mother had an immense amount of laundry to do. Rashela toiled with the heavy iron while Lola took her accustomed place at the copper and the mangle. At the hour when Mordechai's train was to depart for the coast, Lola stared at the gray walls of the laundry, watching the steam condense and trickle down the cold stone. The smell of mold filled her nostrils. She tried to imagine the hard white sunlight that Mordechai had described, silvering the leaves of olive trees, and the scent of orange blossoms blooming in the stone-walled gardens of Jerusalem.

The leader who took Mordechai's place, a young man named Samuel from Novi Sad, was a competent teacher of outdoor skills, but lacked the charisma that had kept Lola awake on meeting nights. Now, more often than not, she fell asleep herself as she waited for her exhausted parents to drop off. She would wake to the *khoja's* dawn prayer call, rallying their Muslim neighbors to devotions. She would realize she had missed a meeting and feel only slight regret.

Other boys and girls did follow Avram and Mordechai to Palestine, each time with a big send-off at the railway station. Occasionally they would write back to the group. Always there was a sameness to the reports; the work was hard, but the land was worth any effort, and to be a Jew building a Jewish land was what mattered most in the world. Lola sometimes wondered about these letters. Surely someone was homesick? Surely such a life could not agree with everyone who tried it? But it seemed as if those who left all became one person, speaking with the same monotonous voice.

The tempo of departures picked up as the news from Germany worsened. The annexation of Austria put the Reich hard up against their borders. But life at the community center went on as usual, the old people meeting for coffee and gossip, the religious for their Oneg Shabbat on Friday night. There was no sense of danger, even when the government turned a blind eye to the fascist gangs who began to roam the streets, harassing anyone they knew to be a Jew, getting into fistfights with the Gypsies. "They are just louts." Lujo shrugged. "Every community has its louts, even ours. It doesn't mean anything."

Sometimes, when Lola was collecting soiled laundry from an apartment in the affluent part of the city, she would catch sight of Isak, always with a heavy book bag slung across his shoulder. He was at the university now, studying chemistry as his father had. Lola wanted to ask him what he thought of the louts, and whether it worried him that France had fallen. But she was embarrassed by the basket of sour-smelling garments she carried. And she wasn't sure she knew enough to ask the questions in a way that would not disclose her as a fool.

When Stela Kamal heard a light knock on the door of her apartment, she reached up to the crown of her head and pulled down her lace veil before she went to answer it. She had been in Sarajevo for a little more than a year, but she still clung to the more conservative ways of Priština, where no traditional Muslim family allowed its women to show their faces to a strange man.

That afternoon, though, her caller was not a man; just the laundress her husband had arranged. Stela felt sorry for the young girl. On her back she carried a wicker pannier laden with pressed laundry. Over the shoulder straps for this, she had slung calico bags full of soiled items. She looked tired and chilled. Stela offered her a hot drink.

At first, Lola could not understand Stela's Albanian accent. Stela threw back the fine piece of lace that covered her face and repeated her offer, miming the pouring of coffee from a *džezva*. Lola accepted gladly; it was so cold outside, and she had walked miles. Stela beckoned her into the apartment and went to the *mangala*, where the embers were still hot. She flung the coffee grounds into the *džezva* and let it boil up once, twice.

The rich aroma made Lola's mouth water. She stared around her. She had never seen so many books. The apartment's walls were lined with them. It wasn't a large apartment, but everything in it had an easy grace, as if it had always been there. Low wooden tables, inlaid with mother-of-pearl in the Turkish style, had yet more books open upon them. Celims in muted colors warmed the gleaming waxed floors. The *mangala* was very old, the copper burnished, the hemispherical cover decorated with crescents and stars.

Stela turned and handed Lola a delicate porcelain *fildžan*, also with a crescent and star glazed into the bottom of the cup. Stela raised the *džezva* high and poured the hot coffee in a long dark thread. Lola wrapped her fingers around the handleless cup and felt the fragrant steam caress her face. As she sipped the strong coffee, she looked over the rim of the cup at the young Muslim woman. Even at home, Stela's hair was tied back beneath spotless white silk, her lace veil lying prettily over it, ready to be drawn down again if modesty required. The young woman was very beautiful, with warm dark eyes and creamy skin. Lola registered, with surprise, that the two of them were probably around the same age. She felt a stab of envy. Stela's hands, holding the *džezva*, were smooth and pale, not red and scaly like Lola's. How nice to have such an easy life, in such a fine apartment, with someone else to do the irksome chores.

Then Lola noticed a silver-framed photograph of the young woman on what must have been her wedding day, although her expression betrayed no joy. The man beside her was tall and distinguished, wearing a fez and a long dark frock coat. But he looked more than twice her age. An arranged marriage, probably. Lola had heard that Albanian tradition required brides to stand stock-still from dawn to dusk on their wedding day, forbidden from taking any part in the celebration. Even a smile was considered immodest and reprehensible. Lola, accustomed to wild rejoicing even at the most observant Jewish weddings, couldn't imagine such a thing. She wondered if it was true, or just one of the rumors that different communities made up about one another. Gazing at the picture, her envy waned. She, at least, would marry someone young and strong. Like Mordechai.

Stela saw Lola scrutinizing the photograph. "That is my husband, Serif effendi Kamal," she said. She was smiling now, and slightly flushed. "Do you know him? Most people in Sarajevo seem to." Lola shook her head. There was no point of intersection between her poor, unlettered family and the Kamals, a large and influential clan of Muslim *alims,* or intellectuals. The Kamals had given Bosnia many muftis, the highest religious office in a province.

Serif Kamal had studied theology at the university in Istanbul and Oriental languages at the Sorbonne in Paris. He had been a professor and the senior official in the ministry of religious affairs before becoming chief librarian at the National Museum. He spoke ten languages and had written scholarly books on history and architecture, although his specialty was the study of ancient manuscripts. His intellectual passion was the literature that had developed at Sarajevo's cultural crossroads: lyric poetry written by Muslim Slavs in classical Arabic, yet following the forms of Petrarchan sonnets that had been carried inland from Diocletian's court on the Dalmatian coast.

Serif had postponed marriage while he pursued his studies, and had finally taken a wife simply to silence all those in his circle who nagged him to do so. He had been visiting Stela's father, who had taught him the Albanian language. His old professor had begun to rib him about his extended bachelorhood. Flippantly, Serif had said he would marry, but only if his friend would give him one of his daughters. The next thing Serif knew, he had a bride. More than a year later, he was still surprised at how happy he was with this sweet young presence in his life. Especially since she had just confided that she was pregnant.

Stela had carefully folded the soiled sheets and garments. She handed them to Lola almost diffidently. She had always done her own laundry. She expected to. But with the baby coming, Serif had insisted on lessening her household chores.

Lola picked up the basket, thanked Stela for the coffee, and went on her way.

On an April morning, when the first snowmelt brought grassy scents from the mountains, the Luftwaffe sent wave after wave of Stuka dive-bombers to raid Belgrade. Armies from four hostile nations poured across the borders. It took less than two weeks for the Yugoslav army to surrender. Even before that, Germany had declared Sarajevo part of a new state. "This is now the Ustashe and Independent State of Croatia," the Nazi-appointed leader declared. "It must be cleansed of Serbs and Jews. There is no room for any of them here. Not a stone upon a stone will remain of what once belonged to them."

On April 16, the Germans marched into Sarajevo and for the next two days, they rampaged through the Jewish quarter. Anything of value was looted. Fires burned unchecked in the old synagogues.

Anti-Jewish laws for the "protection of Aryan blood and the honor of the Croatian people" meant that Lola's father, Lujo, no longer had a job at the finance ministry. Instead, he was forced into a work brigade with other Jewish men, even professionals like Isak's father, the pharmacist. All were forced to wear a yellow star. Lola's little sister, Dora, was expelled from school. The family, always poor, now had to rely on the few coins that Lola and Rashela could earn.

Stela Kamal was troubled. Her husband, usually so courteous, so concerned about her condition, had hardly exchanged six words with her in two days. He had returned home late from the museum, barely touched his dinner, and shut himself up in his study. In the morning he had said little at breakfast, and left early. When Stela went to tidy the study, she found his desk strewn with pages, some heavily corrected with many crossed-out sentences, some balled up and tossed onto the floor.

Serif usually worked calmly. His desk was always impeccably neat and organized. Almost guiltily, Stela smoothed out one of the discarded sheets. "Nazi Germany is a kleptocracy," she read. She did not know the word. "Museums have a duty to resist the plundering of cultural heritage. The losses in France and Poland could have been stanched had not museum directors offered up their skill and expertise to facilitate German looting. Instead, to our shame, we are become one of the most Nazified professions in Europe. . . ." There was nothing else on the sheet. She picked up another crumpled ball. This one had a heading, heavily underlined: ANTI-SEMITISM IS FOREIGN TO THE MUSLIMS OF BOSNIA AND HERZEGOVINA. The page seemed to be an article, or some kind of open letter, decrying the passage of anti-Jewish laws. There was much crossing out, but Stela could read parts of sentences: ". . . only a lightning rod used to draw the people's attention away from their real problems." . . . "Provide help to the poor among the Jewish population, whose number is much higher than commonly estimated. . . ."

Stela crumpled the paper and swept it into a rubbish container. She pressed her knuckles into the small of her back, which was aching a little. She had never doubted that her husband was the wisest of men. She did not doubt it now. But his silences, the crumpled pages, the alarming sentences . . . She thought about speaking to him of these things. All day, she rehearsed what she might say. But when he came home, she poured his coffee from the *džezva* and said nothing.

After a few weeks, the arrests began. In early summer, Lujo was ordered to report for transport to a labor camp. Rashela wept and pleaded with him not to answer the summons, to flee the city, but Lujo said that he was strong, and a good worker, and would manage. He took his wife's chin in his hand. "Better this way. The war cannot last forever. If I run away, they will come for you." Never a demonstrative man, he kissed her, long and tenderly, and climbed aboard the truck.

Lujo did not know that there were no labor camps, only places of starvation and torture. Before the end of the year, he would be marched into the hills of Herzegovina, where the limestone is eaten away in a maze of wormholes. Rivers vanish there, running through the underground caverns, suddenly bubbling up again many miles distant. With other bruised and emaciated men—Jews, Gypsies, Serbs—Lujo stood at the lip of a deep cave whose floor he could not see. A Ustasha guard slashed his hamstrings and pushed him into the abyss.

They came for Rashela when Lola was out delivering fresh-pressed laundry. The soldiers had lists of all the Jewish women whose husbands and sons had already been deported. They herded them into trucks and deposited them at the ruined synagogue.

Lola returned to find her mother and sister gone, the door wide open, their few possessions tossed around in a vain search for something of value. She ran to her aunt's flat, a few streets away, and knocked until her knuckles ached. A Muslim neighbor, a kindly woman who still wore the traditional chador, opened her door and took Lola inside. The woman handed her water and told her what had happened.

Lola fought back the panic that emptied her mind. She had to *think*. What should she do? What *could* she do? The only single idea that made its way through her confusion was that she needed to find them. She turned to go. The neighbor laid a hand on her arm. "You will be recognized out there. Take this." She handed Lola a chador. Lola flung the cloak around her and set off for the synagogue. The front door, splintered by hatchets, hung loose on broken hinges. There were guards there, so Lola crept around to the side of the building, to the small room where the siddurim were stored. The window had been shattered. Lola took off the chador and wrapped it around her hand. She worked a piece of jagged glass loose from its lead surround, reached in, and slipped the catch. The frame, empty of its glass, tilted outward. She pulled herself up to the sill. The small room was in disarray, the shelves pulled down and the prayer books they had contained shredded all over the floor. There was a foul smell. Someone had defecated on the pages.

With the strong arms formed by lifting wet laundry, Lola hoisted her own weight till her ribs rested across the sill. Kicking, scrambling, the lead edge scraping through her clothes, she wriggled her way through the opening and dropped as gently as she could to the floor. Then she cracked open the heavy, polished-wood door. A pungent stink, of fear and sweat, burned paper and sour urine, filled the desecrated sanctuary. The ark that had housed the community's ancient Torah, carried safely from Spain so many centuries ago, gaped open, blackened by flame. The damaged pews and ash-filled aisles were packed with distraught women, old, young, some trying to comfort infants whose cries were amplified by the room's high stone dome. Others hunched over, head in hands. Lola eased her way slowly through the crowd, trying not to call attention to herself. Her mother, her little sister, and her aunt were huddled together in a corner. She came up behind her mother and laid a hand gently on her shoulder.

Rashela, thinking Lola had been caught, let out a cry.

Lola hushed her and spoke urgently. "There's a way out, through a window. I got in that way; we can all escape."

Lola's aunt Rena lifted her fat arms and made a gesture of defeat that took in her wide body. "Not me, my darling girl. My heart's not good. I've got no breath. I'm not going anywhere."

Lola, frantic, knew that her mother would not abandon this beloved older sister. "I can help you," she pleaded. "Please, let's try."

Her mother's face, always lined and careworn, seemed to have fallen suddenly into the deep, folded creases of a much older woman. She shook her head. "Lola, they have lists. They would miss us when they load the trucks. And anyway, where would we go?"

"We can go to the mountains," Lola said. "I know the ways, there are caves where we can shelter. We'll get to the Muslim villages. They'll help us, see if they won't. . . ."

"Lola, the Muslims were here at the synagogue, too. They burned and broke, looted and cheered just like the Ustashe."

"Just a few of them, just the louts—"

"Lola, darling, I know you mean well, but Rena is ill, and Dora is too little."

"But we can do it. Believe me, I know the mountains, I—"

Her mother laid her hand heavily on Lola's arm.

"I know you do. All those nights at Hashomer, I should hope they taught you something." Lola stared at her mother. "Did you really think I was asleep? No. I wanted you to go. I'm not like your father, worried about your honor. I know you are a modest girl. But now I want you to go away from this place. Yes," she said firmly, as Lola shook her head. "I am your mother, and in this you must obey me. You go. My place is here with Dora and my sister."

"Please, Mamma, please let me at least take Dora."

Her mother shook her head. She was struggling hard to contain tears. Her skin had turned blotchy with the effort. "Alone, you have the best chance. She'd never keep up with you."

"I can carry her. . . ."

Dora, clinging to her mother, looked from one to the other of the people she most loved, and, realizing that the result of the argument would be the loss of one of them, began to wail.

Rashela patted her, looking around, hoping the outburst wasn't drawing the guards' attention. "After the war, we'll all find each other." She reached both hands up to Lola's face and stroked her cheeks. "Go now. Stay alive."

Lola dragged her hands through her hair, pulling hard at the tangles until she hurt herself. She threw her arms around her mother and her sister and hugged them hard. She kissed her aunt. Then she turned away and stumbled through the press of sagging bodies, rubbing her eyes with the fleshy part of her hand. When she reached the door to the storeroom, she waited until the guards' eyes were elsewhere before she opened the door and slipped inside. She rested her back against the door, wiping her nose on her sleeve. As she dropped her arm, a small white hand reached out and grabbed it. The hand belonged to a girl with an intense elfin face, eyes huge behind thick glasses and finger planted firmly on lips. She pulled Lola down, hard, then pointed at the window. Lola saw the shape of a German helmet, the muzzle of a rifle, passing by the broken window.

"I know who you are," whispered the girl, who looked about nine or ten years old. "You went to Hashomer with my brother, Isak. I was going to go this year. . . ."

"Where is Isak?" Lola knew he'd been expelled from the university. "Was he taken for forced labor?"

The girl shook her head. "They got Father, but Isak is with the Partisans. There are others from your group, too. Maks, Zlata, Oskar . . . maybe even more now. Isak would not take me with them because I am too young. I told him I can carry messages, I can spy. But he wouldn't listen. He told me it would be safer to stay with the neighbors. But he was wrong. He *must* take me now, because here is nothing but death."

Lola winced. No child her age should talk like that. But the child was right. Lola had seen death in the faces of those she loved.

Lola regarded Isak's little sister. A waif, not much bigger than Dora. Yet her face was animated by the same worried intensity as her brother's. "I don't know," Lola said. "It's going to be hard walking, and dangerous, getting out of the city. . . . I think your brother . . ."

"If you want to know where he is, then you have to take me. Otherwise I'm not telling. And anyway, I have this."

The child reached under her pinafore and pulled out a German Luger. Lola was astonished.

"Where did you get that?"

"Stole it."

"How?"

"When they came to drag us out of the house, I made myself vomit on the soldier who was carrying me to the truck. I had been eating fish stew, so it was disgusting. He dropped me and cursed. While he was trying to clean the sick off himself, I snatched this from his holster and I ran. I was hiding in that building where your aunt lives. I followed you here. I know where my brother is, but I don't know how to get there. Will you take me or not?"

Lola knew this stubborn, wily child would not be tricked or persuaded into telling her where Isak and the others were. Like it or not, they needed each other. As soon as the light began to fade, they scrambled out the window and melted away down the city's back alleys.

For two days, Lola and Ina slept in caves and hid in barns, stole eggs and slurped them raw from the shells, until they reached Partisan territory. Isak had given Ina the name of a farmer, an elderly man with a weathered face and huge ropy hands.

He asked no questions. He opened the door to the cottage and ushered them inside. His wife, tutting and fussing about their matted hair and filthy faces, boiled water in a big black kettle and poured a bowl for each of them to wash. She then set a rich lamb casserole with potatoes and carrots before them, the first real meal they'd had since leaving the city. She treated their blistered feet with salves and put them both to bed for two days before allowing her husband to lead them on to the Partisans' mountain camp.

Lola was glad of the food and rest, as they made an exhausting climb up near-vertical rock faces. As she climbed, the reality of her predicament began to sink in. She had thought only of getting out of the city. She did not feel brave enough to be a resistance fighter. What could a laundress do that would be useful? There had been rumors of Partisan attacks on railway lines and bridges, and terrible reports about wounded Partisans captured by Nazis. One story told how the wounded men had been laid out on the road while the Germans drove a truck over and back across their bodies. Lola clutched the scree and pulled herself up the rock face, her mind filled with these frightful stories.

When they reached a wide ridgeline where the ground flattened and grasses and moss grew in mounds like cushions, she threw herself down, exhausted. Suddenly, a figure in gray emerged from a copse of low trees ahead of them. The uniform was German. The farmer fell prone on the ground and aimed his shotgun. Then he laughed, scrambled to his feet, and embraced the youth.

"Maks!" cried Ina. She bolted toward the youth, and he scooped her into his arms. Maks was one of Isak's best friends. Ina fingered the place where the Nazi insignia had been torn off his uniform. In its place was a crudely sewn five-pointed star, the emblem of the resistance.

"Hello, little sister of Isak. Hello, Lola. So, are you our new *partisankas*?" Maks waited while the girls thanked the farmer and made their farewells. Then he led them along the ridgeline toward a one-story building of heavy beams, lathe, and plaster. Lola recognized Oskar, sitting in the warm grass with his back against the wall. There were two boys she did not know lounging alongside him. All were busy picking lice off their jackets, two of which were German uniforms and one sewn from a piece of gray blanket.

Maks led Lola and Ina past the youths and through the pigsty that formed the entryway to the building's only door. The door opened onto the kitchen. A long, thatched roof over the front of the house made space in the peak for a loft that was reached by a ladder. "Good place to sleep," said Maks. "Warm. A bit smoky." The kitchen floor was of rough-trodden dirt, covered in part by brick, upon which a banked fire burned. The smoke drifted straight up to the rafters and out through the thatch. There was no chimney. A heavy chain held the cooking pots over the fire. Lola noticed several tubs of water near the door. Beyond were two rooms with planked floors. One contained a *pec,* or cement oven. Lola saw the poles for drying laundry suspended above it, and nodded approvingly. It would be possible to get washing dry even on wet and snowy days when it couldn't hang outdoors.

"Welcome to the headquarters of our *odred,*" Maks said. "We are only sixteen . . . eighteen now, counting yourselves, if the commander accepts you. Nine of us you know from Hashomer. The rest are local peasants. Good boys and girls, but young. Though not as young as you," he said, tickling Ina, who giggled. It was the first time Lola had seen the child smile. "Your brother will be surprised. He is second in command of the *odred.* Our commander, Branko, is from Belgrade. He was a secret Communist Party student leader there."

"Where are they?" Lola asked. Despite Maks's friendly manner, the words "if the commander accepts you" filled her with dread. As afraid as she was of being a *partisanka,* she was even more afraid of not being one; being sent back to the deadly city.

"They've gone to collect a mule. Soon enough, we'll be moving on from here. We'll need a mule to carry our supplies when we go on missions. Last time, the explosives and detonators we had to carry took up all the room in our packs. We ran out of food halfway to the section of track we were meant to blow up. We were two days without a crust of bread among us."

Lola's anxiety deepened as Maks talked. She had no idea about explosives or guns. She looked around the kitchen, and suddenly saw something she did know how to do.

"This water, can I use it?" she asked.

"Of course," said Maks. "There's a spring not ten yards from here. Use all you want."

Lola filled the largest of the blackened kettles and hung it over the fire. She stoked the flames and added some wood. Then she went outside.

She stood before Oskar and the two strange youths. With her toe, she scuffed nervously at the turf.

"What is it, Lola?" Oskar asked.

She felt the blush rising.

"I wonder if you . . . if you . . . would give me your jackets and trousers?"

The boys looked at one another and laughed.

"They told us Sarajevan girls were fast!" one said.

"You can't get rid of lice by picking at them." Lola spoke in a rush. "They hide in the seams where you can't find them. If I boil your clothes, it will kill them all. You'll see."

The youths, prepared to do anything to end the infernal itching, handed over their garments, ribbing one another and jostling like puppies as they did so.

"Give her your underpants!"

"Never on your life!"

"Well, I am. No bloody good to get rid of the lice in your coat if they're still running round your balls!"

Later, Lola was hanging the steaming garments—coats, pants, socks, and underpants—over bushes when Branko and Isak emerged from the copse, leading a mule with loaded saddlebags.

Branko was a tall, austere young man with dark hair and eyes that seemed permanently narrowed in an expression of skepticism. Isak came barely up to his shoulders. But Lola noticed, as he swept up his little sister, that he looked stronger across the chest and arms than he had in his student days. His face had lost his indoor pallor and was a little sunburned. He seemed pleased to see Ina; Lola thought his eyes even looked a little moist. But soon he was questioning her closely to make sure she had not made any missteps that would betray their position.

Reassured, he turned to Lola. "Thank you for bringing her. Thank you for coming."

Lola shrugged, unsure what to say. It wasn't as if she'd had a choice, but she didn't want to say that in front of Branko, who would decide if she could stay or not. Little Ina, it seemed, they had a use for. A child could wander inconspicuously around town, observing enemy activities. Lola's uses were less clear to Branko, and Isak's introduction didn't help.

"Lola is a comrade from Hashomer Haza'ir," Isak told Branko. "She came to all the meetings. Well, almost all. She's a good hiker. . . ." Isak, who had never paid the least attention to Lola, ran out of things to say that might recommend her to his commander.

Branko stared at her with his narrowed eyes until Lola felt her face burn. He lifted a corner of the jacket she had spread out to dry. "And a good laundress. Unfortunately, we don't have time for such luxuries."

"Lice." She could barely get the word out. "They carry typhus." She hurried on, before her nerve failed. "In case of infestation, you . . . you have to boil all clothes and linens, at least weekly . . . to . . . to kill the eggs . . . otherwise the whole *odred* could become infected." Mordechai had taught her that. It was the kind of practical information that Lola could understand and remember.

"So," said Branko. "You know something."

"I . . . I . . . know how to splint a fracture, and stanch bleeding, and treat bites. . . . I can learn. . . ."

"We could use a medic." Branko continued to regard her, as if by staring alone he could somehow assess her abilities. "Isak has been doing the job, but he has other heavy responsibilities. He could teach you what he knows, maybe. And later, if you do well, we could send you to one of the secret hospitals to learn about treating wounds. I will think about it."

He turned away then, and Lola let out a breath. Then it seemed he reconsidered and turned his blue stare upon her once again. "Meanwhile, we are in need of a muleteer. How do you feel about mules?"

Lola could hardly say that she didn't know the front of a mule from the back. But she worried that Isak might find her too stupid to be a medic. She looked at the beast cropping the grass. She walked over and lifted the straps where they cut into his hide. The flesh was raw and weeping.

"I know that you should put a saddlecloth under a heavy load such as this," she said, "if you want the beast to work for you." She opened the saddlebags and began removing several of the heaviest packages and carrying them into the house. When Oskar strode over to relieve her of them, she shook her head. "I can manage," she said. She gave a shy smile. "In my family, I was the mule."

Everyone laughed then, including Branko. Nothing more was said, but Lola understood that she had been accepted as a member of the *odred*.

That night, around the *pec*, as Branko spoke to them of his plans, Lola's doubts revisited her. Branko was a zealot. In Belgrade he'd been interrogated and beaten for his political activism. He spoke about Tito and Stalin, and about their own duty to follow these two glorious leaders without question. "Your life is not yours," he said. "Every extra day you are given belongs to those of your families who have died. We will see our country free, or we, too, will die. There is no other future before us."

Afterward, Lola lay awake on her hard pallet feeling lost and alone, longing for the gentle warmth of Dora's rounded little back. She did not want to accept the truth of what Branko had said, that her family was dead. Yet the hollow place inside her left little room for hope. The escape from the city and flight through the countryside had filled her mind. But now, as she listened to the snores of strangers, she felt a dull ache. From then on, everything she did would be like moving through a fog.

. . . . .

Over the next few days, Lola considered the mule. She could do very little with him that he had not already decided to do. The first time she was charged with leading him to a drop point to fetch supplies, the mule rebelled against the gradient and pitched his load into a bramble patch. Lola had to brave thorns to retrieve the boxes of ammunition, with Branko's curses falling on her like blows.

Every day, Lola approached the mule tentatively, smearing salve from their limited supplies on his broken hide while he hawed and brayed as if she were flogging him. Gradually, his raw patches healed. Lola sewed pads to sit under the saddlecloth. She puzzled out an A-frame, made of light willow boughs, that better distributed his loads. On long marches, she asked that the mule be given the opportunity to browse when they came upon a patch of wild anise or clover.

Ill treated, the mule had been ill behaved. But he began to respond to Lola's attentions, and before long would nuzzle her with wet affection. She came to like stroking his velvety ears. She named him Rid, for the carroty color of his coat, and because red was the signature color of the Partisan movement.

Lola soon realized that for all Branko's talk, their *odred* wasn't much of a fighting force. Apart from Branko himself, only Isak and Maks had Sten guns. The farm lads and lasses had arrived with a shotgun each. The brigade commander promised them more weapons, but after every drop it seemed that some other *odred*'s needs were more pressing.

Oskar complained of this more than anyone, until Branko told him that if he wanted a gun so badly, he should capture one. "Ina did it, and she's only ten years old," he taunted.

That night, Oskar left the campsite. He did not return the next day. Lola overheard Isak rebuking Branko. "You goaded him into undertaking a fool's errand. How can he capture a weapon when he has no weapon to use?"

Branko shrugged. "Your sister did." He had taken the Luger from Ina and wore it, with some swagger, on his hip. That night, Lola was helping Zlata gather wood for the cook fire when Oskar came crashing through the trees, the grin on his face wide as a clown's. Over his shoulder he had a German rifle. He was wearing a baggy gray uniform several sizes too large for him, pant legs rolled up and the waist cinched with twine, and carrying a Nazi-issue rucksack bulging with supplies.

He refused to tell the tale of his triumph until Branko, Isak, and the rest of the *odred* had gathered. As he handed around slices of German sausage, he told how he had crept into the nearby occupied village and hidden in some roadside bushes. "I had to lie there almost all day, watching the Germans come and go," he said. "There were always two or three of them together. At last, one comes by, alone. I wait till he passes. I jump out of the bushes, shove a stick between his shoulder blades, and shout, *Stoi*! The ass actually believed I was armed. He raised his hands. I got his gun, and then I told him to strip to his underpants."

Everyone was convulsed with laughter at this point, except Branko.

"And then. You shot him." His voice was flat and cold.

"No, I . . . I didn't see the need. . . . He was unarmed . . . I thought . . ."

"And tomorrow, he will be armed again, and the next day, he will kill your comrade. Sentimental fool. You will give the gun to Zlata. She at least will know how to use it." Lola could not see Oskar's face in the dark. But she felt his silent anger.

The next night, the *odred* was required to help secure and clear a drop site. Lola's job was to keep the mule quiet and calm, ready to carry the arms, radios, or medicines that descended by parachute. While her *odred* hid just beyond the tree line, Partisans from a different *odred*, working under the direction of a foreigner— a British spy, someone said—set out brush and tinder for signal fires, laid across a clearing in a prearranged pattern that the Allied pilot would recognize. Lola trembled from fear and cold. She leaned into Rid's thick pelt, seeking warmth. She had no weapon, aside from the grenade that all Partisans were required to wear on their belts. "If you are about to be captured, you will use it to kill yourself and as many of the enemy as you can take with you," Branko had said. "On no account be taken alive. Use the grenade, and then there is no way you can be tortured into betrayal."

The moon had not yet risen. Lola looked up, searching for starlight. But the thick foliage of the trees denied her even that. Her imagination peopled the dark with Germans, waiting to ambush them. The night crawled on. Just before dawn, the wind rose, threshing the pine boughs. Branko decided that the drop must have been aborted, and signaled Lola to prepare to move off. Wearily, stiff from cold, Lola scrambled to her feet and adjusted Rid's halter.

Just then, the faint buzz of an airplane sounded in the distance. Branko shouted orders to get the fires lit. Isak's fire wouldn't catch. He swore as he struggled. Lola did not think of herself as brave. She would not have described the feeling that took hold of her as courage. All she knew was that she could not leave Isak out there, exposed, struggling, alone. She crashed through the trees and into the clearing. She threw herself prone, blowing hard on the stubborn kindling. A flame leaped just as the dark bulk of the Dakota came into view overhead. The pilot made one run, for reconnaissance, and then swept back around, spilling a rain of packages, each with its own small parachute. Partisans emerged from the surrounding forest, running to gather the precious cargo. Lola slashed at the parachute cords and wrapped up the silk, which she would use to make bandages.

The *odreds* worked fast as the sky began to lighten in the east. By the time dawn broke, Lola was toiling along a narrow ridgeline, a fully laden Rid walking biddably beside her, as they tried to put miles between them and the drop site before the Germans reached the place. Whenever they came to a stream, Branko ordered Maks into the water, to turn over the moss-covered stones. After the *odred* had crossed, the stones were flipped back as they had been, the moss unbroken by boot prints or mule hoofs.

.   .   .   .   .

For seven months, Lola's *odred* lived on the move, rarely spending more than a night or two in one campsite, carrying out demolitions of railway tracks or small bridges. On many nights, they were offered the shelter of a farmer's barn, where they slept in an animal warmth, cushioned by straw. But at other times, they camped in the forest, with only a makeshift blanket of pine needles to keep back the punishing cold. Although never much more than five miles from the nearest enemy post, their *odred* managed to escape ambushes that claimed other units. Branko preened about this as if it were a product of his own leadership. He expected to be served and deferred to like a general officer. Once, at the end of a grueling march, he lay down against a tree to take his rest while everyone else scrambled to gather dry firewood before the darkness overtook them. Oskar, throwing a heavy bundle of branches down beside the prone Branko, muttered something about Communists supposedly doing away with elitist privilege.

Branko was on his feet in a second. He gripped Oskar by the front of his uniform and slammed him hard against the trunk of a tree.

"You sniveling brats are lucky I was assigned to lead you. You should be thanking me every day for keeping you alive."

Isak stepped between them and gently pushed Branko away.

"What keeps us alive," he said quietly, "is not luck, or your *excellent* leadership. It's the loyalty of the civilian population. We wouldn't be able to last five minutes out here without their support."

For a moment, it seemed that Branko was going to strike Isak. But he retained control of himself somehow, and stepped back, spitting contemptuously on the ground.

Lola had sensed Isak's growing impatience with Branko. She knew he deplored Branko's incessant speechifying, late into the night, even after long marches, when the exhausted youths would rather have been sleeping than listening to rambling exegesis on surplus value and false consciousness. Isak would try to bring the political harangues to a close, but many times Branko carried on, oblivious.

The greater frustration lay in the difference between Branko's self-regard and the rather low opinion held of him by the brigade commander in their region. Branko promised better weapons, yet they did not materialize. He told Lola that she would be assigned to a field hospital for training, but this never occurred.

Still, she felt useful in her role as muleteer, and even Branko, who was stinting with praise, from time to time commended her. As winter pressed in upon them, most fell ill. The hacking of their wet coughs became the morning reveille. Lola begged onions from the farmers to make poultices. Isak showed her how to compound the ingredients for expectorants, which she administered diligently. She proposed a redistribution of rations so that those who were recuperating from illness could receive more. Branko promised to move them into winter quarters, but weeks passed and the *odred* remained camped out on the unforgiving mountains. Numbers dwindled. Zlata, ill for weeks with a violent chest infection, was taken in by a local peasant family and died there, in a warm bed, at least. Oskar, tired of the hardships and Branko's constant ill will, deserted in the night, taking Slava, one of the farm girls, with him.

Lola worried about Ina. The child had the same hacking cough as most of the *odred*. But when she raised the subject of finding a winter haven for her with Isak, he dismissed it. "For one thing, she would not go. For another, I would not ask her. I promised her I'd never leave her again. It's that simple."

On a blizzarding day in early March, Milovan, the regional brigade commander, summoned the remnant *odred* to a meeting. As the thin, sickly teenagers gathered around him, he began his address. Tito, Milovan said, had a new vision for his army. It was to be consolidated into tough, professional units that would engage the Germans directly. The enemy forces were to be pushed back to the cities, their lines disrupted, until Partisan control of the countryside was achieved.

Lola, her head muffled in a scarf and her cap pulled down tight over her ears, at first thought she had mistaken what the colonel said next. But the dismay on others' faces confirmed that what she thought she had heard was true. Their *odred* was to be disbanded, effective immediately. "Marshal Tito thanks you for your service, and it will be remembered on the glorious day of victory. Now, those of you who have arms, please stack them for collection. You, mule girl. Take charge of loading them. We will leave now. You will wait till nightfall before moving out."

Everyone looked at Branko, waiting for him to say something. But Branko, his head bowed against the blowing snow, said nothing. It was Isak who was left to protest.

"Sir? May I ask where you propose we go?"

"You may go home."

"Home? What home?" Isak was shouting now. "None of us has a home anymore. Most of our families have been murdered. We, all of us, are outlaws. You can't seriously expect us to walk unarmed into the hands of the Ustashe?" He turned to Branko. "Tell him, damn it!"

Branko raised his head and stared coldly at Isak. "You heard the colonel. Marshal Tito has said there is no longer any place for ragtag bands of children wielding sticks and firecrackers. We are a professional army now."

"Oh, I see!" Isak's voice oozed contempt. "*You* may keep *your* gun—the gun my little sister, a 'ragtag child,' got for you. And the rest of us get a death sentence!"

"Silence!" Milovan raised his gloved hand. "Obey your orders, and your service will be rewarded in the future. Disobey, and you will be shot."

Lola, numb and confused, loaded Rid as she had been commanded. When the few rifles and the bag of grenades had been secured, she took the mule's soft muzzle between her two hands and looked into his eyes. "Be safe, friend," she whispered. "You, at least, they have a use for. May they treat you with more loyalty and care than they are showing to us." She handed the halter to Milovan's aide and gave him a sack in which she kept a precious ration of oats. The aide looked inside the bag, and from his expression, Lola realized Rid would be lucky to see the oats again before they warmed the aide's belly. So she thrust her gloved hands into the sack and pulled up two generous handfuls. Rid's wet breath warmed her hands for a moment. Before he had disappeared into the swirling snow, his saliva had frozen solid on the darned wool. Branko, she noted, did not look back.

The rest of the group gathered around Isak, waiting for him to offer them a plan. "I think we will do best in pairs or small groups," he said. His own intention was to head for liberated territory. Lola sat in silence as the discussion passed from one to another around the fire. Some aimed to go south, into Italian-occupied areas. Others said they would seek out extended family members. Lola had no one, and the thought of an uncertain journey to a strange southern town frightened her. She waited for someone to ask her about her plans, to offer her a place at their side. But no one said anything at all. It was as if she had already ceased to exist. When she got up and left the circle, no one said good night.

Lola found her place in a corner of the clearing and tossed there, restless. She had piled her few belongings into a rucksack and had tied up her feet in layers of cloth she'd saved for bandages. She was lying, awake but with her eyes closed, when she felt Ina's fierce brown gaze. The child was wrapped in her blanket as if it were a cocoon. She had a woolen hat pulled tight over her brow, so that her eyes were all that was visible.

Lola did not realize she had drifted to sleep until she felt Ina's small hand shaking her. It was still dark, but Ina and Isak were up, rucksacks packed. Ina put a hand on her lips to urge silence and then extended a hand to pull Lola to her feet. Scrambling, she rolled her blanket and pushed it into the pack with her few supplies, and trailed after Ina and her brother.

The details of the days and nights that followed would return to Lola in her dreams. But in her waking memory, they remained a blur of pain and fear. The three moved in the dark and hid during the short daylight hours, snatching restless sleep when they could find a barn or a haystack to shelter them, waking in fear to the sound of a dog barking, which could mean a German patrol. On the fourth night, Ina's fever rose. Isak had to carry her, shivering, sweating, murmuring in her delirium. On the fifth night, the temperature plunged. Isak had given his socks to Ina, and wrapped her in his coat, in a vain attempt to stop her wracking shivers. Halfway through the night march, just after they had forded an ice-covered river, he stopped and sank down onto the frozen pine needles.

"What is it?" Lola whispered.

"My foot. I can't feel it," Isak said. "The ice—there was a thin place. My foot went through. It got wet and now it's frozen. I can't walk anymore."

"We can't stop here," Lola said. "We've got to find some shelter."

"You go. I can't."

"Let me see." Lola shone her torch beam on the torn, gaping leather of Isak's boot. The exposed flesh was black with frostbite. The foot had been damaged long before the accident in the stream. She placed her gloved hands over the foot to try to warm it. But it was no good. The toes were frozen solid, brittle as twigs. The slightest pressure would snap them right off. Lola took her own coat off and laid it on the ground. She lifted Ina and placed her on it. The child's breath was shallow and irregular. Lola felt for her pulse and could not find it.

"Lola," Isak said. "I can't walk anymore, and Ina is dying. You have to go on alone."

"I'm not leaving you," she said.

"Why not?" said Isak. "I would have left you."

"Maybe so." She got up and began wrenching frozen sticks from the hard ground.

"A fire's too dangerous," Isak said. "And besides, you won't be able to light it with this frozen wood."

Lola felt exasperation, even anger, rise within her.

"You can't just give up," she said.

Isak made no answer. With difficulty, he struggled to his hands and knees, and then somehow stood.

"Your foot," said Lola.

"It does not have to carry me far."

Lola, confused, reached to pick up Ina. Isak gently pushed her aside.

"No," he said. "She comes with me."

He took the child, so thin now she weighed almost nothing. But instead of going on in the direction they'd been walking, he turned and hobbled back toward the river.

"Isak!"

He did not turn. Embracing his little sister, he stepped off the bank, onto the ice. He walked out into the center, where the ice was thin. His sister's head lay on his shoulder. They stood there for a moment, as the ice groaned and cracked. Then it gave way.

Lola reached Sarajevo just as the first light spilled over the mountain ridges and silvered the rain-slicked alleys. Knowing she could not make it alone all the way to the liberated territory, she had turned back toward the city. She made her way down familiar streets, sidling along the line of the buildings, seeking whatever small protection they afforded from the drizzling rain and from unfriendly eyes. She smelled the familiar city scents of wet pavement, rotting garbage, and burning coal. Starving, soaked, and in despair, she walked without any clear destination until she found herself at the steps of the finance ministry, where her father had worked. The building was still and deserted. Lola climbed the broad staircase. She ran a hand across the dark bas-relief that framed the entrace, and sank down onto her haunches in the doorway. She watched the raindrops hit the stairs, each drop sending out concentric circles that linked for a moment and then dissolved. In the mountains, she had pushed the memories of her family to the back of her mind, afraid that if she opened the door to grief, she would be unable to close it. Here, memories of her father pressed upon her. She wished to be a child again, protected, safe.

She must have dozed for a few minutes. Footsteps, from behind the heavy door, woke her. She shrank herself into the shadows, uncertain whether to run or stay. The bolts slid back with a whine of unoiled metal, and a man in workers' overalls emerged, his muffler high around his chin.

He had not yet seen her.

She uttered the traditional words of greeting. "May God save us."

The man turned, startled. His watery blue eyes widened when her saw the dripping, wraithlike figure cowering in the shadows. He did not recognize her, changed as she was by her months of mountain hardship. But she knew him. He was Sava, a kindly old man who had worked beside her father. She said his name, and then her own.

As he realized who she was, he reached down and lifted her to him in an embrace. Relief at his kindness overwhelmed her and she began to weep. Sava scanned the street to be sure that no one observed them. With his arm still wrapped around her shaking shoulders, he steered her inside, closed the door, and bolted it again.

He took her to the janitors' dressing room and wrapped her in his own coat. He poured fresh coffee from the *džezva*. When she could find her voice, she told him of her exile from the Partisan unit. When she came to Ina's death she could not go on. Sava placed his arm around her shoulders and rocked her gently.

"Can you help me," she said at last. "If not, then please, deliver me to the Ustashe now, because I can't run anymore."

Sava regarded her for a moment without saying anything. Then he rose and took her hand. He led her out of the ministry, locking the door behind him. They walked in silence for one block, two. When they reached the National Museum, Sava led her to the porters' entrance and motioned her to wait on a bench inside an alcove near the door.

He was gone a long time. Lola could hear people beginning to move around the building. She began to wonder if Sava had deserted her there. But exhaustion and grief had made her apathetic. She could no longer take any action to save herself. So she sat and she waited.

When Sava reappeared, there was a tall gentleman beside him. The man was middle-aged and very well dressed, with a crimson fez set atop dark hair streaked with silver. There was something a little familiar about him, but Lola could not think where they might have met. Sava took her hand and pressed it reassuringly. Then he was gone. The tall man beckoned Lola to follow him.

They left the building. He ushered her into the backseat of a small car, signaling that she should lie down on the floor. Only when he had started the motor and pulled out from the curb did he speak. His accent was refined, his voice gentle as he questioned her about where she had been and what she had done.

They had not driven any great distance when he stopped the car and got out, telling Lola to stay where she was. He was gone just a few minutes. When he came back, he handed Lola a chador. Then, he motioned her urgently to stay down.

"May God save us, effendi!"

He exchanged pleasantries with the passing neighbor, pretending to search for something in the car's trunk. When the man turned the corner, he opened the rear door and gestured for Lola to follow. She pulled the chador across her face and kept her eyes down, as she had seen the modest Muslim women do. Inside the building, he rapped sharply on the door, and it opened at once.

His wife was standing just inside, waiting. Lola looked up and recognized her. It was the young wife who had given her coffee when she came to collect the laundry. Stela showed no sign of remembering Lola, which was unsurprising given the great change in her appearance. The year had aged her. She was gaunt and sinewy, her hair cropped short like a boy's.

Stela looked anxiously from Lola's haggard face to her husband's concerned one. He spoke to her in Albanian. Lola had no idea what was said, but she saw Stela's eyes widen. He continued speaking, gently but urgently. Stela's eyes filled, but she wiped them with a lace handkerchief and turned to Lola.

"You are welcome in our home," she said. "My husband tells me you have suffered very much. Come now and wash, eat, rest. Later, when you have slept, we will talk about how best to keep you safe." Serif looked at his wife with a gentle expression of mingled tenderness and pride. Lola saw the glance, and how Stela colored as she returned it. To be loved like that, she thought, would be something indeed.

"I must return to the museum now," he said. "I will see you this evening. My wife will take good care of you."

The feel of hot water and the fragrant scent of soap were luxuries that, to Lola, seemed to belong to another lifetime. Stela gave her steaming soup and fresh bread, and Lola tried her best to eat it slowly, although in her extreme hunger she could have picked up the bowl in both hands and drained it. When she was done, Stela led her to a small alcove room. There was a baby's crib, and in it an infant napped. "This is my son, Habib, born last autumn," she said. She indicated a low sofa along the wall. "This can be your room, too." Lola lay down, and even before Stela returned with a quilt, she had fallen into an exhausted sleep.

When she woke, it was like swimming up through deep water. The crib beside her was empty. She could hear soft voices, one anxious, one reassuring. Then a baby's gentle mewling, quickly quieted. Lola saw that there were clothes set out for her on the bed. They were unfamiliar clothes, a full skirt such as an Albanian Muslim peasant woman might wear, and a large white scarf to cover her cropped hair that could also be pulled across the bridge of her nose to hide the lower part of her face. She knew that her own clothes, Partisan fatigues she'd sewn months ago from a piece of gray blanket, would have to be burned to ashes.

She dressed, struggling a little with the unfamiliar head scarf.

When she entered the book-lined sitting room, Serif and Stela were sitting close together, deep in conversation. Serif had his son, a fine little fellow with a shock of dark hair, perched on his knee. His free hand was entwined with his wife's. They looked up as Lola entered the room, and swiftly withdrew their hands. Lola knew that conservative Muslims felt it was inappropriate even for married couples to express physical affection in the presence of others.

Serif smiled at Lola kindly. "My, you make a fine peasant!" he said. "If you do not mind, the story we will tell to explain your presence here is that you are a maid sent by Stela's family, to help her with the baby. You will pretend to know no Bosnian language at all, and that way you will not need to speak to anyone. In the presence of others, Stela and I will address you in Albanian. You just need to nod to anything we say. It will be best if you do not leave the apartment at all, so very few people will even know you are here. We will need to give you a Muslim name . . . does Leila suit you?"

"I don't deserve this kindness," she whispered. "That you, Muslims, should help a Jew—"

"Come now!" Serif said, realizing that she was about to cry. "Jews and Muslims are cousins, the descendants of Abraham. Your new name, do you know it means 'evening' both in Arabic, the language of our Holy Koran, and also in Hebrew, the language of your Torah?"

"I . . . I . . . we never learned Hebrew," she stammered. "My family wasn't religious." Her parents had gone to the Jewish social club, but never to the synagogue. They tried to dress the children in new clothes at Hanukkah, in years when they could afford to, but apart from that, Lola knew very little of her faith.

"Well, it is a very beautiful and fascinating language," said Serif. "The rabbi and I were collaborating on the translation of some texts, before—well, before this nightmare in which we find ourselves." He rubbed a hand across his brow and sighed. "He was a good man, a very great scholar, and I mourn him."

·   ·   ·

In the weeks that followed, Lola found herself adapting to the rhythms of a very different life. The fear of discovery waned with the passing of time, and before long, the calm, quiet routines of life as the Kamals' baby nurse seemed more real to her than her former existence as a *partisanka*. She grew used to Stela's soft, tentative voice calling her by her new name, Leila. She loved the baby almost from the first time she held him. And she quickly grew fond of Stela, whose physical life in conservative Muslim families had been entirely domestic and private, but whose intellectual horizons, as the daughter and wife of learned people, had been expansive. At first, Lola was a little afraid of Serif, who was almost as old as her father. But his gentle, courtly manners soon put her at her ease. For a while, she couldn't say what it was about him that was so different from other people she had known. And then one day, as he patiently drew her out on some subject or another, listening to her opinion as if it were worthy of his consideration, and then guiding her subtly to a fuller view of the issue, she realized what the difference was. Serif, the most learned person she had ever met, was also the only person who never let her feel the least bit stupid.

The Kamals' day was organized around two things, prayer and learning. Five times a day, Stela would stop whatever she was doing, wash herself carefully, and apply perfume. Then she would spread a small silken rug that she kept only for prayer, and make the prostrations and recitations required by her faith. Lola could not understand the words, but she found the sonorous rhymes of the Arabic soothing.

In the evenings, Stela would work a piece of embroidery while Serif read aloud to her. At first, Lola had retired with Habib at that time, but they had invited her to stay and listen if she wished to. She would sit just a little outside of the circle of yellow light thrown by the lamp and hold Habib on her knee, rocking him gently. Serif chose lively histories or beautiful poems to read, and Lola increasingly found herself looking forward to those evening hours. If Habib fussed and she was obliged to leave the room with him, Serif either waited for her return or summarized whatever she had missed.

Sometimes, she woke in the night, sweaty from a dream in which the Germans' dogs were pursuing her, or in which her little sister cried to her for help as they stumbled through dense woods. In other dreams, Isak and Ina disappeared, again and again, through the cracking ice. When she woke, she would lift Habib from his crib and hug him, taking comfort from the feel of his heavy little body pressed sleepily against her own.

One day, Serif returned early from the library. He did not greet his wife or ask after his son, or even remove his coat at the door, as usual, but went straight into his study.

After a few minutes, he called them. Lola did not usually go into the study. Stela cleaned that room herself. Now, she looked at the books that lined the walls. The volumes were even older and finer than those elsewhere in the apartment; books in a half dozen ancient and modern languages, with exquisite hand-tooled bindings of polished leather. But Serif was cradling a small, simply bound book in his gloved hands. He set it down on the desk in front of him and gazed at it with the same expression he wore when looking at his son.

"General Faber visited the museum today," he said. Stela gasped and clapped a hand to her head. Faber was the feared commander of the Black Hand units, rumored to be responsible for the massacres of thousands.

"No, no, nothing terrible happened. In fact, I think what happened was very good. Today, with the help of the director, we managed to save one of the museum's great treasures."

Serif did not choose to relate a full account of what had taken place at the museum earlier that day. He had not even intended to show them the haggadah. But the presence of the book—in his house, in his hands—somehow overpowered his prudence. He turned the pages so that they could admire the artistry of the book, and told them only that the museum director had trusted it to his care.

.   .   .   .   .

Serif's superior was Dr. Josip Boscovic, a Croatian who managed to negotiate an appearance of complicity with the Ustashe regime in Zagreb while remaining a Sarajevan in his heart. Boscovic had been a curator in old coins before moving into the museum's administration. He was a popular figure in Sarajevo, a fixture at cultural events. His dark hair was slicked back with a highly scented pomade, and his weekly appointment with his manicurist was an immutable rite.

When Faber sent word that he intended to visit the museum, Boscovic realized that his tightrope walk was about to begin in earnest. His own German was poor, so he called Serif into his office and told him he would be needed to translate. He and Serif had different backgrounds and different intellectual interests. But the two men shared the same fierce commitment to Bosnian history and a love for the diversity that had shaped that history. They also shared an unstated recognition that Faber stood for the extinction of diversity.

"Do you know what he wants?" Serif asked.

"He did not say. But I think we can guess. My colleague in Zagreb told me that they looted the museum's Judaica collection. You know, and I know, that what we have here is infinitely more important. I believe he wants the haggadah."

"Josip, we can't give it to him. He will destroy it, as his men have destroyed every Jewish thing in the city."

"Serif, friend, what choice have we? He might not destroy it. I have heard talk that Hitler plans a Museum of the Lost Race, to exhibit the finest Jewish objects, after the people themselves are gone. . . ."

Serif slapped the back of the chair in front of him. "Is there no limit to the depravity of these people?"

"Shhh." Boscovic raised both hands to quiet his colleague. He dropped his own voice to a whisper. "They were joking about it, in Zagreb last month. They called it *Judenforschung ohne Juden*—Jewish Studies Without Jews." Boscovic stepped from behind his desk and laid a hand on Serif's shoulder. "If you try to hide this book, you put your life at risk."

Serif regarded him gravely. "What choice have I? I am *kustos*. Did it survive five hundred years to be destroyed under my stewardship? If you think I can allow such a thing, my friend, you do not know me."

"Do what you must do then. But be quick, I beg you."

Serif returned to the library. With hands that shook, he drew out a box he had labeled ARCHIV DER FAMILIE KAPETANOVIC—TÜRKISCHE URKUNDEN (Archives of the Kapetanovic Family—Turkish Document)s. He lifted a few old Turkish land title deeds from the top of the box. Underneath were several Hebrew codices. He lifted out the smallest one and tucked it under the belt of his trousers, pulling down his coat so that it concealed the bulge. He returned the Turkish deeds to the box and resealed it.

Faber was a spare man, small boned and not particularly tall. He had a gentle voice that he rarely raised much above a whisper, so that people had to pay close attention when he spoke. His eyes were the cool, opaque green of agate stone, set in skin pale and as translucent as the flesh of a fish.

Josip had risen as an administrator because of a charming manner that sometimes bordered on unctuousness. As he greeted the general with a courtly welcome, no one would have known that the back of his neck prickled with nervous sweat. He excused his poor German, apologizing far more profusely than necessary. Serif appeared at the door then, and Josip introduced him. "My colleague is a great linguist; he puts me to shame."

Serif approached the general and offered his hand. The general's grip was unexpectedly soft. Serif felt the flaccid hand lying loosely in his. He was aware of the manuscript shifting slightly against his waist.

Faber did not state the purpose of his visit. In an awkward silence, Josip offered a tour of the collections. As they walked through the vaulted halls, Serif gave an erudite account of the various exhibits while Faber paced behind him, slapping his black leather gloves against a pale white palm and saying nothing.

When they arrived at the library, Faber nodded curtly and spoke for the first time. "Let me see your Jewish manuscripts and incunabula." Shaking slightly, Serif selected volumes from the shelves and laid them on the long table. There was a mathematics text of Elia Mizrahi's, a rare edition of a Hebrew-Arabic-Latin vocabulary published in Naples in 1488, a Talmud volume printed in Venice.

Faber's pale hands caressed each volume. He turned the pages with exquisite care. As he fingered the rarest of the codices, peering at the faded inks and delicate, veined parchments, his expression changed. He moistened his lips. Serif noted that his pupils were dilated, like a lover's. Serif looked away. He felt a mixture of disgust and violation, as if he were witness to a pornographic spectacle. Finally, Faber closed the binding of the Venetian Talmud and looked up, his brow raised in a question.

"And now, if you please, the haggadah."

Serif felt a rivulet of scalding sweat run down his back. He turned up his palms and shrugged. "That's impossible, Herr General," he said.

Josip's face, which had been flushed, turned quite pale.

"What do you mean, 'impossible'?" Faber's quiet voice was cold.

"What my colleague means," said Josip, "is that one of your officers came here yesterday and requested the haggadah. He said it was wanted for a particular museum project of the Führer's. Of course, we were honored to give him our treasure for such a purpose. . . ."

Serif began to translate Josip's words, but the general interrupted him.

"Which officer? Give me his name." He stepped toward Josip. Despite his slight build, the general suddenly seemed to ooze menace. Josip took a step backward, knocking against the bookshelves.

"Sir, he did not give me his name. I . . . I . . . did not feel it was my place to ask it. . . . But if you would come with me to my office, I might be able to give you the paper he signed for me, as a receipt."

As Serif translated his director's words, Faber sucked in his breath. "Very well." He turned on his heel and headed for the door. Josip had only an instant to exchange a glance with Serif. He made it the most eloquent glance of his life. Then, in a voice as calm as a lake on a still day, Serif called after the general. "Please, sir, follow the director. He will lead you to the main stair."

Serif knew he had very little time. He hoped he had divined the director's plan correctly. He scribbled out a receipt with the haggadah's catalog numbers and then, in a different pen, signed below them in an illegible scrawl. He called for a porter and told the man to take the paper to the director's office. "Use the service stair, and be as quick as you can. Put it on his desk where he can see it the instant he walks in."

Then, deliberately, forcing himself to slow his movements, he walked to the hat stand and reached for his overcoat and fez. He sauntered out of the library and across the hall to the museum's main entrance. He made eye contact with Faber's waiting entourage, nodding in acknowledgment of their presence. Halfway down the museum stair, he stopped to confer with a colleague who was ascending. He passed the large black staff car waiting at the curb. Smiling and greeting his acquaintances, he stopped at his favorite café. He sipped his coffee slowly, as a real Bosnian is supposed to, savoring every drop. Then, and only then, he headed for home.

As Serif turned the pages of the haggadah, Lola gasped at the splendor of the illuminations.

"You should be very proud of this," he said to her. "It is a great work of art that your people have given the world."

Stela wrung her hands and said something in Albanian. Serif looked at her, his expression firm and yet kindly. He answered in Bosnian. "I know you are concerned, my dear. And you have every right to be. We already shelter a Jew, and now a Jewish book. Both very much wanted by the Nazis. A young life and an ancient artifact. Both very precious. And you say that you do not care about the risk to yourself, and for that I commend you, and am proud. But you fear for our son. And what you fear is very real. I, too, fear for him. I have made plans for Leila with a friend of mine. Tomorrow, we will meet him. He will guide her to a family in the Italian zone who can keep her safe."

"But what about the book?" said Stela. "Surely the general will uncover your deception. After they search the museum, won't they come here?"

"Don't worry," said Serif calmly. "It is by no means certain he will uncover us. Dr. Boscovic had the presence of mind to tell Faber one of his men had come for the book. The Nazis are looters at heart. Faber knows that his officers are schooled in theft. He probably has a half dozen men he believes capable of having stolen the book to enrich themselves. And in any case," he said, wrapping the small volume in its cloth, "after tomorrow, it will not be here."

"Where will you take it?" said Stela.

"I am not sure. The best place to hide a book might be in a library." He had thought about simply returning the book to the museum, misshelving it somewhere among the many thousands of volumes. But then he recalled another library, much smaller, where he had spent many happy hours studying at the side of a dear friend. He turned to Stela and smiled. "I will take it," he said, "to the last place anyone would think to look."

The next day was Friday, the Muslim Sabbath. Serif went to work as usual, but excused himself at midday, saying he wished to attend the communal prayers. He returned to his home to collect Stela, Habib, and Lola. Instead of heading for the local mosque, he drove out of the city, up into the mountains. Lola held Habib during the drive, playing his favorite games of peep-o and handy pandy, drawing him close whenever she could, trying to memorize the smell of his head, which reminded her of the sweet fragrance of mown grass. The road was a difficult one, narrow and switchbacked. Now, in midsummer, the light was as rich as butter, golden on the small fields of wheat and sunflowers that filled each sliver of flatland between the swift, steep rises of the mountains. When winter came, the snows would make these ways impassable until spring thaw. Lola concentrated on Habib to stop herself from feeling nauseated by the car's movement and by her own anxiety. She knew it was wise to leave the city, where the risk that she would be discovered was constant. But she hated to leave the Kamals. Despite the grief she carried and the fear that stalked her, the four months in their household had brought her a serenity she'd never experienced before.

It was sunset when they came through the final narrow pass and saw the village open like a flower in its small hanging valley. A farmer was bringing his cows in from the fields, and the call to evening prayer mingled with the whine and groan of the moving cattle. Up here, in the isolation of the mountains, the war and its privations seemed very far away.

Serif stopped the car at a low stone house. The walls were white, each stone laid alongside the next with the precision of an elaborate jigsaw puzzle. The deep, niched windows were tall and narrow, with thick shutters, painted cerulean blue, that could be closed against winter storms. Wild larkspur, a deeper blue, grew in profusion around the building. A pair of butterflies drifted lazily amid the blossoms. An old mulberry tree spread its boughs over the courtyard. As soon as the car pulled up, a half dozen small faces peeped out of the glossy foliage. The tree was thick with children, perched on its branches like bright birds.

One by one, the children dropped out of the tree and swarmed around Serif, who had brought a sweet for each of them. From the cottage, a slightly older girl, her face veiled like Stela's, emerged, rebuking the children for the ruckus. "But Uncle Serif is here!" the children cried excitedly, and Lola could see the girl's eyes smiling over her veil.

"Welcome, most welcome!" she said. "Father has not yet returned from the mosque, but my brother Munib is inside. Please, come, and be comfortable." Munib, a scholarly looking youth of about nineteen, was seated at a desk, magnifying glass in one hand, tweezers in the other, carefully mounting an insect specimen. The table shimmered with fragments of wings.

Munib turned as his sister called to him, looking cross that his concentration had been disturbed. But his expression changed when he saw Serif. "Sir! What an unexpected honor." Serif, knowing his friend's son's great passion for insects, had secured work for Munib as an assistant in the museum's natural history department during school vacations.

"I am glad to see that you keep up with your study, despite the difficult times," Serif said. "I know your father still hopes to send you to the university one day."

"*Insha'Allah,*" Munib said.

As Serif took a seat on a low couch under an arched window, Munib's sister ushered Stela and Lola into the women's parlor, as the younger children carried in a seemingly endless parade of trays: grape juice, pressed from the family's own vines, tea—a rarity now in the city—homegrown cucumbers, and handmade pastries.

So Lola was not present when Serif Kamal asked his good friend, Munib's father, the village *khoja,* to hide the haggadah. She did not see the enthusiasm on the *khoja*'s face as he impatiently brushed aside his son's work to clear a space on the table for the manuscript, or the wonder in his eyes as he turned its pages. The sun had set, bathing the room in a warm red afterglow. Tiny motes shimmered and danced in the fading light. As a child entered carrying a tray of tea, one small piece of butterfly wing rose on the slight breeze from the open door and fluttered to rest, unnoticed, on the haggadah's open page.

Serif and the *khoja* took the haggadah into the library of the mosque. They found it a narrow place on a high shelf, pressed between volumes of Islamic law. The last place anyone would think of looking.

Later that night, the Kamals drove back down the mountain. They stopped just outside the city, at a fine house with a high stone wall. Serif turned to Stela. "Say good-bye now. We can't linger here." Lola and Stela embraced. "Farewell, my sister," Stela said. "God keep you safe until we meet again." Lola's throat closed, and she could not answer. She kissed the baby's head and handed him to his mother, then she followed Serif into the dark.

Hanna

Vienna, Spring 1996

PARNASSIUS.

Great name for a butterfly. It had a kind of loftiness, and I felt elevated as I walked out through the manicured gardens of the museum toward the swirling traffic of the Ringstrasse. I'd never found butterfly remains in a book before. I couldn't wait to get to Werner's place and tell him all about it.

The traveling scholarship that brought me to Vienna after my undergraduate degree could have taken me anywhere. Jerusalem or Cairo would have made most sense. But I was determined to study with Werner Maria Heinrich, or Universitätsprofessor Herr Doktor Doktor Heinrich, as I'd been told to address him, the Austrians being the opposite of Australians in insisting on giving a separate title for each degree earned. I'd heard about his expertise in traditional techniques—he was the world's best at spotting forgeries because he knew more than anyone about the original crafts and materials. He was also a specialist in Hebrew manuscripts, which I found intriguing for a German Catholic of his generation. I offered myself as his apprentice.

His reply to my first letter was polite but dismissive—"honored by your interest but unfortunately not in a position," etc. My second letter yielded a shorter, slightly more exasperated turndown. The third got a flat and rather testy one-liner that translated into Aussie as "no bloody way." But I came anyway. With an immense amount of front, I presented myself at his apartment on Maria-Theresienstrasse, and begged him to take me on. It was winter, and, like most Australians on their first trip to a seriously cold place, I'd come unprepared for the brutal weather. I thought my rather fetching, cropped leather jacket was a winter coat, since it served that purpose in Sydney. I had no idea. So I must've cut a pathetic figure when I lobbed up on his doorstep, shivering, the snowflakes that'd melted in my hair turned to little icicles that clinked when I moved my head. His innate courtliness made it impossible for him to turn me away.

The months I spent grinding pigments or polishing parchments in his spacious flat-cum-workshop, or sitting beside him in the conservation department of the nearby university library taught me more, I think, than all my formal degrees combined. The first month was very stiff: "Miss Heath" this and "Herr Doktor Doktor" that, correct and rather chilly. But by the time I left I was his "Hanna, *Liebchen*." I think we each filled a vacancy in the other's life. We were both rather shorthanded in the family department. I'd never known my grandparents. His family had been killed in the Dresden firebombing. He'd been in Berlin, in the army, of course, although he never talked of it. Nor did he speak about his childhood in Dresden, abbreviated by war. Even in those days, I had enough tact not to press it. But I noticed that when I walked with him near the Hofburg, he always went out of his way to avoid Heldenplatz, the Hero's Square. It was only much later that I came across the famous picture of that square, taken in March of 1938. In the photograph, it is packed with people, some of them clinging to the gigantic equestrian statues to get a better view, all of them cheering as Hitler announced the incorporation of his birth nation into the Third Reich.

After I left Werner to go to Harvard for my PhD (where I probably wouldn't have been accepted without his glowing recommendation), he wrote to me occasionally, telling me about interesting projects he was working on, offering me career advice. And when he came to New York a couple of times, I'd take the train down from Boston to see him. But it had been a few years since then, so I wasn't prepared for the frail figure waiting for me at the top of the marble-clad staircase that led up to his flat.

He was leaning on an ebony cane with a silver top. His hair, too, was silver, rather long, brushed back from his forehead. He was wearing a dark velvet jacket with pale lemon piping on the lapels. At his neck he wore a bow tie in the nineteenth-century fashion, a long piece of patterned silk tied loosely under the collar. He had a little white rosebud for a boutonniere. I knew how particular he was about appearances, so I'd taken more than usual pains with my own grooming, making my French twist fancy rather than functional and wearing a fuchsia suit that looked good with my dark hair.

"Hanna, *Liebchen*! How beautiful today! How beautiful! More lovely each time I see you!" He grasped my hand and kissed it, then peered at the chapped skin and made a little *tsk*. "The price of our craft, eh?" he said. His own hands were rough and gnarled, but I noted that his nails were freshly manicured, which mine, alas, were not.

In his mid-seventies, Werner had retired from the university, but he still wrote the rare paper and occasionally consulted on important manuscripts. The minute I stepped into the apartment, I could see—and smell—that he hadn't stopped working with the materials of old books. The long table by the tall Gothic windows, where I'd sat beside him and learned so much, remained cluttered with agate stones and foul-smelling gallnuts, antique gold-beater's tools, and parchments in all states of preparation.

He had a maid now, and as he ushered me into the library—one of my favorite rooms in the world, since every volume in it seemed to come with a story—she served the *kaffee*.

The rich cardamom scent made me feel like a twenty-year-old student again. Werner had taken to drinking his coffee Arabic style after a visiting professorship at the Hebrew University in Jerusalem, where he'd lived in the Christian quarter of the Old City, among Palestinians. Every time I smelled cardamom it reminded me of him, and of this apartment, washed with the pale gray European light that is so easy on the eyes when you're working for hours on fine details.

"So. It is good to see you, Hanna. Thank you for taking the time to come out of your way and humor an old man."

"Werner, you know I love to see you. But I was hoping you might be able to help me with something, as well."

His face lit up. He leaned forward in his wing chair. "Tell me!"

I'd brought my notes, so I referred to these as I told him what I had done in Sarajevo. He nodded, approving. "It is exactly as I myself would have done. You are a good student." Then I told him about the *Parnassius* wing fragment, which intrigued him, and then the other artifacts—the white hair, the samples of stain and the salt, and finally I got to the oddity of the grooved boards.

"I agree," he said. "Definitely it seems they were prepared to take a pair of clasps." He looked up at me, his blue eyes watery behind gold-rimmed glasses. "So, why are they not there? Most interesting. Most mysterious."

"Do you think the National Museum would have anything on the haggadah, and the work that was done there back in 1894? It's a long time ago. . . ."

"Not so very long for Vienna, my dear. I am sure there will be something. Whether it is something useful is another matter. But it was a tremendous fuss, you know, when the manuscript came to light. The first of the illustrated haggadot to be rediscovered. Two of the foremost scholars of the day traveled here to examine it. I am sure the museum has their papers, at least. I think that one of them was Rothschild, from Oxford; yes, that's right, I'm sure of it. The other was Martell, from the Sorbonne—you read French, yes? The binder's notes, if they kept them, they would be in German. But perhaps the binder left no notes. As you saw for yourself, the rebinding was disgracefully mishandled."

"Why do you think that was, when the book was the center of so much attention?"

"I believe there was a controversy over who should keep the book.

Vienna, of course, wanted to retain it. Why not? The capital of the Austro-Hungarian empire, the center of Europe's artistic energy . . . But remember, the Hapsburgs only *occupied* Bosnia at that time— they didn't annex it until 1908. And the Slav nationalists hated the occupation." He raised a crooked finger and waved it—it was a mannerism of his when he had something he thought particularly interesting to say.

"By coincidence, the man who started World War I was born the very year the haggadah came here, did you know that?"

"You mean the student who shot the Hapsburg guy in Sarajevo?" Werner drew in his chin, grinning smugly. He loved to tell people something they didn't know. We were alike in that way.

"In any case, I think fear of inciting nationalism might have been why the book was eventually returned to the Bosnian Landesmuseum. My guess is that the clumsy binding was Vienna's revenge, a little piece of petty snobbery: if it has to go to the provinces, then a cheap binding is good enough. Or it may have been something more sinister." His voice dropped a little, and he drummed his fingers on the brocaded arm of his chair. "I don't know if you are aware of it, but those fin de siècle years saw a great surge in anti-Semitism here. Everything Hitler said and some large part of what he did with regard to the Jews was rehearsed here, you know. It was the air he breathed, growing up in Austria. He would have been, let me see, about five years old, starting kindergarten in Braunau, when the haggadah was here. So strange, to think about such things. . . ." His voice trailed off. We had begun to tread rather close to forbidden ground. When he looked up at me and spoke again, I thought at first that he was trying to change the subject.

"Tell me, Hanna, have you read Schnitzler? No? You must! You cannot understand anything about the Viennese, even today, without Arthur Schnitzler."

He groped for his cane and stood, with difficulty, treading slowly and carefully toward the bookcases. He ran his finger along the spines of volumes that were almost all first or rare editions. "I have only the

German and you still do not read German, do you? No? Great pity. Very interesting writer, Schnitzler, very—forgive me—erotic. Very frank about his many seductions. But also he writes a great deal on the rise of the *Judenfressers*—that means Jew Eaters, because the term *anti-Semitism* was not yet coined when he was a boy. Schnitzler was Jewish, of course."

He drew a book from the shelf—"This is called *My Youth in Vienna*. It's a very nice edition—an association copy, Schnitzler to his Latin master, one Johann Auer, 'with thanks for the Auerisms.' Do you know, I found this in a church book sale in Salzburg? Remarkable that no one had spotted it. . . ." He leafed through the book until he found the passage he sought. "Here, he apologizes for writing so much on 'the so-called Jewish question.' But he says that no Jew, no matter how assimilated, was allowed to forget the fact of his birth." He adjusted his glasses and read aloud, translating. " 'Even if you managed to conduct yourself so that nothing showed, it was impossible to remain completely untouched; as for instance a person may not remain unconcerned whose skin has been anesthetized but who has to watch, with his eyes open, how it is scratched by an unclean knife, even cut until the blood flows.' " Werner closed the book. "He wrote that in the early 1900s. The imagery is very chilling, is it not, in the light of what followed. . . ."

He replaced the book on the shelf, then drew a crisply ironed white handkerchief from his pocket and wiped his brow. He sat down heavily in his armchair. "So it is possible that the rebinding was careless because the binder was one of Schnitzler's Jew Eaters."

He sipped the last of his coffee. "But maybe it was none of these things. At that time, it wasn't appreciated, what even the most dilapidated binding might be able to tell. Much information was lost when old bindings were stripped and discarded. Every time I have had to work on such a volume, it pains me to think of it. Most likely, if the book arrived in Vienna with clasps of some kind on the old binding, they would have been the original . . . but one cannot be sure. . . ."

I nibbled at a small piece of a devastatingly rich cake called Waves of the Danube, which was Werner's favorite. He rose, dusting the crumbs from his jacket, and shuffled to the telephone to call his contact at the museum. After an animated conversation in German, he put down the receiver. "The Verwaltungsdirektor can see you tomorrow. She says the papers from that era are archived in a depository some distance away from the museum. She will have them sent to her by noon tomorrow. When do you need to be in Boston?"

"I can stay another day or two," I said.

"Good! You will call me, yes, and let me know if you find something?"

"Yes, of course," I said. I got up to go. At the door, I leaned down—he was slightly stooped now and just a little shorter than I was—and kissed his papery cheek.

"Werner, forgive me for asking, but, are you quite well?"

"*Liebchen,* I am seventy-six. Very few of us are 'quite well' at that age. But I manage."

He stood at the doorway as I walked down the stairs. I turned in the ornate entranceway, looked up, and blew him a kiss, wondering if I'd ever see him again.

Later that afternoon, I sat on the corner of my narrow bed in the pension near Peterskirche with the phone in my lap. I'd badly wanted to tell Ozren about the *Parnassius.* But when I pulled my notebook from my document case, the envelope with Alia's brain scans had fallen out. I felt suddenly guilty about flouting Ozren's will and butting into his private suffering. He'd probably go ballistic all over again if he found out what I'd done. He was right; it was none of my damn business. Much as I wanted to talk to him about the butterfly wing, the fact of my own deception hung over me like a wet sack. Finally, when it was well past the time I thought he'd be at the museum, I got up the nerve to call. He was there, working late. I blurted out the news about the book, and could hear the pleasure in his voice.

"There has always been a big question about where the haggadah was during World War II. We know that the *kustos* somehow kept it from the Nazis, but there were various stories: that he concealed it within the library among some Turkish documents, that he took it to a village in the mountains and hid it in a mosque. Your wing seems to be evidence for the mountains. I can look at the elevations and see if I can narrow down a village, and then ask around to see if he had any special ties in any of them. It would be very nice to know who we have to thank for hosting the haggadah during the war. Too bad no one ever asked him when he was alive. He suffered a lot, after the war, you know. The Communists charged him with being a Nazi collaborator."

"But he saved the haggadah. How could he be a collaborator?"

"Not just the haggadah. He saved Jews, too. But a charge of collaboration was a useful way for the Communists to get rid of anyone who was too intellectual, too religious, too outspoken. He was all of those things. He fought with them a lot, especially when they wanted to tear down the Old City. Horrible urban renewal plans they had, for a while. He helped stop that madness, but it cost him. Six years in solitary confinement—absolutely terrible conditions. Then, suddenly, they pardoned him. That was how it went at that time. He got back his old job at the museum. But probably the time in jail destroyed his health. He died in the 1960s, after a long illness."

I raked a hand through my hair, pulling out the pins that secured it.

"Six years in solitary. I don't know how anyone copes with that."

Ozren was silent for a moment. "No, I don't know, either."

"I mean, it wasn't like he was a soldier or even a political activist . . . people like that, you think, well, they know what the stakes are. But he was just a librarian. . . ."

As soon as I said that, I felt like an idiot. Ozren, after all, was "just" a librarian, and that hadn't stopped him acting with guts when he'd had to.

"I mean . . ."

"I know what you mean, Hanna. So, tell me: what are your plans?"

"I'm going to check out the archives at the National Museum tomorrow. See if there's anything about clasps. Then I'll be in Boston for a couple of days and I can do some tests on the stains at a friend's lab there."

"Good. Let me know what you find out."

"I will. . . . Ozren . . ."

"Hmmm?"

"How is Alia?"

"We're almost finished *Winnie-the-Pooh*. I thought perhaps I'd read him some Bosnian fairy tales next."

I hoped the static on the phone line masked the way my voice went all weird as I mumbled a reply.

Frau Zweig, the chief archivist at the Historisches Museum der Stadt Wien, was not at all what I expected. In her late twenties, she was dressed in high black boots, a teensy plaid skirt, and a tight, electric blue jersey that emphasized an enviable figure. Her dark hair was cropped in a jagged bob and streaked in various shades of red and yellow. There was a silver stud in the side of her retroussé nose.

"You are a friend of Werner?" she said, shocking me further by being the only Viennese I'd ever heard call him by his first name. "He's a trip, isn't he? With the velvet suits and that whole last-century thing he's got going on. I just *adore* him."

She led me down the back stairs of the museum, into the warren of basement rooms. The *clip clip* of her high-heeled boots echoed on the stone floor. "Sorry to set you up in such a dump," she said, opening the door to a storeroom whose functional metal shelves were filled with the familiar accoutrements of exhibition spaces—bits of old frames and mounting boards, dismantled display cases, jars of preservative. "I would have put you in my office, but I'm in meetings there practically all day—staff review time, you know. *Sooooo* boring." She rolled her eyes like an adolescent resisting a parental directive. "Austrian bureaucracy sucks, you know? I trained in New York City. It was hard to come back here to all this formality." She wrinkled her small nose. "I wish I could move to Australia. Everyone in New York thought I was from there, you know? I'd say Austria and they'd go, 'Oh! Such cute kangaroos!' I let them think that. You guys have such a better reputation than we do. Everyone thinks, Australians: relaxed, funny. Austrians: Old World, stuffy. Should I move there, you think?" I didn't want to disillusion her, so I didn't let on that I'd never seen anyone quite as unstuffy as she was in a senior archivist position in Australia.

There was an archival box on the workbench in the center of the room. Frau Zweig took a box cutter and broke the seals. "Good luck," she said. "Let me know if you need anything. And give Werner a big kiss from me." She closed the door, but I could hear the *clip* of her boots receding down the corridor.

There were three folders in the box. I doubted anyone had looked at them in a hundred years. All of them were embossed with the museum seal, and the abbreviation K.u.K, which stood for *Kaiserlich und Königlich*—imperial and royal. The Hapsburgs had the title "emperor" in Austria and "king" in Hungary. I blew the dust off the first folder. It contained just two documents, both in Bosnian. I could tell that one of them was a copy of the bill of sale to the museum from the family named Kohen. The second was a letter, in very fair handwriting. Luckily, there were translations attached to it, probably made for the visiting scholars. I scanned the English version.

The author of the letter introduced himself as a teacher—hence the careful handwriting. He was, he said, an instructor of the Hebrew language at Sarajevo's *maldar*. The translator had added a note explaining that this was the name for the elementary schools run by Sephardic Jews. "A son of the Kohen family, being my pupil, brought the haggadah to me. The family, recently bereaved of its breadwinner, desired to alleviate their financial strains by realizing something on the sale of the book . . . sought my opinion as to its value. . . . While I have seen dozens of haggadot, some of them very old, I have never seen illuminations of this kind. . . . On visiting the family to learn more, I found that there was no information regarding the haggadah beyond the fact that it had been in the Kohen family "many years." The widow said her husband had related that the book had been used when his grandfather conducted seder, which would put it in Sarajevo as early as the mid-eighteenth century. . . . She said, and I was able to confirm, that the Kohen grandfather in question was a cantor who had trained in Italy. . . ."

I sat back in the chair. Italy. The Vistorini inscription—*Revisto per mi*—put the haggadah in Venice in 1609. Had the Kohen grandfather trained in Venice? The Jewish community there would have been much larger and more prosperous than Bosnia's, and the musical heritage of the city was rich. Had he perhaps acquired the book there?

I imagined the family, with its educated, cosmopolitan patriarch, gathered at the seder table; the son, growing from child to man, burying his father in due season and taking his place at the head of the table. Dying himself, probably suddenly, since his family had been left in such precarious circumstances. I felt sad for the widow, struggling to feed her kids, raising them alone. And then even sadder, realizing that the kids of those kids must have perished, because there wasn't a single Jew by the name of Kohen left in Sarajevo after the Second World War.

I made a note to myself to look into exchanges between the Jewish communities of the Adriatic in the 1700s. Maybe there was a particular Italian yeshiva where Bosnian cantors went to study. It would be great to make an educated guess as to how the haggadah reached Sarajevo.

But none of this had to do with clasps, so I set that folder aside and reached for the next one. Herman Rothschild, ancient Near Eastern manuscripts specialist of the Bodleian Library, Oxford, unfortunately had handwriting a great deal less legible than the Hebrew teacher's. His report, ten densely scribbled pages, might as well have been in Bosnian, it was so difficult for me to decipher. But soon enough I discovered that he hadn't dealt with the binding at all. He had been so dazzled by the fact of the illuminations that his entire report was more of an art history treatise, an aesthetic evaluation of the miniatures in the context of Christian medieval art. I read through his pages, which were erudite and beautifully expressed. I copied down a few lines to quote in my own essay. But none of it was relevant to the matter of the clasps. I set the pages aside and rubbed my eyes. I hoped his French colleague had taken a broader view.

M. Martell's report was a complete contrast to that of his British counterpart. In point form, very terse, it was entirely technical. I was yawning as I paged through it, the usual boring enumeration of quires and folios, until I got to the last page. And then I stopped yawning. Martell described, in technospeak, a worn-out, stained, and damaged binding of eroded, ragged kid. He noted that the linen threads were missing or frayed, so that most of the quires were no longer attached to the binding at all. Amazing and fortunate, according to what he described, that pages hadn't been lost.

And then there were several short sentences that had been crossed out. I pulled the desk light down to see if I could read what M. Martell had had second thoughts about. No luck. I turned the paper over. Sure enough, the force of his hand had made a partially legible imprint under the strikeout. For several minutes, I puzzled over the letters I could decipher. Reading incomplete French words backward was tricky. But eventually I had most of it, and I knew why it had been crossed out.

"Pair nonfunctioning, oxidized Ag clasps. Double hook and eye, mechanically exhausted. After cleaning w. dilute $NaHCO_3$, reveal motif of flower enfolded by wing. Chasing = embossed + repoussé. No hallmark." Here in this museum in 1894, M. Martell had worked his soft cloth and his small brushes over the old and blackened pieces of metal until the silver once again gleamed in the light. For just a moment, the very dispassionate M. Martell had lost his head.

"The clasps," he had written, "are extraordinarily beautiful."

Feathers and a Rose

Vienna, 1894

Vienna is the laboratory of the apocalypse.

—Karl Kraus

"Fräulein Operator in Gloggnitz? May I have the honor to wish you a splendid good afternoon? I trust that your day has passed pleasantly so far. The party at this end of the wire, Herr Doktor Franz Hirschfeldt, presents his compliments and would like to extend to you a most grateful kiss on the hand for the favor of completing this connection."

"And a very fine afternoon to you, my dear Fräulein Operator in Vienna. Thank you for your good wishes, and please accept in return my most sincere felicitations. I am happy to reply to your kind inquiry by remarking that my day has been very agreeable and I hope that you and your party are likewise enjoying the very delightful summer weather. As the humble representative of my party, may I venture to say that His Excellency the baron looks forward to the opportunity to add his good wishes and . . ."

Franz Hirschfeldt held the telephone away from his ear and tapped a pencil against his desk. He had no patience for this time-wasting stream of pleasantries. The words going through his mind were by no means so polite. He longed to cut in, to tell the women to shut up and make the damned connection. He tapped the pencil so hard against the desk's nickel edge that a portion of it snapped, flew off, crossed the surgery, and landed on the white-sheeted examination table. Didn't these women know there was a ten-minute time limit on calls out of the city? Sometimes, it seemed to Hirschfeldt as if the entire allotment was squandered before he even got his party on the line. But the last time he'd been short with an operator she'd dropped the connection entirely, so he held his peace.

It was just another small irritation, like the rub of the shirt collar that the laundress *would* overstarch, despite his express instructions. There were too many such annoyances in this city: the tedious obsequiousness, the fashion for strangulating collars. It provoked him that he had to be so constantly provoked. He was thirty-six years old, father of two attractive children, married to a woman he still admired, discreetly entertained by a series of mistresses who amused him. He was professionally successful, even prosperous. All this, and he lived in Vienna, which was undoubtedly one of the greatest cities of the world.

Hirschfeldt lifted his gaze from the desk and let it travel beyond the corniced window as the fräuleins continued to drape their compliments over the length of the telegraph wires. The city had been confident enough to raze its own medieval fortress walls and replace them with the welcoming new sweep of the Ringstrasse; pragmatic enough to embrace the industrialization that dusted the horizon with the haze of prosperity.

Here was his city, in all her magnificence, capital of an empire that stretched from the Tyrolean Alps, across the Bohemian Massif and the Great Hungarian Plain, to the Dalmatian coast and the wide golden lands of the Ukraine; a cultural hub that attracted the best intellects and the most creative artists—only last night his wife, Anna, had dragged him out to hear that man Mahler's latest, very strange composition, and wasn't he from Bohemia or somewhere of that sort? And the exhibition of paintings by Klimt that they'd looked in on—that was something different. Artistic license, he supposed one called it, but the man had a very odd conception of the female anatomy.

It wasn't as if nothing moved in Vienna. On the contrary, the city pulsed with the frantic energy of its own great invention, the waltz. And yet . . .

And yet seven centuries of Hapsburg monarchy had encrusted

the imperial capital with an excess of its own grandeur, buried it under twirls of plaster, mired it in swirls of thick cream, weighed it
down with curlicues of gold braid (even the *dustmen* had epaulets!),
and stupefied it by this stream—no—this cataract, of unctuous cour-
tesies. . . .

"... if it is still convenient for Herr Doktor Hirschfeldt to entertain the connection, His Excellency the baron would be only too
pleased . . ."

Well, he *would* be pleased, thought Hirschfeldt. The fräulein was
right about that. The baron would be very pleased. Pleased to hear
that he had an inconveniently located boil and not a raging case of
syphilis. No need for the near-toxic dose of mercury or the visit to
the malaria ward to contract a fever torrid enough to burn out the
worse infection. With any luck, the baron hadn't yet made any fool-
ish, guilty confessions to the baroness. The doctor had counseled
him to take his weeping member away, alone, to his mountain lodge,
until Hirschfeldt had a chance to examine his paramour.

The baron's lover had turned out to be a naive girl whose young
flesh was sound and whose story held up to Hirschfeldt's tactful and
astute interrogation. She had just left the surgery, her cornflower
eyes red from a little cry. They always had a little cry; the infected
from despair, the healthy from relief. But this girl had wept from
humiliation. The sheet on the examination table still held the impression of her slender body. She'd been as pale as the sheet, and trembling, when Hirschfeldt had required her to spread her thighs. No
hardened courtesan, this one. Hirschfeldt had felt her shame and
handled her with delicacy. Sometimes, when prying into the details
of a patient's intimate life, one had to play the bully to get to the
truth. But not with this delicate creature, who had been only too
willing to recount the short history of her seductions, the first by a
literary gentleman, who as it happened was also a patient of
Hirschfeldt's and known to him as a man with a jealous regard for his
physical soundness. After no very lengthy affair, he had passed her on
to the attentions of the baron.

Hirschfeldt had taken care to make a note of her address in his private diary. Perhaps, after a decent interval, when there could be no question of breaching the doctor-patient relationship, he might arrange an encounter. One could, in this city, do a great deal worse.

The baron's rumbling, bluff baritone finally vibrated the wire, replacing the twittering of the fräuleins. Hirschfeldt, however, watched his words. The fräuleins were notorious eavesdroppers.

"Baron, good day. I just wanted to let you know at the earliest opportunity that the plant we were trying to identify is very likely, almost certainly, not the invasive weed you were concerned about."

Down the line, he heard the baron exhale.

"Hirschfeldt, thank you. Thank you for letting me know so promptly. It is a very great relief to me."

"Don't mention it, Excellency. But that plant still requires some cultivation"—the boil should be lanced—"and we need to attend to it."

"I will see you as soon as I return to the city. And thank you, as ever, for your discretion."

Hirschfeldt put down the phone. Discretion. That was what they paid him for. All the aristocrats, their kid gloves covering the rashes on their palms. All the so-respectable bourgeoisie terrified by the canker sores pulsing in their pantaloons. He knew very well that many of them would not have a Jew defile their drawing room, or even keep him company over a coffee. But they were only too pleased to entrust to him the care of their private parts and the confidences of their private lives. Hirschfeldt had been the first in town to advertise the availability of a "sequestered" waiting room, for the use of those with "secret diseases." But that was when he had first raised his shingle. It was many years since he had needed to advertise.

Discretion: a valuable commodity in this city, capital of carnality, where scandal and gossip were the fuels that stoked the social engine. And *so* much to gossip about. Six years since the crown prince and his paramour had done away with themselves in the hunting lodge at Mayerling, and still one never tired of new rumors regarding that tragedy, or farce, depending on one's degree of romanticism or cynicism. Of course, the royal family's determination to hush up the affair had only fanned the blaze of gossip, as such attempts ever will. The Hapsburgs may have had the power to haul off Mary Vetsera's corpse in the middle of the night with a broom handle shoved up her back to disguise the fact that she was forty hours dead. But while they could erase her name from the Austrian press, they could not keep foreign newspapers from finding their way across the border and under the seats of Vienna's cabs, where the cabbie would, for a stiff fee, deliver them to the avid eyes of his passengers.

Hirschfeldt, who trained under the royal physician, had known the crown prince, Rudolf. He had liked him. They were the same age, and of a similar liberal bent. In their few meetings, he had sensed how thwarted the prince was, how frustrated by a role that was never more than ceremonial. It was no life for a grown man, being kept out of the counsels of state, required only as a dress dummy at banquets and balls. Waiting for a destiny that shimmered and retreated each time he attempted to approach it. And yet Hirschfeldt could not condone the ridiculous suicide pact. What was it Dante wrote, about the pope who abdicated his throne to become a contemplative and yet is condemned to one of the lowest circles of hell? Something about being punished for having turned his back on a great opportunity to do good in the world. . . . And ever since the prince's shocking death, Vienna had been in almost imperceptible decline—a decline of mood rather than matter. But with no liberal face left in the Hofburg to stare them down, the *Judenfressers* grew louder year by year.

Who would have thought that a single suicide—or a double suicide, more properly—could put an entire city in a sour temper? Vienna valued its suicides, especially those that were dramatic, conducted with some flourish—like the young woman who had decked herself in full bridal regalia before flinging herself from a speeding train, or the circus artist who, in the midst of his performance, had cast away his pole and leaped from the high wire to his death. The audience had applauded, because he jumped with such verve that all believed it was part of his act. It was only as the blood began to pool under his shattered body that the cheers turned to gasps and the women turned their faces away, understanding that this man had added another digit to a suicide rate already the highest in Europe.

Suicide and sexual diseases. Two great killers of the Viennese, from the highest born to the lowest.

Hirschfeldt finished his notes on the baron's case and called on his secretary to send in the next patient. He glanced at his daybook. Ah yes. Herr Mittl, the bookbinder. Poor fellow.

"Herr Doktor, Kapitän Hirschfeldt is here to see you. Should I send him in first?"

Hirschfeldt uttered an almost inaudible groan of irritation. Why was David bothering him at the clinic? He hoped his self-absorbed brother had had tact enough to stay clear of the sequestered waiting room. Herr Mittl was a nervous, highly proper little man who had paid a high price for some momentary indiscretion in his distant youth. He felt the shame of his condition deeply and as a result had been reluctant to seek treatment in the early stages of his disease, when there might have been some hope. He, of all people, would be mortified to encounter an officer of the Hoch- und Deutschmeister.

"No, give the captain my compliments but ask him to wait. Herr Mittl has troubled to make an appointment. He must have precedence."

"Very well, Herr Doktor, but . . ."

"But what?" Hirschfeldt ran his finger under his collar, which was even more stiffly starched than usual.

"He is bleeding."

"Oh, for goodness' sake. Show him in."

How typical, he thought, as his half brother, a foot taller but a full thirteen years younger, strode into the surgery clutching a piece of red-stained silk to the side of his sculpted jaw. Little ruby orbs of blood glinted among the blond hairs of his wide mustache.

"David, what in the name of God have you done now? Another

duel? You're not a youth anymore. Why on earth can't you learn to control your temper? Who, this time?"

Hirschfeldt had risen from behind his desk to lead his brother toward the examining table. Then he remembered he had not had the nurse in to change the sheet. Better safe than sorry. He propelled him instead to a chair by the window and then carefully lifted the saturated silk—a fine cravat, ruined—away from the gash.

"David." His voice was heavy with reproof. He ran a finger over an old, white cicatrix that inscribed an arc above his brother's right eyebrow. "One dueling scar is, I suppose, excusable, even perhaps, in *your* circles, desirable. But two. Two is positively excessive." He applied alcohol to the new wound as his brother winced. There would be a scar, no doubt. The rapier cut was short but quite deep. Hirschfeldt judged it would heal without stitches if the sides of the wound were taped together and bandaged firmly. But would his vain brother leave the bandage in place? Probably not. He turned to reach for a suture.

"Are you going to tell me? Who?"

"No one you'd know."

"Oh? You would be surprised whom I know. Syphilis is no respecter of army rank."

"It wasn't an officer."

Hirschfeldt paused, the bright point of the suture needle poised above his brother's flesh. He turned his brother's face toward his own. A pair of sleepy eyes, the same dark blue as the young captain's well-cut jacket, gazed back at him insouciantly.

"A civilian? David. You go too far. This could be disastrous."

"I don't think so. In any case, I couldn't abide the way he said my name."

"Your name?"

"Oh, come on, Franz. You know very well how some people pronounce Jewish names. How they can make each syllable into a little one-act farce of derisiveness."

"David, you are oversensitive. You see slights everywhere."

"You weren't there, Franz. You can't stand in judgment on me in this matter."

"No, I wasn't there, this time. But I've seen it all before."

"Well, even if I was oversensitive, even if I was mistaken in the matter of the name, what happened next proved otherwise. When I called him out, he proclaimed that I was in no position to demand satisfaction, being a Jew."

"Whatever did he mean?"

"He was referring, of course, to the Waidhofen manifesto."

"The what?"

"Ach. Franz. Sometimes I wonder what city it is that you live in. The Waidhofen manifesto has been the talk of every coffeehouse in Vienna for weeks. It's the German nationalist faction's damnable re-action to the fact that a great number of Jews, both at the university and in the officer corps, have become proficient and dangerous fenc-ers. Well, and so they had to, simply to defend themselves from the increasing provocations. In any case, the manifesto states that a Jew is without honor from the day of his birth. That he cannot differenti-ate between what is dirty and what is clean. That he is ethically sub-human and dishonorable. It is therefore impossible to insult a Jew and from this it follows that a Jew cannot demand satisfaction for any insult."

Franz expelled a long breath. "Good lord."

"You see?" David laughed, then grimaced, as the muscle in his lacerated cheek protested. "Even you, my wise elder brother, might have taken a scalpel to the fellow."

The irony was that David Hirschfeldt, unlike Franz, was not a Jew. A year or two after Franz's mother had died of consumption, their father had become smitten with a Bavarian Catholic. He had converted to her faith in order to woo her. Their son, David, had been raised amid the scent of Sunday incense and fresh-cut Christmas pines. The only Jewish thing about the blond, blue-eyed, half-Bavarian rising star of the Vienna Hausregiment was his name.

"There's more."

"What?"

"There are rumors I'm to be bounced from Silesia."

"David! They couldn't possibly. You're their champion, ever since the gymnasium. Is it because of this latest . . . adventure?"

"No, of course not. Everyone in Silesia has been in an illegal duel at some point. But it seems my Bavarian *Mutti* no longer provides enough pure blood to counteract the taint of our father."

Franz couldn't think of anything to say. His brother would be devastated if he were expelled from his fencing club. And it would hurt the club to lose its best competitor. If David was right, and not merely being hypersensitive, then the state of things was much worse than he'd imagined.

Hirschfeldt was distracted as his last patient of the day was shown in. "I'm so sorry to have detained you, Herr Mittl, but there was an emergency. . . ." He looked up then, and noticed Mittl's gait. At once, the man's deteriorated condition got his full attention. Mittl lumbered on stiff legs held wide apart until he stood nervously by the examination table, twisting his hat in his hands. His face, a narrow face always, was drawn and gray. There was a stain on his shirt, which was unusual; Hirschfeldt recalled Mittl as being most particular about his grooming. Hirschfeldt spoke to him gently. "Do sit down, Herr Mittl, and tell me how you are."

"Thank you, Herr Doktor." He eased himself carefully onto the table. "I've not been well. Not well at all."

Hirschfeldt conducted his examination knowing what he would find: the gummy tumors, palpable around the joints, the optic atrophy, the muscle weakness.

"Are you still managing to work, Herr Mittl? It must be difficult for you."

There was a flash of fear in the man's eyes. "Oh yes. I must work. Must work. No choice. Even though they conspire against me. They give the lucrative work to their own, and I get the dregs. . . ."

Suddenly Mittl stopped and clapped a hand to his mouth. "I forgot that you—"

Hirschfeldt interrupted, to save them both embarrassment. "How do you manage with the fine work, your eyesight deteriorating as it is?"

"I have my daughter to help me with the sewing. Only one I can trust. The other apprentices are all in league against me, stealing everything, down to my linen thread. . . ."

Hirschfeldt sighed. The paranoid delusions were as much a symptom of tertiary-stage disease as the physical disabilities. He wondered that Mittl was getting any commissions at all, given his impairment. The man must have a very loyal clientele.

Suddenly Mittl fixed him with a lucid gaze. His voice dropped back into its normal pitch. "I think I am losing my mind. Is there nothing you can do for me?"

Hirschfeldt turned away and walked to the window. How much should he tell him? How much could he take in? He was reluctant to mention experimental treatments to patients who could not perhaps grasp the full risks, the very uncertain rewards. And yet these treatments were too drastic to try on anyone who was not late stage and terminal. To do nothing was to condemn poor Mittl to his miserable decline until death overtook him.

"There *is* something," Hirschfeldt said at last. "A colleague of mine is working on it in Berlin. The results are promising, but the treatments are extensive, painful, and I'm afraid very costly. It requires as many as forty injections over the course of a year. The agent my colleague has developed is very toxic, based on arsenic. His idea is that the compound harms the diseased parts of the body more than it harms the sound parts, which will, in time, recover. But the effects can be severe. Pain at the injection site is very common, as are gastric disorders. But my colleague has documented some dramatic results. He even claims cures, but I must warn you that I think it is too early to make such assertions."

Mittl's cloudy eyes had become avid. "You said 'expensive,' Herr Doktor. How much?"

Hirschfeldt sighed and named the sum. Mittl buried his head in his hands. "I haven't got it." And then, to Hirschfeldt's deep embarrassment, the man began to sob like a child.

Hirschfeldt did not like the last patient of the day to be a hopeless case. It wasn't the mood he liked to be in when he left his clinic. He had intended to call upon his mistress, but as he reached the turn to her street, he hesitated and walked on. It wasn't just Mittl. It had been ten months; Rosalind's wide-hipped, fleshy beauty was beginning to bore him. Perhaps it was time to look elsewhere . . . the image of the slender, trembling girl with the cornflower eyes came to him unbidden. He wondered idly how long it would be before the baron was sated with her. Not, he hoped, too long. . . .

It was a delicious late-summer evening, the slant of the low sun warming the cold plaster nudes that cavorted across the entablature of some rather ostentatious new apartments. Who would buy such places, he wondered. The new industrial class, perhaps, wanting some physical proximity to the Hofburg. The only proximity they could hope for. All their wealth would never raise them up to the social plane of the aristocracy.

The warmth had tempted all kinds of people into the streets. Hirschfeldt took comfort in their diversity. There was a family, the wife veiled, the man wearing a fez, who had probably come all the way from Bosnia to see the heart of the empire under whose protection their lands had fallen. There was a Bohemian Gypsy woman, her spangled hem jingling in time to her swayed-hip walk. And a Ukrainian peasant with a red-cheeked boy riding on his shoulders. If the German nationalists wanted to purify this state of foreign influence, they would have many more obvious exotics to weed out before they got to the Jews, much less to a totally assimilated man like his brother, David. Still, a small voice nagged at him. The Bosnians and the Ukrainians weren't dominant figures in the arts, in industry, in finance. A few colorful tourists—perhaps even the German nationalists could find them appealing, a picturesque element in the urban landscape. What they apparently *did not* find appealing was the prominence of Jews in every field of Austrian endeavor, even, these days, in the officer ranks of the army.

Hirschfeldt had watched the young limes and the sycamore saplings taking root on the malls of the Ringstrasse. Now they had grown high enough to throw slender stripes of shadow across his path. One day they would provide shade. His children, maybe, would live to enjoy it. . . .

He would go home, yes, to his children; that was the thing to do. He would propose to his wife that they go for a family stroll in the Prater, perhaps. He would speak with her about David; she would understand his concerns. But his wife was not at home when he got there, and neither were the children. Frau Hirschfeldt had gone to call on the Hertzls, the maid said. And the nanny had already taken the children for an airing in the park. Franz felt put out, even as he knew that the sentiment was unreasonable, since he so often claimed to be detained at the clinic at this hour. Still, he wanted his wife's company and he had grown very used to having what he wanted. And what did she see in that vapid wife of Hertzl's? What did Hertzl see in her, for that matter? But even as his mind framed the question, Franz knew the answer.

Frau Hertzl's blond beauty and her frivolous painted fingernails were perfect foils for Theodor's dark, rabbinic gravity. With his Julie on his arm, he appeared less Jewish, and Franz was aware that this was beginning to matter to his literary friend. But the woman had so little to say. Her whole existence seemed framed by fashion. His own thoughtful, educated wife could hardly find her engaging. That Anna should be wasting her time on such an unprofitable friendship, when he wanted her home, was yet another annoyance. He retreated to his bedchamber and threw off the shirt with its bothersome collar. He put on a smoking jacket. Better. He tilted his head from left to right, releasing the tension in his neck. He made for the salon, called for a glass of schnapps, and retreated behind the broadsheets of his daily newspaper.

Anna did not see him as she swept through the door. Her head was down, her hands busy extracting hat pins. She turned to the mirror in the hallway as the wide straw hat came off. Franz saw her face reflected in the glass. She was smiling at some private joke as her fingers fluttered around thick swirls of hair that had come loose with the hat. Franz put down his glass silently and moved behind her, taking one of the twists of hair in his hand and stroking the backs of his fingers along her neck. His wife gave a startled shudder.

"Franz! You frightened me," she protested. Her face, as she turned to him, was flushed. But that alone would not have been enough to pierce Hirschfeldt with sudden, unwelcome knowledge. Before she turned, he had noted that one of the tiny, muslin-covered buttons on the back of her bodice had been fastened into the wrong buttonhole. Her maid, who was fastidious, would never have allowed such a thing. Such a small thing; a tiny betraying detail of a very great betrayal.

Hirschfeldt took his wife's face between his hands and stared at her. Was it his imagination, or did her lips have a softened, bruised look? Suddenly he did not want to touch her. He let go of her face and rubbed his hands down the side of his trouser seams, as if wiping off uncleanliness.

"Is it Hertzl?" he hissed.

"Hertzl?" Her eyes scanned his face. "Yes, Franz, I went to see Frau Hertzl, but she was not at home so I—"

"Don't. Don't trouble to lie to me. I spend my life among the sexually reckless, the cuckolders, and their trollops." He pushed his thumb hard across her lips, mashing them against her teeth. "You have been kissed." He reached behind her neck and pulled hard on the muslin so that the buttons tore from the delicate loops of fabric that held them. "You have been undressed." He leaned in close. "Someone has fucked you."

She took a step away from him, trembling.

"I ask you again: was it Hertzl?"

Her brown eyes brimmed. "No," she whispered. "Not Hertzl. No one you know."

He found himself repeating what he'd said to his brother not so many hours earlier. "You'd be surprised who I know." His mind was full of images: the baron's boil-cratered penis, the yellow pus oozing from a girl's eroded labia, the gummy tumors eating away at poor demented Mittl. He couldn't breathe. He needed air. He turned away from his wife and walked out the door, slamming it behind him.

Rosalind, having given up on seeing Hirschfeldt that evening, was dressing for a concert. There was an attractive second violin in the Behrensdorf Quartet who had stared at her across his bow all through a recital at a private salon the previous evening. After the performance, he had sought her out and made a point of telling her that he would be playing at the Musikverein tonight. She had just dabbed scent behind her ears and was contemplating whether to risk the delicate lemon silk of her bodice to the pin of a small sapphire brooch when Hirschfeldt was announced. She felt a slight stab of irritation. Why had he not called at the usual hour? He burst into her boudoir, looking entirely odd in his smoking jacket and with such an expression on his face.

"Franz! How very peculiar! Don't tell me you wore that in the street?"

He did not answer, simply unbuttoned the frogs on the jacket with impatient fingers and threw it on the bed. Then he strode up to her, slid the strap of her gown off her shoulder, and commenced kissing her with an urgency he hadn't displayed in months.

Rosalind submitted to, rather than participated in, the untender coupling that followed. After, she raised herself on one elbow and gazed at him. "Would you care to tell me what is going on?"

"Not really."

She waited a few moments, but when he said nothing more, she rose, picked up her gown where it had fallen on the floor, and commenced to dress again for the Musikverein. If she hurried, she could get there before the first interval.

"You are going out?" He sounded aggrieved.

"Yes, if you are going to lie there with a face like a stone. I am most certainly going out." She turned to him, angry now herself. "Franz, do you realize it has been a month since you have taken me anywhere, brought me a gift, made me laugh? I think perhaps it is time I took a vacation. I might go to the spa at Baden."

"Rosalind, please. Not now." He was chagrined. It was he who should decide when to end the affair, not she.

She picked up the brooch. The sapphires looked well against the lemon, and drew attention to her lively eyes. She jabbed the pin into the delicate fabric. "Then, my friend, you had best give me a reason to stay."

With that, she stood, swirled a light stole over her creamy shoulders, and left the room.

In the gathering dark of early evening, Florien Mittl clutched at the slender trunk of a lime tree to steady himself as fur-hatted Hassids poured out of their synagogue and filled the street with their uncouth Yiddish babble. His gait was too uncertain to risk trying to make his way against the tide. He would have to wait till they passed. In the upper-Austrian burg where he had been raised, it was the Jews who would make way for a Christian, they who would wait for him to pass. Vienna was too liberal; there was no doubt of it. These Jews had been allowed to forget their place. And was there no end to them? It was not Saturday, so he supposed it must be some Jewish festival or another that brought them out in such numbers, in such strange finery.

Perhaps it was the very festival commemorated in the book he had been given to rebind. He didn't know. Nor did he care. He was glad to have the work, even if it was a Jewish book. Typical that they would give him a *Jewish* book, destined for the obscurity of a provincial museum. He, who once had been entrusted with the gems of the imperial collection, the finest psalters, the most beautiful Books of Hours. . . . Well, it was months since the museum had sent anything at all his way, so it was no use dwelling on the past. He would do his best. He'd started on the boards for the new binding, cut them, grooved them for the clasps. The book must have had a remarkable binding once, judging by those clasps. They were as finely wrought as anything in the imperial collection. Four hundred years ago, and some Jew was already rich. Always knew how to get money, them. Why not he? Bring the binding back to that standard, that was what he must strive for. Impress the museum director. Prove he wasn't ready for the scrap heap. Get more work. He must get more work. Scrape together the funds for the Jew doctor's cure. Of course, the doctor probably lied about the cost. He wouldn't charge another Jew such a usurious rate, Mittl would wager on it. Bloodsuckers, all of them, growing fat on Christian suffering.

Bitter, frightened, in pain, Mittl made his way along the street, dreading the moment he would have to turn into the *platz*. The small square might as well be the wastes of the Sahara, so difficult to make the crossing. He hugged the periphery of the square, staying close to the walls of the buildings, grateful for fence railings to grasp against a sudden gust of wind that might topple him. At last he arrived at his own building. He did battle with the heavy door, and then leaned, exhausted, against the newel post at the foot of the stairs. He rested there for a long moment, gathering his wind and his will, before the slow ascent. He feared the stairs. He saw himself dead at the base of them, his head pulped, a broken leg twisted grotesquely. He clutched at the banister, pulling himself up hand over hand like an alpinist.

The apartment was dark, and smelled bad. The usual scents of leather and size were overlaid with ranker aromas of unwashed clothes and rancid meat. He lit a single gas lamp—all he could afford—and unwrapped the slice of mutton his daughter had left for him, oh, several days ago. Why did the girl neglect him so? She was all he had, since her mother . . . since Lise . . .

With the thought of his wife, guilty regret swept over him. What a wedding present he had given her. Did his daughter know? He couldn't bear it if his daughter knew. But perhaps that's why she had grown distant, helping him only as far as mean duty demanded. Probably he disgusted her. Certainly he disgusted himself. Like the meat. Rotten. Rotting inside. The mutton had a greenish tinge, and was slimy to the touch. He ate it anyway. There was nothing else.

He had intended to start again on the work. He wiped his hands on a piece of rag and turned toward his workbench, where the book in its damaged binding lay waiting for his attentions. Years, centuries, since anyone had repaired it. A chance for him to show his skill. Do it quickly, impress them, so that they might send him more commissions. Dazzle them. That was what he must do. But the light was so poor, and the pains traveled up and down his arms without respite. He sat down, and pulled the lamp close. He picked up the knife, and then placed it down again. What was it he was supposed to do? What was the first thing? Remove the boards? Release the quires? Prepare the size? He had rebound hundreds of books—valuable, rare books. But suddenly he couldn't recall a sequence of steps that had been as natural to him as breathing.

He put his face in his hands. Yesterday, he hadn't been able to remember how to make the tea. Such a simple thing. A thing he'd done without thinking, several times a day, most of the days of his life. But yesterday it had loomed at him like the frightening staircase, too many steps. He had put the tea leaves into the cup, and the sugar into the teapot, and scalded himself with the water.

If only the Jew doctor could be persuaded to give him the cure. He had to save what was left of his mind, what was left of himself. There must be something other than money he could offer him. No. Nothing. Jews were only interested in money. There must be something he could sell. His wife's wedding ring. But his daughter had that; hard to ask her for it back. Only a drop in the ocean anyway. Not such a very fine ring. She deserved better, poor Lise. Poor dead Lise.

How could he think, how could he work, with this worry constantly gnawing him? He would lie down, perhaps, for just a little while, and then he would be better. Then he would remember, and be able to go on.

Florien Mittl woke, fully dressed, when the light of late morning finally won its struggle with the grime that coated his window. He lay there, blinking, trying to collect his scattered thoughts. He remembered the book. Then he remembered the dread of the evening before. How was it that he could remember *not* remembering, and yet the fugitive facts themselves remained so elusive? How could a man misplace the skills of a lifetime? Where did such knowledge go? His thoughts were like an army in retreat, ceding ever more territory to the enemy, his illness. No, not a retreat. Not lately. More like a rout. He turned his head stiffly. A beam of sunlight lay like a stripe of yellow ribbon across the workbench. It hit the sad, tattered, untouched cover of the book. And then it flared on the freshly polished silver of the clasps.

Hirschfeldt did not fast on the Day of Atonement. Racial solidarity was one thing; he had made a dutiful appearance at the synagogue, nodded to those to whom he needed to nod, and slipped out at the first seemly moment. But unhealthy dietary practices were something else. He thought such customs superstitions from a bygone, primitive age. Generally, Anna agreed with him. But this year she had fasted, creeping around the flat as the day wore on with a hand pressed to her temple. Dehydration headache was Hirschfeldt's silent diagnosis.

As the light faded, the children huddled together on the balcony, waiting for the glimmer of the third evening star, which signaled the end of the fast. The two of them had gone without sustenance only the short hour since nursery tea, but they loved the semblance of ritual. There were several squeals, several false alarms, before the moment when the silver trays laden with good things—poppy-seed cakes and sweet crescent pastries—officially became permitted fare.

Hirschfeldt placed a small square of torte, Anna's favorite, on a plate. He poured some cool water from the silver ewer into a crystal glass and carried these things to his wife. His rage at her had subsided quite suddenly. So suddenly that he had surprised himself, giving himself immense plaudits for his magnanimity, his maturity, his sophistication. He had not thought of himself as quite such a man of the world. That he had returned home the morning after his discovery to find her tearful, penitent, and full of pleadings, this had surely helped. But the odd thing was that the idea of her, desired by another, had rekindled his own passion. The erotic appetite was a fascinating thing, he mused, as he kissed a sweet crumb from the corner of her hungry lips. That man Freud, whose rooms were so close to his own, he must get to know him better. Some of his writings were full of insight. He had barely thought of Rosalind, away in Baden, or the girl with cornflower eyes.

"I don't know, Herr Mittl. I've never taken a payment like this before. . . ."

"Please, Herr Doktor. I have removed them from the Mittl family Bible, you must see they are very fine. . . ."

"Very fine, Herr Mittl. Lovely. Not that I know anything about silversmithy, but anyone can appreciate the detail in this . . . work of a real craftsman . . . an artist, indeed."

"They are pure silver, Herr Doktor, not plate."

"Oh, I don't doubt it, Herr Mittl. That's not the issue. It's just that I . . . we . . . Jews in general, we don't have family Bibles. Our Torah is kept in the synagogue, and in any case, it is a scroll. . . ."

Mittl frowned. He wanted to blurt out that the clasps had come off a Jewish book, but he could hardly reveal that fact without exposing himself as a thief. Was it a measure of his madness, or of his desperation, that he had persuaded himself no one from the museum would miss the pair of clasps? If they did, he had determined to assert that the clasps had never come to him. He would throw suspicion on the foreign scholars instead.

But this negotiation was not going well. He squirmed in his seat. He had been convinced that the doctor, in his avarice, would fall on the bright metal as instinctively as a bowerbird.

"Even you Jews must have some kind of . . . of prayer book?"

"Yes, of course we do. I, for example, have a siddur, for services, and we have a haggadah, for Passover, but I really don't think either of them is equal to silver clasps. Pedestrian editions, I'm afraid. Contemporary bindings. One should have better, I suppose. I've often meant to—"

Hirshfeldt stopped himself in midsentence. Damn it. The little man was going to cry again. A woman's tears were one thing. He was used to them; he did not mind them. They could even be charming, in a way. One enjoyed consoling a woman. But a man's tears. Hirschfeldt cringed. The first time he had seen a man really weep was his father, the night his mother died. It had been harrowing. He had believed his father impregnable. For him, it had been a night of double loss. His father's uncontained grief had turned his own childish tears into a howling, heaving fit of hysteria. He and his father had never treated each other quite the same way, after that night.

And this, too, was harrowing. Hirshfeldt had unconsciously wrapped his hands around his ears, trying to shut out the sound of it. Horrible. How desperate Mittl must be, to weep like this. How desperate, to have vandalized his own family Bible.

And then, quite suddenly, Hirschfeldt stepped out from behind the wall that years of training and experience had erected. He allowed himself to be exposed to the broken, sobbing figure in front of him, and to be moved, not as a doctor is moved by a patient, to a safe and serviceable sympathy, but as a human being who allows himself full empathy with the suffering of another.

"Please, Herr Mittl. There is no need for this. I will send to Dr. Ehrlich in Berlin and request a course of his serum for you. We can begin the treatments early next week. I can't promise you results, but we can hope. . . ."

"Hope?" Florien Mittl looked up and took the handkerchief the doctor held out to him. Hope. That was enough. That was everything.

"You mean it? You will?"

"Yes, Herr Mittl." As he saw the transfiguration of Mittl's narrow, rodent face, Hirschfeldt felt an even greater surge of magnanimity. He took the clasps in his hand and stood. He walked around his desk to where Mittl sat, breathing raggedly, dabbing at his eyes. He was about to hand the clasps back, to tell him to restore them to their rightful place.

But then the light gleamed on the silver. Such delicate roses. Rosalind. He needed a farewell gift for her when she returned from Baden. One must begin and end an affair with some panache, even if one hasn't behaved impeccably throughout. He shifted the clasps in his hand and studied them more closely. Yes, a skilled jeweler— he knew just the man—could make a pair of earrings from the roses, a perfect pair of fine studs. Rosalind, whose beauty was of a large and overstated variety, preferred such subtle, smaller pieces for her jewels.

What did he owe to the Mittl family Bible, after all? At least it existed. Not like the mountains of Talmuds and other Jewish books consigned to flames over centuries by order of Herr Mittl's church. What did it matter if it had no clasps? Ehrlich charged an exorbitant sum for his serum. Earrings for Rosalind were only a partial recompense for what he would have to spend. He looked again at the clasps. He noted that the feathers, made to enclose the roses, had a curve that suggested an enfolding wing. It would be a shame if one did not use those, too. The jeweler could make a second pair of earrings, perhaps. For an instant, he thought of delicate, birdlike limbs, and cornflower eyes. . . .

No. Not for her. Not yet. Perhaps never. For the first time in years, he felt no urgency for a mistress. He had Anna. He had only to think of her, and imagine a strange hand touching her, to be overcome with desire. He smiled. How very appropriate. A pair of wings, to gleam amid the dark hair of his own Fallen Angel.

Hanna

Vienna, Spring 1996

MY HANDS WERE SHAKING as I put down the report. Where were they, these silver clasps, so beautiful that they'd moved a dry old stick like Martell? And who'd crossed out his notes?

My mind raced through scenarios. The clasps had been loose on the binding when it arrived. Black and encrusted, so that their value wasn't immediately apparent. Why had the Kohen family not kept them polished? Perhaps they never realized that the black metal was silver. "Nonfunctioning," "mechanically exhausted," Martell had said, which probably meant they weren't hooking together, serving their original purpose of keeping the parchments pressed flat. In any case, they would have been removed by Martell for cleaning, and handed on to the binder already detached from the book, to be fixed onto the new binding. That's if they *had* been handed on. Maybe Martell, who had fancied them so much, had boosted them. But no: that couldn't be. The boards had grooves. The binder had prepared for clasps. So Martell wasn't the villain.

The clasps had gone to the bindery. Or maybe not: maybe they'd gone to a silversmith for repair of the mechanism. Had they come back to the museum? That was the next question. I pulled out the last file in the box.

There were ten documents, all in German. One seemed to be a bill, or an invoice. The handwriting was awful, but there was a signature. To have a name, it's what you pray for. A name is like the beginning of the ball of thread that'll lead you through the labyrinth. There were marginal notes scribbled on the bill, in a different, much clearer hand. The other documents were correspondence between the Staatsmuseum of Vienna and the Landesmuseum of Bosnia. Looking at the dates, I could see it spanned several years. It seemed to be about arrangements for the return of the haggadah, but beyond that I was in the dark.

I had to find Frau Zweig. It wasn't really the done thing, to walk around someone else's museum with one of their archive boxes under your arm, but I couldn't leave the documents unattended, and I couldn't wait. When I found my way to her office, she was deep in conversation with a small gray man—gray hair, gray suit, even his tie was gray. In the corridor, a pimply youth, clad all in black, was waiting his turn to see her. Frau Zweig looked like a rainbow lorikeet locked up by mistake in an aviary of pigeons. When she saw me hovering, she gestured that she'd be only a few more minutes.

True to her word, she ushered out the gray man with some dispatch, and asked young Mr. Black to kindly wait. We went into her office.

I closed the door. "Ohh," she said. "I hope that means you have found a *scandale*! Believe me, this place needs one!"

"Well, I don't know," I said, "but I have established that there were silver clasps on the book when it got here, and according to all sources, they weren't on the book when it left."

I quickly summarized what I'd read and then handed her the documents in German. She pulled out a pair of reading glasses with lime green frames and perched them on her ski-jump nose, just above the stud. The invoice was, as I'd hoped, from the binder, and there was a name, or part of one. "Something or other Mittl. The signature is terrible, I can't make out the first name. But Mittl . . . Mittl . . . I've seen it before. I think he was a binder the museum used quite a bit, at one period. . . . I seem to remember it in connection with the imperial collections. I can easily check that. We just computerized the entire records last year." She turned to the keyboard on her desk and tapped away. "Interesting. Florien Mittl—the Christian name is Florien—completed more than forty commissions for the museum, according to this. But guess what?" She paused dramatically and pushed herself back from the computer, twirling in her office chair. "The haggadah was the last." She turned back to the invoice. "This note, here in the margin, is interesting. . . . It's someone quite senior, from the tone of it. He is directing that the invoice not be paid 'until outstanding matters are resolved.'"

She scanned the other letters. "These are weird. This one is a long list of excuses why the haggadah can't be returned to Bosnia at this time. Pretty flimsy excuses, most of them. . . . It seems like the Staatsmuseum is stalling on the return of the book, and the Bosnians are . . . how do you say? Piss? Pissed?"

"Australians say 'pissed off.' *Pissed* means drunk. *Piss* is alcohol. To take the piss—that means to send someone up, make fun of them." (Why was I telling her all this?)

"So the Bosnians. They are very *pissed off* about it. Between the lines, here is my guess: Mittl stole the clasps, or lost them, and it cost him his commissions from the museum. The museum hushed it up so as not to upset the Bosnians. But then they had to stall returning the book for as long as possible, hoping that by the time it went back no one would notice that a pair of broken old black clasps had been left off the new binding."

"In which case, they were lucky," I mused. "History helped them out quite a bit, I'd say. By the time the book finally went home, everyone who knew anything was either dead or preoccupied. . . ."

"Speaking of preoccupied, I have to deal with these so-stupid evaluations. . . . When do you leave for the States? I can look into Mittl for you, yes?"

"Yes, please, that'd be great."

"And tonight, please let me take you out to a part of Vienna where you can't get Sacher torte and I can absolutely guarantee that you won't hear a waltz."

Thanks to Frau Zweig's late-night tour of S-and-M clubs, jazz basements, and conceptual art studios (one artist, naked and trussed like a chicken, was suspended from the ceiling, and the big event of the night was when he peed on someone in the audience below), I slept all the way to Boston. Waste of a first-class ticket. I might as well have been back there in cattle class, as per bloody usual.

I took the T from Logan airport to Harvard Square. I hate driving in Boston. It's the traffic that drives me spare, and the absolutely terrible manners of the motorists. Other New Englanders refer to Massachusetts drivers as "Massholes." But there's a whole other reason not to drive there: the tunnels. It's really hard to avoid them; you're always being one-wayed or no-left-turned into their gaping maw. In general, I don't have anything against tunnels. My cowardice usually doesn't extend that far. I don't have any trouble with the Sydney Harbour Tunnel, for instance. It's bright down there, clean and shiny, confidence inspiring. But when you go into Boston tunnels, they're really creepy. They're dim, and the tiles are leak stained, as if Boston Harbor is oozing its way through flaws in substandard concrete that some Irish mafia conned the city into buying. They look like they're going to crack open any minute, like something in a Spielberg movie, and the last thing you hear will be the roar of freezing water. My imagination can't handle it.

The T is the oldest subway system in the United States, and I figure if it has lasted this long, it must have been built right in the first place. The train I took from the airport gradually filled with students. They all seemed to be wearing T-shirts with messages on them. Signaling each other like fireflies. NERD PRIDE, said one, and on the back: A WELL-ROUNDED PERSON HAS NO POINT. Another one: THERE ARE ONLY 10 KINDS OF PEOPLE IN THE WORLD. THOSE WHO UNDERSTAND THE BINARY SYSTEM AND THOSE WHO DON'T. Both got off at the MIT stop.

Sometimes, I think if you took all the universities and all the hospitals out of greater Boston, you'd be able to fit what's left into about six city blocks. Harvard straddles both sides of the river and segues into MIT on one side and Boston University on the other. All three campuses are absolutely huge. Then there are Brandeis, Tufts, Wellesley, and a bunch of little ones like Lesley and Emerson and dozens more you've hardly heard of. You can't spit without hitting a PhD. And I was here because of one of them: the bezillionaire who had paid for my ticket from London was an MIT math genius who'd invented an algorithm that led to some kind of toggle switch that was used in every silicon chip. Or something like that. I'd never quite gotten it when someone explained it to me, and I'd never actually talked to him face-to-face. He'd arranged for the Houghton librarians to show me the codex he was interested in, and I was there when the library opened and able to do my appraisal in plenty of time to make my other meeting of the morning, with my mother.

She had left a terse message on my answering machine at home in Sydney, explaining that her only free moment was a brief tea break the very morning I flew in. I could just hear her brain ticking: "Maybe she won't call in to her machine, and I can get out of seeing her." But I checked my messages before I left Vienna. I grinned to myself as I listened to her voice, tentative and distracted. "There is no escape, Captain Kirk," I muttered. "You *will* be seeing me in Boston."

Nevertheless, it was a job locating her. Like the universities, the big hospitals in Boston merge into one another—Mass General, Brigham and Women's, Dana Farber—it's like a giant industrial park devoted to illness. The conference center was an offshoot of the complex, purpose-built for humongous medical meetings. I had to ask directions four times before I finally found the lecture theater where she had said she would be. I'd picked up a program at the registration desk and saw she had one of the coveted keynote addresses, scheduled when no one else was speaking. Lesser lights had to compete for attention with other doctors' presentations, while the lowliest made do with a poster about their research displayed with dozens of others in a big hall.

Mum's talk was humbly titled "How I Do It: Giant Aneurysms." I slipped into the back row. She was at the podium, stylish in a cream cashmere dress tailored to emphasize her athletic figure. She paced as she talked, showing off her long legs. Almost everyone else in the auditorium was a balding guy in a dark rumpled suit. She had them transfixed. They were either staring at her, rapt, or scribbling like mad in their notebooks as she unfolded the fruits of her most recent research, which had to do with a new technique she'd pioneered. Instead of opening heads, she snaked a catheter up into the brain and shot little metal coils into the aneurysms, blocking them off and preventing them from bursting.

She was one of the rare breed who still did this kind of "bench and bedside" medicine, developing a technique in the lab, then taking it to the OR. Personally, I think she liked the austerity of the science a lot better than dealing with actual patients, whom she tended to see not as human beings with ambitions and affections so much as complex data sets and problem lists. But she also loved the strut and swagger of being a top surgeon, a top *woman* surgeon.

"You think it's for me?" she'd said one day when, in the middle of some blue or other, I'd accused her of loving the way everyone at the hospital kowtows to her. "It's not for me. It's for every nurse or female intern who has had to put up with being belittled and demeaned, having her backside fondled or her intelligence questioned. It's for you, Hanna. And all the women of your generation, who'll never have to be harassed and leered at in a workplace again, because women like me struggled, and survived. And I run things now, and I don't let anyone forget it."

I don't know how true it was, the whole altruism riff, but I know she believed it. Anyway, I loved to see her taking questions in a setting like this, although I averted my eyes from the viscous, slimy things up on the big screen behind her. She was in complete control of her data and responded to what she considered to be good points or queries with a gracious eloquence. But woe to anyone who asked something half-baked, or questioned her conclusions. She would fix them with this charming smile, but you could hear the chain saw revving. Without a hint of anger or arrogance in her voice, she'd dismember them. I really couldn't bear to watch her do it to students, but this room full of blokes was another matter. They were supposedly her peers, and therefore fair game. She certainly knew how to work a crowd. The applause, when she finished, was more like the sound at a rock arena than a medical convention.

I slipped out while they were still clapping and waited on a bench in the hall. She emerged surrounded by a scrum of admirers. I got up and moved into her line of sight. I was going to join in the chorus of compliments about her great presentation, but when she spotted me her face actually fell, and I realized that she really had been hoping I wouldn't make it. It was almost comical, the way her expression changed, and then changed back again as she remembered to rearrange it.

"Hanna. You made it. How nice." Then, as soon as the other doctors had melted away, "But how pale you look, darling. You really should *try* to get outside sometimes."

"Well, I'm, you know, working. . . ."

"Of course you are, darling." Her blue eyes, nicely made up with some kind of dusky brown shadow, traveled from my boots to the top of my head and back again. "We all work, don't we? It doesn't mean we can't get out and exercise. If *I* can find the time, dear, then *you* should certainly be able to. How is your latest tatty little book, anyway? Fixed all the dog-eared pages?"

I took a deep breath and let that one go right through to the keeper. I didn't want to piss her off till I got what I'd come for. She looked at her watch. "I'm so sorry I don't have more time. We'll have to get tea in the cafeteria, I'm afraid. I have meetings just back-to-back and then I simply *have* to make an appearance at the predinner drinks this evening. They've got some *Nigerian* writer, Wally Something, for the keynote speaker. Just because the current president of the Neurosurgical Congress is a Nigerian, we have to have some obscure African, in Boston, when there are probably a dozen decent local writers who at least speak English that they could have asked."

"Wole Soyinka did get the Nobel prize for literature, Mum. And, actually, they do speak English in Nigeria."

"Well, you would know that sort of thing, of course." She had a hand on the back of my jacket and was already propelling me down the hallway.

"I, um, I was wondering. I've got some films. The man I was working with in Sarajevo, the librarian, his kid got shot during the war, there was swelling. . . . I wondered if you—"

She stopped in the hallway. There was a minute of silence.

"Oh. I see. I knew there was some reason why I was being honored by your attentions."

"Oh, cut it out, Mum. Will you take a look, or not?"

She snatched the manila envelope out of my hands and turned back down the corridor. We had to walk about a mile to a footbridge linking to the medical suites. We stepped into the lift. The door was closing when some elderly gent in a dressing gown tottered toward us. There's a word a friend of mine coined for that feeble gesture we make as if we're going to hold the door, when in reality we've got no intention of it. He calls it "to elefain." My mum's elefain was the lamest ever; the door closed right in the old bloke's face. We let the floors pass in silence, and then I waited while she asked an intern where to find a light box.

She hit a switch and a dazzling wall of white appeared. *Snap, snap, snap.* She flung the films against the light and then glanced at each scan for about two seconds.

"Toast."

"What?"

"The kid's toast. Tell your friend he might as well pull the plug now and save himself some medical bills."

The anger rose swiftly: hot, stinging. To my intense chagrin, I also felt tears in my eyes. I grabbed the films off the light box. My wrists were actually limp with rage. I could barely get the scans stuffed back into the envelope. "What is it with you, Mum? Were you absent the day they taught bedside manner?"

"Oh, Hanna. For goodness' sake. People die every day in hospitals. If I got choked up every time I saw an adverse scan . . ." She gave an exaggerated sigh. "If you were a doctor, you'd understand these things."

I was too upset to reply. I turned away to wipe my eyes. She put out a hand and turned me back toward her. She scanned my face.

"Don't tell me," she said, her voice saturated with contempt. "Don't tell me you are *involved* in some way with this child's father. Some threadbare bookworm from an Eastern European *backwater*. And aren't they all Islamics or something, in Sarajevo? Isn't that what all the fighting was about? *Don't* tell me you've involved yourself with a Muslim? Really, Hanna, I thought I'd raised you as enough of a feminist to draw the line at that."

"Raised me? You?" I slammed the envelope down on the desk. "You didn't raise me, unless you count signing checks to housekeepers."

She'd been gone when I woke in the morning and rarely back before my bedtime. My most vivid early memory of her was tail-lights in the driveway in the middle of the night. We had an automatic gate that made a grinding noise that often woke me. I'd sit up in bed and look out the window and wave to the departing Beemer. Sometimes, I wouldn't be able to get back to sleep, and I'd cry, and Greta, the housekeeper, would come in, drowsy, and say, "Don't you know your mother is saving someone's life tonight?" And I would feel guilty for wishing she was home, in the next room, where I could crawl into bed beside her. Her patients needed her more than I did. That's what Greta always said.

She put a hand to her gleaming hair, as if to tidy her already flawless updo. For once I'd actually gotten to her. I felt a little rush of satisfaction at that. But she rallied quickly. Never one to concede a point. "Well, you certainly didn't get this tendency to overwrought self-pity from me. How was I to know you had an emotional investment in this case? You're always telling me you're a scientist. Forgive me for treating you like one. Oh, sit down, for goodness' sake, and stop glaring at me. Anyone would think *I* shot the blessed child."

She pulled out a chair from behind the desk and patted it. I sat down, warily. She perched on the edge of the desk and draped one well-toned leg over the other.

"What I am saying is simply this, in plain, unvarnished layman's terms. The child's brain at this point is mostly dead tissue, a spongy mess. If you continue to keep the body alive by artificial means, the limb contractures will worsen, there will be a constant battle against decubitus ulcerations of the skin, against pulmonary and urinary infection. This child will never wake up." She raised both hands, palms up. "You asked for my opinion. Now you have it. And surely the doctors over there already told the father this?"

"Well, yes. But I thought—"

"If you were a doctor, you wouldn't have to think, Hanna. You'd know."

We went and had our tea—don't ask me why. I made some rote conversation: a question about the paper she'd delivered and when it would be published. I have no idea what she answered. I kept thinking about Ozren, and Winnie the bloody Pooh.

I was still chewing on it as I took the Harvard shuttle back across the river to see Razmus Kanaha, chief conservation scientist at the Fogg. Raz was an old postdoc mate of mine. He'd had a pretty rapid career rise and was very young to be heading up the oldest art research center in the United States. He'd come at conservation through chemistry, as I had, but he'd kept closer to that side of the work. He was noted for his analysis of carbohydrates and lipids in marine environments, which had led to a whole new paradigm in the treatment of art recovered from shipwrecks. He'd grown up in Hawaii, which perhaps explained his maritime obsession.

The security at the Fogg was pretty intense, for obvious reasons: the museum housed one of America's finest collections of impressionist and postimpressionist masterworks, as well as a handful of fabulous Picassos. The visitor's pass had some kind of computer-chip-looking thing in it, so as to track my movements around the building. Raz had to come down and personally sign me in.

Raz was one of those vanguard human beings of indeterminate ethnicity, the magnificent mutts that I hope we are all destined to become given another millennium of intermixing. His skin was a rich pecan color from his dad, who was part African American and part native Hawaiian. His hair, straight and glossy black, and the almond shape of his eyes came from his Japanese grandmother. But their color was the cool blue he'd inherited from his mum, a Swedish windsurfing champion. I'd been quite taken with him when we were postdocs together. It was just my kind of relationship; light, easy, fun, no strings. He'd go off on long marine salvage gigs somewhere, gathering research for his dissertation, and when he came back, we'd pick up the relationship, or not, depending on what mood we were both in. There were never any hard feelings if one or the other of us was otherwise engaged.

After the Harvard years, we hadn't seen a lot of each other, but we'd kept in loose touch. When he married a poet, I sent them a beautiful little nineteenth-century edition I'd found with woodcuts of famous shipwrecks. The wedding photo they sent me back was something. Raz's wife was the daughter of an Iranian-Kurdish mother and a Pakistani-American father. I couldn't wait to see their kids: they'd be walking Benetton ads.

We hugged awkwardly, the way you do in a workplace, not quite knowing whether to air kiss once or twice, getting it wrong, banging skulls, and wishing you'd just shaken hands. We walked across the light-drenched atrium and up the stone stairway past the galleries. There was a metal security gate sealing off the top floor, where Raz and the other conservators did their work.

The Straus Center for Conservation was a strange mix: an absolutely up-to-date science facility coupled with an attic-style assembly of collections gathered by its founder, Edward Forbes. Early last century, Forbes traveled the world, trying to obtain a sample of every known pigment ever used in art. The walls of the stairwell were lined with shelves holding his finds: a rainbow spectrum of vitrines full of ground lapis and malachite as well as real rarities, such as Indian

Yellow, made from the piss of cows fed only on mango leaves. This wonderful, lime-tinged, lemony pigment doesn't really exist anymore. The British banned its production during the Raj because the restricted diet was too cruel to the cattle.

At one end of a long studio, someone was working on a bronze torso. "She's comparing a cast made in the sculptor's lifetime with one made later to see what differences there are in the finishes," Raz explained. Down at the other end stood the bench that housed the spectrometer. "So, what have you got for me?" Raz asked.

"They're specimens I lifted from a stained parchment. Wine, I'm betting." I drew out the photograph I'd taken of the stained page, the russet blooming across the pale cream ground. I'd marked the photos to show where I'd lifted the two minute samples. I hoped I'd taken enough. I handed Raz the glassine envelope. He took up a curved scalpel and placed the first dot of stained matter onto a kind of round microscope slide with a sliver of diamond at the center for the specimen to rest on. He ran a roller over the sample, to squash it flat against the diamond so that infrared light could pass through it. He slipped the slide under the lens.

He peered through the microscope to make sure the specimen was centered, and adjusted the two snake lights on either side to illuminate it correctly. In any other lab, including mine at home, it took hours to get a dozen spectra. Every molecule gives off light in various colors of the spectrum. Some substances tend more to the blue end, others to the red, and so on. That means the spectrum of a molecule is like a fingerprint that can be used to identify it. Raz's new toy was the latest thing: it could get two hundred spectra in less than a minute. I felt a stab of envy as the computer screen next to us came alive with green lines that leaped and dived up and down a grid that measured light absorbance. Raz studied the graph.

"That's odd," he said.

"What?"

"Well, I'm not sure. Let me look at the other sample."

He fiddled around again with the glassine envelope and mounted the second dot. This time, the squiggles on the screen seemed to map an entirely different mountain range.

"Ha," he said.

"What do you mean, 'Ha'?" I was actually sweating.

"Just a minute." Raz changed the slides again, and again the graph rose and fell across the screen. He tapped some keys on the computer keyboard. Other graphs, in yellow, red, orange, and blue, leaped up around the green line.

"Ha," he said again.

"Raz, if you don't tell me what it is that you are seeing, I'm going to run you through with your own scalpel."

"Well, what I'm seeing doesn't make a lot of sense. This is a Hebrew manuscript, right? Didn't you say a haggadah?"

"Yes." I almost barked.

"So any wine that would have been spilled on it, we can assume pretty safely that it would be kosher?"

"Yes, of course. Kosher for Passover, strict as strict can be."

He leaned back in his chair and pushed away from the desk so that he was facing me.

"Do you know anything about kosher wine?"

"Not a lot," I said. "Just that it's usually sweet and undrinkable."

"Not these days. There are some perfectly quaffable kosher wines being made, especially in the Golan Heights, but other wineries too."

"How come you're such an expert? You're not Jewish. Or are you?" Raz's ancestry was so mixed up anything was possible.

"I'm not. But you could say I'm religious about wine. Remember I spent six months at the Technion in Israel, working on artifacts recovered from a Mediterranean wreck? Well, I got friendly with a woman whose family owned a vineyard in the Golan. Lovely spot. Spent a lot of time there, one way and another, especially during the vintage. Which is, I have to say, lucky for you." He had his hands behind his head and was leaning back in the chair, grinning smugly.

"Raz, that's great. I mean, whoop-de-do. But for God's sake, what has it got to do with this stain?"

"Keep your shirt on and I'll tell you." He turned back to the graph and pointed to a tall spike. "See that? That nice spike of absorbance there? That's protein."

"So?"

"So there shouldn't be any protein in kosher wine. In traditional wine making they've pretty much always used egg white as a clarifying agent, so you can expect to get traces of protein. But the use of any animal product is prohibited in kosher wine. Traditionally, they use a kind of fine clay instead, to do the same job." He rattled a couple of keys and brought up the graph from the second specimen. "This one looks the way you'd expect it to."

"So what are you saying? That they spilled two different kinds of wine on the same page? Pretty far-fetched."

"No, what I'm saying is that there's something else mixed in with the wine in places." He tapped another key, and the screen came alive again with a variety of lines in various colors. "I've called up the library of all the spectrometry we've done here, looking for something that matches the profile. And there it is. See that blue line? It tracks almost exactly over the green line generated by the first specimen. I'd say that's what you've got there on the page, mixed in with the wine, staining your parchment."

"So?" I was almost yelling, at this point. "So what is it?"

"That blue line?" he said calmly. "That's blood."

Wine Stains

Venice, 1609

Introibo ad altare Dei.

—Latin Mass

THE BELLS—silvery, shivering—rang in his head as if the clappers were striking the raw red interior of his skull. The wine lapped the cup as he replaced it on the altar. When his knee touched the floor, he rested his brow against the crisp linen. He stayed there a moment, letting the cold of the marble seep through the altar cloth. When he got up, there was a small damp patch from his sweat.

The old mothers at this early Mass were too devout to notice that he staggered slightly as he rose. Their heads, wrapped in threadbare shawls, were bent in devotion. Only the altar boy, his eyes bright as a newt, drew his brows together. Damn the young and the clarity of their judgments. He tried—God knows how he tried—to keep his own mind centered on the holy mystery. But the faint stink of his own predawn vomit would not leave his nostrils.

He was dry. The words stuck to his tongue like ashes of burned parchment. Like the ashes that had fallen in a warm rain after the last book burning. A piece had landed on his cassock, and as he raised a hand to brush it away, he noticed that the words were still legible, pale ghost letters against the charred ground. And then they turned to dust and blew away.

"Per ipsum"—he held the Body over the Blood and made the sign of the cross—"et cum ipso"—curse his tremors—"et in ipso"—the Bread of Heaven was dancing over the chalice like a bumblebee— "est tibi Deo Patri omnipotenti, in unitate Spiritus Sancti, omnis honor et gloria." He raced through the Pater Noster, the Libera Nos, the Agnus Dei, and the prayers for peace and sanctification and grace until, Deo *gratias,* he finally tilted the chalice and felt the Precious Blood—cool, astringent, delicious—washing away the bile and the bitterness and the terrible tremor in his flesh. He turned to give Communion to the server. The boy's eyes, thankfully, were closed, their judgment hidden behind the thick hedge of his lashes. Then he made his way to the altar rail and placed bright white hosts on a half dozen furry old tongues.

In the sacristy after the Mass, Giovanni Domenico Vistorini felt the boy's appraising gaze again, lingering on the tremor in his hands as he drew off his stole and struggled with the tie on his cincture.

"What are you dawdling about for, Paolo? Take off your cassock and get along. I saw your grandmother at Mass. Go on now. She will have need of your arm."

"As you wish, Father." The boy spoke, as ever, with an exaggerated politeness. There was even the hint of a bow. Vistorini sometimes thought he might have preferred open insolence. But Paolo was graceful and precise, at the altar and away from it, and gave him nothing to complain about. The boy's contempt was conveyed only in long, assessing glances. He gave the priest one of these lacerating stares and then turned away to disrobe, his efficient, economical gestures mocking Vistorini's fumbling. He was out the door without another word.

Alone in the sacristy, Vistorini opened the cabinet that contained the unconsecrated Communion wine. The cork came out of the decanter with a wet, sucking sound. He licked his lips. The cool jug was misted with condensation, so Vistorini raised it carefully, for his hands were still trembling, and took a deep swallow. Then another. Better.

He was about to replace the stopper in the decanter, but then he considered the morning stretching before him. The office of the pope's Inquisitor in Venice was not noted for its liberality. The rooms the doge had assigned to the members of the Inquisition were gloomy, badly furnished, and poorly provisioned. Vistorini believed that the doge was trying to make a point; that the minions of Rome held a subordinate position in the state where only he, and the Ten, made decisions of significance. In any case, it might well be past the noon hour before he could procure another drink. He raised the jug again and let the velvet liquid course down his throat.

Vistorini's step was almost jaunty as he closed the side door of his church and stepped out into the milky light of early morning. The sun was just high enough to reach into the narrow *calle,* throwing dappled reflections from the canal that silvered the stone in bright, dancing patches. The chime of the Marangona bell sounded, deeper and more resonant than any other bell in the city. It signaled the start of the workday for *arsenalotti,* and the opening of the gates at the nearby Geto. Shutters rattled as merchants opened for trade on the *campiello* in front of the church.

Vistorini breathed deeply. Even after thirty years in the city, he still loved the light and the air of Venice, its mingled scents of brine and moss, mold and moist plaster. He had been only six years old when he came to the city, and the brothers at the orphanage had encouraged him to shed all memories of the past, along with his accent and his foreign manners. They had conveyed to him that reminiscence was a shadowy and shameful thing, indicating lack of gratitude for his present blessings. He had been schooled to push away thoughts of his dead parents and the short life he had shared with them. But sometimes, fragments broke through, in dreams, or when his will was weakened by intoxication. And in those fragments, the past was always lit by a wincing glare and tasted of dust carried by scorching winds.

As he moved over the bridge, past the bargeman delivering meat to the butcher and the washerwomen at work by the canal, he recognized several of his parishioners. He greeted them with a pleasant word or a kind inquiry, depending on the family's condition. A legless beggar propelled himself forward on the stumps of what should have been his arms. Great God. Vistorini formed a mental prayer for the man, whose deformity was so grotesque that even a surgeon would be hard pressed to lay eyes on him without recoil. He placed a coin on the beggar's oozing extremity and then, fighting his revulsion, laid a hand on his scabby head and blessed him. The beggar responded with an animal grunt that seemed to be an expression of gratitude.

As a parish priest, Vistorini tried his best to feign interest in the little lives of his flock. Yet the work of ministry didn't really engage him. His principal service to his church lay elsewhere. Vistorini's abilities had been recognized by the brothers who had taken him in as an orphan. They had been impressed by his facility with languages, but also with his superior understanding of complex, abstract theology. They had educated him in Greek and Aramaic, Hebrew and Arabic, and he had absorbed it all. In those days, his thirst for knowledge had been great; now, it was the other thirst that ordered his existence.

In 1589, when Pope Sixtus V proclaimed a ban on any books by Jews or Saracens that contained anything against the Catholic faith, the young priest Vistorini had been a natural choice to work as censor of the Inquisitor. For seventeen years, almost his entire life in Holy Orders, Domenico had read and passed judgment on the works of alien faiths.

As a scholar, he had an innate reverence for books. This he had been required to subdue when his mission was to destroy them. Sometimes, the beauty of the Saracens' fluid calligraphy moved him. Other times, it was the elegant argument of a learned Jew that gave him pause. He would take his time considering such manuscripts. If, in the end, he determined that they had to go to the flames, he would avert his gaze as the parchments blackened. His job was easier when the heresy was patent. At those times, he could watch the flames, rejoicing in them as a cleansing thing, ridding human thought of error.

He had such a book with him this morning, a Jewish text. His morning's work would be to draft the order for all copies in the city to be surrendered to the Inquisitor's office, from whence they would go to the fire. The words, the blasphemous words, danced in his head, the Hebrew letters as familiar to him as Latin script:

Christian worship of Jesus is an idolatry much worse than the Israelites' worship of the golden calf, for the Christians err in saying that something holy entered into a woman in that stinking place . . . full of feces and urine, which emits discharge and menstrual blood and serves as a receptacle for men's semen.

Sometimes, Vistorini wondered how such words still came to be committed to paper, after more than a hundred years of Inquisition. Jews and Arabs had been fined, imprisoned, even put to death, for lesser blasphemies than these. He supposed that the proliferation of printing houses in Venice was to blame. Officially, Jews were banned from the trade of publishing, and yet their houses thrived under the flimsy front of some Christian willing to lend his name in exchange for a few gold sequins.

Not every man who wished to set up as a printer should be approbated to do so. Some of them, evidently, were ignorant or malicious. He would have to discuss this with Judah Aryeh. The Jews should exercise more control, or the Inquisitor would be obliged to do it for them. Better to keep the Office of the Inquisition outside of the Geto walls. Surely even a lesser intellect than Judah's would see the sense of that.

As if his thoughts had conjured him up out of the stones, Vistorini saw the scarlet hat of the rabbi Judah Aryeh, making a furtive way through the crowd in front of him on the Frezzeria, where the arrow makers crafted their wares. He was walking with the stooped, head-down posture he always affected when outside the Geto. Vistorini raised a hand to hail the man, but hesitated. He watched the rabbi for a moment, considering him. How many small humiliations had it taken to bow him over into that cringing stoop: the abusive pranks of loutish boys, the jeers and spittle of the ignorant. If only the stiff-necked fellow would embrace the truth of Christ, he could end all such abasements.

"Judah Aryeh!"

The rabbi's head came up like a deer expecting one of the craftsmen's arrows. But when he saw Vistorini, his wary expression eased into a smile of real pleasure.

"Domenico Vistorini! It has been too long, Father, since I have seen you in my synagogue."

"Ah, Rabbi, a man can take only so many reminders of his own shortcomings. One may wish to learn from you and yet at the same time feel humiliated by your eloquence."

"Father, you mock me."

"No need for false modesty with me, Judah." The rabbi was so famous for his silver-tongued biblical exegesis that he preached at four different synagogues on the Jewish Sabbath, and many Christians, including friars, priests, and noblemen, entered the Geto just to hear him. "The bishop of Padua, whom I brought to hear you last, agreed that he had never had the book of Job so well explicated," Vistorini said. He did not add that he had heard the bishop preach on the same text some weeks later, in the Padua cathedral, and had thought the bishop's sermon nothing more than flour already ground between the millstones of the rabbi's intellect. Vistorini was sure that no few of the priests who came to listen did so in order to steal the rabbi's words. For himself, it was not so much the content, but the polished and passionate mode of delivery that he wished to emulate. "Would that I held the congregation in my hand, as you do. I try to learn your secrets, to better deliver the word of Mother Church, but alas! they remain opaque to me."

"A man's thoughts and the ability to express them come from God, and if my words find favor, may it be to his honor." Vistorini suppressed a sneer. Could the rabbi really believe such unctuous platitudes? Aryeh noticed Vistorini's displeased expression and changed his tone. "As to secrets, Father, I have but one: if the congregation expects a sermon of forty minutes' length, then give them one of thirty minutes. If they expect thirty, then give them twenty. In all my years as rabbi, I have never once had a soul complain to me that a sermon was too short."

The priest smiled at that. "Now it is you who mock me! But walk with me a little, if you will, for I have a matter to discuss with you."

Judah Aryeh had straightened as he spoke to Vistorini, and now, protected by his eminent companion, he walked upright, his shoulders thrown back and his head erect. His dark hair escaped from the scarlet fabric of his cap in springy curls that were lit, like his beard, with chestnut highlights. Vistorini envied Judah's physique, tall and well made, if somewhat spare, with an olive-gold skin unlike the pale flesh that marked so many scholars. But the impression was marred by that lurid head covering.

"Judah, why do you wear that hat? You know it is not impossible for you to get leave to wear a black one." The scarlet color was meant to recall the blood of Christ that the Jews had brought down upon their own heads. Yet Vistorini knew a number of Jews who had been granted exemption.

"Father Dom, I know very well that with friends and money one may do almost everything in Venice. Money, as you well know, I have not. But friends, yes, I have several who would spare me this imposition. With a word here or there, I could, as you say, wear a black hat and pass about unmolested. But if I did so, I would not know life as the people in my congregation know it. And I do not want to be separate from them. I am vain enough to have my daughter sew my caps from velvet and line them with silk, but I will do as the law requires, for a man's worth does not come from what he wears on his head. A red hat, a black hat: what matter? Neither one can cover up my mind."

"Well said. I might have known you would have your reasons as well tended as a Benedictine's garden."

"But I do not think you asked me to walk with you to discuss millinery."

Vistorini smiled. He did not like to admit it, even to himself, but sometimes he felt closer to this witty, intelligent Jew than to any priest in his own order.

"No, I did not. Sit a moment, if you will." Vistorini gestured toward a low wall by the canal. "Read this," he said, passing the book, opened at the offending passage.

Aryeh read, swaying slightly, as if he were in synagogue. When he had finished, he gazed across the canal, avoiding his friend's eyes. "Clearly in contravention of the Index," he said. His tone was carefully neutral, expressing no strong emotion. Vistorini had often noted with chagrin that although Aryeh, like himself, had come to Venice from elsewhere, the Jew spoke with the inflections of a born Venetian; the soft, lilting dialect of the city, overlaid by the distinctive cadences of his own particular *sestiere,* the Cannaregio. The priest had tried to make his own speech sound native, but he could never completely shed the accents of his childhood.

"It is a little more serious than that," Vistorini said. "This kind of deliberately provocative text will bring the attention, the wrath of the Holy Office down upon the whole Geto. You would do well, my friend, to deal with this matter yourself, before we are obliged to do so. You should close down these printers."

Judah Aryeh turned to face the priest. "The author of this text did not write to provoke, but merely to express a truth as he conceives it. Your own theologians have tied logic in knots to advance a doctrine addressing this very same point. What is the Annunciation, after all, but the fumbling of minds striving to deal with the indelicate realities of the body? We Jews are merely more forthright about such matters."

Vistorini sucked in a deep breath and was about to protest when Aryeh raised a hand to forestall him. "I do not want to waste such a fine morning arguing theology with you. I think we learned long ago, you and I, how little profit there is in it. The merits or demerits of this particular work aside, I think you need to look realistically at where your office now stands with the state of Venice. The number of cases the Inquisitor is able to bring to trial here is falling year following year. And most of those that do come to court are quashed there for lack of evidence. I am not saying that we do not fear you, but we do not fear you as we once did. I will tell you what my people say of your office: that your poison has congealed, and that you have lost the recipe to brew more."

Vistorini picked at the lichen growing on the stone beside him. There was, as always, sense in what his friend asserted. The late pope, Gregory XIII, had identified the very weakness of which the rabbi spoke. "I am pope everywhere except in Venice," he had said. But Vistorini sensed a dangerous mood with the new pope in Rome. He might not confront the doge and the Ten directly, but he could do it through the city's Jews. Even a wounded beast can gather its strength for one last lunge of the claw.

"Rabbi, I hope—and I say this sincerely—that you do not have cause to learn again the meaning of terror. Surely those among you who are descendants of the Spanish exile still remember the bitter conditions under which their grandparents were got hither?"

"We have not forgotten. But *there* is not *here*. *Then* is not *now*. The Spanish Inquisition was a nightmare from which many of us still cannot awaken. And yet we Ponentinis, whose forebears experienced that great dispossession, are just one group, one set of memories. There are Hollanders, Tedeschis, Levantinis. How can we not feel secure here, when every noble family has its Jewish confidante, and when the doge does not even allow your Inquisition to force conversionist sermons upon us?"

Vistorini sighed. "I myself counseled the Inquisitor against such sermons," he said. "I told him it would only exasperate your people, not edify them." The real reason: he had not wanted to expose the inferiority of his own preaching to congregations who had heard Judah Aryeh.

The rabbi rose to his feet. "I must be about my business, Father." He tugged at his hat, wondering whether it was safe to speak his mind. He decided that the priest had a right to know his reasoning. "You know that your church has always taken a view on these matters very different from ours, from the day that the first printing press was assembled. Your church did not want your holy scriptures in the hands of ordinary people. We felt differently. To us, printing was an *avodat ha kodesh*, a holy work. Some rabbis even likened the press to an altar. We called it 'writing with many pens' and saw it as furthering the spread of the word that began with Moses on Mount Sinai. So, my good father, you go and write the order to burn that book, as your church requires of you. And I will say nothing to the printing house, as my conscience requires of me. *Censura praevia* or *censura repressiva,* the effect is the same. Either way, a book is destroyed. Better you do it than have us so intellectually enslaved that we do it for you."

Vistorini had no ready response to the rabbi, and that irritated him. He became aware of a dull thudding in his temple. The two men took a cool farewell of each other, and Judah Aryeh left the priest, still seated, by the canal. As the rabbi walked away, his heart beat hard. Had he been too forthright? Anyone overhearing their exchange would have gasped at his insolence and wondered that Vistorini didn't have him sent to the Leads. But anyone overhearing would not have known the history that stood between them. They had been friends, in so far as such a word had meaning in their circumstances, for ten years. So why, the rabbi asked himself, was his heart pounding so?

As soon as he turned off the *fondamenta* and out of sight of Vistorini, Aryeh leaned against the wall and breathed shallowly. The breaths hurt. He had had the pains for many years. He remembered well how his chest had ached the first day he met the priest, in the office of the Inquisitor. Judah Aryeh had taken a great risk. Few went willingly to the Holy Office, but he had asked to be heard there. He had spoken for more than two hours, in eloquent Latin, trying to obtain a partial lifting of the ban on the Talmud. The two-part work was the distillation of Jewish thought since the days of exile, and to be deprived of it had been a hardship, an intellectual fast that had begun to feel like starvation. For the Mishnah, the main body of the work, he knew there was no hope of reprieve. But for the second part of the Talmud, the Gemara, he felt he could make a case. The Gemara was an exchange of rabbinical opinions, a collection of arguments and disputes. This, he argued, could be seen as helping rather than harming the church, as it demonstrated that even rabbis disagreed on aspects of Jewish law. Surely the evidence of such divisions within Judaism could be used to strengthen the church's case against his faith?

Vistorini had stood behind the Inquisitor's chair, his eyes narrowed. He knew the Hebrew texts intimately, having confiscated and destroyed so very many copies of the Talmud. He knew that any moderately learned rabbi could take the Gemara and reconstruct from it the text of the accursed Mishnah for his students. But the Inquisitor let himself be wrapped inside the rabbi's skein of clever words. He gave the Jews leave to keep such copies of the Talmud as they had in hand, so long as they were properly expurgated.

Although he had lost the match of wits, Vistorini had been impressed by Aryeh; by his learning, by his courage, but also by his cunning. It was, he thought to himself, like watching an alchemist show a deceptive increase. You knew there was some trick being played, yet observe as closely as you could and still the moment and the means of adding the extra ore would remain obscure to you.

As the rabbi, giddy with relief at saving his texts, made to leave the Inquisitor's chamber, Vistorini had leaned in close and whispered, "Judah the Lion. Better they should have named you Judah Shu'al." The rabbi looked into the priest's eyes and saw, not anger exactly, but the ambivalent emotion a loser has toward a worthy opponent. The next time Aryeh came to the Holy Office, he took a chance. He had the curate announce him to Vistorini as "Rabbi Judah Vulpes."

Vistorini came to enjoy sparring with Aryeh, who could appreciate a wordplay in three languages. The priest had led a solitary life. At the orphanage, his thick accent and the shame that seemed to shadow mentions of his past made him shy with the other boys. At the seminary, his interests and abilities had set him off from his peers.

But with Aryeh, he could wrestle with an intellectual equal. He appreciated that Aryeh never wasted his time by trying to defend blatant heresy or clear violations of the Index. Sometimes, Vistorini allowed the rabbi to convince him. He would redact rather than destroy, and once or twice he raised his pen to reprieve a threatened text, writing the necessary words of authority on the first of its pages.

His interest in Aryeh eventually led him to conquer a long-standing distaste, and cross the little bridge to the Geto. When he had been a seminarian, many of his fellow students had gone there regularly. Baiting the Jews had been a favorite sport for some of the youths; others had gone in an honest spirit of evangelism, to win souls. A few had gone to risk their own by taking part in illicit entertainments. But Vistorini had found the very idea of the Geto repellent. He would not willingly enter a gated neighborhood crawling with nothing but Jews. The very idea made him feel trapped, suffocated, unclean.

The first Jews to settle in Venice in 1516 had been German loan bankers. Others followed, but were allowed to pursue only three trades: pawnbrokers, providing inexpensive credit to poor Venetians; *strazzaria* dealers, buying and selling used goods; or foreign traders, using their ties to the Levant to facilitate the city's vast export and import business. They were permitted to live only in the small area that had once been the city's iron foundry, or Geto, a walled island of ash, joined to the rest of the city by only two narrow bridges, gated and locked each night.

But as the years passed, some Venetians had warmed to the presence of the Jews, hiring them to perform their haunting music, seeking them out as physicians or financial advisers. For the Jews, the fact that their property rights were respected and that they had protection of the law made Venice a promised land compared with conditions elsewhere.

So they had kept coming: the Ponentini, expelled from Spain and then from Portugal by the Catholic monarchs. Then the Tedeschis, fleeing pogroms in the German cities; and the ever-restless Levantinis from lands such as Egypt and Syria. The community had swollen to near two thousand souls, their dwellings piled one atop the other, six or seven large families together, until the Geto had the densest population and the tallest structures in Venice. When Vistorini asked the way to Judah's synagogue, he was directed to a tall, narrow apartment building. At the top of a steep, dark stairwell, the rabbi's house of worship shared roof space with a dovecote and a chicken coop.

Although he had first been drawn to the rabbi as a kindred intellect, it was weakness, not strength, that had sealed their bond. One afternoon, Judah had happened to be walking in the area between the Geto and the priest's church, taking the narrowest *callettos* and *rughettas* so as to escape harassment on the more crowded thoroughfares. He had interrupted a cutpurse who was bending over the body of his victim. The man ran off, and Judah recognized Domenico, drunk, his head bleeding from the robber's blow, his cassock soaked in urine. The rabbi had taken a great personal risk, missing curfew, to obtain clean linens and help the priest get sober, so that his church never knew what a shameful spectacle its representative had made of himself.

When Domenico tried to thank Judah, the rabbi muttered that he too had a weakness that Satan exploited from time to time. He would not say more. And yet that weakness gnawed at his mind, distracting him from his prayers by day and from the tender exchanges with his wife by night. As he slumped against the wall in the *calle,* he knew that the pain in his chest did not come only from the boldness of his exchange with the priest. Nor was it his morning's errand—illicit, dangerous—that had set his heart skipping and thumping. Both those things combined with the nagging voice in his head, the tempter's voice that he could not quiet. He had tried, God his witness knew how he had tried, to arrange to leave Venice before Carnivale was to begin in just a few days. He had wanted to put himself out of reach of sin. The ability to go behind a mask, to be another man, to do what a Jew may not do—the temptation overwhelmed him. The year before, he had managed to get a position as a tutor outside the city. But the season of Carnivale had been extended year by year, and suitable appointments had become hard to find. He had applied to tutor a youth in Padua, and to take the bimah for a sick rabbi in Ferrara. But neither situation had been offered to him.

As Carnivale drew closer, his wife, knowing the danger, had gone through his box, searching among his clothes for the mask and cape that would make him indistinguishable from a Venetian Gentile. Eventually, she found where he had concealed them, among the notions and bolts of cloth belonging to their daughter, the seamstress. She had taken both items directly to the *strazzaria* and sold them. He had thanked her for it, kissing her tenderly on the forehead. For a day or so, he felt profound relief that the props of his disgrace had been put beyond his reach. But soon, all he had been able to think about was Carnivale, and the opportunity it afforded him.

Even now, when he needed his wits, the serpent wrapped itself around his every thought, squeezing out reason and conscience. He made his way to the set of steps near the Rialto where he had been told to wait. He did not like to stand so, exposed, in the heart of the city. He sensed people staring at him. Citizens pushed past him, muttering disparaging comments. It was with great relief that he saw the gondolier expertly poling the boat toward the steps. The boat was painted an austere black, the color mandated by laws to discourage Venetians from ostentatious displays of their wealth. The uniform color, as well as the legendary discretion of the gondoliers, helped trysting lovers maintain their anonymity.

Aryeh made his way gingerly down the slippery stone steps, aware that the sight of a Jew boarding a gondola was no very common thing. He was nervous, and the fluttering of his heart made him a little dizzy. A Venetian would have reached out to take the gondolier's elbow as a way of steadying himself as he boarded, but Aryeh was unsure how the gondolier would feel about being touched by a Jew. The superstition that such a touch could be used for Jewish witchcraft, to pass evil spirits to Christians, was widespread among

Venetians. Just as he placed his foot in the boat, the wake from a passing craft tipped the deck. Aryeh wobbled, waving his arms like windmills, and landed on his rear. From the Rialto came coarse laughter. A gob of spittle traveled over the canal wall and landed on his hat.

"*Dio!*" the gondolier cried, reaching down and grasping the rabbi with forearms well muscled from plying the oar. When the rabbi was on his feet, the gondolier brushed his clothing solicitously and then hurled a raft of salty invective that shut the mouths of the laughing youths ashore.

Aryeh chided himself for his thoughts about the gondolier. Of course, Doña Reyna de Serena would hardly have a Jew hater in her employ. She was sitting, waiting for him, in the cushioned privacy of the *felze*.

"Quite an entrance, Rabbi," she said, raising an eyebrow. "Not the most discreet way to come aboard. But sit now." She gestured at the embroidered silken cushions opposite her own. Outside, the *felze* curtain was a discreet black sailcloth. But inside, it was lined with gold-threaded brocades that made a joke of the sumptuary laws.

Reyna de Serena had come to Venice in some state a decade earlier. Having fled Portugal a Jew, she had arrived in Venice professing herself a devout convert to Christianity. She had taken a new name, one that indicated her gratitude to her place of refuge. As a Christian, she had been able to establish herself outside the crowded precincts of the Geto, in a magnificent palace, right beside the Venetian mint. Some Venetians joked that the Serena house contained even more gold than its neighbor, for Serena was heiress to one of the greatest Jewish banking fortunes in Europe. Because the family had spread its operations well beyond the Iberian Peninsula, only a portion of the wealth had been lost to the plundering royals of Spain and Portugal. Although she no longer answered to her family's Jewish name, there was little doubt in most minds that she still had access to its funds.

But Serena did not spend her great wealth only on her brocade hangings and her entertainments, which were attended by the cream of the nobility. In secret, she was Aryeh's chief source of alms for needy members of the Geto community. Furthermore, he knew she aided Jews in many other cities, through the banking network her family had established. He also knew that her public face as a devout Catholic was a mask she wore, putting it on as casually as a Carnivale disguise.

"So, Rabbi. Tell me your needs this day. How can I help you to help our people?"

Aryeh despised himself for what he was about to do. "My lady, the wings of your generosity have already enfolded a great many of our sons and daughters, protecting them from the cruelties of exile. You are a fountain of clear water where the parched may drink, you are—"

Reyna de Serena raised a jeweled hand and waved it in front of her face, as if warding off a bad smell. "Enough. Just tell me how much you need."

Aryeh named a sum. His mouth was dry, as if the lie had parched it. He watched her face, grave and lovely, as she considered the amount for an instant, and then reached into the pile of cushions beside her and drew out two fat purses.

Aryeh licked his lips and swallowed hard. "My lady, the families will bless your name. If you knew the details of their hardship . . ."

"I do not need to know anything more than that they are Jews, they are in need, and you think them worthy of my help. I have trusted you with my secret, Rabbi; how then not trust you with a few sequins?"

As the rabbi felt the weight of the gold, he wondered at her definition of *few*. But the word *trust* made his heart contract as if a fist had suddenly squeezed it.

"Now, Rabbi, I have a service to ask of you."

"Anything, my lady." The fist eased its grip a little, at the hope he might be able to do something in partial atonement for his dishonesty.

"I hear you are a friend of the censor at the Holy Office."

"I would not say 'friend' exactly, my lady." He thought of the terse exchange by the canal. "But we know each other, we speak together often, and with civility. In fact, I am just come from him. He wants to close the printing office of Abraham Pinel—the one that the Bernadotti lend their names to."

"Does he so? Perhaps I might have a word with Lucio de Bernadotti. I am sure he would prefer to avoid such an embarrassment. Perhaps he can arrange to have the house commission a work in praise of the pope, so that a sudden closure by the Holy Office would become less politically expedient?"

Aryeh smiled. No wonder Reyna de Serena had survived, even thrived, in an exile that had crushed so many. "But how can I help my lady with the censor?"

"I have this," she said, reaching once again under the cushions at her side and drawing out a small, kid-bound book with finely wrought silver clasps. She handed it to the rabbi. Aryeh took the book in his hands.

"It is very old," he said.

"Indeed. More than a hundred years. Like me, a survivor from a world that no longer exists. Open it."

Aryeh released the catches, admiring the talent of the silversmith. Each clasp, closed, was in the form of a pair of wings. As the delicate catch released—still smoothly, after more than a century—the wings opened to reveal a rosette enfolded within. Aryeh saw at once that the book was a haggadah, but unlike any he had ever seen before. The gold leaf, the rich pigments . . . he stared at the illuminations, turning each page eagerly. He was delighted, yet a little disturbed, to see Jewish stories told in an art so like that of the Christians' prayer books.

"Who made this book? These pictures?"

Reyna de Serena shrugged. "How I would love to know. It came to me from an elderly manservant of my mother's. He was a kindly man, ancient by the time I knew him. He used to tell me stories, when I was little. Such terrible stories, filled with wicked soldiers and pirates, storms at sea and plagues on land. I loved them, as a child will, who does not yet know enough of the world to perceive what is real and what is fable. Now, I am ashamed to recall how I pressed him for those stories, for I think they were the true stories of his own life. He said he was born in the very month of the Spanish expulsion, and that his mother had died in a shipwreck not long after that, trying to find a safe haven in which to raise him. He somehow came under the protection of my family—many orphans did, over the years. As a youth he worked for my grandfather, not in the bank, but in the secret business of helping Jews to escape from Portugal. In any case, the book was his; his oldest and dearest possession. When he died, he left it to my mother, and when she she died passed it down to me. And I have treasured it, because it is lovely, but also because it reminds me of him, and the suffering of so many like him.

"Rabbi, I need the censor to examine and pass this book. But I cannot take any chances with it. I must know he will pass it before I bring it to his attention. And, of course, no one must know it is mine. Catholic ladies have no need of haggadot."

"Doña de Serena, let me take it and study it. I know very well what form of words violates the Catholics' Index. I will make sure in the first place that there is indeed nothing offensive to the church, and then I will bring it to Father Vistorini in a way most assured to bring a satisfactory outcome."

"You will be sure of it? I think I could not bear it if this book, having traveled so far and through so much, should be consigned to the flames."

"So, that is why I must ask you, my lady, if I might: although I am confident I can get what you seek from the censor, why, if you keep the book in secret, do you need to have it passed? Surely you can have no reason to fear that your personal property would ever be searched or examined? No one in Venice would dare—"

"Rabbi, I propose to leave Venice—"

"My lady!"

"—and at that time, who knows what scrutiny my goods might become subject to. I need to be meticulous."

"But this is grievous news indeed! I shall miss you. All the Jews of Venice will miss you, even though they do not know the name of their generous patroness. You have no idea how many undeserved blessings I get from my people as a result of the alms you allow me to dispense to them."

She raised her hand, again impatient with his praise.

"I have lived well here. But I have learned something about myself, as the years have passed. I have discovered that I cannot live my whole life as a lie."

"So, you propose to drop the pretense of your conversion? You know it is a risk, weak as the Inquisition is, it still—"

"Rabbi, do not trouble yourself. I have arranged safe passage."

"But where will you go? Where is this happy place where one may live and prosper as a Jew?"

"Not so very far. Just across the sea that stands between us and the lands under the governance of the Sublime Porte. The Ottoman sultans have long welcomed us—for our skills and our wealth. When I was younger, I did not choose to go there, but much has changed since then. The community has grown. In several places we have our doctors, our Hebrew poets. The sultan has invited me, and even now is sending a *chaus* from his court to the doge with a message to arrange my safe passage. It is not without risk. Many will be glad to know that what they have long suspected is true: that I have pretended Christianity in order to live freely here. But if I stay, I must live my life alone. I cannot marry a Christian man and keep from him the secret of my Jewish soul. There, perhaps, it will not be too late to make a match, to have a child. Perhaps you will come and make the blessings at his brit? They say the city of Ragusa is very lovely—not so lovely as Venice, to be sure, but at least it will be an honest life. I will have my own name back again. Now, enough. Pray with me, for I yearn to fill my ears with the sound of Hebrew."

A short time later, Aryeh disembarked from the gondola in a *canaletto* some distance from the bustle and inquisitive eyes of the Rialto. His pockets heavy with Doña de Serena's purses, the small book pressed against his waist, he had every intention of going home. He was walking, head down, eyes on the stones. He had passed the *mascarer*'s workshop without even looking up to see what masks the artisan had placed on display. But at the corner, he stopped. The gold in his pockets anchored him there.

Usually, Judah knew his obsession for what it was: a temptation of Satan. But sometimes his reason and learning allowed him to convince himself otherwise. Had not the tribes of Israel been assigned their lands by the casting of lots? Had not the Hebrews selected their first king just so? How could something be from Satan if the Torah sanctioned it? Perhaps it wasn't Satan who had instructed him to cheat Doña de Serena. Perhaps the hand of the Lord had given him these purses. It might be divine Providence, requiring him to risk all, so that he would win even greater riches for his people. He would dispense such wealth to the needy as would uplift the entire Geto. Even as his heart flipped and shuffled in his chest, Judah felt himself suffused with pleasure at the thought. He turned, retraced the few steps to the mask-maker's workshop, and entered.

Vistorini rose from his desk, looking for a cloth to mop his brow. He had occupied the morning dealing with the seizure orders for the heretical book. It was too late in the year, and too early in the day, to be so hot. His sweat smelled sour, a reminder that he had not bathed in some time. The argument with the Jew had set his head throbbing, and now the pain grew sharp. A small knot of anger formed in his unsettled stomach. He told himself that he was affronted, that the rabbi presumed too much upon their friendship. He could not admit the truth; that he did not like being bested in argument. His gut tightened. He needed the latrine. He moved into the hall of the Holy Office with the unsteady gait of a sick old man.

It was cooler, at least, in the hall. Generally, the mildewed walls oppressed him, but on this day he was glad of a little respite from the closeness of his chamber. As he turned the corner, he almost collided with the serving boy, carrying the tray that contained his sparse lunch. He took the napkin from the tray and wiped his face, then handed the sweat-smeared cloth to the boy, who accepted it gingerly, and with an expression of distaste. Damn him, thought the priest, continuing to the latrine. Damn all these youths and their judgmental airs. It was bad enough to have to put up with that insolent altar boy, Paolo, an educated child of a good family. But how dare a servant look at him with such contempt?

Vistorini's bowels leaked their contents into the malodorous drain, but the pain in his gut barely eased. Perhaps he had a canker sore developing. He went reluctantly to the refectory table, looking for the wine. He had no appetite for the cook's watery broth or the bread to sop it. A single goblet, not more than half filled, had been set at his place. When he called for more, the boy said that the wine cupboard had already been locked by the steward. He thought he saw a shadow of a smirk, quickly suppressed, cross the youth's face as he reported this.

Back in his office, his mood worse, Vistorini set about the routine business of redacting. His pen laden with heavy black ink, he went through pages, rendering illegible any Hebrew references to Christians, to the uncircumcised, to Jew haters, to "observers of strange rites" unless the passage was unambiguously referring to the idolaters of antiquity and was not a coded reference to the church. He fell upon words such as *wicked kingdom* or *Edom* or *Roman* that might possibly be read as referring to Christians. He also expurgated any mention of Judaism as the one true faith, all references to *the Messiah yet to come,* any use of the words *pious* or *holy* when applied to Jews.

On days when Vistorini felt well, he would handle the books more gently, sometimes even performing his duty by emending an objectionable passage, rather than striking it out. If he added the words *star worshippers* after a reference to *idolater,* he could exclude the implication that veneration of images of Christian saints was idol worship.

But now his head throbbed and his mouth tasted like dung. His pen slashed through the words with heavy cross lines. Sometimes, he scored so hard that the nib of the pen tore through the vellum. He felt as if he might be sick. He paged through the book, deciding there were too many errors. Vindictively, he cast it aside, destined for burning. That would show Judah Aryeh, the arrogant ass. Why not burn them all and be done with it? Then he could go home, where at least his servant would bring him a drink. He brought his arm across the desk, sweeping half a dozen unread volumes into the pile marked for the fire.

Judah Aryeh sat up slowly in the dark, so as not to awaken his wife. The moonlight lit the curve of her cheek, and her unbound hair, always modestly hidden by day, spilled across the pillow in a wild profusion of black and silver. It was all he could do to refrain from caressing it. When they were first married, he had tangled his hands in that hair, clutched at it, been aroused by the feel of it against the bare skin of his chest as they made the wild, unpracticed love of the very young.

Sarai was a lovely woman still, and even after two dozen years he could grow hard if she looked at him a certain way. Sometimes, he wondered about Vistorini, and how he could live a life without a woman's warmth in his bed. Or children. What would it be, to miss the sight of them, sweet-faced infants growing, changing, year by year, finding their paths to an honorable maturity? He wondered if the wine his friend drank so excessively was a way to blunt those needs, so natural, so God given.

It was not that Aryeh despised the life disciplined by faith. To the contrary, he knew the ascetic beauty of such a way of being. He lived every moment mindful of the 613 commandments of the Torah. It was natural to him to separate the milk from the meat, to refrain from labor on the Sabbath, to abide by the laws of family purity in his relations with his wife. The disciplines of that monthly abstinence had only sharpened desire and sweetened their reunion. But to be without a wife entirely . . . that, to him, was no fit life for a man.

The door creaked as Aryeh closed it. He waited on the stair for a moment to see if the sound had roused anyone. But the crowded building was never quiet, even at this late hour. An old man's hacking cough came through the thin wooden partition between their apartment and the next. If one needed to build ever upward, the walls had to be of the thinnest and lightest materials. From the floor below, the cry of a hungry newborn pierced the night. And from above came the incessant crowing of the damned cockerel that seemed to lack all sense of dawn or dark. Someone should have the *shochet* dispatch that benighted fowl to the pot, Aryeh thought, as he picked his way carefully in the dark down the creaking wooden staircase. Outside, he made for the narrow place that divided his building from the next one. Dropping to his knees, he passed a hand through the slimy stones and tugged out the canvas sack he had hidden there. Stealing down the alley, he waited until he was in the deepest shadow to open the sack and shake out the contents. After a few moments, he went on toward the Geto gates.

The hardest part of the night's deception lay ahead of him. The gates had been closed several hours earlier. Gentiles whose business in the Geto had detained them past curfew could easily obtain egress simply by bribing the guards. But the only way out, for a Jew, demanded nerve and guile. Aryeh lingered in the shadows and waited. The rabbi's distinctive chestnut curls escaped from beneath the tricorn hat of a patrician. The damp air penetrated even the fine wool of the nobleman's cloak that, with the mask, completed his disguise. Almost an hour passed. He flexed his shoulders to relieve their stiffness and shook his legs, one after the other, to prevent cramps. Soon, he would have to give up for the night and try again the next. But just as that thought took shape, he heard the sounds he had been waiting for. Ragged voices, raucous laughter. Soon, a party of Gentile youths straggled into the *campiello*. Using the license of Carnivale, they had been snatching some illicit foreign pleasures among immigrant Jews whose condition was so low that they pandered their sons and daughters for the purpose.

There were six or seven of them, staggering toward the gate-house, crying up the guardsmen to let them out. All wore the dark cloak of Carnivale and the masks of characters from the commedia dell'arte. Aryeh's heart flipped and fluttered in his chest. He had only a moment to act, to fall in with the party and hope that in the dark and their inebriation they would not raise a fuss. He touched a hand to his mask, nervously checking the ties for the tenth time in as many minutes. He had chosen a common and popular design: the long beak of the plague doctor. No doubt there were, that night in the city, a horde of men dressed just alike. But at the last moment, as he stepped from the scalloped shadows and into the square, doubts swarmed his mind. Surely it was too great a risk. Surely the youths would challenge him. He should go back as he had come, anony-mous in the dark, and fling the damnable mask into the sewer as he went.

But then he thought of the candlelight dancing on piles of gold sequins, the dizzying ecstasy in the moment the card turned and re-vealed its secrets. Aryeh swallowed hard. The pleasure of the thought was so great he could taste it at the back of his throat. He stepped forward and into the youths' noisy wake. Be bold, he thought. He threw an arm over the shoulder of the nearest youth and attempted to feign a laugh that came out in a strange, nervous falsetto.

"Help me, young sir. My legs are gone from too much drink and I don't wish to draw the attention of the guards." The youth's eyes, through the crescent slots of an Arlecchino mask, were unintelligent as a cow's. "Awright, uncle, on we go," he slurred. His breath, Aryeh thought, could have fueled a lamp.

It was just an instant, passing under the lit gate, but Aryeh felt sure his pounding heart—how could they not hear it?—would give him away. But then he was through and on the narrow bridge. Three steps up, three steps down, into the Gentiles' Venice. As he left the bridge, he reclaimed his arm from the youth's shoulder and melted away toward a shadowed overhang. He rested his head against a rough stone wall and tried to breathe. It was some minutes before he was able to go on.

As he turned back into the *canaletto,* the crowd swept him up into itself. The dark brought no rest in Venice during Carnivale. At sunset, torches and chandeliers shed light on a continuum of celebration. The city was mobbed; its main thoroughfares more crowded, for once, than those of the Geto. The costumed nobles drew pickpockets and mountebanks who hoped to prey on them; jugglers, acrobats, and bear baiters who hoped to entertain them. Class, for the moment, was expunged. The tall man in the long-nosed Zanni mask bearing down upon Aryeh might well be a servant or a porter, like his character, or he might be one of the Ten. "Good evening, Mr. Mask," was all the greeting required.

Aryeh touched his hat as he sidled by the tall Zanni and merged again into the throng, allowing it to carry him along toward a *ridotto,* which lay no great distance from the bridge. He entered, one masked nobleman among so many abroad in the night. He climbed to the second floor and passed into the room of sighs. The salon was fitted up in a gaudy taste, the light from many chandeliers too bright to flatter the wrinkled necks of the masked women who lolled listlessly upon sofas, comforting their losing partners. There were husbands with mistresses, wives with the *cicisbeos* meant to be their chaperones but often, in fact, their lovers. There were also prostitutes, panderers, and police spies. All wore masks to equalize their condition. All, that is, except the bankers. These men, all of them members of the aristocratic Barnabot family, were the only Venetians approbated to fill this role. Each Barnabot, dressed alike in long black robe and flowing white wig, stood behind his own table in the next salon. Their bare faces proclaimed their identity for all to know.

There were more than a dozen tables from which to choose. Aryeh watched as the bankers shuffled and dealt hands of basset and panfil. He ordered wine and ambled over to observe a high-stakes game of treize. There was just a single player, matching his luck with the bank. The deal passed back and forth between them several times before the player scraped his sequins into a small purse and went off, laughing, to his friends. Aryeh stepped into his place, and two other men joined him. The banker stood between tall candles, shuffling the cards as the players laid out their piles of sequins, each of them betting against the luck of the dealer. It was a simple game: the dealer had to name the cards from one to thirteen—ace to king—as he dealt. If the card fell as he named it, he collected the wagers and retained the deal. If he reached the king without matching a call to the dealt card, he had to pay the wagers and relinquish the deal to the player on his right.

His voice, when he commenced the deal, was low and even. *"Uno,"* he said, as the five of spades hit the table. *"Due,"* as the nine of hearts appeared. *"Tre,"* and luck was still against him as the eight of spades appeared. The count had risen to *"nove"* and still the dealer had not dealt the card he was naming. Just four more chances, and Aryeh's gold sequin would be doubled.

"Fante," the banker called. But the card that he dealt was a seven of diamonds, not a jack. Just two more chances. Aryeh eyed his sequin.

"Re." The last card, the king. But the dealer had turned up an ace. The dealer's long white fingers reached for the pile of sequins beside him. He placed one before Aryeh, four before a man in a lion mask, and, with a slight bow, seven before the high-wagering man in the Brighella mask. The dealer, having lost the hand, surrendered the deal to the Brighella. Aryeh loosened his mask to mop his brow. He reached into Doña Reyna's purse and placed two more sequins on the table beside his original wager and his winnings from the first hand. His wager was now four gold pieces. He thought he noticed the men on either side of him give small nods of approval.

"Uno." The voice from behind the Brighella mask was deep and resonant. The card he turned over was a nine of clubs. *"Due."* A jack,

much too soon to be of use to him. *"Tre, quattro, cinque, sei . . . fante, cavallo . . ."* The Brighella's voice seemed to get deeper on each card, as none matched the number he cried out. Aryeh felt his own heart beating faster. He was about to win another four sequins. At this rate he would double Doña Reyna's purse in no time. *"Re!"* cried the Brighella. But the card he turned was a seven of spades. The Brighella reached into his purse and placed sequins on each player's pile. His eyes glittered through the half-moon slits above the mask's bulbous cheeks.

The deal passed to Aryeh. He watched as the lion, the Brighella, and the impassive-faced noble of the Barnabot family placed their piles of sequins. The Brighella, chasing his losses, placed twenty gold sequins on the table. The Barnabot wagered a modest two sequins. The lion played four, as he had each hand.

Aryeh's hands were deft and steady as he shuffled the deck. He felt exhilaration rather than dread, even with twenty-six sequins at stake. *"Uno!"* he cried exultantly, and, as if he had the power to summon the card from the deck, the single, vivid red blot of the ace of diamonds gleamed in the candle glow.

Aryeh scooped the winnings toward himself. As winner, the deal remained with him. Once again, the players laid their bets; the Brighella chancing another twenty sequins, the Barnadot two, the lion four.

"Uno!" Aryeh's voice lilted, even though the card he turned over was a nine. *"Due! Tre! Quattro!"* It wasn't until he reached *fante,* the jack, that his throat began to tighten at the prospect of loss. But the secret to Aryeh's gambling compulsion was contained in that moment, when the dread began to spread through him like ink in a glass of clear water. For he welcomed the feeling, that dark, terrifying sensation of risk. To teeter on the edge of loss, or to win the hand, the point was the intensity of the sensation. He never felt so alive as he did in those moments, poised between the one outcome and the other.

"Cavallo!" he cried, and the card was an ace of diamonds—the same ace that had brought him fortune on the last hand had betrayed him on this one. He had only one chance more. His flesh tingled.

"Re!" he cried out, and the king he had named stared back at him from the table. The others shuffled uneasily. This man in the plague doctor mask had uncanny luck. To win one hand on the first card, and then to win another on the last card. A strange chance, indeed.

Aryeh watched the candlelight dance on the Barnabot's ruby ring as the Barnabot slowly drew out two more sequins, and then, slowly, added two more. The nobleman was betting that the plague doctor's luck must turn.

The Brighella gazed at him, his eyes glassy now, as he laid forty sequins upon the table. Only the lion held his ground, placing the same four sequins at risk.

For just under an hour, Aryeh's fortune waxed, and he basked in the pleasure of his mounting pile. He had more than doubled the value of Doña Reyna's first purse. The lion mask left the table and made an unsteady way to the room of sighs. He was replaced by a Pulcinella who seemed intoxicated and played with a reckless flourish, crying out ostentatiously at every ill turn in his fortunes. The Barnabot nobleman maintained his aloof and dignified demeanor, but his bare face began to show some lines of strain. The Brighella, the biggest loser, grasped the table. His knuckles had turned quite white. A small gallery of the curious had gathered on the edge of their circle.

Finally, inevitably, Aryeh reached the king without naming a card correctly. The Pulcinella gave a raucous cry of glee. Aryeh bowed and paid out the wagers—eighty sequins to the Brighella, ten to the Pulcinella, four to the Barnabot. He passed the deal to the Brighella and considered his next wager.

It had been a magical hour. He felt as light as one of the colored balloons that rose above the city during Carnivale. Truly, the large pile of winnings could do much for the poor in his congregation. He stood there, his hand hesitating over the gold. Perhaps Satan had lured him here, but God had given him this moment of choice. He would listen to the voice of reason in his head. He would take these winnings and leave the *ridotto*. He had fed his beast, had felt the blood rise in terror and exhilaration. It was enough. He swept the pile toward the mouth of his purse.

A hard hand, the Brighella's, landed on his own. Aryeh looked up, startled. The eyes behind the other man's mask were black, the pupils dilated. "No *gentleman* quits the game after having the advantage of the deal."

"Quite right," slurred the Pulcinella. "Not done, making off with a man's money. Think more of gold, do you, than of having a good time? Not the spirit of Carnivale. Not a gentleman. Not even a Venetian, I'll wager."

Aryeh flushed deeply beneath his mask. Did they know? Had they guessed? By raising the issue of "otherness," the drunken Pulcinella probed very close to the vein. He withdrew his hand from under the Brighella's and placed it over his heart. He stepped back from the table and made a deep bow. "Gentlemen," he said, in his soft, lilting, unmistakably Venetian accent. "Forgive me. A momentary lapse, merely. Truly I do not know what I was thinking. By all means, let us go on."

For the next hour, the game continued, each man winning and losing in his turn. Aryeh judged that enough time had passed, and once again made to leave the table. Once again, the Brighella stayed his hand as he reached for his still-significant winnings. "Why such a hurry?" the low voice said. "Do you have a tryst?" And then his voice dropped even lower, and the bulbous mask loomed closer. "Or do you have a curfew you must keep?"

He knows, Aryeh thought. Beneath his cloak, he began to sweat.

"Give us one hand more, at decent stakes, Mr. Plague Doctor! A hand in friendship, eh?" The Brighella reached beneath his cloak then and laid a full purse upon the table. Aryeh, his hand shaking now, pushed all of his winnings forward. The fear of loss—intense, delicious—overwhelmed him.

The Barnabot nobleman had the deal again. *"Uno. Due. Tre . . . "*

Aryeh's head felt light.

" . . . Otto. Nove . . ."

He was finding it hard to breathe through the mask. His heart thumped and banged in his chest. He was about to win again.

" . . . Fante. Cavallo . . ."

The exhilaration and the terror held him in their delicious, equal grip. And then, the terror won, pulling him down, smothering him, as the Barnabot turned over a king. The roar in Aryeh's head muffled the sound of the syllable slowly forming on the noble's lips. *"Re!"*

The Barnabot reached for the pile of gold and swept it to himself, bowing slightly in the direction of the Brighella.

"Now, dear Doctor. Now you may leave us, if you are so very tired of our company."

Aryeh shook his head. He could not leave. Not now. He had lost not only his winnings, but a full half of his stake. One of Doña Reyna's purses lay flaccid and empty at his side. He had been determined to wager one purse only. Half to gamble, half to spend on the needs of his flock. That was what he had told himself. But now he fumbled at his other hip for the second purse. As his fingers closed on its reassuring bulk, Aryeh felt as if he were bathed in radiance. He felt complete conviction that the magical luck of the early evening was with him again. Not his own hand, but the very hand of the divine will directed him as he pushed the full purse forward upon the table.

For once, even the impassive face of the Barnabot registered emotion. The eyebrows rose to the edge of his frosted wig, and he gave an almost imperceptible bow toward Aryeh. Then he began to deal.

Aryeh had just a few seconds to feel the exquisite pleasure-pain to which he was enslaved. The card that cost him the purse was an eight. The round vowels of the word *otto* seemed to fall from the Barnabot's lips and merge with the curved infinity symbol of the number itself, elongating into a tunnel that seemed to suck the soul from the rabbi.

He stared in disbelief at all that gold, pushed into gleaming towers on the dealers' side of the table. He raised a hand and called for a quill. He shook as he wrote a note for another hundred sequins. The Barnabot nobleman took the note between two fingers, glanced at it, and shook his head in silence. Aryeh felt the blood rise, scalding, to his scalp.

"But I have seen you play with a loser upon his word to the value of ten thousand ducats!"

"The word of a *Venetian* is one thing. Why don't you go to a Jew bloodsucker if you want credit." He let the note fall to the floor.

There was a sudden silence at the nearby tables. Masked faces turned in unison, a flock of buzzards sensing carrion.

"A Jew!" the Pulcinella slurred. " 'Splains it. I knew he was no Venetian!"

Aryeh turned, knocking over his wine goblet, and stumbled from the salon. In the room of sighs, a whore reached out a fleshy arm, attempting to pull him down upon her couch. "What's the rush?" she said, her voice low and seductive. "Everyone loses sometimes. Sit with me and I'll make you feel better." Then she raised her voice. "I've always wanted to taste a circumcised one!" He shrugged her off and staggered down the stairs to the street, humiliated by laughter closing behind him like water.

In the gray light of the sanctuary, Judah Aryeh pulled his tallis over his head and bowed low before God. "I have trespassed, I have dealt treacherously, I have robbed. . . ." Tears wet his cheeks as he rocked forward and back, reciting the familiar words of the prayer of atonement. "I have acted perversely, and I have wrought wickedness, I have been presumptuous, I have framed lies and I have spoken falsely . . . I have committed iniquity and I have transgressed. . . . I have turned away from your commandments and judgments that are good, and it has profited me naught. What shall I say before you, who dwellest on high, and what shall I declare before you, thou who abidest in the heavens? Dost thou not know all things, hidden and revealed? May it therefore be thy will, O Lord, our God and God of our fathers, to forgive me, to pardon my iniquity, and to grant atonement for my transgressions. . . ."

He sank down upon a bench, exhausted and heartsick. God might forgive sins against his laws, but Aryeh knew—he had preached it often enough—that forgiveness also must be sought from, and atonement made to, those who had been damaged by sinful acts. He thought with despair of returning to Reyna de Serena to confess his deception. And of the humiliation he must face before his own congregation. He would have to admit to taking the bread from the mouths of the hungriest, the medicines from the dying. And then he, poor man that he was, would have to make good the sum he had stolen. This would require the most stringent economies. He would have to pawn his books, perhaps even move the family to cheaper quarters. With six persons in two small rooms, their home was hardly lavish, yet one of the rooms had a window, and both high ceilings. Aryeh thought about the cheaper alternatives: the *shochet* had shown him a lightless, one-room place hard by his butchery that he had on offer for very fair terms. Privately, Judah had called the place the cave of Makhpelah, but he had promised to keep it in mind if any in his congregation was in need of housing. Rooms were in such short supply in the Geto that even such grim quarters at a fair rent would find many takers. But how could he ask Sarai to move to such a gloomy place? And his daughter, Ester, who worked at home, how would she have space for her bolts of cloth and seamstress bench? How could she sew without daylight? The sin was his, not his family's. How could he make them suffer so?

Aryeh rubbed his hands over his cheeks. His flesh, in the growing light, was gray and haggard. Soon, the minyan would begin to gather. He would have to prepare a face to greet them.

He left the sanctuary and descended to his rooms. The aroma of frying told him that Sarai was already up. Usually, Aryeh loved the crisped frittatas she made, hot and golden brown. He would sit at the crowded table with his three sons and his beloved daughter, and let their babble and banter flow around him. But this morning the scent of the hot oil assailed him. He felt ill.

He steadied himself against a chair. Sarai was working with her back to him, her hair caught up modestly in a fine wool scarf she had knotted fetchingly at the nape of her neck. "Good morning," she said. "You were up before the birds. . . ." She turned to glance at him over her shoulder, and the smile on her lips turned to a concerned frown. "Are you ill, husband? You look so pale. . . ."

"Sarai," he said. But he could not go on. His oldest sons stood together in the corner, making their morning prayers. The youngest, who had completed his, was already at the table with his sister, enjoying their frittatas. He could not speak of his shame before them, even though soon enough the whole Geto must know of it.

"It is nothing. I could not sleep." That last, at least, was true.

"Well, you must rest, later. You need to be refreshed to greet the Bride Shabbat." She smiled. For a husband and wife to make love on the Sabbath was a commandment, and it was one requirement of the faith that both of them observed with joy. He gave a weak smile back, and then turned to pour a basin of water. He splashed his face and wet his hair, then replaced his *kippah* and climbed the stairs to the sanctuary.

The minyan had already gathered in the pale light. In these times, thought Aryeh, it was all too easy to gather ten. An outbreak of plague, not quite one year earlier, had claimed so many lives that above twenty eldest sons still came to pray each day, marking their season of sorrow, reciting the prayer for their dead.

Aryeh made his way to the bimah. A blue velvet cloth, the color of midnight, lay across the table. It had been sewn by his daughter when she was still a little girl. Even then, her stitching had been fine and even. But the cloth had grown shabby now, like almost everything in the little room. Aryeh had worn the nape off the velvet at the places where his hands gripped the bimah. This did not trouble him, any more than the benches that wobbled or the floor that rippled unevenly underfoot. These things were signs of use, signs of life, evidence that human beings came here, many of them and often, trying to talk to their God.

"Magnified and sanctified may his great name be. . . ." The voices of the mourners rose as one. Kaddish had always been one of Aryeh's favorite prayers—the prayer for the dead that did not mention death, or grief, or loss, but only life and glory and peace. The prayer that turned its face away from burial plots and moldering remains and set its eyes on the firmament: "May a great peace from heaven—and life!—be upon us and upon all Israel, and say all, amen! May he who makes peace in his high places make peace upon us and all Israel, and say all, amen!"

Aryeh did not linger after the morning service. He exchanged just a few brief words with his congregants on the way out. Neither did he remain at home, where he feared the intuitive scrutiny of Sarai's loving gaze. He left her, still cooking, calmly preparing the food they would eat that night, and the next day, for on Shabbat itself no work would be done. When he left, she was patiently peeling apart each onion, layer by layer, inspecting the pieces with meticulous attention lest the tiniest insect lay within. To eat such an insect, even by accident, would be to violate the commandment against consuming any of those living things that swarm.

Aryeh made his way to the home of a *strazzaria* dealer who had prospered enough to set aside part of his house as a library. Because Aryeh had tutored the man's sons, he had been invited to use the room for his own quiet study. There, he carefully unwrapped Doña de Serena's haggadah, which he had protected in a piece of linen cloth. If he were to go to her to confess his lies and theft, at least he would not go empty-handed. He would read the book carefully to determine if it was safe to submit it to the Holy Office, and if so, he would take it to Vistorini that very day. With luck he would be able to retrieve it, with the necessary words safely inscribed, and visit Reyna de Serena after the Sabbath.

He eased the silver clasps open. What a place must Sepharad have been that the Jews who lived there could make such a book as this! Did they live like princes, these Jews? They must have done, to afford such an amount of gold and silver leaf, to pay such craftsmen as the silversmith and artists of the rank of this illuminator. And now, their descendants wandered destitute over the face of the earth, looking for any safe place that would allow them to lay down their heads in peace. Perhaps there had once been many books like this one, just as fine, all ashes now. Gone and lost and forgotten.

But he could not afford to give in to lament, or to bedazzlement. No good wondering about the illuminator—surely a Christian? For what Jew would have learned to make images such as the Christians made?—or about the *sofer*, who had inscribed the text in such a lovely and accomplished hand.

These stories, intriguing as they were, he had to put from him. Instead, he had to put himself into the mind of Giovanni Domenico Vistorini, a hunter's mind, fierce in pursuit of the slightest hint of heresy. A suspicious and perhaps a hostile mind. Aryeh hoped that Vistorini, the scholar, would appreciate the book for its beauty and its antiquity. But Vistorini the censor had burned so many beautiful books.

So Aryeh turned the pages of illumination until he arrived at the first pages of Hebrew text. "This is the bread of affliction. . . ." He began to read the familiar story of the Passover as if he were encountering it for the first time.

Vistorini raised the glass to his lips. Not bad, the wine the Jew had brought him. He did not recall drinking kosher wine before. He took another swallow. Not bad at all.

No sooner had he set his glass down than the Jew reached for the wineskin and refilled it. He noted, with pleasure, that it was a very large wineskin, and that the Jew's own glass stood, barely touched, glowing red in the low afternoon light. He would have to draw this business out, that would be the wise thing. For, once he had said what he proposed to say, the Jew would leave, and likely take his wineskin with him.

"This book of yours, are there many like it, hiding under bushels in your Geto?"

"None that I have ever seen. Truly, I think very few such books have survived from the community of Sepharad."

"Whose book is it?"

Aryeh had expected the question, and dreaded it. He could not betray Reyna de Serena. "Mine," he lied. Aryeh hoped to use whatever modicum of friendship or its simulacrum that stood between himself and the priest.

"Yours?" The priest's eyebrow rose skeptically.

"I had it from a merchant who came here from Apulia."

The priest gave a short laugh. "Did you so? You, who are always crying poor? You could afford to buy a codex as fine as this?"

Aryeh's mind raced. He could say he received it for a service, but that seemed unlikely. What service could he do that would be of such a value? Because his sin was at the forefront of his mind, he blurted out the next thing that came into it. "I won it from him, at a game of chance."

"Strange stakes! Judah, you amaze me. What game?"

The rabbi colored. The conversation was veering rather too close to the marrow. "Chess."

"Chess? Hardly a game of chance."

"Well, the merchant had a rather inflated view of his skills. He took a chance in wagering his book upon them. So in his case, yes, one might say that chess was a game of chance."

The priest laughed again, this time really amused. "Words. To you, they are just sweetmeats in your mouth. I forget that, when I do not see you." He took another large swallow of wine. He was feeling more warmly toward the rabbi. What had it been that had irritated him so on their last meeting? He couldn't now quite recall it. Pity he had to disappoint the fellow, really.

"Well, I am glad to hear that this was the way of it. For what comes by chance will be the more easily let go."

Aryeh sat up, rigid in his chair. "You can't mean . . . ? You don't mean to say that you will not pass this book?"

The priest leaned across the desk and placed a hand on Aryeh's shoulder. It was unlike him to willingly touch a Jew. "I regret to say it, but yes, that is precisely the situation."

Aryeh shrugged off the priest's hand and stood up, anger and disbelief animating him.

"On what possible grounds? I have read every page of text, every psalm, every prayer, every song. There is nothing, not one word of it, that contravenes the Index in any particular."

"You are right. There is nothing of that nature in the text." Vistorini's voice was low and calm.

"Well, then?"

"I do not speak of the text. There is, as you say, nothing against the church in the *text*." He paused. Aryeh's pounding heart seemed loud to him in the silence. "There is, I regret to say, a grave heresy in the illumination."

Aryeh covered his eyes with his hand. It had not even occurred to him to closely study the illuminations. He had been dazzled by them, but had not lingered to parse their meaning in any detail. He sat down again, heavily, in the priest's carved chair.

"Which one?" he said, his voice a whisper.

"Oh, more than one, I am afraid." The priest reached across the desk for the codex, bumping his wineglass as he did so. Aryeh put out a hand, reflexively, to steady it. Then, in the vain hope of mellowing the priest, he reached for the wineskin and filled the glass to the brim.

"One need not look far," said Vistorini, opening the book at the first set of illuminations. "See, here? The artist tells the story of Genesis. He gives us the division of light from dark. So, and very nicely done, the severe contrast of the white and black pigments. Austere and eloquent. Nothing there of a heretical nature. The next one: 'And the spirit of God moved on the face of the waters.' Lovely, the use of the gold leaf to indicate the ineffable presence of God. Again, nothing heretical. But the next, and the next, and the three that follow. Look, and tell me: what do you see?"

Aryeh looked, and his head became light. How could he have *not* seen? The earth on which the Almighty created the plants and the animals—in each and every illumination, it was shown as an orb. That the earth was round, and not flat, was now the opinion of a majority of theologians. Interesting that this artist of a century earlier, when Christians were being sent to the stake for this belief, espoused it. But that, alone, would not condemn the book. The illuminator had ventured further into dangerous territory. In the top right corner of three of the paintings, above the earth, was a second gold-leafed orb, clearly meant to be the sun. Its placement was ambiguous.

Aryeh looked up at Vistorini. "You believe this implies the heliocentric heresy?"

"'Implies'! Rabbi, don't be disingenuous. This is clearly in support of the heresy of the Saracen astronomers, of Copernicus, whose book is on the Index, of that man in Padua, Galileo, who will soon enough be brought before the Inquisition to answer for his errors."

"But the drawings—one need not read them that way. The orbs, the concentric rings, they might be decoration, merely. Surely, if one were not looking for it, the implication could pass unnoticed. . . ."

"But I am looking for it." Vistorini drained his glass, and the rabbi, distracted, refilled it. "Because of that man Galileo, the church is now especially concerned with the promulgation of this heresy."

"Dom Vistorini, I implore you. For any kindness I may have done you in the past, for the many years we have known each other. Please, spare this book. I know you are a man of learning, a man who respects beauty. You see how beautiful this book is. . . ."

"All the more reason to burn it. Its beauty might one day seduce some unwitting Christian to think well of your reprehensible faith." Vistorini's mood was elevated. He was enjoying this. The rabbi was entirely in his power. The man's voice, that mellifluous voice, was breaking. Vistorini had never known him to care quite so passionately about one book. He had a sudden idea that would prolong the pleasure of this afternoon. He held up his empty glass to the window, as if studying the fine curve of the goblet.

"Perhaps . . . but no. I should not suggest it—"

"Father?" Aryeh leaned forward, his eyes avid. He fumbled for the wineskin and filled the priest's glass.

"Well, I might redact the offending pages." He ran his finger over the vellum, flipping it back and forward. "Four pages—not so very many—and then there would still remain the key drawings, of the flight from Egypt, that is the main point of the work. . . ."

"Four pages." Aryeh imagined the knife detaching the vellum folios. He felt actual pain in his chest, sharp, as if the knife were stabbing him.

"Here's an idea," said Vistorini. "Since you say you won this book in a game of chance, what do you say if we play another to determine its fate? You win, I will redact and spare the book. I win, it goes to the flames."

"What game?" Aryeh whispered.

"What game?" Vistorini sat back in his chair, sipped the wine, and pondered. "Not, I think, chess. I have a premonition that you would best me there, as you did the merchant from—where did you say?"

Aryeh, tense and upset, could not for the moment recall his fabrication. He feigned a coughing fit to mask his confusion.

"Apulia," he blurted at last.

"Yes, Apulia. So you said. Well, I do not want to risk emulating the fate of that unfortunate man. Cards, I have none, nor die to cast." He continued, idly, turning the pages. "I have it. Let us play a version of lots, but fit the game to the wager. I will write the words of censor's permission, *Revisto per mi,* each one on a slip of parchment. You shall draw them blind. As you draw them, if the order of words is correct, I will inscribe that word in the book. If you draw the word out of order, I will not complete the inscription, and you lose."

"But that means a game in which I have to win a three-to-one wager three times. The odds, Father, are too steep."

"Steep? Yes, perhaps so. Say this, then: if your first draw is correct, you may remove that slip from the second draw. Then your odds improve to even. I think that sounds a fair game."

Aryeh watched the priest's hand inscribe the longed-for words on parchment scraps and drop them, one by one, into an empty coffer on his desk. His heart skipped as he noticed something the priest, who was already quite drunk, had not perceived. One of the scraps he had chosen was of a lower grade than the other two, just a little thicker. It was the scrap on which Vistorini had scrawled the middle word, *per*. Aryeh thanked God. Suddenly, his odds were much improved. He prayed to God to guide his hand as he reached within the box. His fingers quickly identified the thicker parchment, and rejected it. Now it was even odds. Right or wrong. Light or dark. The blessing or the curse. Therefore, choose life. He closed his hand on the scrap, drew it out, and handed it to the priest.

Vistorini's expression did not change. He placed the scrap facedown on his desk. Then he reached for the haggadah, opened it to the last page of Hebrew text, dipped his quill, and wrote, in a fine hand, the word *revisto*.

Aryeh tried not to let the joy show in his face. The book was saved. He had only to select the thick scrap and this terrible game would be over. He reached again into the coffer, this time giving silent thanks to God.

He handed the thick scrap to Vistorini. This time, the priest's face did not remain impassive. The corners of his mouth turned down. He pulled the haggadah toward him, angrily, and wrote the next two words: *per mi*.

Then he glared at Aryeh, who was beaming. "It is worth nothing, of course, unless I sign and date it."

"But you . . . but we . . . Father, you gave your word."

"How dare you!" Vistorini stood up suddenly, bumping against his heavy oak desk. The wine lapped in his glass. The liquor had worked in him to that sour point at which anger banishes euphoria.

"How dare you talk about 'my word.' You come to me with this implausible fabrication—this, let us be frank, this patent lie on your lips about winning this book, and you talk about the giving of *my* word! You presume on my goodwill, you dare to infer we are friends. Would that the boat that carried your accused forebears here from Spain had never reached dry land! Venice gives you a safe home, and you do not keep within the few rules she requires of you. You set up printing houses against the laws of the state and pass around your filth about our Blessed Savior. You, Judah, God has given you wit and made you learned, and yet you harden your heart to his truth and turn your face from his grace. Get out of here! And tell whoever really owns this book that the rabbi lost it in a game of chance. That way you will spare them the thought of all that fine gold leaf going up in flames. You Jews love your gold, I know that."

"Domenico, please . . . I will do anything you ask . . . please. . . ." The rabbi's voice was ragged. He could not get his breath.

"Get out! Now. Before I charge you with promulgating heresy. Do you want to serve ten years on a galley with your feet in chains? Do you want a dark cell in the Leads? Get out!"

Judah fell to his knees and kissed the priest's cassock. "Do what you will to me," he cried. "But save the book!" The priest's only answer was a shove that sent the rabbi sprawling. He rose to his feet with difficulty and staggered from the room, down the hall, and outside, into the *canaletto*. He was weeping and gasping, tearing at his beard like a man in mourning. All around him, pedestrians turned to stare at the mad Jew. He felt their eyes, their hatred. He began to run. The blood eddied, trapped and sluggish, in the fissured chambers of his breaking heart. As his feet landed on the hard stone, fists seemed to strike his chest, the blows of a giant.

When the boy came with the taper, Vistorini had just poured the last glass from the now-empty wineskin. At first, in dim light and in his drunkenness, he thought it was Aryeh, come back to beg from him, and he snarled. But then the boy swam into focus, and Vistorini signaled that yes, he should light the candles on his desk.

When the boy went out, he pulled the haggadah into the pool of light. He began to hear the voice in his head, the voice he didn't usually allow himself to hear. But at night, sometimes, in dreams, and when he'd had too much to drink . . .

The voice, the dark room, the sense of shame, the prickling fear. The carved Madonna in the niche to the right of the doorstep. The child's hand, enfolded in a larger, calloused one that guided the tiny fingers to touch the polished wood of her toe. "You must do this, always." The blowing sand of that desolate town. The voices: Arabic, Ladino, Berber? He did not know any longer which language. And the other one, the language he must not speak.

"Dayenu!" He cried the word aloud. "Enough!"

He dragged a hand through his greasy hair, as if he could drag the memories from his mind and cast them away. He knew now, perhaps he had known always, the truth of that past about which he must not think, must not even dream. He saw the smashed foot of the Madonna, the small roll of parchment that fell out. He had been screaming, terrified, and struggling in some rough grip, but through his tears, he had seen it. The Hebrew script. The hidden mezuzah. Through his tears, he had seen the words *"Love the lord thy God with thy whole heart. . . ."* He had seen the Hebrew letters, crushed into the dirt beneath the boot of the man who had come to arrest his parents and put them to death as crypto-Jews.

There had been a haggadah, also; he was sure of that. Hidden in that secret closet where they went to speak the forbidden language. Her face, when she lit the candles. So lined, so weathered in the flaring light. But her eyes, so kindly when she smiled at him. Her voice, when she sang the blessings over the candles. So soft, just a whisper.

No. This was wrong. It never was so. Too many Hebrew books had addled his mind. These were dreams, merely. Nightmares. Not memories. He started to pray in Latin, to drown out the fragments of the other voices. He lifted the glass. His hand shook. Wine spilled onto the parchment but he didn't even notice. "I believe in one God, the father almighty. . . ." He tightened his grip on the glass, raised it to his lips, and drained it. "And in Jesus Christ, his only son, our Lord. . . . Begotten but not made . . . and in one holy Catholic and apostolic church. I acknowledge one baptism for the forgiveness of sins. . . ." His cheeks were wet.

"Giovanni Domenico Vistorini. I am! Giovanni. Domenico. Vistorini." He murmured the name, over and over. He reached for the glass. Empty! His hand tightened. The thin Venetian glass shattered, and a shard pierced the fleshy part of his thumb. He barely felt it, though the blood dripped and mingled with the wine stain already blooming on the parchment.

He closed the haggadah, smearing the russet stain. Burn it, Giovanni Domenico Vistorini. Burn it now. Do not wait for the auto-da-fé. I will go to the altar of God. I, Giovanni Domenico Vistorini. I will go, because I am. Giovanni Domenico Vistor— I am . . . I am . . . Am I . . . am I? Am I Eliahu ha-Cohain?

No! Never so!

Suddenly, the pen was in his injured hand. He flipped the pages until he found the place. He wrote: *Giovanni Dom. Vistorini*. That is who I am, in this Year of Our Lord 1609.

He flung the pen across the room, laid his head down on the desk, on the cover of the haggadah, and wept as his world spun and whirled.

Hanna

Boston, Spring 1996

"IT'S TOO BAD," Raz said, reaching for the basket of warm pappadams, "that we'll never know what really happened."

"I know." I'd been thinking about little else all evening. I looked out the restaurant window onto Harvard Square, one floor below. Students with their necks wrapped in scarves made their way past the homeless people panhandling in their accustomed doorways. Middle of April, and the temperature had plunged again, leaving the last remnants of ashy, unmelted snow pushed into stubborn clumps on the street corners. Harvard Square could feel like a party on a warm night, full of energy and privilege and promise. Or it could seem like one of the bleakest places on earth—an icy, windswept rat maze where kids wasted their youth clawing over one another in a fatuous contest for credentials.

After the initial exhilaration of discovering the bloodstain, I'd fallen into a funk. It was a familiar feeling for me; an occupational hazard. It was as if I was up against some genie who lived within the pages of old books. Sometimes, if you were lucky, you got to release him for an instant or two, and he would reward you with a misty glimpse into the past. Other times, *pouf*—he'd blow it all away before you could make sense of it, and stand there, arms crossed: *Thus far, and no farther.*

Raz, oblivious to my mood, just kept rubbing it in. "Blood is potentially so dramatic," he said, swirling the pinot in his glass.

Raz's wife, Afsana, stayed in Providence three nights a week because she'd scored an assistant professorship teaching poetry at

Brown. So we were dining alone and could talk shop as much as we liked. But all we could do was speculate, and that was annoying me.

"I don't know how you drink red wine with Indian food," I said, trying to change the subject. I sucked on my beer.

"Could've been some big drama," Raz continued, undaunted. "Passionate Spaniards, fighting for possession of the book—sabers drawn, daggers—"

"More likely some bloke was carving the Passover roast and his hand slipped," I interrupted grumpily. "Don't look for zebras."

"What?"

"Just a saying. 'If it has four feet, a long nose, and it eats hay, look for a horse before you go searching for a zebra.'" It was my mother's saying, actually; something to do with her residents. Apparently inexperienced docs always want to diagnose rare syndromes, even if the patient's symptoms fit some perfectly common condition.

"Oh, you're just a wet blanket. Zebras are *much* more exciting." Raz reached for the bottle and recharged his glass. The haggadah wasn't his project; he didn't feel the frustration the way I did. "You could run a DNA test, I suppose. . . . Find out the ethnic origins of the person whose blood it is. . . ."

"You could. Except you can't. You'd have to violate the parchment to extract a big enough sample. And even if I recommended it, which I wouldn't, I doubt they'd let me." I broke a piece of pappadam—flat, crisp, like matzoh. Like the matzoh the mysterious black woman held in the haggadah illumination. Another mystery I wouldn't be able to solve.

Raz went rabbiting on: "It'd be great if you could transport back in time and be there when it happened. . . ."

"Yeah, I bet the wife yelled at him: 'You klutz! Look what you've done to our book!'"

Raz grinned, defeated at last by my sour mood. He'd always had a romantic streak. That's what had drawn him to shipwrecks, I suppose. The waiter arrived with a bowl of searing vindaloo. I dribbled the fiery sauce over my rice, took a forkful, and felt my eyes water. I loved this stuff. I had lived on it when I was at Harvard. The burn was as close as I'd found to my favorite food in the world: the king prawn sambal at the Malayan restaurant at home in Sydney. Food can be very restorative sometimes. After a few bites I started to feel a bit better.

"You're right," I said. "It *would* be something, to be back there, when the haggadah was still just some family's book, a thing to be used, before it became an exhibit, locked up in a vitrine. . . ."

"Oh, I don't know," Raz said. He was poking at the vindaloo suspiciously. He served himself a scant spoonful and loaded the rest of his plate with dal. "It's still doing what it was meant to do, or it will be, as soon as it goes into the museum. It was made to teach, and it will continue to teach. And it might teach a lot more than just the Exodus story."

"What do you mean?"

"Well, from what you've told me, the book has survived the same human disaster over and over again. Think about it. You've got a society where people tolerate difference, like Spain in the *Convivencia,* and everything's humming along: creative, prosperous. Then somehow this fear, this hate, this need to demonize 'the other'—it just sort of rears up and smashes the whole society. Inquisition, Nazis, extremist Serb nationalists . . . same old, same old. It seems to me the book, at this point, bears witness to all that."

"Pretty profound, for an organic chemist." I could never resist a chance to take the piss. Raz scowled at me, then he laughed, and asked what I was planning to talk about at the Tate. I told him I was giving a paper on the structural features and conservation problems of Turkish manuscripts. Their binding format often leads to damage in use, and it's amazing how many conservators still don't know how to deal with it. From there we drifted into gossip about my bezillionaire client and the pros and cons of university deaccessioning programs. Raz's lab did all the important work on Harvard's holdings, so he had some strong views on the subject.

"It's one thing if a manuscript is in a university library, accessible to scholars, another if it gets passed off to a private collector and locked away in a vault somewhere. . . ."

"I know. And you should see this guy's vault. . . ." My client lived in one of the huge old mansions on Brattle Street, and he'd excavated a safe room that was state of the art and absolutely stuffed with treasures. Raz, who had access every day to fantastic things, was pretty hard to impress. But even his eyes widened when I told him, in strict confidence, about a few of the things this guy had managed to acquire.

From that discussion we moved on to museum politics in general and from there to spicier shop talk: sex in the stacks, a.k.a. the love lives of librarians. And that pretty much was the whole conversation for the rest of the evening. At one point I was fiddling with the saltshaker. In all the excitement of checking out the bloodstain, we hadn't looked at the scraping of salt crystals I'd taken off the parchment. I told Raz I'd need to trouble him again the next day because I really wanted to get a look at those crystals under his video spectral comparator.

"You're very welcome. Anytime. You know we'd love to have you at Straus. Permanently. There's a job for you, whenever you raise your hand."

"Thanks, matey, that's very flattering. But there's no way I'd leave Sydney."

I guess all the chatting about who was doing who in our little world had something to do with what happened next. We were leaving the restaurant when Raz put a hand on my hip. I turned and looked at him.

"Raz?"

"Afsana's not here," he said. "What's the harm? Auld lang syne and all that."

I looked down at his hand, picked it up between my thumb and forefinger, and removed it from my person. "Guess I'll have to rename you."

"Huh?"

"I'll have to call you 'Rat' from now on, instead of Raz."

"Oh, come on, Hanna. When did you turn into such a prude?"

"Ah, let's see—perhaps that would be two years ago? When you got married?"

"Well, I certainly don't expect Afsana to live like a nun when she's in Providence, with all those juicy young undergrads sitting dewy-eyed at her feet, so I don't see—"

I covered my ears with my hands. "Spare me. I don't need to know the details of your marital arrangements."

I turned away from him and hurried down the stairs. I suppose I am a bit of a prude, about some things, anyway. I like loyalty. I mean, do what you like when you're single. Live and let live. Lay and get laid. But why bother to be married at all, if you don't want the commitment?

We walked the few blocks to my hotel in an awkward silence and parted with a stilted good night. I went up to my hotel room feeling ticked off, and a little bit desolate. If I found someone I loved enough to marry, I wouldn't be as reckless about it as Raz.

Weirdly, when I fell asleep, I dreamed about Ozren. We were downstairs from his apartment, in the bakery at Sweet Corner, except the stove was my DēLonghi, from the flat in Bondi. We were cooking muffins, of all things. When I took the tray out of the oven, he came up behind me so that his forearm rested against mine. The muffins were perfectly risen, steaming, fragrant, bursting out of their patty pans. He held one up to my lips. The crust gave way in my mouth and I tasted something creamy and rich and delicious.

Sometimes a muffin is just a muffin. But not in that dream.

I woke to the insistent bleating of the telephone. Thinking it was just my wake-up call, I rolled over, lifted the receiver, and dropped it back into the cradle. Two minutes later, it was ringing again. This time I sat up and noticed the time winking red on the digital clock. Two-thirty. If it was my wake-up call, four hours early, the desk clerk was going to have hell to pay. I muttered a grumpy, *"Huhgn?"*

"Dr. Heath?"

"Mmmm."

"This is Dr. Friosole, Max Friosole. I'm calling from Mount Auburn Hospital. I have a Dr. Sarah Heath here. . . ."

Anybody else in the world would have been wide-staring awake and in an anxiety attack right then. But the fact that my mother was at a hospital in the middle of the night struck me, in my sleepy stupor, as perfectly ordinary. *"Mmmhuh?"* I grunted.

"She's seriously injured. I believe you are next of kin?"

Suddenly I was sitting up, groping for the light switch, disoriented in the strange hotel bed. "What's happened?" My voice was husky, like I'd swallowed a toilet brush.

"It was an MVA. She was ambulatory on scene with pain on palpation suggesting pulmonary—"

"Wait. Stop. Speak English, will you?"

"But I thought . . . Dr. Heath . . ."

"My mother's an MD, I'm a PhD."

"Oh, uh. She was in a car accident."

I thought of her hands first. She's so protective of her hands.

"Where is she? Can I speak to her?"

"Well, I think you should come down here. She . . . she's, well, to put it frankly, she's been a bit difficult. She signed herself out AMA— ah, that's 'against medical advice'—but she suffered a syncope—I mean fainted— in the hospital corridor. She has a ruptured spleen— massive hemoperitoneum—blood in the abdomen. We're prepping her for surgery now."

My hands shook as I took down the hospital details. By the time I got there, she'd been moved from the ER and up to the OR. Dr. Friosole turned out to be a junior resident with a five o'clock shadow and a gaunt, sleep-deprived look around the eyes. In the very short time it took me to throw on some clothes, find a cab, and get over there, he'd dealt with a gunshot wound and a heart attack, so he could hardly remember who I was. He looked up the admitting info for me and established that Mum had been a passenger in the car, driven by an eighty-one-year-old woman who had been DOA. They'd hit a crash barrier on Storrow Drive. No other vehicle involved. "The police took a statement from your mother at the scene."

"How come? I mean, are they allowed to do that, if someone is seriously injured?"

"She was lucid when they got there, administering CPR to the other victim, apparently." He glanced again at the notes. "Argued with the EMTs—wanted to intubate the woman at the scene and was quite difficult when the EMTs insisted on proceeding to the ER."

That'd be right, I thought. I could just hear her. "But if she was in good shape then, what happened?"

"That's the spleen for you. Sneaky. You're a bit sore but basically fine and you don't know you're hemorrhaging until much later, when your BP crashes through the floor. She diagnosed herself, you know, just before she passed out. . . ." I must have looked a little green at this point because he stopped talking about oozing guts and asked if I wanted to sit down.

"The old lady . . . do you have a name?"

He flicked the paper on his clipboard. "Delilah Sharansky."

It didn't mean anything to me. I tried to follow the directions Friosole was giving me to the part of the hospital where Mum was, but my mind was working so hard on the whole idea of this unlikely accident that I made about six wrong turns getting there. I sat down on a hard plastic chair—buttercup yellow, almost obscenely bright against the gray sludge color of everything else in the hospital. Then there was nothing for me to do but wait.

She looked absolutely awful when they wheeled her out of recovery. She had IVs the size of garden hoses in her arm, and one cheek was all bruised and swollen where it must have slammed into the side of the car. She was groggy, but she recognized me straightaway and gave a crooked grin that might have been the most sincere smile she'd ever given me. I took the hand that didn't have the large-bore IV in it.

"Five on this one," I said. "And five on the other one. Surgeon Heath, still in business."

She groaned softly. "Yes, but doctors who work in hospitals need their spleens," she whispered. "Can't fight infections. . . ." Her voice broke and her eyes watered and big fat tears traveled down her poor smashed cheek. I had never, in thirty years, seen my mother cry. I picked up her hand and kissed it, and then I started crying, too.

They let me stay in her room on a kind of Barcalounger chair. The sedation and the painkillers knocked her out again within about fifteen minutes, which was a good thing because she was pretty upset. I couldn't get back to sleep on the damned chair so I just zoned out, waiting for the sky to get light and listening to the gathering sounds in the corridors outside as the morning shift got ready to do meds and BPs and prep the poor sods arriving for elective surgery. I thought of all the things I needed to do—call the Tate and cancel my presentation. Call Mum's secretary, Janine, and get her to work on rescheduling the appointments waiting for Mum back in Sydney. Call the police, and find out what Mum's legal obligations were, if any. In Sydney there'd be an inquest, probably, if an accident resulted in a fatality. I imagined Mum would be pretty dark if she had to stick around Boston to appear at something like that.

Eventually I got so agitated about all this that I went off to find a phone and get going on the calls. It was still business hours in London, and there'd be someone on duty at the hospital in Sydney even though it was the middle of the night. When I got back to the room, Mum was awake. She must have been feeling better because she had her Dr. Heath, chair of neurosurgery, voice back, giving the nurse who was trying to change her IV a hard time about the placement of the cannula. I saw her eyes on me as I came into the room.

"Thought you'd gone," she said.

"Nup. Can't get rid of me so easily. I was just leaving a message for Janine to, you know, let her know. . . . How are you feeling?"

"Bloody ghastly." Mum never swore, except for the occasional four-letter word, delivered like a bludgeon. Colloquial, casual Aussie swearing was beneath her.

"Can I get you something?"

"A competent nurse."

I gave the nurse a look meant to express apology for my mother's rudeness, but she wasn't a bit fazed. She just rolled her eyes and shrugged and went on taking Mum's vitals. Actually, it wasn't a bit like Mum to be rude to a nurse. I knew then that she had to be in real pain. It was one of the things I really had to give her: the nurses at her hospital worshipped her. One of them, a nurse who'd gone to med school and was then an intern, had taken me aside after she'd overheard the two of us going at it in Mum's office one day. I must have been in take-no-prisoners mode, for her to bother. Anyway, she said there was a side of Mum I didn't know, or I wouldn't say such terrible things to her. She said Mum was the only surgeon who actually encouraged nurses to ask questions, to take on more skilled tasks. "Most surgeons get their backs up if you question them, treat you like you're up yourself or something. But your mother—she was the one who got me the application for mature-age admission to med school, wrote the recommendation that got me in."

I remember I was pretty surly with that intern, at the time. Basically told her to butt out and mind her own business. But inside, somewhere, what she said made me really proud. The trouble was, what was great for her was poison for me. When it came to medicine, Mum was a real evangelist. And I was like the minister's daughter who grows up apostate.

When the nurse left the room, Mum signaled weakly. "Yes, actually, you can get me something. A pen and paper. Write down this address."

I took down the street name she gave me, an avenue somewhere in Brookline.

"I want you to go there."

"What for?"

"It's Delilah Sharansky's home. Tonight they will be sitting shivah. It's the Jewish mourning ritual."

"I know what it is, Mum," I said, a trifle curtly. "I've got a bloody degree in biblical Hebrew." I wanted to say, The big surprise is that *you* know what it is. I'd always suspected she was a bit of an anti-Semite. Mum's bigotries were very bifurcated. When it came to patients, she didn't see skin color. But watching the news, she'd make casual ethnic slurs about "the lazy Abos" or the "bloodthirsty Arabs." Likewise, she'd given plenty of bright Jews coveted spots in her residency program, but I never recall her inviting one home to dinner.

"These people, the Sharanskys? They don't know me from soap. They won't want a stranger there."

"They will." She shifted her weight in the bed, and winced from the effort. "They will want you there."

"But why would they? Who was Delilah Sharansky, anyway?"

She took a deep breath and closed her eyes.

"It's no good now. All bound to come out at the inquest, or whatever damn thing they have here."

"What? What are you talking about?"

She opened her eyes and looked right at me. "Delilah Sharansky was your grandmother."

I stood on the steps of the tall redbrick house for a long time, trying to get up the guts to knock on the door. It was in my favorite part of Brookline, the edgy part right near Alston where the burrito joints give way to the kosher groceries and the street life is equal parts art-student goth and Jewish *frum*.

There's a very good chance I never would have knocked at all, if another group of mourners hadn't arrived behind me and just sort of swept me inside with them. The door opened on a dozen or so loud voices, all talking at once. Someone handed me vodka in a shot glass. Somehow, I hadn't pictured shivah like this. I guess that was the Russian part of Russian Jewish.

The house also wasn't at all what you'd expect, going by the conventional exterior or by the fact that an eighty-one-year-old woman had lived here. The inside had been all opened up, in a very contemporary way, with white walls and light pouring in from well-placed skylights. There were tall, spare ceramic vases with twisted branches in them, and Mies chairs and other vintage-modern, Bauhaus-y pieces.

On the far wall, there was a very large painting. The kind of painting that knocks your breath out of you. It was a gorgeous, burning expanse of Australian sky with just a strip of hard red desert implied in a few lines of paint in the lower quarter of the canvas. So simple, so powerful. It was one of the pictures that had made the artist's name in the early 1960s. You could see one from that series in just about any major museum that bothered at all with Australian art. But this was one of the greats. The best I'd seen. We had one ourselves—I mean, Mum did—at the house in Bellevue Hill. I'd never thought about it that much. She had quite a few trophy paintings: Brett Whiteley, Sidney Nolan, Arthur Boyd. Always the big boys with the big names. No reason why she wouldn't have an Aaron Sharansky.

That morning, Mum and I had talked for quite a while, until I could see I was exhausting her. I'd got the nurse to give her something, and when she fell asleep, I went to Widener Library to look up the facts of Aaron Sharansky's biography. It was all there, easily retrieved. Born in 1937. Father, survivor of Ukrainian concentration camp, professor of Russian language and literature at Boston University. He brought his family to Australia when he was invited to create the first Russian language department at the University of New South Wales in 1955. Aaron attended art school at East Sydney Tech, went jackarooing in the Northern Territory, started doing the paintings that made him famous. Became an enfant terrible of Aussie art. Outspoken, outrageous. Deeply political when it came to the desert environment and the mining industry's destruction thereof. I remembered seeing him on the news, being arrested at some sit-in, protesting a bauxite mine, I think it was. He'd had long black hair, and the rozzers—who were rough in those days—were using it to drag him through the sand. There was a big scandal about it, I remembered that. He refused the bail conditions, that he not go back to the mining site, and sat in jail for a month with a dozen Aboriginal men. He came out of it with a lot to say about the terrible treatment of Aboriginal people in custody. He was quite the hero in some circles after that. Even conservatives had to listen politely, if they wanted a crack at buying one of his paintings. Every time he had a show, there was a kind of frenzy to get one, no matter how high the prices rose.

Then, at twenty-eight, the story took a different turn. His vision started to fail. Turned out he had a tumor, pressing on his optic nerve. Risked delicate surgery to remove it. A few days later, he died of "postoperative complications."

What was not noted in any of the profiles or the numerous obits was the name of the neurosurgeon who had performed the operation. Australian doctors weren't allowed to be named in the press in those days—some kind of medical ethics policy. Although I wasn't in a position to know for sure, I suspected that, in her early thirties, my mother already had the complete lack of self-doubt that would have made it possible for her to operate on his difficult tumor. But had she? If so, she'd gone against a long-standing tradition, that doctors don't operate on those with whom they are emotionally involved.

Sarah Heath and Aaron Sharansky were lovers. At the time of his surgery, she was four months pregnant with his child.

"You thought I didn't love your father?"

The look on her face was one of absolute astonishment. It was as if I'd said there was a hippopotamus in the hand basin. I'd returned to the hospital from Widener in the afternoon. She was still asleep when I got there, and it was all I could do not to shake her awake. When she finally opened her eyes, I was almost standing over her, crazy with questions. We talked then, questions, answers, and long silences. It was the longest conversation we'd ever had that wasn't an argument.

"Well, why wouldn't I think you didn't love him? You never mentioned him. Ever. Not once. And when I finally got up the nerve to ask you, you just walked away with a disgusted look on your face." The memory of that moment still hurt. "D'you know, for a long time after that, I was convinced that I was the child of a rape, or something. . . ."

"Oh, Hanna. . . ."

"And it seemed clear that you couldn't stand the sight of me."

"Of course that wasn't true."

"I . . . I thought I must remind you of him, or something. . . ."

"You *did* remind me of him. You looked so much like him, right from the minute you were born. That dimple you've always had, the shape of your head, your eyes. Later, your hair—the exact color and texture of his. The expression on your face when you concentrate—it's the same look he had when he was painting. And I thought, All right, she looks like him, but she'll be like me, because she's with me. I'm raising her. But you weren't like me. You were interested in the things he loved. Always. Even your laugh is like his, the way you look when you are angry. . . . Every time I looked at you I thought of him. . . . And then, when you hit adolescence, and you seemed to hate me so much . . . it was as if that was part of my punishment."

"Punishment? What do you mean? Punishment for what?"

"For killing him." Her voice was suddenly very small.

"Oh, for goodness' sake, Mum. You're the one who's always telling *me* not to be self-dramatizing. Losing a patient is hardly the same as killing him."

"He wasn't my patient. Are you mad? Haven't you learned anything about medicine from living with me all those years? What kind of a doctor would I be if I'd operated on someone I was absolutely, passionately in love with? Of course I didn't operate on him. I did the tests, got the diagnosis—he presented complaining of blurred vision. He had a tumor. Benign, slow growing, not life threatening at all. I recommended radiation, and he tried that, but the visual impairment persisted. He wanted the surgery, risks and all. So I referred him to Andersen."

The legendary Andersen. I'd heard the name all my life. Mum practically worshipped him.

"So, you sent him to the best. How can you blame yourself for that?"

She sighed. "You wouldn't understand."

"You could give me a chance to—"

"Hanna, you had your chance. A long time ago." She closed her eyes then, and I sat there, squirming. I couldn't believe we were falling into the same old, same old. Not at a time like this, when there was so much I needed to know.

Outside, it would have been getting dark, but in the bowels of the hospital there was no way to know that. Corridor sounds of clanking gurneys and beeping pagers filled the silence. I wondered if she'd drifted back into a medicated doze. But then she stirred, and started speaking. She still had her eyes closed.

"You know, when I applied for a neurosurgical residency, they didn't want to give it to a woman. Two of the assessors said straight-out that it would be a waste of training, that I'd marry and have kids and never practice."

Her voice rose and hardened. In her mind, I could tell she was back there in that room, facing the men who wanted to deny her the future she'd set her heart on. "But the third assessor was the chair of the department. He knew I'd had the highest marks of anyone in my year, that I'd consistently excelled during my internship. He said to me, 'Dr. Heath, I am going to ask you just one question: is there anything, anything in the world, that you can imagine yourself doing, other than being a neurosurgeon? Because if the answer is yes, then I urge you to withdraw your application."

She opened her eyes then, and looked at me. "I didn't hesitate for a second, Hanna. There wasn't anything else, for me. Not a thing. I didn't want to be married. I didn't want a child. I'd let go of all those ordinary, normal desires. I tried to make you understand it, Hanna, how utterly amazing and wonderful it is, to be able to do it—the hardest surgery, the surgery that matters most. To know that you have a person's thoughts, their personality, under your fingertips and that your skill— I don't just save lives, Hanna. I save the very thing that makes us human. I save souls. But you never . . ." She sighed again, and I shifted in my seat. The evangelist was back in her pulpit. I'd heard it all before and knew where it went from here, and that was no place I wanted to go. But she changed gears suddenly.

"When I got pregnant, it was a mistake, and I was so angry with myself. I had no intention of having a baby, ever. But Aaron was thrilled, and he made me thrilled, too." She was still holding me in a direct blue gaze, and her eyes started to glisten.

"In some ways, Hanna, we were the most unlikely lovers. He was this tomato-tossing lefty iconoclast, and I was—" She broke off. Her hands were traveling nervously across the sheet, smoothing nonexistent wrinkles. "Until I met him, Hanna, I'd never looked up. I'd never voluntarily spent a minute of my time on anything that didn't lead to being a doctor, and then, when I was one, to being a better one. Politics, nature, art—he introduced me to all those things. I don't believe in clichés like love at first sight and all that, but that was what it was, with us. I'd never felt anything like it. Never have, since. He walked into my surgery, and I just knew—"

A nurse's aide backed into the room, pulling a tea cart. Mum's hands were shaking, so I held the cup for her. She took a few sips and then waved it away. "Americans can't make decent tea." I plumped the pillows, and she adjusted her position, wincing with the effort.

"Do you want me to ask them for something?"

She shook her head. "Dopey enough already," she said. She took a deep breath, gathering her strength, then she went on. "That first day, when I got home, there was a painting waiting for me—the one that hangs over the sideboard in the dining room."

I whistled. Even then, that painting must've been worth a hundred grand. "Most I ever got from a would-be suitor was a bunch of flowers, wilted, actually."

Mum gave a crooked grin. "Yes," she said. "It was quite a statement of intent. There was a note from him, with it. I still have it. Always. It's in my wallet. You can see it if you like."

I walked over to her locker and took out her handbag.

"The wallet's in the zip compartment. Yes, that's right, there."

I pulled it out. "It's behind my driver's license."

It was short, just two lines, written with an artist's charcoal pencil in big, swooping letters.

What I do is me, for that I came.

I recognized the line. It was from a poem by Gerard Manley Hopkins. Underneath, Aaron had written:

Sarah, you are the one. Help me to do what I came for.

I was staring at the words, trying to imagine the hand that had written them. My father's hand, which I had never held.

"I called him, to say thank you for the painting. He asked me to come over to his studio. And after that . . . after that, we spent every spare moment together. Until the end. It wasn't long. Just a few months, really. I've often wondered if it would have lasted, what we had, if he'd lived. . . . He might have ended up hating me, just like you."

"Mum, I didn't—"

"Hanna, don't. There's no point. I know you've never been able to get past the fact that I wasn't a 24/7 mother to you, when you were little. By the time you hit adolescence you might as well have been a cactus plant, as far as I was concerned. You wouldn't let me get near you. I'd walk into the house and I'd hear you and Greta laughing together. But when I came up to you, you'd shut down. If I asked what the joke was, you'd just give me this stone for a face and say, '*You* wouldn't get it.'"

It was true. I'd done exactly that. My little way of punishing her. I let my hands fall open in my lap in a gesture of surrender. "That's all a long time ago, now," I said.

She nodded. "All of it. All a long time ago."

"What happened, with the operation?"

"I didn't tell Andersen about our relationship when I referred Aaron to him. I was already pregnant, but no one knew. Amazing what you can hide under a white coat. Anyway, Andersen invited me to scrub in, but I said no—made some lame excuse. I remember how he looked at me. Usually I'd walk over hot coals for a chance to scrub in with him. For that type of tumor, you go in through the skull base. You peel back the scalp and—"

She broke off. I realized I'd involuntarily raised my hand to my ears, to shut out the gruesome description. She gave me a lacerating stare. I dropped my hands like a guilty child.

"In any case, I didn't choose to scrub in. But I did find some reason to be hanging around the OR when Andersen came out. He was pulling off his gloves, and I'll never forget his face when he looked up. I thought Aaron must have died on the table. It took everything I had, just to stand there, upright. 'It was a benign meningioma, as you diagnosed. But the optic nerve sheaths were extensively involved.' He'd tried to peel the tumor off the sheaths to get the blood supply back to the nerves, but there was too much of it. Anyway, I knew from what he said that Aaron wouldn't be able to see. And I knew right then and there that Aaron wouldn't consider it living. As it happened, he never woke up to find out he was blind. That night, there was a bleed, and Andersen missed it. By the time they took your father back into the OR to evacuate the clot—"

The nurse came in then. She gave Mum an appraising look. It was obvious how agitated she was. The nurse turned to me. "I think you'd better let the patient rest for a while," she said.

"Yes. Go." Mum's voice sounded strained, as if even those two small words required a huge effort. "It's time. It's time you were with the Sharanskys."

"Hanna Heath?" I turned away from the painting on Delilah Sharansky's wall and found myself looking into a familiar set of features. Mine, translated onto the face of a much older man.

"I'm Delilah's son. Her other son. Jonah."

I held out a hand, but he grabbed me around the shoulders and drew me to him. I felt desperately awkward. When I was a little girl, I'd longed for family. Mum had been an only child and not close to her parents. Her dad had made a pile in the insurance business and taken his wife off to a tennis and golf retirement community in Noosa before I was even born. I think I'd met my grandmother once before she died suddenly, of a heart attack. My grandfather rather hastily married someone else, a tennis coach. My mother didn't approve, so we never visited.

Suddenly, here I was, surrounded by strangers who were my blood relations. There were quite a few of them: three cousins, an aunt. There was another aunt, apparently, who was working as a trade rep in Yalta. And there was Uncle Jonah, the architect who had renovated this house for Delilah.

"We were so relieved to hear that your mother is recovering," he said, flipping back a troublesome strand of straight black hair in a nervous gesture that was, I realized, a mirror of one of my own. "None of us wanted Mom to keep driving after she turned eighty, but she was a stubborn old bat." She'd been a widow for more than fifteen years, he said, and had grown used to calling her own shots. "Ten years ago she went back and got her PhD—so I suppose it's understandable that she wouldn't let us tell her what to do. But we all feel terribly about your mother. If there's anything we can do . . ."

I assured him that Mum was being well taken care of. Once word had got around the neurosurgical meeting, the whole doctor network had sprung into action, the way it does for one of its own. I doubted there was a patient in Boston who was getting more attentive care.

"Well, Mom would be glad that this tragedy has brought us you, at last."

"Yeah, it's too bad you and your mum didn't stay in Australia—it would have been nice to have a granny when I was a kid."

"Oh, but we did stay there, for a few years. Mom wanted to give me the chance to finish my architecture degree. I was a night student at the Institute of Technology and I worked for the NSW Government Architect during the day. I designed the loos at Taronga Park Zoo. If you ever have occasion to take a piss there . . ." He grinned. "Well, they're really nice, as loos go. . . ." He put his glass down and looked at me as if he was trying to decide whether or not to say something. "You should know. Mom begged Sarah to let us see you, to make you part of the family. But Sarah said no. She insisted that there be no contact."

"But you just said your mother didn't take orders from anyone. Why would she listen to Sarah?"

"I think it came hard to her. But she knew we were moving back here. I suppose she thought it was unfair to create a big disruption in your life and then vanish. But she found out where you went to pre-school, you know, and would go there and watch for you, in the afternoon, when the housekeeper came to collect you. She worried about you. She said you looked like a sad little kid. . . ."

"Well, that was pretty perceptive of her," I said. My voice, much to my embarrassment, was breaking, and I couldn't keep the tremble from my lip. How bloody cruel. Cruel to Delilah, who must have yearned for her grandchild, all she had left of her son. And cruel to me. I would have been a different person if I'd had this family.

"But why did Mum keep in touch, then? I mean, why were they together last night?"

"Estate matters. Aaron's trust—he willed his copyright to create the Sharansky Foundation."

"Of course," I said. It was one of Mum's boards. She was in big demand for boards—corporate, charity. She'd take the director's fees and the prestige, but I'd never got the sense she cared that much about any of them. The Sharansky Foundation had always seemed an odd one for her; its interests weren't exactly aligned with the Establishment.

"Aaron wrote a will just before his operation, creating the Foundation. He named Delilah and Sarah as trustees. I guess he thought he'd bind them together that way."

Someone else came up then, and Jonah turned to speak to her. I stared at the pictures on the bookshelf. There were just a few, in plain silver frames. There was one of Delilah as a young woman, dressed in a white organza frock with a silver-spangled collar. She had huge dark eyes, all lit with excitement over whatever event it was that she'd dressed up so beautifully for. And there was a picture of Aaron, in his studio, paint-spattered, considering the canvas in front of him as if the photographer wasn't even there. There were family group shots, bar mitzvahs, I suppose, brises, maybe. . . . Good-looking people with arms over one another's shoulders, smiling eyes, body language that said they were glad to be together.

They were all so warm—plying me with food, hugging me even. I'm not used to being hugged. I was trying to recast myself as someone who belonged in this setting, someone half Russian Jewish. Someone who could have been going through life named Hanna Sharansky.

The vodka bottle was sitting on the glass table, and I kept gravitating toward it. I lost count of how many I'd had. I kept tossing them down, glad of the numbing buzz. Everyone was telling Delilah stories, Jonah's wife was telling how, when she first got married, Jonah kept saying her matzoh balls weren't like his mom's. "I tried whipping the egg whites separately, combining everything gently by hand, and making these lovely, airy matzoh balls, but no, they were never like Delilah's. And then one day I got fed up and just threw everything in the blender. They were golf balls. So tough. And what does Jonah say? 'Just like Delilah's!'"

There were other stories in the same vein. Delilah hadn't been a stereotypical Jewish mother, or grandmother, for that matter. Jonah's son, a bloke a bit younger than I, talked about the first time his parents had left him alone for a weekend, supposedly staying with his granny Delilah. "She met me at the door and she had two take-out chickens in foil bags. She thrust them at me and said, 'Now go home and have a nice weekend with your friends. Just don't get yourself— or me—into any trouble.' It was an overprotected fourteen-year-old's dream, I tell you."

Jonah and his wife buried their faces in their hands in mock horror. "If we'd known . . ."

I said I had to go not long after that. I said I had to look in on Mum, which I didn't have any intention of doing. But I did have to get out of there. I was reeling, partly from the vodka shots, but only partly. It was going to take me more than one night to catch up with thirty years of missing information. Missing love.

By the time I got back to the hotel, all the confusing new feelings I'd been having about my mother since her accident had resolved themselves into the familiar little angry knot I'd had with me most of my life. It wasn't enough to know that she had once been a woman capable of a great love. Yeah, sure, she'd suffered. Lost the love of her life, and carried a gutful of blame over it. And yes, I hadn't been perfect by any means. Needy and unforgiving and a nightmare adolescent. But it still wasn't enough. Because in the end, she'd made all the decisions, and I'd paid for them.

I went into the bathroom and threw up, which is something I hadn't done—at least from too much drinking—since I was an undergrad. I lay on the bed with a wet washcloth on my face and tried not to notice the room spinning. As the headache started to kick in, I decided that I wouldn't cancel my Tate talk after all. Let Mum's fellow docs take care of her. I knew they would. She'd always put her work first. . . .

And so did he. The voice in my head was her voice. *He was the one who really chose work over love.* He needn't have risked his life with a dangerous operation. He had so much. A lover, a family. A child on the way. But none of it was as important to him as his work.

OK, then, bugger the both of them. Better just get on with it, like they would.

I had a wicked hangover, which is just what you don't want on a seven-hour plane trip. At least I was in the pointy end again, courtesy of the bezillionare. I took the piece of seared salmon the flight attendant offered me, thinking of all the poor sods in the back struggling through their cardboard chicken and rubber pasta. But even in first class, airline food is crap. The fish was seared, all right; cooked to perfection, and then left on the griddle for another hour and a half. All I really wanted was water, anyway. While I waited for someone to take the tray, I picked up the little plastic saltshaker, letting a few grains drop into my hand. After Mum's accident, I hadn't thought of getting back to Raz's lab. When I hadn't shown up, he'd assumed I was still dark with him. He'd done the analysis without me, as a goodwill gesture. He'd left a message, scribbled by hand, at the desk of my hotel. I had it out on the linen-covered tray table in front of me.

You were right: NaCl. But sea, not rock. Ck. how they made kosher salt in C.15th? 16th? Maybe not table salt? Maritime adventures? Fits yr known locations, Spain and Venice??? Sorry fr being an oaf last night. Let me know how goes Lon. Your mate,
Rattus Raz

I smiled. Typical Raz. Looking for zebras again. And, of course, his shipwreck obsession would lead him to think of maritime mishaps. But I would take his advice and look into it. What made salt kosher, anyway? I had no idea. It was another line of inquiry, another thread to follow. Perhaps the genie in the book would give me a glimpse of something.

I let the white grains fall from my hand onto a weary, rust-edged lettuce leaf. Thousands of feet below, the salty waves of an unseen ocean heaved and crashed in the dark.

Saltwater

Tarragona, 1492

The word of YHVH is refined
As silver and gold are refined.
When these letters came forth, they were all refined,
Carved precisely, sparkling, flashing.
All of Israel saw the letters
Flying through space in every direction,
Engraving themselves on the tablets of stone.

—The Zohar

DAVID BEN SHOUSHAN was not a rude man, it was just that his mind was on higher things. His wife, Miriam, often chastised him for this, for passing within feet of her sister in the marketplace without a nod of acknowledgment, or failing to hear when the mackerel sellers were hawking their fish at half the usual price.

So he was never quite able to explain why it was that he noticed the youth. Unlike the other beggars and peddlers, this one did not cry out, but just sat, silent, his eyes searching the faces of the passing crowd. Maybe it was his very stillness that caught Ben Shoushan's attention. In all the clamor and bustle, he was the one quiet, centered thing. But perhaps that was not it at all. Perhaps it was merely a beam of thin winter sunlight, glinting on gold.

The youth had claimed a small patch of ground at the edge of the market, hemmed in by the city wall. It was a damp, windy spot at this time of year; a poor place to attract customers, which was why the local merchants left it for the itinerant peddlers or the ragtag of war-fleeing Andalusians who drifted through the city. The wars in the south had set so many adrift. By the time they reached this far, what little they'd had of value was already sold. Most of the refugees who found places on the market's edges were attempting to sell worthless things: threadbare cales and surcoats or a few worn-out household goods. But the youth had a piece of leather unrolled in front of him, and on it, bright and arresting, was a collection of small painted parchments.

Ben Shoushan stopped and fought his way through the press to get a better look. He squatted, pressing his fingers into the chill mud for balance. It was as he thought; and the pictures were dazzling. Ben Shoushan had seen illuminations in the Christians' prayer books, but never anything like this. He stooped and peered, unable to believe his eyes. Someone well acquainted with the Midrash had done these, or at least directed the artist. An idea occurred to Ben Shoushan, an idea that pleased him immensely.

"Who made these?" he asked. The youth stared at him, the bright brown eyes blank with incomprehension. Assuming he did not understand the local dialect, Ben Shoushan switched to Arabic, then Hebrew. But the blank stare did not change.

"He's deaf-mute," said a one-armed peasant, hawking a much-mended dough trough and a pair of wooden spoons. "I met up with him and his black slave on the road." Ben Shoushan looked at the youth more closely. His clothes, though travel stained, were very fine.

"Who is he?"

The man shrugged. "The slave told some wild tale—claimed he's the son of a physician who served the last emir. But you know how it is with slaves, they like to make up tales, eh?"

"Is the boy a Jew?"

"He's circumcised, so he's not Christian, and he doesn't look like a Moor."

"Where is this slave? I'd like to know more about these pictures."

"Slipped off one night not long after we reached the coast at Alicante. Trying to get home to Ifriqiya, no doubt. My wife's taken a liking to the youth; he's a willing soul and he surely doesn't give her any backchat. But when we got here, I made him understand that he'd have to sell something to pay his way. The pictures are all he had with him. That's real gold on them, you know. You want one?"

"I want all of them," said Ben Shoushan.

Miriam slapped the meat onto the quadrae so hard that David's slice broke, letting a trickle of juice dribble onto the table.

"Now look what you've done, you filthy man!"

"Miriam . . ." He knew that the source of her anger was not the broken piece of bread. His daughter, Ruti, had leaped to her feet and was already wiping up the spill. David saw the girl's shoulders drooping as his wife continued her scolding. Ruti hated raised voices. Sparrow, David called her, for she reminded him of a nervous little bird. Like a sparrow, she was a dull brown thing, with dun-colored eyes and a muddy complexion, who often smelled bad from tending the kettles where he boiled the gallnuts, resins, and copper vitriol that made his inks. Poor Sparrow, he thought. Gentle, willing to work, at fifteen she could have been married to some kindly young man and out of reach of her mother's bitter tongue. But Ruti lacked both fortune and a fair face. And from the observant Torah families, who did not set such store in those things, she was excluded by the taint of her brother's conduct.

Miriam, tough as an old saddle, had no patience with the girl's timidity. She shoved her daughter roughly and snatched the clout from her hand, rubbing at the table with exaggerated vigor. "You know better than me how few commissions you have, and yet you go and spend two months' income on pictures! And Rachela says you didn't even bargain with the boy."

David tried to quash his unneighborly thoughts about Rachela, who always seemed to know the business of the entire Kahal in its most minute particulars.

"Miriam . . ."

"As if we haven't enough expense coming up, with your nephew's wedding!"

"Miriam," said David, raising his own voice in a way that was highly unusual for him. "The pictures are *for* the wedding. You know I am making a *haggadah shel Pesach* for Joseph's boy and his bride. Don't you see? I can have the quires with these pictures bound into the book, and then we will be able to give a gift of substance."

Miriam pursed her lips. She tucked a curl of hair into her linen headdress. "Oh, well, in that case . . ." Miriam would rather suck a

gall than back down in an argument, but this information brought
with it the ease of removing an ill-fitting boot. She had been troubled
about this wedding gift. One could hardly come with a trifle to the
wedding of Don Joseph's eldest son and the daughter of the Sanz
family. She had worried that a plain haggadah from David's own
hand would seem a paltry gift to those great families. But these pictures, with their gold and lapis and malachite, these, she had to admit, had quality.

David Ben Shoushan cared nothing for money and less for position; that he was the poorest man in the entire Ben Shoushan family
bothered him not at all. But he did care for the peace of his household. Seeing that he had pleased his refractory wife was a relief to
him. The idea of the thing satisfied him, too. A decade ago, he might
have hesitated at the propriety of images, even religious ones such as
these. But his brother was a courtier: he held banquets and enjoyed
music and was—though David would never say it to his face—barely
distinguishable from a Gentile. Why should his son not have a book
to rival the finest Christian psalter? The great Rabbi Duran, after all,
had insisted on teaching his students only from beautiful books.
These, the rabbi said, strengthened the soul. "It has been one of the
virtues of our nation that the rich and important in every generation
have tried to produce beautiful manuscripts," the rabbi had said.

Well, he was neither rich nor important, but by the help of the
Almighty, these fine paintings had been put into his hands—hands
that had already been gifted with the skill to produce harmonious
script. He intended that the book he made would be a glory. Most
of the time, he found it hard to explain to his wife that his work as a
sofer—a scribe of God's holy languages—made him rich, despite the
very few maravedis it earned them. But as he looked at her, smiling
slightly as she cleared the table, he was glad that for once she seemed
to understand him.

He was at work in the first gray light of morning, waving away
Miriam when she came to offer breakfast. Their house, like most in
the Kahal, was a tiny tilted thing, just two rooms perched one above

the other, so Ben Shoushan had to work outdoors, even in the chill of winter. It was barely ten paces from the street door to the house, and the space was crammed with vats of skins soaking in lime, and others stretched on frames waiting for the few pale beams of sunlight that would slowly dry them. There were skins still thick with their fat and blood vessels, awaiting the careful parings of his rounded blade. But he had a small pile of scraped skins, and these he sorted carefully, looking for those of mountain sheep, that matched the parchments of the illuminations. When he had selected the perfect skins, he set Ruti to work, rubbing them smooth with pumice and chalk. He washed his hands in the chill water of the courtyard fountain, and sat down heavily at his *scriptionale*, carefully ruling up the readied pages with his bone stylus. His letters would hang from these faint lines. When the ruling was done, he passed his cold hands over his face.

"*Leshem ketivah haggadah shel Pesach*," he whispered. Then he took up the turkey quill and dipped it in the ink.

הא לחמא עניא

Ha Lachma an'ya. . . . This is the bread of affliction. . . .

The fiery letters seemed to burn into the parchment.

. . . which our fathers ate in the land of Egypt. Whoever is hungry, let him enter and eat . . .

Ben Shoushan's stomach growled, protesting his missed breakfast.

Whoever is in need, let him enter and celebrate.

There were many in need this year, thanks to the taxes imposed by the king and queen for their interminable wars in the south. Ben

Shoushan tried to rein in his racing thoughts. A *sofer* must fill his mind with only the holy letters. He could not be distracted by daily things. *"Leshem ketivah haggadah shel Pesach,"* he whispered to himself again, trying to quiet his mind. His hand formed the letter *shin* — the letter of reason. What reason could there be in this constant fighting with the Moors? Had not the Muslims, Jews, and Christians shared these lands in contentment—in *convivencia*—for hundreds of years? What was the saying? Christians raise the armies, Muslims raise the buildings, Jews raise the money.

This year here, and the next year in the land of Israel.

This year here, thanks to Don Seneor and Don Abravanel, may their names be inscribed for a blessing, who have dazzled the eyes of Ferdinand with gold, and kept the royal ears closed to the hateful murmuring of jealous burghers.

This year slaves . . .

Ben Shoushan thought of the slave who had served the mute youth. How he wished he had been able to speak with him, to find out something of the history of those marvelous paintings. The *sofer*'s hand moved from ink bottle to parchment as his imagination conjured a lean black figure, walking with a staff along a dusty yellow road toward a settlement of mud-brick houses where a family waited who had imagined him dead. Well, likely he *was* dead, by now, or chained to a galley oar with a bloodied back.

He went on so, all day until the light failed, battling the distractions of his busy mind to set down letter after careful letter. At dusk, he asked his Sparrow to bring him a clean robe, and he walked to the *mikvah*, hoping that by a ritual immersion he might clear himself of the daily clamor and open his mind fully to his sacred work. Returning refreshed, he bade Sparrow fill a lamp so he could work on into the night. When Miriam smelled the rich scent of the lit wick, she came flying from the house like a wasp, scolding about the price of the oil. But David spoke to her with unaccustomed sharpness, and she retreated, muttering.

It was in the still of the early hours, when the stars blazed in the black sky, that it happened. His fasting, the chill, the brilliant flare of the lamp: suddenly the letters lifted and swirled into a glorious wheel. His hand flew across the parchment. Every letter was afire. Each character raised itself and danced spinning in the void. And then the letters merged into one great fire, out of which emerged just four, blazing with the glory of the Almighty's holy name. The power and the sweetness of it were too much for Ben Shoushan, and he fainted.

When Ruti found him in the morning, he was slumped unconscious under the *scriptionale*. A light frost whitened his beard. But his script, every letter and word of it perfect, covered more pages than a *sofer* could complete in a week of constant labor.

Ruti put him to bed that morning, but in the afternoon he insisted on rising and getting to his work again. His hand was once again an ordinary *sofer's*, his mind the usual unruly tangle of mundane thoughts, but his heart remained touched by the night's mystical bliss. The feeling stayed with him the following day, and the text progressed steadily and well.

On the fourth day, when the work of what should have been weeks was nearing completion, a light tapping came on the outer door. Ben Shoushan hissed with exasperation. Ruti, skittering in her silent, birdlike way through the clutter of the courtyard, flung back the crossbar and opened the door. When she recognized the woman who stood there, Ruti straightened, her hands fluttering to adjust her head cover. Her eyes, when she turned to her father, were wide and frightened.

As the woman moved to step across the threshold, Ben Shoushan flung down his quill, outraged. How dare she, whom he would not name, how dare she come to his door? His anger acted on his empty stomach like acid, sending a searing pain through his gut. Ruti, startled by his expression, fluttered back from the street door, heading toward the house.

The woman was speaking in that mellow, whorish voice of hers.

Determined not to hear her, Ben Shoushan muttered in Hebrew: "The lips of the strange woman drip honey, but her rear end is bitter as wormwood." They were the last words he had said to his son—his son! his Kaddish, apple of his eye and root of his heart!—before he left through that very door to go to the baptismal font and then to the altar. David Ben Shoushan had rent his coat that day. Two years gone and still, wherever he turned, the memory of his boy was there, vivid and searing. And now here *she* was, source of his heartbreak, speaking a name no longer uttered in his house.

"I have no son!" he shouted, turning his back and following Ruti toward the inner door.

Two paces and he stopped. What had she said?

"The *alguazil* came with the bailiff in the night. He struggled, so they beat him, and when he cried out, they forced a metal gag into his mouth—one of them held him while the other turned the screws to make it widen until I thought they would break his jaw." She was weeping now. He could tell because her voice was no longer mellow, but ragged. He still had not brought himself to look at her. "They have him at the Casa Santa—I followed them there, begging to know the charges, to know who has accused him—but they turned on me then, and said I was guilty of polluting Christian blood by carrying the child of a Marrano heretic. I am a coward, for I left the place, ran away. I can't bear the thought that my child might be born in the dungeons of the Inquisition. I come to you because I do not know where else to turn. My father has no money for a ransom." Her honey voice, as she mouthed this lie, sounded thin and reedy as a child's.

David Ben Shoushan did look at her then, at her swollen belly. She was very near her time. The mixture of love and loss he felt at that moment seemed to melt the marrow of his bones. His grandchild, who would not be a Jew. Reeling, as if he had drunk too much wine, he traversed the small courtyard toward the heavy wooden door and closed it in her tear-streaked face.

The young man spoke with difficulty. When they had unscrewed the gag and pulled the metal bulb from his mouth, four fractured teeth had gone with it. His lips were torn at each corner, and when he opened them to speak, a fresh spurt of blood trickled down his chin and dripped onto his stained smock. He tried to raise a hand to wipe his mouth, but the manacles prevented him.

"How can I confess, Father, when you do not tell me of what I stand accused?"

They had brought him here in his nightdress, and he shivered. The room inside the Casa Santa was windowless, its walls hung with black cloth. The only light came from six candles set on either side of a picture of Christ crucified. The table, also, was draped in black.

The Inquisitor's face was invisible in the recess of his hood. Only his pale hands, fingertips pressed together beneath an unseen chin, were discernible in the candlelight.

"Reuben Ben Shoushan . . ."

"Renato, Father. I was baptized Renato. My name is Renato del Salvador."

"Reuben Ben Shoushan," the priest repeated, as if he had not heard. "You would do well to confess now, for the sake of your immortal soul, and . . ." He paused for a long moment, the fingertips lightly tapping. "And for the sake of your mortal body. For if you will not declare your sins freely to me, here, you surely shall do so in the place of relaxation."

Renato felt the contents of his bowels liquefying. He clutched his manacled hands hard against his belly. He swallowed, but there was no saliva in his mouth. His voice was a rasp.

"I know not what it is you imagine that I have done!"

In the corner, a scribe scraped away with his pen, taking down every word Renato uttered. The sound carried Renato home, to the courtyard of the Kahal and the sound of his own father's stylus on parchment. But his father wrote only words of glory. Not like this man, whose job it was to note down every desperate plea, every moan and cry uttered by the accused.

"Why do you do it to yourself? Admit, and be reconciled. Many have done so, and walked from here. Better, surely, to wear the penitent's San Benito for a season or two than to forfeit your life to the fire?"

A groan escaped from Renato. He could smell the acrid smoke of the last auto-da-fé. It had been a humid day, and the stink of burning had hung low over the city. Six had gone to the fire. Three, confessing heresy at the last moment, had been strangled before the flames were lit. The others, burned alive, had uttered screams that haunted his dreams.

An exaggerated sigh came from within the hood. The white hands fluttered. A third man, tall, his head covered in a leather mask, moved forward from the shadows.

"Water," the priest said, and the masked head nodded. The priest rose then and left the room. The huge man reached for Renato, and roughly stripped his smock. Reuben Ben Shoushan had spent his boyhood as a scholar, hunched over the *scriptionale*, training to follow his father's profession. But in the two years since he had become Renato, he had worked outdoors every day, doing hard physical labor in Rosa's father's groves, or at the olive press. He would never be a large man, but his arms were strong now, muscled and browned from the sun. Yet naked, with the hooded man looming over him, he looked vulnerable. There were bruises blooming on his shoulders from the blows of the *alguazil*.

The guard prodded him roughly forward, and they passed from the black room, down the stairs toward the place of relaxation. When Renato saw the ladder tilted over the large stone basin, the bindings still bloodied from the last prisoner's writhings, the wooden pegs that would be stuffed in his nostrils, he could hold his sphincter no longer. A terrible stench filled the chamber.

. . . .

David Ben Shoushan dressed with care. He put on his least frayed tunic and arranged the *garde-corps* so that the long hood fell gracefully over each shoulder. Ruti wiped away tears as she struggled to darn a small hole in her father's only pair of hose.

"Here, give me that, you stupid girl," said Miriam, snatching the stocking from her. Ruti's hands, coarsened by her work with the skins, were not as skilled at fine work as her mother's. Swiftly, Miriam caught the fabric together with stitches so small they were barely visible. "We have need of haste here!" she said, flinging the stocking to her husband. "Who knows what they are doing to my boy!"

"You have no boy," said David, roughly. "Do not forget that. We sat *shivah* for our son. I go to do what I can for a stranger who has fallen into grave misfortune."

"Tell yourself what brings you peace, fool," said Miriam. "But stop your preening and go, I beg you!"

David walked the narrow alleys to his brother's house with the bile rising in his throat. He had never felt his poverty weigh so heavily. Every Jew, and every *converso,* knew that the Inquisition was as much about filling the royal purse as purifying the Spanish church. For payment of a rapacious fine, most prisoners could walk—or hobble, or be borne on a litter, depending on how long they had been held—from the doors of the Casa Santa. But would Joseph wish to spend such a sum on an apostate nephew, one whose own father had declared him dead?

David was so bound up with his own shame and sorrow that he was before the gates of his brother's fine house before he recognized the commotion under way inside. Joseph, who prided himself on his refinement, usually kept a tranquil home, his servants discreet and unobtrusive. But this day the courtyard rang with the sound of harried voices. David reviewed the date in his mind—the wedding was not until the following month. So this bustle could not be part of preparation for that celebration. His brother's gatekeeper recognized him and ushered him within. He saw Joseph's best gelding being brought from the stable, and the horses of guards and servants being packed for a journey.

Joseph himself emerged from the house at that moment, dressed for the road, deep in conversation with a weary-looking, travel-stained man. It took David a moment to recognize the traveler as the secretary to Don Isaac Abravanel. At first, Joseph was so engrossed in his talk that his eye passed right over his brother, where he stood amid the stir of busy servants. But then his glance returned to the still, hunched figure, and his face softened. Joseph Ben Shoushan loved and revered his pious younger brother, even though their relative importance in the world had placed a barrier between them. The older man held out his hand to the younger and drew him into a close embrace.

"Brother! What brings you here with a face like a funeral?"

David Ben Shoushan, having rehearsed his request all the way to the villa, suddenly found himself tongue-tied. His brother was clearly preoccupied with his own momentous business, and his brow, too, was furrowed with concern.

"It is my . . . it is a person who has suffered—that is, who has fallen into a misfortune," he stammered.

A flicker of impatience, quickly stifled, passed across Joseph's face.

"Misfortunes beset us from all sides!" he said. "But come, I am about to take bread before my journey. Come eat a hasty meal with me and tell me what I may do."

David reflected that his brother's "hasty meal" would have been counted a banquet at his own meager table. The meat was fresh, not salted, and served with fruit, hard to find in winter, and the lightest pastries. David could bring himself to taste none of it.

When David had unburdened himself, Joseph shook his head and sighed. "Any other time, I would ransom this young man. But his fate overtakes him on an evil day. This day, I fear we must think first of the Jews—forgive me, brother—and let those who have left our faith face the consequences that their own choice has brought upon them. I go now, in the greatest haste, to Granada, with every crusata I can scrape together. Don Abravanel's secretary here"—he nodded to the gentleman, who was slumped, exhausted, against the pillows—"has ridden to me with the gravest news. The king and queen are preparing an expulsion order—"

David sucked in his breath.

"Yes, even as we have feared. They have taken the capitulation of Granada as a sign of divine will that Spain be a Christian country. It is, then, their intention to thank God for their victory by declaring Spain a land where no Jew may remain. The choice is to convert, or depart. They have hatched this plan in secret, but finally the queen has confided it to her old friend Don Seneor."

"But how could the king and queen do such a thing as this? It is Jewish money—or at least Jewish money raising—that has secured them the victory over the Moors!"

"We have been milked, my brother. And now, like a dry cow, we are to be dispatched to the slaughterhouse. Don Seneor and Don Abravanel are preparing one last offer—bribe, let us be frank—to see if this can be gainsaid. But they are not hopeful." Joseph waved his lamb shank at the exhausted man in the corner. "Tell my brother what the queen has said to Don Isaac."

The man ran a hand over his face. "My master told the queen that the history of our people shows that God destroys those who would destroy the Jews. She replied that this decision did not come upon us from her or from her husband. 'The Lord hath put this thing into the heart of the king,' she said. 'The king's heart is in the hands of the Lord, as the rivers of water. He turns it wheresoever he will.'"

"The king, for his part"—interrupted Joseph—"puts all the burden for this upon the queen. But those nearest the royal couple know that the very timbre of the queen's words echo her confessor, may his name be rubbed out."

"What can you possibly offer them more than what we have rendered up to them in the past?"

"Three hundred thousand ducats."

David buried his face in his hands.

"Yes, I know; a staggering sum. More than a king's ransom; ransom of a people. But what choice have we?" Joseph Ben Shoushan stood then and offered his hand to his brother. "You see why I have nothing to spare for you this day?"

David nodded. Together, they walked back out into the busy courtyard. The armed outriders and servants were already mounted. David accompanied his brother to his horse. Joseph mounted, then leaned down from the saddle and spoke into his brother's ear. "I do not need to tell you, I am sure, to say nothing of our conversation. There will be panic when this news gets abroad. No need for tears and wailing if we are able to turn their majesties again toward us." The horse, fresh and restless, strutted in place, fretting to be gone. Joseph tugged sharply on the reins and reached for his brother's hand. "I am sorry about your son."

"I have no son," David replied, but his words came out as a quavering whisper, lost in the ring of iron on stone as the party passed swiftly through the gate.

For four days, Renato moved in and out of consciousness. He woke with his cheek pressed to a stone floor strewn with urine-soaked straw and rat feces. When he coughed, there were clots of blood, but also long ribbons of clear tissue that fell apart in his fingers. It was as if his insides were sloughing off; his body falling apart from the inside. He was thirsty, but at first he could not reach the water jar. Later, when he was able to grasp it between shaking hands and pour a trickle into his mouth, the pain of swallowing made him pass out again. In his dreams, he was once again bound on the sloping ladder, the water cascading into his mouth, his own involuntary swallowing pulling the narrow length of linen farther and farther into his gut.

Renato had not known that such pain was possible. Silently, for speech was impossible, he prayed to die. But his prayers went unanswered, for when he woke, he was still lying there, the red eyes of the rats glinting at him in the dark. By the fifth day, he was awake more than unconscious, and by the sixth, he could drag himself into a sitting position, propped against the wall. All he had to do now was wait, and remember.

It had been after the fifth ewer of water, when the linen was well down his throat, that the Inquisitor had come into the place of relaxation. They had set the ladder upright then, as he gagged and choked and writhed in panic. And then Renato saw it, at last, the evidence against him, and finally he knew what it was he had to confess. The priest held, between two fingers, as if it were a piece of ordure, a long brown leather strap, a small square box. Inside it was the word of God, inscribed in his father's impeccable hand.

"You false *conversos* are a dry rot, eating away at the heart of the church," the priest said. "You pray your filthy prayers in secret and then pollute our church with your lying presence among us." Renato couldn't reply, either to confess or to repudiate the charges. Speech was not possible with the cloth wadded tight in his throat. The priest stood there as they inverted the ladder, poured another ewer of water, and then finally, with sudden, shocking force, tugged forth the cloth, which had penetrated to his gut. Renato felt as if his entrails were being pulled up through his throat. He had passed out, and when he came to himself, he was alone again in the cell.

· · · · ·

Shin. Fe. Kaf.
Pour out your wrath upon the nations who know you not. . . .

Because he had not known what else to do, David Ben Shoushan had returned to his *scriptionale* and gone right back to work on the Shefoch Hamatcha, near the conclusion of the haggadah. But his mind, like his ink vats, boiled in a poisonous stew. His hand trembled, and his letters were unlovely. From inside the house, he could hear Miriam, her grief warring with her rage, as she poured out torrents of abuse on the name of his brother and shouted at poor Sparrow, who, he gathered, was trying unsuccessfully to comfort her. He had said nothing of his brother's large mission, or the fate that now hung over all of them. His thoughts swirled from Reuben *in the house of oppression,* to their own plight *beset by enemies,* to poor little Sparrow. *Rise up, my love, and come away.* He had to find her a husband, and swiftly. If they were to take the uncertain road into exile, she would need more protection than he could give her. His mind ran through the list of possible candidates. Avram, the *mohel,* had a son of the right age. The boy stuttered, and had a squint, but his character was good enough. But Avram might not be able to overlook the taint that Ruti carried as sister to a *converso.* Moise, the *shochet,* was a strong man with strong sons, who would be better protectors, but the boys were all headstrong and ill-tempered, and as well, Moise liked money, which David would not be able to provide.

It did not even occur to David to consult Ruti herself about this, or any other matter. Had he done so, he would have been most surprised by the result. He did not realize it, but his love for his daughter marched hand in hand with a kind of contempt for her. He saw his daughter as a kind-hearted, dutiful, but vaguely pitiable soul. David, like many people, had made the mistake of confusing "meek" with "weak."

For Ruti had a secret life of which her father could not conceive. For more than three years, Ruti had been immersed in the study of the Zohar, the Book of Splendor. Alone, in secret, she had become a practitioner of the Kabbalah. These studies were forbidden to her, on account of both her age and her gender. Jewish men were supposed to be forty years old before they approached the dangerous realm of mysticism. Women were never thought worthy to undertake it. But the Ben Shoushan family had produced famous Kabbalists, and from the time she was a child, Ruti had been aware of the Zohar's power and importance in her father's spiritual life. When her father's small group of trusted scholars had met at the house to study, Ruti had struggled to listen as they discussed the difficult text, keeping herself awake while feigning sleep.

If Ruti's soul had a secret life, so too did her dumpling body. She could not study from her father's books: he would never have permitted it. But she had seen the volumes she needed at the bindery, when she had taken her father's work there. Micha, the binder, was a young man grown too soon old, with pale jowls and sparse hair that he tugged at nervously whenever his wife entered his workshop. She was frail and drab, often ill, worn out by the bearing of children, several of whom always seemed to be trailing after her, crying.

Ruti remembered the new way the binder had looked at her when she told him what she wanted. At first, she told him her father had asked to borrow the books, but Micha saw through that deception at once; everyone in the Kahal knew that David Ben Shoushan, poor as he was, owned a remarkable library. He guessed what she was about, and he knew the weight of the taboo that she was violating. If she was prepared to break such weighty rules as these, he reasoned, then perhaps there were other areas of transgression into which she might be tempted. In return for the use of the books, he had lain her down upon the soft scraps of hide fallen from the binder's workbench. She had breathed in the rich scents of fine leather while the binder's hands, skilled at working flesh, touched her hidden places. She had been terrified, the first time she agreed to this transaction. She had quivered when he had lifted up the rough brown wool of her smock and spread apart her dimpled thighs. But his touch had been subtle, and soon delightful; opening her up to a pleasure she had never guessed existed. When he put his tongue between her legs and lapped at her like a cat, he had brought her to a physical ecstasy akin to the spiritual one she felt on the rare nights in her cave when the letters lifted for her, and soared.

She came to think of it as right, somehow, that these two forbidden ecstasies should be linked: that her femaleness, which should have barred her from this study, actually made it possible for her; the yielding up of her now-willing flesh providing the means to acquire delight of the soul. It was because she knew the power of lust and the pleasures of the body that she had found a way to understand, if not forgive, her brother's betrayal of his family and his faith. She believed if her father had been less exacting and less rigid, had hinted to Reuben earlier on the mysteries and beauties of the Zohar, her brother would not, could not, have fallen into the thrall of another faith.

But Reuben had been raised by the letter of the law. Every day, he hunched over the *scriptionale,* doing only the most routine of work, with his father always finding fault. She could still hear her father's voice, always calm, never raised, constantly critical: "The space in the middle of the letter *beit* should be exactly equal to the width of the top and bottom lines. Here, on this line, see? You have made it too narrow. Scrape it off and do the page again. Reuben, you must know by now that the lower left corner of the *tet* is squared, the right corner rounded. You have reversed it here, see? Do the page again." Do it again, and again, and again.

Never once did her father open the door for Reuben to the glory that swirled in the dark ink. Her own mind was incandescent with it. Any tiny letter was a poem, a prayer, a gateway to the splendor of God. And every letter its own road, its own special mystery. Why had her father not shared some of this with her brother?

When she thought of the letter *beit,* it was not of the thickness of lines or the exactitude of spaces. It was of mysteries: the number two, the dual; the house, the house of God on earth. "They will build me a temple and I will dwell in them." *In them,* not *in it.* He would dwell within her. She would be the house of God. The house of transcendence. Just a single, tiny letter, and in it, such a path to joy.

In time, Ruti's heart had opened to the bookbinder, and affection had grown between them. When the bookbinder had suggested some clandestine code they could use when either of them desired the touch of the other, she had proposed the letter of union, *beit.* She would see it scrawled on a corner of one of her father's bills, and know that Micha's wife was gone from the house. She would add it to the notes of instruction her father sent to the bindery, to say without words, if other customers were present, that she had time and would not be missed at home if she tarried. She wondered if Reuben had also had a secret signal with his beloved, a mark on a tree, or a cloth placed just so. It would have to have been something like that, for Rosa, like most Christians, could not read.

Reuben had lived for the moment, at the end of every day, when he was finally released from the *scriptionale* to go and run errands. Ruti had watched the way he sprang up, suddenly alive. And she had noticed how a certain errand increasingly brought a smile to his face and a special spring to his step.

When he had been sent to buy olives or oil from Rosa's father, how could he not have noticed the daughter who was also ripening? Ruti could guess exactly how it had come about, though her brother would never have thought to taint what he believed were her inno-cent ears with confidences about his physical passions.

After the conversion, the marriage, and the estrangement, Ruti and her brother had met by chance in the marketplace. She knew she was supposed to ignore him, as if he were just another Gentile stranger to be passed with lowered eyes. But her heart could not be schooled so. She let the crowd carry her toward him, and under cover of the press of bodies, she reached out and grasped his hand. How different it felt, how coarse it had become, released from the pen to serve the pruning hook. She squeezed it, pouring all the affection she could into the gesture, before hurrying away.

The next time, a couple of weeks later, he was ready for her. He pushed a note into her palm, imploring her to meet him. He had named the place; south of the town, Esplugües. *Esplugües* means "caves," and this dry white hillside was riddled with them. One in particular, deep and hidden, had been a favorite retreat of their childhood. Later, he had brought Rosa to it during the secret days of their courtship. He did not know it was the same cave Ruti used now for her clandestine studies. Their first meeting was strained: much as she loved him, she could not help blaming him for the pain and disgrace he had brought upon her family. But her brother was a good man, she knew that in her heart, and most of the kindness she had felt as a child had come from him, not from her querulous mother or her abstracted father. Soon, they met there weekly. On the day he told her news of the baby, due in the springtime, he wept.

"It is only when you are to be a father yourself that you finally know what it is that your own father feels for you," he whispered. Ruti pulled his head into her lap and stroked her brother's hair. His voice was muffled. "Does he never speak of me?"

"Never," she said, as gently as she could. "But I believe that not an hour goes by when he does not think of you." She ran her hand over the bleached, pitted stone. The place reminded her of bones, an ossuary forged of the remains of unloved dead. The hectic flesh of her ruddy palm was so impermanent, after all. They would all be dead, soon enough, their bones sucked dry, porous as lace. And who would care then that her brother had let a priest dribble water on his forehead and say a few Latin prayers? Ruti, in this very cave, had felt the presence of God. She had trembled before an immanence that would scorch away the water and suck the very breath from the priest's mouth.

It was at that moment that an idea occurred to her. How harmless it seemed, to give her brother that memento of shared hours between a father and a son, standing together before God.

"I could bring you something," she said. And the next week, she did.

David Ben Shoushan looked around impatiently for his daughter. "Sparrow!" he called. "I need you, girl. Do make haste, for once, and stop your dawdling."

Ruti tossed the scrubbing brush into the pail and rose from her hands and knees, rubbing at the place where the tiles had bitten into her flesh. "But I haven't finished the floor, Father," she said softly.

"Never mind that, I have an errand that won't wait."

"But Mother will be—"

"I will manage your mother." There was something furtive in her father's manner that Ruti had never experienced before. His eye was on the street door. "I need you to take this packet to the binder. He has my detailed instructions already. He knows what to do with it. The book must be ready to present to Don Joseph when he returns. They are expecting him in time for Shabbat. Now go, daughter, and be quick. I don't want to give the rogue an excuse for tardiness."

Ruti moved to the well. Quickly but with care, she washed and dried her hands before she took the packet, wrapped in a piece of cloth. Her father's hand, usually so steady, was trembling. As she felt the shape of the fabric-wrapped metal, she recognized it at once. She had polished it often enough, nervous lest she drop it or damage the silver filigree. It was the one precious thing in the household. Her eyes widened.

"What are you staring at? The work does not concern you."

"But this is the scroll case from Mother's *ketubah*!" she exclaimed. The *ketubah* itself was the most beautiful Ruti had seen. David had made it himself, the young *sofer* entranced by the idea of this bride, whom he hardly knew, writing every letter of every word of the marriage contract as a perfect tribute to the woman he believed then would be his soul mate. When his own father had seen the work, he had been so proud of his son that he had spent more than he had intended to buy a fine case for it.

"Father," squeaked Ruti, "you can't be meaning me to give this in payment to the binder?"

"Not in payment!" David's own guilt and uncertainty made him terse. "The haggadah must have worthy covers. Where else would we get silver to embellish it? The binder has found a smith from outside of Tarragona who will do the work for nothing because he wants to recommend himself to the Sanz family. He is waiting at the bindery, so go now. Be off with you!"

He had first thought of selling the *ketubah* case as part of the ransom for his son. But the case was inscribed with the word of God, and to sell it to a Christian who would melt it down for coin silver was shameful, probably sinful. Yet at the heart of his faith was a fundamental teaching, that the saving of human life should take precedence over all other *mitzvot,* or commandments. Then he saw the way. He could use the silver to embellish the haggadah, so that the sacred would remain sacred. Surely then so fine a gift would open the hand of his brother. How could it not do so? David had convinced himself of this. It was the one slim hope to which he clung. With extreme annoyance, he noticed that Ruti was still standing before him, holding the packet out as if to give it back to him.

"But Mother cannot possibly have agreed to this. . . . I . . . I . . . am afraid she will be angry with me."

"Most assuredly, my Sparrow, she will be angry. But not with you. There is a reason for this that is not your concern, as I have said. Now hurry before that rogue uses your lateness as an excuse to delay the work."

As it happened, her father need not have worried on that score. Whatever else Micha may have been, he was a proud craftsman, and he knew that the illuminations and text presented to him by Ben Shoushan held the promise of a book of exceptional beauty. It could make his reputation among the wealthiest Jews in the community. Such opportunities didn't come his way every day, and he had set aside all his lesser commissions to attend to this one.

The haggadah sat on the workbench, bound in the cover he had fashioned of the softest kid, embossed with intricate tooling. There was a blank space at the center of the cover.

The silversmith was a young man, just out of his apprenticeship but gifted in design. He took the packet eagerly from Ruti, unwrapped it, and examined the *ketubah* case. "Very fine. A shame to undo such work. But I promise your mother I will fashion something worthy of her sacrifice." He had a small parchment with him, which he unrolled on the workbench. He had drawn a design for the cover's central medallion, which showed the wing of the Sanz family emblem entwined with roses, the symbol of the Ben Shoushan family. He had also designed a set of beautiful clasps, also ingeniously formed of wings and roses.

"I will work all night, if necessary, so that the book will be ready by Erev Shabbat, as your father desires," he said. He wrapped the book and the case carefully and took his leave then, anxious to cover the miles from Tarragona in daylight, before the brigands began their nightly work.

Ruti ran her finger over a section of stitched quires, pretending to examine the sewing, stalling until the smith left the workshop. She had seen the letter of union, their secret *beit*, scribbled on a parchment scrap on the workbench.

The binder turned from the doorway. He licked his lips. She felt his hand on the small of her back as he propelled her toward the alcove. Inside, the familiar, rich scent of leather aroused her, and she turned to him, circling her plump arms around his thin hips, tugging away his apron and then working loose the garment beneath. The taste of him was sharp and salty in her mouth.

She could still taste him as she stood outside the street door of her house. She was late for the evening meal, but she was afraid to go in. She expected her parents to be at war over the missing case. But when she finally plucked up her courage and entered, as she knew she must, she found her mother nagging, just as she always did, about her father's everyday inadequacies. There was no tempest, just the usual low tide of bile. Ruti kept her eyes on her bread and did not look at her father, although she wanted to. She wondered what lie he had told and wanted very badly to ask him. But some things on earth were possible, and some were not, and Ruti knew the difference.

When Renato was to be put to the question for the third time, he was too weak to stand. The *alguaziles* had to drag him, one on each side. He sat in the black-draped room, smelling the scent of candle wax and the rank stink of his own fear.

"Reuben Ben Shoushan, do you confess that you did have in your possession those things required for a Jewish man to pray?"

He tried to speak, but the sound from his raw throat was a whisper. He wanted to say that he had not prayed as a Jew, as the phylacteries suggested. He had walked away from Hebrew prayer when he left his father's house. It was true that he had loved Rosa before he had loved her church. But the priest who had baptized him explained that Jesus often worked his will just so, and that the love he felt for Rosa was but a particle of the Lord's love, given to him as a foretaste of the sweetness of salvation. He had wrestled, in his mind, until he could believe that Jesus was indeed the Messiah for whom the Jews had waited. He had liked the priest's hopeful account of heaven. Perhaps most of all, he liked the idea of a wife whose body would be free to him at almost any time, rather than the hard discipline of abstinence that awaited him for half of every month with a Jewish bride.

He had kept the phylacteries not because he missed Jewish prayer, but because he missed his father, whom he loved with all his heart. When he rose, and before he slept, he clasped the leather straps to him, not to pray, but just to think for a moment of his father, and the love with which he had inscribed the parchment within. But to love a Jew and his works was itself a sin to these priests of the Inquisition.

And so he nodded.

"Let the record show that the Jew, Reuben Ben Shoushan, has confessed to Judaizing. Now, admit that you have corrupted your wife with these things. An informant says you have been seen praying together."

Renato felt a new surge of fear. His wife. His innocent, ignorant wife. Surely he was not to be the cause of her suffering. He shook his head as vigorously as his depleted state allowed.

"Admit it. You taught her your vile prayers and forced her to pray with you. There was a witness."

"No!" Renato rasped, finally finding his voice. "They lie!" He dragged the words from his shredded throat. "We prayed the Pater Noster and the Ave Maria. Only those. My wife had no idea I had brought Jewish things into our house."

"Did you have these things with you when you contracted the sacrament of marriage?"

Renato shook his head.

"How long, then, have you been a Judaizer?"

He opened his cracked lips and whispered, "Only one month."

"You claim you have been a Judaizer for only one month?"

He nodded.

"Then who supplied you with these things?"

Renato winced. He had not foreseen this.

"Who supplied you? Name the man!"

Renato felt the room begin to spin and clutched his chair.

"Name him! I give you one chance more."

The priest signaled, and the masked hulk moved toward him. The *alguaziles* grasped Renato and tugged him from the chair. He held his peace as they dragged him from the room and down the dimly lit stairs. He held his peace as they tied him to the ladder and inverted it over the basin. Dry sobs wracked his body as he heard the well water pouring into the ewers. Still, he held his peace. It was when they picked up the linen and forced open his jaws that he cried out. The pain of the one word seared his throat.

"Sparrow!"

When an *alguazil* made an arrest in the Christian quarters, he took care to do it at dead of night. That way, their victim would be at his lowest ebb, confused, unlikely to put up significant resistance or raise a fuss among neighbors who might complicate the business. But the Holy Office of the Inquisition did not send its own soldiers into the Kahal. It was concerned with the rooting out of heresy among those who pretended to have accepted Christ, not with those who persisted in their old, erroneous faith. The crimes of Jews who meddled with Christians and tempted them from the true religion were a matter for the civil authorities, and they sent their soldiers at any time they chose.

So it was afternoon, and still light, when a preemptory banging shattered the peace of the Ben Shoushan house. Only David was within; Miriam had gone to the *mikvah,* and Ruti to the bindery to see if her father might collect the finished work that evening in time to deliver it to his brother, whose return was expected. David had noticed, with annoyance, that she was late returning from the errand, as usual.

He shuffled to the door, crying out as he went against whatever uncouth caller had the effrontery to pound so on his door. As he flung the bar back and saw who stood there, the imprecations died in his mouth. He took a step backward.

The men moved into the courtyard. One spat into the well. Another turned, slowly and purposefully, letting the tip of his sword's scabbard catch on the edge of the bench that held David's delicate writing implements. Ink bottles tumbled to the ground.

"Give us Ruth Ben Shoushan," the tallest of the armed men commanded.

"Ruti?" said David in a small voice, his eyes widening in surprise. He had been sure the men had come for him. "There must be a mistake. You can't want Ruti."

"Ruth Ben Shoushan. Now!" The man raised a booted foot with an almost languid motion and kicked over David's *scriptionale*.

"She . . . she is not here!" said David, his scalp prickling with fear. "She went out on an errand for me. But what can you possibly want with little Ruti?"

In reply, the soldier drew back his fist and struck the *sofer* in the face. David reeled, lost his balance, and fell backward, landing hard on his buttocks. He wanted to howl in pain, but the air had been forced from him, and when he opened his mouth, no sound came.

The soldier reached down and tore off his head cover, then grasped the knot of silver hair in his fist and pulled him up off the ground.

"Where did she go?"

David, wincing, cried out that he didn't know. "My wife sent her and I—"

Before he could finish his sentence, the soldier wrenched on his hair, flinging him to the ground. A boot landed hard against the side of his head.

His ear roared and rang. He felt a burning on the side of his face, then wetness.

Another kick landed against his jaw. He felt the bones grind against each other.

"Where is your daughter?"

Even had he wanted to reply, his broken jaw would not open to form words. He tried to raise an arm to protect his fractured skull, but it was as if a lead weight had been tied to it. His left side would not move. He lay there, powerless under the blows, as the blood leaking into his brain spread further, and extinguished the light entirely.

Rosa del Salvador had not slept properly in days. Her huge belly would not let her find a comfortable position. Her face throbbed from the blows her father, in his rage, had landed on her earlier in the evening. Even when exhaustion dragged at her and she dozed, a terrible dream always came. Tonight the dream had been of an old horse from her childhood, a black gelding with a white star on his forehead. He had been the blindfolded horse who worked the oil press, plodding in patient circles. One day the horse had fallen lame, and her father had sent for the knacker. Rosa remembered how the man had put the iron bolt to her old friend's head, right on the star, and given the great hammer blow. As a little girl, she had cried for the death of the horse. But in her dream, the horse did not die, but reared, screaming, with the metal bolt embedded in his head and blood flying from his tossing mane.

Rosa awoke, sweating. She sat up in the dark and listened to the night sounds of her family's *masía*. The farmhouse was never really silent. There was always the creaking of the old beams, the ragged snores of her father in his wine-drenched slumber, the scratching of mice among the amphorae where the grain was stored. Usually these sounds soothed her, but not tonight. She rubbed her hands over her belly. These dreams, surely, were curdling the blood that should nurture her child. She feared that the child inside her might be turning monstrous.

Why had she let herself love a Jew? Her father had warned her. "Don't trust him. He says he will give up his faith for you, but they never do. In the end, he will blame you, and the bitterness will poison your later years."

Well, if only that was all that had happened. A commonplace misery, such as a marriage gone sour in old age. Now it was likely that neither of them would see their old age. Without ransom, which her father refused to pay, her husband faced the stake. She had begged her father to buy her husband's life, and received blows for it. Her stubborn choice in marriage had put them all at risk, he said. The entire family was now suspected of being secret Jews. Any jealous neighbor who wished for one less competitor in the oil market, any greedy man who eyed their fine groves, could make an accusation against them. It could be some trifling thing: that her mother had choked on a piece of ham, that her father had changed his shirt on a Friday, that she, Rosa, had lit candles too early in the evening. Her father feared it, that was plain. Every evening he tormented himself, running through lists of his competitors, of customers who might have a grievance, of relatives with whom he had not been open-handed enough in their times of need. He would berate her mother for having once, long ago, bought kosher meat because it was selling cheaper at market than the cuts of the Christian butcher. At such times, Rosa tried to be anywhere in the *masia* that would keep her from falling under his eye. Once, when he beat her, he had cried out that he wished she would miscarry, that her infant, with its Jew-polluted blood, might be born dead. Rosa's great guilt was that, as the blows fell, she, too, began to wish for it.

Agitated, she eased herself up off her pallet and reached for her mantle. Air, that was what she needed. The heavy farmhouse door creaked as she pressed against it. The night was mild; the scent of loamy earth carried the first hint of spring. She threw a blanket around her shoulders but did not take a lamp; her instep knew the path to the grove that she had traversed all her life. She loved the trees, the gnarly strength of them. The way they could be blasted by lightning or charred by a brushfire, and look quite dead, then send forth a new green shoot out of the old wood and keep living, in spite of everything. She would have to be like an olive tree, she decided. She ran her hand over the rough bark.

She was there, in the groves, when the *alguazil* and the bailiff came on horseback up the path that led from the town. She watched, hidden in the tree shadows, as the lamps flared in the house. She heard her mother's cries of fear, her father's shouts of protest, as the bailiff took note of the contents of the farmhouse. Everything they owned would be forfeit to the crown if the charges against them were proved. She shrank to the ground, pulling the dun-colored blanket tight to hide the whiteness of her bed gown, covering herself in earth and leaf litter, afraid lest the torches move toward the groves. But her father must have told some lie about her whereabouts to the *alguazil,* for he did not even make a cursory search. She watched, helpless, as her parents were led away. And then she ran, with her strange, slow, pregnant gait, through the groves, across the neighbor's fields. She could not go to them for help; she could not know if they were the Inquisition's informants. Beyond the neighbor's fields, the land rose abruptly toward Esplugües. She could hide there, in the cave where she and Renato had met in secret courtship. Why had she gone to him? Why had she brought this misery upon their heads? The bulk of the baby compressed her lungs so that she could barely breathe as she climbed. The sharp stone scraped her bare feet. She was cold. But fear drove her on.

When she reached the mouth of the cave, she collapsed, gasping. When she felt the first pain, she thought it was a stitch. But then it came again, not harsh, but unmistakable; a pressure like a girdle drawn too tight. She cried out, not because the contraction hurt her, but because her child, whom she did not want, this baby, who might have turned into a monster, was about to be born, and she was all alone and very much afraid.

Ruti and Micha were together in the storeroom when they heard the door to the bindery open. The binder cursed. "Stay in here and be silent, for pity's sake." He closed the heavy door to the storeroom and stepped out, tugging at his leather apron, trying in vain to hide the bulge beneath. Stifling his annoyance, he arranged his face to greet the client.

His expression changed when he saw that it was a soldier, and no client, who had entered his workshop. The haggadah, complete, splendid, with its gleaming clasps and burnished medallion, sat on the counter, where he and Ruti had been admiring it until their desire had overtaken them. Micha, offering a polite greeting, moved between the soldier and the bench, deftly pushing the book under a pile of parchments.

But the soldier did not care for books and barely noticed his surroundings. He had picked up a thick needle from the workbench and was working it under his nails, sloughing greasy matter in a little cascade of motes that fell, Micha noted with dismay, onto a sheet of prepared parchment.

"Ruth Ben Shoushan," the soldier said, without preamble.

Micha swallowed hard and made no answer. His inner panic expressed itself in a blank expression that the soldier took for witlessness.

"Speak, dullard! Your neighbor, the wine seller, reports that she came in here."

No point denying it. "The daughter of the *sofer,* you mean? Ah yes, now that you mention it. She did come, indeed, on an errand for her father. But she left with . . . ah . . . a silversmith . . . I think from Perello. Her family had business with him, it seems."

"Perello? She has gone there, then?"

The bookbinder wavered. He did not want to betray Ruti, but he was not a brave man. If he gave false information to the authorities, and was discovered . . . But then, if Ruti was found in his store cupboard, that was already enough to indict him.

"Sh . . . she did not confide her plans to me. You must know, sir, that unmarried Jewish women do not speak with men outside their families, except briefly, on necessary matters of business."

"How would I know what your Jewess whores do?" said the soldier, but he turned for the doorway.

"May I ask . . . that is, might your lordship tell me, why so important an officer would concern himself with the humble daughter of the *sofer*?"

The young man, like most bullies, couldn't resist a chance to instill fear. He turned back into the shop with an unpleasant laugh. "Humble, maybe, but not the daughter of the *sofer* anymore. He's already on his way to hell with the rest of your damned race, and she'll be joining him soon. Her brother's for the stake, and she's to go with him. He confessed that she tempted him to Judaize."

Miriam returned from the *mikvah*, ready to greet her husband as a bride. There had been signs, the past year, that told her there could not be many more months in which the purification ritual would be required of her. She knew she would miss it: the restraint of abstinence, the anticipation of renewed union.

For the previous ten days, since the start of her period, David and Miriam had not even touched hands, according to the ancient laws of family purity. Tonight they would make love. As much as their personalities had grated one against the other, their physical union had always been a mutual pleasure, and no less as their bodies aged.

Miriam was spared from finding her husband dead in his blood on the stones of her courtyard. The whole alley had heard the rough, raised voices, and known all too well what they meant. As soon as the armed men were gone from the Kahal, they had come to do what was necessary and right for their neighbor.

When Miriam saw her house already prepared for shivah, she thought at once of Reuben. They had sat shivah for Reuben for seven days after his baptism as a Christian, to signify that he was dead to them. But now it fell into her heart that her son was truly dead. His father had relented and decided to accord him Jewish rites. She grasped the doorpost.

The neighbors supported her, brought her inside, and gradually made her understand the truth. David's body had been washed and clad in white. Now the neighbors wrapped the body in a linen sheet and carried it to the burial ground. Shabbat was approaching, and Jewish law required burial without delay.

As soon as her husband was buried, Miriam lit the *yizkor* candle. She wanted to give herself up to grief. Her husband dead, her son convicted and sentenced to death in the Casa Santa, her daughter . . . where was she? The soldiers, in their callousness, had invaded the graveside, crudely interrogating the mourners as to the whereabouts of the deceased's daughter. Miriam struggled to think clearly. For the first of her tragedies, David's death, she could do nothing but grieve. For the second, her incarcerated son, she could do little but pray. But the third, Ruti, was another matter. There, it might not be too late. If the girl could be found, warned, hidden or spirited out of the city . . .

Just as she was thinking these things, the neighbors parted, jostling to make room as Joseph Ben Shoushan, still wearing his travel clothes, crossed to his sister-in-law to offer his condolences. His eyes were red from road weariness and grief.

"The servants told me the news as I arrived at my house. I came directly here. Sorrow heaps upon sorrow. David! My brother . . . if only I had ransomed your son as he asked me, this might not—" His voice broke.

Miriam spoke with a harsh urgency that startled the grieving man. "You did not, and what is done is done and God will judge you. But now you must save our Ruti—"

"Sister," Joseph interrupted. "Come with me now to my house. I am taking you under my protection."

Miriam, her eyes blank and uncomprehending, could not focus

on his words. She could not leave her house during shivah, surely he knew that. And poor as she was, she did not intend to walk away from her own home to become a charity case in her brother-in-law's. How could he think she would abandon her little house and all its memories? Miriam's querulous voice sounded almost normal as she started to list her objections to her brother-in-law.

"Sister," he said quietly, "soon, very soon, we shall all be forced to leave our homes and our memories, and we all of us shall be charity cases. I wish I could offer you a place in my home. All I am able to offer you is a place at my side on the uncertain road that now faces us."

Slowly, painfully, Joseph explained to the crowded room the events of the preceding weeks. Husbands and wives, who usually would not touch each other in public, fell upon each other, weeping. Anyone passing by the little house and hearing the lamentation would have thought, Indeed, David Ben Shoushan was a good and pious man, but who would have known his death would provoke such an outpouring?

Joseph did not tell Miriam's neighbors, simple people like the fishmonger and the wool comber, all the arguments and stratagems that had been tried in the monthlong struggle for the heart and soul of the monarchs. He told them, simply, that their leaders had done their best. Pressing the case for the Jews had been Rabbi Abraham Seneor, eighty years old, the queen's friend, who had helped negotiate her secret marriage to Ferdinand. He had served as treasurer of her own *hermandad* police force and as tax collector for Castile. Seneor was such a wealthy and important man that when he traveled, it took thirty mules to accommodate his retinue. With him was Isaac Abravanel, renowned Torah sage and the court's financial adviser. He had won his post in 1483, the very same year that the queen's confessor, Tomás de Torquemada, had been named Grand Inquisitor of the Holy Inquisition Against Depraved Heresy.

It was Torquemada who pushed the case for the Jews' expulsion. He had been unable to act on his hatreds during the Reconquest, when the monarchs relied on Jewish money and tax collecting to fund the war against the Moors; Jewish merchants to supply the troops over miles of difficult, mountainous terrain; Jewish translators, fluent in Arabic, to facilitate negotiations between Christian and Muslim kingdoms. But with the conquest of Granada, the war was over; there were no more Arab rulers to deal with; and sufficient Jewish skills, such as translation and scientific knowledge, craftsmanship and medicine, could be found among the *conversos*.

Four weeks passed between the day the monarchs signed the edict of expulsion and the day they finally ordered its proclamation. During that time, they required strict secrecy on the matter, and this encouraged Seneor and Abravanel to hope that their minds were not fixed, that the right persuasions might be effective. Every day during this time, the two men worked to raise more money, to muster more supporters. Finally, Abravanel and Seneor knelt before the king and queen in the throne room of the Alhambra palace. A gentle light, from an alabaster-latticed window behind and above the monarchs, fell on their tired, troubled faces. Each, in turn, argued his case. "Regard us, O King," said Abravanel. "Use not thy subjects so cruelly. Why do thus to thy servants? Rather exact from us our gold and silver, even all that the house of Israel possesses, if we may remain in this country." Then Abravanel made his offer: three hundred thousand ducats. Ferdinand and Isabella looked at each other and seemed to waver.

A hidden door to an anteroom flew open. Torquemada, who had been listening, repelled, to every word praising Jewish loyalty and lauding Jewish contributions to the kingdom, swept into the throne room. The light from the high windows glanced off the gold crucifix he held out before him.

"Behold the crucified Christ whom Judas Iscariot sold for thirty pieces of silver!" he thundered. "Will Your Majesties sell him again? Here he is, take him." He placed the crucifix on a table before the two thrones. "Take him, and barter him away." He turned, in a swirl of black cassock, and strode from the room, not even seeking the monarchs' leave to go.

Abravanel glanced at his old friend Rabbi Seneor and saw a look of defeat. Later, out of hearing of the monarchs, he vented his anger. "As the adder closes its ear with dust against the voice of the snake charmer, so the king hardened his heart against us with the filth of the Inquisitor."

The bookbinder was the very last of David Ben Shoushan's close acquaintances to present himself at shivah. He had waited until the nearing hour of Shabbat had driven the other mourners to their homes. He wanted to speak to Miriam as privately as he could.

His strategy worked. Miriam, who had refused to leave with Don Joseph despite her brother-in-law's sincere entreaties, was alone save for one servant that Don Joseph had required to stay with her. She was irritated when the servant announced Micha. She needed time to think. How could she leave the Kahal, the only world she had ever known? She had been born there. Her parents had lived and died there. Their bones, and now the body of her husband, were buried in the Jewish graveyard. How could a people leave its dead untended? And among Christians! When the Jews were gone, they would plow the land for gain, disturbing the rest of all the beloved dead. And what of the old, the ill, those who could not travel, the women nearing their time? Her mind skipped to the wife of her condemned son. She, at least, would be safe. Able to give birth in her own home, with family to tend to her. Give birth to the grandchild whom Miriam would never see. Her tears began again, and now here was the fool of a bookbinder, and she must try to compose herself.

Micha expressed the usual condolences and then approached Miriam more closely than propriety allowed. He put his face to her ear. "Your daughter," he said, and she stiffened, ready to receive the blow of even more bad news. Swiftly, Micha told of the soldier's visit. Any other time, Miriam's shrewd brain would have led her to wonder why Ruti had tarried so long at the bindery, since her sole purpose in being there was to bring her father news of when he might collect the haggadah. She would have demanded to know what business Ruti had in the binder's storage alcove. But grief and worry had dulled Miriam's mind, and her entire focus was on what the binder said next.

"What do you mean, 'gone'? How can a young girl be gone, alone, on the southern road, at night, with Shabbat beginning? What nonsense is this?"

"Your daughter told me that she knows of a safe hiding place that she could reach before Shabbat. Her intention is to hide there and send you word when she is able to do so. I gave her bread and a skin of water. She said there is food in the hiding place."

Micha took his leave then, hurrying home through the narrow streets of the Kahal. Miriam was so lost in her worry—what secret place could Ruti know?—that she had failed to ask Micha for the haggadah.

But the bookbinder had given the haggadah to Ruti, at her insistence. As he walked toward his house, he wondered if he had done right. He reached his door just as the notes sounded marking the beginning of Shabbat. As he stepped through the door, the thin cry of the ram's horn joined with the wailing of his infants within, and he pushed the thoughts of the girl, and her troubles, away from him. Surely he had enough problems of his own.

As Ruti made the familiar approach to her cave, she, too, heard a faint wailing. Ruti was sure-footed in the dark. She had made this illicit night journey many times, creeping from the room in which her parents slept to snatch a few hours of secret study. But the unexpected sound made her stop suddenly on the steep path, and a scatter of smooth stones loosed themselves and clattered off the path and onto the dry rock below.

The wailing stopped abruptly. "Who is there?" a weak voice called. "For the love of the Savior, help me!"

Ruti barely recognized Rosa's voice. Dehydration had swollen her tongue; terror and pain had exhausted her. For twenty hours she had writhed alone, the contractions mounting. Ruti scrambled into the cave, crying out reassurance and fumbling for the hidden lamp and flints she kept there.

The light flared on a forlorn, bruised figure. Rosa sat with her back to the rock wall, her knees pulled up hard to her chest. Her nightdress was smeared with blood and other fluids. She mouthed the word *water* through cracked lips, and Ruti quickly held the skin to her mouth. Rosa swallowed too much and a second later was bent over, heaving. In the midst of her vomiting, another contraction seized her.

Ruti tried to control her own fear. She had only the most vague idea of how infants came into the world. Her mother had been reticent about matters of the body, considering that Ruti did not need to know such things until she was betrothed. The Kahal was crowded, its homes pressed one against another, so she had heard the cries of laboring women and knew it was a painful, sometimes dangerous, business. But she hadn't conceived of so much blood and excrement.

She looked around for something to wipe the vomit from Rosa's face. All she could find were the pungent cloths in which she had wrapped some dry cheeses for her sustenance during the long nights of study. When she brought these near Rosa's face, the girl heaved again. But this time there was nothing left to vomit.

The night stretched on. The pains came, in the end, without respite. Rosa screamed until her throat was too raw to utter more than a rasping cry. Ruti could only bathe Rosa's forehead and cradle her shoulders through the spasms. Would this baby never be born? She was afraid to know what was happening between Rosa's legs, but as the girl began to scream and flail in a new agony, Ruti reluctantly moved from her position and knelt in front of this woman, whom her brother had loved so much. The thought of him, and the agonies he might very well be undergoing even at the same moment, gave

Ruti a kind of courage. Gently, she eased Rosa's knees apart and gasped with a mix of awe and panic. The baby's dark crown was forcing its way against taut, straining skin. With Rosa's next contraction, Ruti overcame her fear and touched the head, trying to position her fingers so that she might grasp the small skull and ease its passage, but Rosa was too weak to push. For minutes, an hour, there was no progress. They were all three of them trapped. The infant in the unyielding birth canal, Rosa in her agony, Ruti in her dread.

She moved on her hands and knees close to Rosa's battered face. "I know you are tired. I know you suffer," she whispered. Rosa groaned. "But there can be only two endings to this night. Either you find the strength to push this baby out or you will die here."

Rosa howled and raised a hand in a weak attempt to strike at Ruti. But the words moved her. When the next spasm slammed her, she mustered what little strength remained in her body. Ruti saw the crown of the head straining, the flesh tearing. She cupped her hand around the head and eased it out. Then the shoulders. All in a rush, the baby was in her hands.

He was a boy. But the long struggle to be born had been too much for him. His tiny arms and legs flopped limply in Ruti's hands, and no cry came from his still face. With distaste, Ruti hacked at the cord with her small knife and wrapped the infant in some cloth she had torn from her own mantle.

"Is he . . . is he dead?" whispered Rosa.

"I think so," said Ruti somberly.

"Good," breathed Rosa.

Ruti rose up from her knees and carried the baby away to the back of the cave. Her knees stung from the pressure of the stone, but that wasn't why her eyes filled with tears. How dare a mother rejoice in her own infant's death?

"Help me!" Rosa cried. "There's something—" She screamed. "It's the monster! It's coming out!"

Ruti turned. Rosa was squirming, trying to crawl up the wall away from her own afterbirth. Ruti looked at the glistening mass and shuddered. Then she remembered the cat that had birthed her kittens in a corner of the courtyard, and the messy afterbirth that had followed. Stupid, superstitious Christian whore, she thought, giving vent to all the anger and jealousy she felt for this woman. She laid the limp bundle down, took a step toward Rosa, and would have struck her, if the bruises on her face, visible even in the dim lamp light, had not called on her pity.

"You grew up on a farm. . . . haven't you seen afterbirth before?"

Ruti's anger and grief made further conversation with Rosa impossible. Without speaking, she divided the few supplies in the cave—the cheese, the bread and water she'd had from Micha. Half she set beside Rosa.

"Since you care so little for your son, then I do not suppose it is any great matter to you if I bury him according to Jewish rites. I will take the body and see it into the ground as soon as Shabbat ends at sunset."

Rosa let out a great sigh. "Since he isn't baptized, it makes no difference."

Ruti tied her small bundle of provisions in what remained of her mantle. She slung this over one shoulder. Over the other, she placed a sack that contained a small packet, carefully wrapped in layers of hides and tied up with thonging. Then she reached for the body of the stillborn child. The baby moved in her hands. Ruti looked down and saw the eyes of her brother, warm, kindly, trusting eyes, gazing back at her, blinking. She said nothing to Rosa, who had curled herself up into a ball and was already halfway to exhausted sleep, but passed quickly out of the cave. As soon as she was on the path, she descended as fast as was safe with her burdens, fearful lest the child should cry and give away the secret that he lived.

On Sunday, just after the noon bell, all across Spain, royal heralds sounded a fanfare, and citizens gathered in town squares to hear a proclamation from the king of Aragon and the queen of Castile.

Ruti, dressed in the manner of a Christian woman, in ill-fitting clothes she had pilfered from the box in Rosa's bedroom, made her way through the gathering crowd in the fishing village's main square until she was close enough to hear the herald. It was a lengthy text, setting out the perfidies of the Jews and the insufficiency of measures so far taken to stop their corruption of Christian belief.

"Therefore we command . . . all Jews and Jewesses, of whatever age they may be, that live, reside, and dwell in our said kingdoms and dominions . . . by the end of the month of July next, of the present year 1492, they depart from our said kingdoms . . . and that they not presume to return to, or reside therein, or they shall incur the penalty of death." Jews were not to leave with gold or silver or gems; they had to pay all outstanding debts but were not in a position to collect any monies owed to them. Ruti stood there, as the hot spring sunshine beat on her unaccustomed head covering, and felt as if the world had cracked wide open. All around her, people were cheering, praising the names of Ferdinand and Isabella. She had never felt more alone.

There were no Jews in the village, which was why Ruti had chosen to walk there after taking what she could from the Salvador *masía*. She had not considered it theft, as the things she took were for the support of the Salvadores' grandchild. In the village, she had sought out a wet nurse, concocting an implausible story about her sister having been lost at sea. Fortunately, the woman was ignorant and dull, and did not question Ruti's account, or why a woman just delivered of a newborn should have been at sea at all.

As the crowd dispersed, singing and crying out slanders against the Jews, Ruti stumbled across the square toward a fountain, and sat down heavily on its stones. Every path before her was a road into the dark. To go home to her mother was to put herself in the hands of the Inquisitors. To carry on the tenuous pretense of being a Christian was impossible. She had fooled a dull peasant woman, but when she had to find lodging or buy food, the flimsy nature of her story would almost certainly be exposed. To become a Christian—to convert, as the monarchs urged all Jews to do—was unthinkable.

Ruti sat there as the afternoon waned. Anyone who looked closely at the dumpling girl would have seen that she was rocking gently, back and forth, as she prayed to God for guidance. But Ruti had never been the kind of girl that people noticed.

Finally, as the slanting light turned the white stones orange, she arose from her place. She pulled off the head cover of a Christian woman and discarded it by the fountain. From the sack beside her she drew out her own scarf and her surcoat, marked with the distinctive yellow button of a Jew. For once, she did not lower her eyes as she walked through the square, past the staring Christians, but held their gaze and returned it with one of anger and resolve. And so she made her way to the dockside shanty where the wet nurse waited with the baby.

When the sun had set and darkness sheltered her from the eyes of the curious, Ruth Ben Shoushan walked into the sea, the nameless infant tight against her breast, until she stood waist-deep. She unwrapped him, throwing the swaddling cloth over her head. His brown eyes blinked at her, and his small fists, free of constriction, punched at the air. "Sorry, my little one," she said gently, and then thrust him under the dark surface.

The water closed around him, touching every inch of his flesh. She had a firm grip around his upper arm. She let go. The water had to take him.

She looked down at the small, struggling form, her face determined, even as she sobbed. The swell rose and slapped against her. The tug of the receding wave was about to pull the infant away. Ruti reached out and grasped him firmly in her two hands. As she lifted him from the sea, water sluiced off his bare, shining skin in a shower of brightness. She held him up to the stars. The roar in her head was louder now than the surf. She cried out, into the wind, speaking the words for the infant in her hands. *"Shema Yisrael, Adonai eloheinu, Adonai echad."*

Then she drew the cloth from her head and wrapped the baby. All over Aragon that night, Jews were being forced to the baptismal font, driven to conversion by fear of exile. Ruti, exultant, defiant, had made a Gentile into a Jew. Because his mother was not Jewish, a ritual immersion had been necessary. And now it was done. Even as the emotion of the moment brimmed within her, Ruti was counting up the days. She did not have very long. By the eighth day, she would need to find someone to perform his brit. If all went well, this would be in their new land. And on that day, she would give the child his name.

She turned back toward the beach, hugging the baby tightly to her breast. She remembered she had the book, wrapped in hide, slung in a shoulder sack. She pulled on the straps to raise it out of the reach of the waves. But a few drops of saltwater found their way inside her careful wrappings. When the water dried on the page, there would be a stain, and a residue of crystals, that would last five hundred years.

In the morning, Ruti would begin to look for a ship. She would pay the passage for herself and the baby with the silver medallion that she had pried off the leather binding, and where they made landfall—if they made landfall—would rest in the hand of God.

But tonight she would go to her father's grave. She would say the Kaddish and introduce him to his Jewish grandson, who would carry his name across the seas and into whatever future God saw fit to grant them.

Hanna

London, Spring 1996

I LOVE THE TATE. I really do. Despite the fact that its collection of Australian art is pretty sketchy. Not a single Arthur Boyd painting, for one thing, which has always bugged me quite a bit. I went straight, of course, to the Sharansky. I had a compulsion to look up all his works. I knew the Tate had something by him, and I knew I must've seen it, but I couldn't remember the painting. When I finally found it, I knew why. It's not very memorable. Small, early, hardly hinting at the power of the other things that were coming. Typical Tate, I thought. Get the Aussies on the cheap. Still, it was his. I stood there, thinking: My father made it.

Why hadn't she told me? At least I would have grown up with this, which is not nothing: the ability to look at the beauty he left behind. To feel pride in my father, rather than the undertow of shame that had always pulled at my thoughts about him. As I gazed at the picture, I wiped at my eyes with the sleeve of my sweater, but it was no good. Big tears just kept welling up. Standing there, with a class of English schoolkids dressed in kilts and blazers swarming around me, I lost it. I started to sob. First time in my life it had happened to me. It freaked me out. I started to panic, and that had made it worse. Great big embarrassing, overwhelming sobs. I backed up against the wall and tried to brace myself against it while I struggled for self-control. It didn't work. I felt myself sliding slowly down until I was a puddle on the floor. I crouched there, my shoulders shaking. The Brits gave me a wide berth, as if I were radioactive.

After a few minutes, one of the guards came up to me and asked if I was ill, and did I need help. I looked up at him, shook my head, and gulped air, trying to stop the sobbing. But I couldn't get a hold of myself. He crouched down beside me and patted my back. "Somebody died?" he whispered. His voice was very kind. Strong regional accent. Yorkshire, maybe. Yes, I nodded. "My father."

"Ah, well, then. That's hard, luv," he said.

After a while, he held out an arm, and I took it, and together we scrambled awkwardly up. I stammered thanks, then I let go of his arm and stumbled through the gallery, trying to find my way to the exit.

Instead, I found myself in the room with all the Francis Bacon paintings. I stopped in front of the one I've always loved best. It's not a really well-known one and they don't always hang it. There's a man, walking away, sort of leaning into the wind, while a black dog does a tail-chasing swirl in the foreground. It's somehow ominous and innocent at the same time. Bacon just got the dog thing. Absolutely nailed it. But this time, looking at it with my eyes all teary, what registered with me wasn't the dog at all. It was the bloke. Walking away. I stared at it for a long time.

The next day, I woke up in my Bloomsbury hotel room feeling light and washed out. I've always been suspicious of people who advocate a good cry as a remedy for anything. But I really did feel much better. I determined to focus on the conference. There were actually a couple of useful papers, if you could overlook the twit accents of the people delivering them. The art world in England is an absolute magnet for the second sons of threadbare lords, or women named Annabelle Something-hyphen-Something who dress in black leggings and burnt orange cashmeres and smell faintly of wet Labrador. I always find myself lapsing into Paleolithic Strine when I'm around them, using words I'd never dream of using in real life, like *cobber* and *bonza*. In the United States, it's the opposite. Despite my best efforts, I really have to watch myself or I fall right into what they call "linguistic accommodation." I start losing the *t* out of *water* and plopping down a *d* instead, or start saying "sidewalk" and "flashlight" when I mean "footpath" and "torch." I guess I resist it more diligently in England because Mum has always affected a kind of plummy, haut-Pom accent I associate with her snobbery. When I was little, she'd actually wince when I talked to her. "Really, Hanna, your vowels! They sound like a lorry has run over them. Anyone would think I was sending you off to the western *suburbs* every morning instead of the most expensive crèche in Double Bay."

To pull myself out of the funk I'd allowed myself to fall into, I decided to focus on the haggadah catalog essay. What with all the drama back in Boston, I'd fallen behind on the writing, and the printer's deadline was closing in. A journo friend, Maryanne, who was back visiting her family in Oz, had offered me her cottage in Hampstead, so as soon as the conference was over, I holed myself up there for a couple of days. It was a fantastic little wooden house beside a lumpy graveyard, with deep blue ceanothus and climbing roses cascading over mossy garden walls. It was an old house, creaky, with hobbit proportions—low doorways and wavy ceiling beams that looped down to brain the unwary. Maryanne was short, unlike me. Woe to anyone over five feet ten—which was the height of the kitchen ceiling. I'd been to parties there where the tall guests spent all night hunched over, like furtive gnomes.

I thought I'd better call Ozren and let him know where I was at with the essay, but when I rang the museum, the assistant librarian answered with a terse, "Not here."

"When are you expecting him?"

"Exactly, I do not know. Maybe here after tomorrow. Maybe no." I tried his apartment, but the phone rang into empty space. So I just got on with it. I liked writing in Maryanne's little study, a tiny room under the eaves at the top of the house. It had great light and a view all the way across London. On rare days, when it wasn't raining or misty or too polluted, you could see the outlines of the South Downs.

I was pretty confident about the essay. While I hadn't come up with the big drumroll discovery I always hoped for, I felt that the insights about the *Parnassius* and the missing clasps broke new ground. I was leaving the finishing touches till after I'd checked out the white hair sample I'd extracted from the binding. I'd asked Amalie Sutter about it. She'd said I could have any number of zoologists at the museum look at it. "But the people who really know hair—animal, human—are the police." She thought a forensics lab would be the place. Having read rather too many P. D. James novels, I'd decided to leave it till London. I had a fancy to see how the real thing squared with the fiction.

Lucky for me, Maryanne had really good contacts at the Metropolitan Police. She was a contributing editor at the *London Review of Books*, and had written a lot about Salman Rushdie, right after the Iranians threatened to top him. She'd been one of the few people Rushdie had trusted enough to see regularly during the worst years, and she'd wound up getting seriously involved with one of the blokes in his Scotland Yard detail. I'd met him once at a party at Maryanne's—he was definitely a kitchen croucher since he was about six-two and a gorgeous specimen, even when scrunched. He'd finagled an appointment for me at the Metropolitan Police hair-and-fiber lab. "It's against policy," Maryanne warned me, "so you'll need to be discreet about it. But apparently the lab person was just really intrigued by the story about the book and she wanted to do it for you on her own time."

I was also keen to know if Ozren had had a chance to follow up on the *Parnassius,* on checking out which mountain village the haggadah had been hidden in during World War II. If he had any more info, I wanted to include it in the essay. Generally, these kind of essays are dry as Lake Eyre. Very technical, like the report by the French guy in Vienna, Martell. Full of riveting stuff like how many quires there are and how many leaves per quire, the state of the binding threads, the number of sewing holes, and so on, and on, ho hum. I wanted this one to be different. I wanted to give a sense of the people of the book, the different hands that had made it, used it, protected it. I wanted it to be a gripping narrative, even suspenseful. So I wrote and rewrote certain sections of historical background to use as seasoning between the discussion of technical issues. I tried to give a sense of the *Convivencia,* of poetry parties on summer nights in beautiful formal gardens, of Arabic-speaking Jews mixing freely with Muslim and Christian neighbors. Although I couldn't know the story of the scribe or the illuminator, I tried to give a sense of each of them by explaining the details of their crafts and what medieval pavilions of the book were like and where such artisans fitted into the social milieu. Then, I wanted to build up a certain tension around the dramatic, terrible reversals of the Inquisition and the expulsion. I wanted to convey fire and shipwreck and fear.

When the writing stalled, I called up the local Hampstead rabbi and quizzed him on salt— What made it kosher? "You'd be surprised how many people ask me that," he said, a trifle wearily. "Generally speaking, it's not the salt that's kosher, it's the fact that it's the right kind of salt for koshering meat—brining it, in other words, to get the traces of blood out, because Jews who keep kosher don't consume blood."

"So what you're saying is any salt with a large crystal structure could be kosher salt? It doesn't matter if it's mined rock salt or evaporated from the sea or what?"

"That's right," he said. "And also it should have no additives. If it had, say, dextrose, which is added to some salt along with iodine, that would be an issue at Passover, because dextrose comes from corn."

I didn't bother to get him to explain to me why corn wasn't kosher at Passover, since I was pretty sure no one was adding dextrose to any salt that would have been used around the haggadah. But I did use the fact that the salt stains came from sea salt as a way into describing the haggadah's sea voyage, probably at the time of the expulsion, working in quotes from some vivid contemporary accounts of those terrible forced journeys.

I'd got as far as Venice, the Jewish community there in the original ghetto, the pressures of censorship in general and on Jewish books in particular, the threads of commerce and culture that bound the Jewish communities of Italy with those across the Adriatic, the suggestion that the book might have come to Bosnia with an Italian-trained cantor named Kohen. I was so engrossed in the writing—it can get that way, on good days, when you fall down a rabbit hole and the rest of the world disappears—that I almost exploded when the doorbell rang.

I could see a courier's van parked in the lane and I went down to open the door, unreasonably pissed off that some package for Maryanne had broken my concentration. But what the courier had was an envelope for me, from the Tate. I signed and opened it, wondering what it could be. Inside was an express letter that had already been forwarded once, from Boston. The damn thing had been chasing me around the world.

I slit the envelope, curious. Inside was a copy of an ambrotype and a screed in flamboyant handwriting from Frau Zweig. The photo was of a man and women, formally posed—she seated, he standing behind with his hand on her shoulder. Someone, Frau Zweig, I assumed, had drawn a circle around the woman's head, which was turned in three-quarter profile. An arrow pointed to her earring.

Frau Zweig's letter had no preamble, no salutation. It was the written version of a squeal.

"Check it out!!!

"Is the Frau wearing part of our missing clasp??? Remember Martell's description of the wing??? Turns out Mittl died of arsenic poisoning just after he worked on the haggadah. He had the clap (like at least half the citizens of Vienna!) and this Frau's husband, Dr. Franz Hirschfeldt, was his clap doctor. I was only able to find all this because they actually TRIED Hirschfeldt for Mittl's murder. He got off—he was only trying to help the guy—but the case has been written up a lot lately as part of our long-stalled soul search into Austrian anti-Semitism.

"Call me when you get this!"

·   ·   ·

Of course, I got right on the phone.

"I thought you'd never call! I thought, I know Australians are laid back, but how blasé can she be?"

I explained about the letter, and how I'd just that minute received it. "Now, if we can only find the other piece—the roses. I'm still on the hunt, believe me. It's MUCH more fun than anything else I have to do here. . . ."

I glanced at my watch and realized that if I didn't hoof it, I was going to miss my appointment at the Yard. I blathered an effusive thanks to Frau Zweig and shrugged on a jacket as I tried to find the number of a cab. I was way too late to get there on the Tube. While I waited for the cab to show up, I tried Ozren again. I wanted to tell him the news about the clasps, and also maybe have a little brag to him about how well the writing was going. The assistant at the museum was as brusque as she'd been the day before: "Not here. Call back."

I'd ordered a gypsy cab because London black cabs have gotten ridiculously expensive. I almost had a seizure on the way in from Heathrow when the meter for the trip hit the equivalent of a hundred Australian dollars and we weren't even out of Hammersmith. The cab that turned up was a shabby gray van, but the driver was a great-looking West Indian, with wonderful long dreads. The van smelled faintly of ganja. He gave a textbook double take when I said where I wanted to go.

"You Babylon, mon?"

"What?"

"Are you filth?"

"Oh. You mean a rozzer? No way, mate. Just visiting the rozzers."

He stopped a couple of blocks short of the actual address, anyway. "They got sniffer dogs there, mon," he explained. Since he charged me only ten quid for a trip that would've set me back about sixty in the black cab, I didn't complain, even though it was raining. The rain in London isn't like the stuff in Sydney. There, it doesn't rain a whole lot, but when it does, you know about it: big, lacerating downpours that turn the roads into cataracts. In London the drizzle is more or less constant, but it's hardly even worth putting up your umbrella, it's so fine. I've actually won quite a few drinks from people in London, betting on which of the two cities has the higher average rainfall.

There was a woman hovering just inside the main entrance. She came out as soon as I started climbing the steps.

"Dr. Heath?"

I nodded. She was a tweedy matron of about sixty, built like a brick dunny. She looked more like the stereotype of a prison guard than a scientist. She shook my hand in a hard grip and, without letting go, sort of rotated me on the steps and propelled me back down toward the street.

"I'm Clarissa Montague-Morgan." Another Something-hyphen-Something, although this one lacked the Sloany style, and the faint smell she gave off was lab chemicals, not Labs. "I'm terribly sorry I can't invite you in," she said, as if I'd arrived at her flat for high tea or something. "But there are quite strict protocols here, protecting the chain of evidence and so forth. It really is extraordinarily difficult to get permission for a nonstaff visitor, especially a non-law enforcement individual."

I was disappointed; I'd wanted to see how she went about evaluating the hair, and said so.

"Well, I can tell you all about that," she said. "But why don't we just pop in here, out of the rain? I'm on tea break, I have about fifteen minutes."

We were outside a dreary little Laminex-table sandwich shop. There were no other customers. We both ordered tea. Even in crummy establishments in London, you can generally get proper tea, in a pot, unlike the bag on the side of a cup of tepid water that you often get even in high-end American places.

As soon as the tea came, piping hot and very strong, Clarissa started in on the subject of hair analysis. She spoke in clipped, clear, very precise sentences. I wouldn't have wanted her as a witness against me in court.

"The first question we would ask, if it were a crime-scene matter, is, human or animal? That's very easily determined. You look first at the cuticle of the hair. The hair scales on humans are readily identifiable and rather smooth, but on animals they're various—petal shaped, spinous—depending on the species. You make a scale cast to see the pattern more clearly. In the rare case the scales are not definitive, there's always the medulla—the central core of the hair. Cells there are very regular in animals but amorphous in humans. And then there's pigment. Pigment granules in animal hair are distributed toward the medulla, in humans it's toward the cuticle. Have you got the sample there?"

I handed it to her. She put on her glasses, held the envelope up to the fluorescent light, and peered at it.

"Unfortunate," she said.

"What?"

"No root. Under magnification it can reveal a wealth of information. And the DNA's there, of course, so you're out of luck with that. You always get root tissue in hair that has been naturally shed—mammals are shedding about a third of their hair at any given time, you know. . . . But I'd say this hair has been cut; not shed, not pulled. I'll verify all this when I get back to the lab."

"Have you ever solved a crime with a hair sample?"

"Oh, quite a few. The least challenging are the ones where you've got human hair on the body of the victim that you can DNA match with the suspect. Puts the suspect at the crime scene for you. My favorite cases are a bit more involved. There was the chap who strangled his ex-wife. He'd moved to Scotland after the marriage broke up, she still lived in London, and he'd been ever so careful to build a good alibi. Said he was at his parents' home in Kent all day. Well, he *was* there, part of the day. The investigating officer noticed that the parents had a yappy little Peke. The hairs from that dog matched hairs found on the victim's clothing. That wouldn't have been definitive, but it certainly got the investigating officer's attention. A search of the chap's house in Glasgow turned up a recently dug flower bed. We excavated it, and found he'd buried the clothes he wore to do the murder, and they were covered in Pekingese dog hair."

Clarissa glaced at her watch then, and said she'd best be getting back to work. "I'll look at this tonight for you. Call me at home around nine p.m.—here's the number—and I'll tell you what I've found."

I took the Tube back to Hampstead since I wasn't in a rush, and went for a nice soggy walk on the heath. Back at Maryanne's, I heated a mug of soup and went upstairs with it, to polish up my essay. I decided to see if I could reach Ozren at his flat.

Someone picked up the phone on the first ring. A man's voice, not Ozren's, answered with a muted, *"Molim?"*

"Excuse me, I don't speak Bosnian. Is—is Ozren there?"

The man switched easily into English, but kept his voice so low I could hardly make out what he was saying. "Ozren, he is here, but he is not taking calls right now. Who is this, please?"

"My name's Hanna Heath. I am a colleague of Ozren's—I mean, I worked with him for a few days last month, I—"

"Miss Heath." He cut me off. "Could I suggest that someone else at the library help you? It is not a good time. Just now, my friend is not thinking about his work."

I got that feeling you get when you're about to ask a question and you already know the answer, and you don't want to hear it.

"What's happened? Is it Alia?"

The voice at the other end gave a long sigh. "Yes, I am sorry to say. My friend got a call from the hospital the night before last, saying that the boy had a high fever. It was a massive infection. He died this morning. We bury him soon."

I swallowed hard. I didn't know what to say. The conventional thing in Arabic is to say, "May all your sorrows now be behind you." But I didn't have a clue what Bosnian Muslims said to each other to express condolences.

"Is Ozren all right? I mean—"

He cut me off again. Apparently Sarajevans didn't have a lot of time for the easy sentiment of outsiders. "He is a father who has lost his only son. No, he is not 'all right.' But if you mean is he going to jump into the Miljacka, then no, I do not think so."

I felt bleak and sick to my stomach, but this unwarranted sarcasm curdled all those feelings into a clot of anger. "There's no need to take that tone, I'm just trying—"

"Miss Heath, I mean, Dr. Heath. The other book expert said you were Dr. Heath, I should have remembered that. I am sorry I was rude. But we are all very tired here, and rather busy with the funeral arrangements, and your colleague stayed such a long while—"

"What colleague?" It was my turn, now, to be abrupt.

"The Israeli, Dr. Yomtov."

"He was there?"

"I assumed you knew. He said you were working together on the haggadah."

"Oh, uh, sort of." Amitai may well have left a message at my Sydney lab saying he was going to Sarajevo and someone there forgot to tell me. But I doubted it. His presence in the city was baffling. And I couldn't think why on earth he would go to Ozren's apartment. With the man grieving for his dead son, it was beyond peculiar. But I wasn't going to get anything more out of this bloke, that was clear. The handset was practically in the cradle at his end as I was in the middle of asking him to tell Ozren how sorry I was.

I had been of two minds about going on to Sarajevo from London. But suddenly I was calling the airline to arrange a ticket. I told myself it was to find out what Amitai was up to. As I said, I'm not a soggy Kleenex kind of person. A grieving father isn't really my thing at all, so the thought of seeing Ozren again, under these circumstances, could hardly figure into the decision.

I was on hold with the airline for quite a while, working out connections, and as soon as I put the phone down, it rang.

"Dr. Heath? It's Clarissa Montague-Morgan from the Metropolitan Police Forensics Unit."

"Oh, hi. I was going to ring you at nine, I . . ." I wondered how she'd gotten the number at Maryanne's, since I hadn't given it to her. But then, I guess if you work at Scotland Yard, you can easily find out that sort of thing.

"Never mind, Dr. Heath. I just thought that my findings were rather interesting, and I wanted to share them with you. It's a cat hair, we can be definitive about that. The cuticle scales are prototypically sharp and pointed. But there's something quite odd about your sample."

"What's that?"

"It's the cuticle, you see. There are trace particles there, where you don't see them in animals, of very strong dyes in the yellow spectrum. You might see such particles in human hair—if a woman had colored or highlighted her hair, for example. But I've never seen it in an animal sample before. I think you'd agree with me that cats, in general, do not dye their hair."

A White Hair

Seville, 1480

My eyes seep sorrow; water skins with holes.

—Abid bin al-Abras

WE DO NOT FEEL the sun here. Even after the passage of years, that is still the hardest thing for me. At home, I lived in brightness. Heat baked the yellow earth and dried the roof thatch until it crackled.

Here, the stone and tile are cool always, even at midday. Light steals in among us like an enemy, fingering its narrow way through the lattices or falling from the few high panes in dulled fragments of emerald and ruby.

It is hard to do my work in such light. I must be always moving the page to get a small square of adequate brightness, and this constant fidgeting breaks my concentration. I set down my brush and stretch my hands. The boy beside me rises unbidden and goes to fetch the sherbet girl. She is new here, in the house of Netanel ha-Levi, and I wonder how he came by her. Perhaps, like me, she was the gift of some grateful patient. If so, a generous one. She is a skilled servant, gliding across the tiles silent as silk. I nod, and she kneels, pouring a rust-colored liquid that I do not recognize. "It is pomegranate," she says, in an unfamiliar tribal accent. She has green eyes, like the sea, but her skin gleams with the tones of some southern land. As she bends over the goblet, the cloth at her throat falls away and I note that her neck is the golden brown of a bruised peach. I puzzle on what hues I would combine to render this. The sherbet is good; she has mixed it so that the tartness of the fruit still tells beneath the syrup.

"God bless your hands," I say as she rises.

"May the blessings be abundant as rain upon your own," she murmurs. Then I see her eyes widen as they fall upon my work. As she turns, her lips begin to move, and though her accent makes it difficult to be sure, I think that the prayer she whispers is of a different import entirely. I look down at my tablet then and try to see my work as it must appear to her. The doctor gazes back at me, his head tilted and his hand raised, fingering the curl of his beard as he does when he considers some matter that interests him. I have him, there is no doubt of it. It is an excellent likeness. One might say he lives.

No wonder the girl looked startled. It puts me in mind of my own astonishment when Hooman first showed me the likenesses in the paintings that had enraged the iconoclasts. But it is Hooman who would be astonished if he could see me now: me, a Muslim, in the service of a Jew. He did not think he was training me for such a fate. For myself, I have grown accustomed to it. At first, when I came here, I felt ashamed to be enslaved to a Jew. But now my shame is only that I am a slave. And it is the Jew, himself, who has taught me to feel this.

I was fourteen when my world changed. The valued child of an important man, I never thought to find myself sold into bondage. The day the traders brought me to Hooman, it seemed that we passed by the workshops of every trade in the known world. They had a sack over my head so that I would not try to escape, but even through the jute, smells and sounds told which guilds we walked among. I remember the stench rising from the tanners, the sudden sweet tang of the esparto grass in the street of the espadrille makers, the clang of the armorers, the dull beat of the carpet looms, and the stray, discordant notes of the instrument makers testing their wares.

Finally, we came to the pavilion of the book. The guard pulled off my blindfold then, and I saw that the calligraphers' studio occupied the highest ground and faced south, enjoying the best light. The painters' studio was set beneath. As the trader led me through the rows of seated figures, not one raised his head from his work to steal a glance at me. The assistants in Hooman's workshop knew he demanded complete concentration, and how harshly he could punish failure.

A pair of cats lay sleeping, curled together on a corner of his silk carpet. With a wave of his hand, he shooed them off, and signaled me to kneel in their place. He spoke coldly to my guard, and the man bent to slash the filthy rope that bound my wrists. Hooman reached out, lifted my hands and turned them over, examining the places where the twine had cut deep. He barked harshly at the guard before dismissing him. Then he turned to me.

"So, you claim you are a *mussawir*." His voice, as he said this last, was a whisper, the swish of brush across polished paper.

"I have painted since I was a child," I answered.

"So long as that?" he said. The lines around his eyes tightened with amusement.

"I will be fifteen before the end of Ramadan."

"Is that so?" He reached out and ran a long-fingered hand over my beardless chin. I flinched from him, and he raised his arm sharply, as if to strike me for it. But then he let it fall instead to his side and reached into the pocket of his robe. He said nothing, just looked at me until I felt the heat in my face and dropped my head. To fill the silence, I blurted, "Plants, especially, I am skilled at."

He withdrew his hand then, and I saw that there was a small bag of embroidered silk pinched between his thumb and forefinger. From it, he drew a grain of rice of the elongated staple such as Persians prize. He handed it to me. "Tell me, *ya mussawir,* what do you see?"

I stared at the grain, and I suppose my mouth fell slack, like a simpleton's. Upon it was painted a polo match—one player galloping, his horse's tail flying as he bore down upon finely wrought goalposts, another sitting his mount as a servant handed him his stick. You could count the braids in the mount's mane and feel the texture of the rider's brocade jacket. As if this were not astonishing enough, there was an inscription also:

Into one grain, there come a hundred harvests
In a single heart is a whole world contained.

He took back the grain then, and placed into my palm a second one. This was plain—a rice grain such as any. "Since you are 'especially skilled' at plants, you shall give me here a garden. I will have in it such foliage and flowers as you think best reveal your abilities. You have two days. Take your place over there, among the others."

He turned from me then, and picked up his brush. He had only to glance across the room and a boy leaped up, the scarlet he had mixed bright as fire, licking the sides of the bowl he cradled between careful hands.

I do not think it will come as any great surprise when I say I failed his test. I had spent my days, before my capture, making drawings of plants known to my father for their medicinal virtues. Thus, healers separated from him by many miles, and even many languages, might know precisely which plant was meant, no matter by what name they might be used to call it. I had thought it exacting work, and had taken pride that my father thought me fit to do it.

My father, Ibrahim al-Tarek, was already an old man when I was born. I arrived into a house so crowded with offspring that I never expected to win any notice from him. Muhammad, the eldest of my six brothers, was more of an age to have been my father; indeed, he had a son born two years before me who proved, for a while, the chief tormentor of my childhood.

My father was a tall man, even with his slight stoop; handsome, even though the flesh of his face was sunken and scoured with lines. After evening prayers, he would come to the courtyard and sit on the woven mats set beneath the tamarisk, listening to the women's accounts of their day, admiring their weaving, and asking gentle questions about us—the youngest ones—and how we did. When my mother was alive, he sat longest of all with her, and I took secret pleasure in my half-formed understanding of her special place with him. We quieted our voices when he came, and while our games did not stop, they lost intensity. Somehow, we would find ourselves playing nearer and nearer to the place where he sat, ignoring our mothers' meaning frowns and shooing hands. Finally, he would reach out a long arm and clasp one of us to him, and set that lucky one beside him on the mat for a gentle word. Other times, if we played at hide-and-seek, he would let one or other of us use the long folds of his robe as a hiding place, and laugh at our squeals when we were discovered there.

His rooms—the plain cell where he slept, the library dense with books and scrolls, and the workroom crowded with delicate beakers and jars—these we were never to enter. And I would not have dared to do so, if the lizard who had become my secret companion had not escaped my pocket one afternoon and scurried off along the beaten-earth floor, always just out of reach of my pursuit. I was seven at the time, and my mother had been dead for almost a year. The other women had been kind to me, especially Muhammad's wife, who was nearer to my mother's age than my father's other wives. But despite their care, longing for her ate at my heart, and I suppose the little lizard was one of the many ways I tried to fill the hollow places.

I was just outside the library when I finally caught up with him. My hand hovered over his lacquered skin. His tiny heart beat hard. I lowered my hand, and in an instant he poured like liquid through my fingers and, shrinking himself somehow flat as a riyal, vanished under the library door. My father was out, or so I thought, and so I hesitated for just a moment before pushing the door and entering.

He was an orderly man, in general, but that order did not extend to his books. Later, when I worked beside him, I came to know very well the cause of the chaos that greeted me in his library that afternoon. His scrolls lay along one wall of the room, pressed close, floor to ceiling, so that the circular ends of them were forced a little flat, like the cells of a honeycomb. Somehow, there was an order in which he had laid them, and this he held in his head, for he would pull out a scroll without hesitation, open it on his workbench, and then lean down with his forearms across it. He would stay so, for many minutes or very few, then straighten suddenly so that the scroll snapped closed. He would push it aside then and pace to the other wall, where he kept some score or so of bound volumes. Choosing one, he would leaf through its pages, grunt, pace some more, sweep it, also, to one side and grope for his writing stuffs, scrawl some lines on a parchment, fling down his brush, and then repeat the whole again. By the end of it, there would be as many items on the floor as on the bench.

My lizard had chosen an excellent place to elude me, I thought, as I crawled under the bench, pushing aside papers and fallen volumes. I was down there when my father's sandaled feet appeared. I abandoned pursuit of my lizard then, and stayed as still as I could, hoping he had come in search of a single scroll and that he would leave again and allow me to slip away undiscovered.

But he did not leave. He had a branch of some glossy green plant in his hand. He set this down and embarked upon the restless ritual I have described. A half hour passed so, then an hour. I grew stiff. My foot, on which my weight rested, fizzed and prickled beneath me. But I did not dare move. As my father worked on, pages of his writing, started and then pushed aside, fell from the bench, along with the branch he had carried in. When one of his pens landed by me, I had grown bored and daring enough to reach for it. I studied a leaf from the branch. I liked the way the blade was divided by ribs into a pattern that seemed as regular and purposeful as the mosaics that lined the walls in the room where my father and my older brothers received their guests. On a corner of my father's discarded page, I began to draw that leaf. The brush was a marvel to me—a few fine hairs set into the shaft of a feather. With it, if I steadied my hand and concentrated my thought, I could capture exactly the delicacy of the thing I drew. When the ink dried, I replenished it from the spots that fell liberally onto the floor from my father's impatient scratchings.

Perhaps my movement caught his eye. His large hand reached out and grabbed my wrist. My heart fluttered. He drew me out and stood me before him. I did not take my eyes from the floor, so fearful was I of finding anger in that beloved face. He said my name then, softly and without rancor.

"You know you are not permitted to be here."

In a trembling voice, I told him of my lizard, and begged his pardon, "but I thought he might perhaps be eaten by one of the cats."

His grip eased as I spoke. He enfolded my hand in his larger one, and patted it gently. "Well, the lizard has his own fate, as do we all," he said. "But what is this?" He lifted my other hand then, where I still clutched the page on which I'd made my drawing. He studied it for a moment and said nothing. Then he shooed me out of the room.

In the courtyard that evening, I hung back and did not seek his notice, hoping that he might not think to mention my transgression. Later, when I went, unpunished, to my mat with the others, I congratulated myself on the success of this plan.

The next day, after he led the household in morning prayer, my father called me to his side. My stomach heaved. I thought that I was to be punished after all. But instead my father had brought a fine pen, some ink, and an old scroll only partly scribbled over with his jottings. "I want you to practice," he said. "Your skill, if it is developed, could be of much help to me."

I worked hard on those drawings. Every morning, after I set aside the wooden plank on which I learned to write the verses of the Holy Koran—my father insisted that every one of his children attend these lessons—I did not join the games or the chores of the others, but took out my parchment and drew till my hand grew stiff. I relished my father's notice and wished above anything to be of use to him. By the time I was twelve, I had developed some competence. Almost every day after that, I spent some part of my time in his company, helping him to make the books that mended the health of strangers across a score of countries.

By late afternoon of that first day in Hooman's studio, I felt as if those sweet years and all their learning had deserted me entirely. As the daylight waned and my hand trembled from the strain of strokes so minute that an observer could not see that any movement had been made, I lay down on my mat in a corner of the workshop and felt both worthless and afraid. Tears stung my tired eyes, and a sob must have escaped me, for the man settling himself upon a mat nearby whispered gruffly that I mustn't mind. "Be glad that you were not sent instead to the bindery," he said. "There, the apprentices must learn to draw out a strand of gold so fine it may thread through a hole in a poppy seed."

"But Hooman will not keep me if I cannot do this work, and yet it is the only skill I have." On the journey here, after my capture, I had seen other foreign youths my age, clinging terrified to the ship's rigging in a wild sea, breaking rock in the white-hot glare of the quarries, or coming, hunched and filthy, from the dark mouths of the mines.

"You will not be the first to fail, believe me. He will find some task for you."

And so he did. He barely glanced at my rice grain before casting it aside. He sent me off to work with the "preparers of the ground"—those painters and calligraphers whose sight had weakened or hands lost their steadiness. All day I sat with those bitter men, rubbing each parchment with mother-of-pearl, perhaps a thousand times, until the page was polished smooth. After a few days of this, the flesh of my fingers puckered and peeled away in shreds. Soon, I could not hold a paintbrush. That was when I gave way to the despair that I had held back since my capture.

I had not allowed myself to think of home, or how we had left it, in celebration, my father's wives ululating with joy as the hajj caravan departed to the sound of drums and cymbals. I had not allowed myself to think of my father as I saw him last. But now I could not gainsay the images of him, his silvered hair stained with blood and pale gray tissue, a bubble of crimsoned spittle forming on his lips as he tried to mouth the words of his last prayer. His eyes, his desperate eyes, searching my face as the Berber held me, the arm across my throat hard and wide as a tree branch. Somehow, I struggled free of that grip just long enough to shout the words for my father, the words that he no longer had the breath to say: "God is most great! There is no God but God!" I felt a blow and fell to my knees, still crying out for him: "I rely on God!"

There was another, harder blow then. When I came to consciousness, my mouth tasted of iron. I was sprawled facedown in a cart, among our looted goods, moving northward. Painfully, I raised my pounding head to peer through the slatted sides. My father lay there, in the distance, a bundle of rags stirring in the hot desert wind: indigo rags, and atop them, the glossy black feathers of the first vulture.

I lived three months with the preparers of the ground. And now, when I can look back at that time without the fear that attended it—that I would spend my entire life in the tedium of pounding and rubbing and bitter reminiscence—I can accept that I learned a great deal there, especially from Faris. Faris, like me, had been born across the sea in Ifriqiya. Unlike me, he had traveled here voluntarily, to practice his art in the rump state that remained of the once-mighty nation al-Andalus. Unlike the others, he did not boast all the time of the great skill he had once possessed. Nor did he engage in the constant nagging and bickering, as ceaseless as the drone of blowflies.

Faris's eyes were cloudy as a winter sky. Disease had claimed his sight when he was still quite young. Finally, after I had come to know him, I asked why he had not gone to one of the great doctors of the city. I knew there was an operation that sometimes restored the sight of clouded eyes. I had not seen it myself. My father healed with plants rather than probes, but he had shown me once a fine series of drawings on how such a thing might be done by one who had the skill: a delicate slicing into the eyeball, pushing open the clouded window and tipping it backward into the space behind.

"I had this cutting," Faris said. "Twice it was tried on me by the emir's own surgeon. But as you see, the effect was not successful."

"God put him in the fog and keeps him there in penance for the paintings he made." The quavering voice came from old Hakim, who had been a calligrapher. He boasted that he had copied twenty Korans in his career, and that the holy words were etched on his heart. If so, they had not softened it. The only gentle words that came from his pursed mouth were his prayers. The rest of his speech was a relentless stream of bile. Now, he rose from his mat, where he had been dozing, shirking his share of toil. Leaning on his stick, he came hobbling to where we sat at our work. He raised the staff and poked it at Faris. "You wanted to create as God creates, and God has punished you for it."

I touched Faris gently on the arm, questioning, but he shook his head. "Ignorance and superstition," he muttered. "To celebrate God's creation is not the same as competing with the Creator."

The old man raised his voice. "The makers of figured pictures are the worst of men," he intoned, his speech slipping into the orna-mented Arabic of prayer. "Are you so arrogant that you doubt the word of the Prophet?"

"May peace be upon him, I could never doubt his word." Faris sighed. He had clearly had this argument too many times. "I doubt those who claim that saying as a true one. The Koran, which is be-yond all doubt, is silent on such matters."

"It is not silent!" The old man was shrieking now, hunched over, his yellowed beard almost resting on Faris's bowed head. "Does not the Koran use the word *sawwara* to describe how God forms man from a clot? Therefore, God is a *mussawir*. To call yourself one is usurping him who formed us all!"

"Enough!" Faris had raised his voice now. "Why don't you tell the boy the truth of why you are here? There is no tremor in his hand, and he sees as well as a falcon. He was dismissed for defacing the art of painters."

"Dismissed for doing God's work!" the old man cried. "I cut their throats! Beheaded them all! Murdered them to save the soul of the emir!" He was cackling, as if at some private joke.

I was confused. I looked at Faris, but his whole person was trembling. Sweat had formed on his brow. A bead of it dripped onto the polished paper before him, spoiling the hard effort of a morning. When I placed my hand on his arm, he shook it off. Tossing his piece of pearl shell aside, he rose to his feet and pushed the old man harshly out of his way.

Hooman sent for me two days after. I walked through the studio, noticing things that fear had blurred the first time: the bright shards of lapis lazuli waiting to be ground into blue pigment, the flare of light on wafers of silver, and the old man in a screened alcove, shielded from the slightest breeze, as he picked shimmering patches of color from a pile of butterfly wings. Hooman signaled me to kneel where I had knelt before, on a corner of his carpet. He had one of the cats resting across his arms. He lifted it up to his chin and buried his face in the dense fur for a moment, then, unexpectedly, he held it out to me.

"Take her!" he said. "You're not afraid of cats, are you?" I shook my head and reached for her. My hands—work ravaged and hardened now with calluses—sank into her softness. The cat appeared large, but was in fact a tiny thing encased in a cloud of fur. She mewled once, like an infant, then curled herself on my lap. Hooman held out a sharp knife, hilt toward me. I winced. Surely he didn't want me to kill his cat? My face registered my dismay. The lines around his eyes tightened for a moment.

"And where did you think we got the fine hairs for our brushes?" he asked. "The cats are kind enough to supply them." He lifted the second cat into his own lap and stroked under her chin until she rolled over and stretched her neck. He pinched no more than five or six of the long throat hairs and slid the knife under them.

When he looked at me again, the cat in my lap had stretched herself, pulling back my sleeve so that one white paw lay along my forearm.

"Your skin," said Hooman softly. He stared at me. I tried to pull the sleeve of my robe down over my wrists, but he put out his hand and stopped me. He continued to stare without seeing me. I knew the look. It was the way my father had studied a tumor, forgetting as he examined it that there was a person to whose body the thing attached. When Hooman spoke again, it was to himself and not to me. "It is the color of blue smoke . . . no . . . it is like a ripening plum, with the pale down still dusting it." I fidgeted, misliking this close attention. "Be still!" he ordered. "I must paint this color."

And so I sat there until the light failed. When that happened, he dismissed me abruptly, and I went to a vacant pallet in a corner of the studio, not knowing why I had been summoned.

The next day, Hooman handed me the new brushes he had ordered to be made, the cat's hairs secured in a feather shaft. There were brushes of various sizes. A few contained just a single hair, for the making of the very finest of lines. He gave me, also, a piece of polished parchment. "Give me a portrait," he said. "You may choose for a subject anyone in the studio."

I chose the boy who assisted the gold beaters, thinking that his smooth, almond-eyed face best resembled the ideal youths pictured in so many of the finest books. Hooman tossed the page aside after barely looking at it. He stood, abruptly, and signed for me to follow him.

Hooman's private quarters were set at a little distance from the studio, down a high-vaulted passageway. The room was large, the divan covered in brocade and piled with cushions. In a corner stood a set of small coffers, boxes for the keeping of books. Hooman knelt before the finest of them and opened its carved lid. He lifted the little book inside with great reverence and placed it on the reading stand. "This is the work of my master, the pearl of the world, Maulana of the delicate brush," he said. He opened the book.

The image shimmered. I had never seen a painting like it. Within the bounds of a small page, the painter had made a world of life and movement. The script, in Persian, I could not read, but the illumination was eloquent enough. The scene depicted a princely wedding. There were hundreds of figures, yet no two of them were alike: every turban was of a different fabric, variously tied. Every robe was of a diverse design, embroidered or appliquéd with a hundred kinds of arabesques. Looking at the painting, you could hear the rustle of silk and the swish of damask as the crowd swirled around the royal bridegroom. I had been used to see the people in pictures depicted face-on or in profile, but this painter had not restricted himself so. The heads he drew were caught in every aspect—some three-quarter profile, some tilted downward, others chin raised. One man's head was turned completely from the painter, so that all we saw was the back of an ear. But more striking still: every face was unique, as in life. There was such expression in the eyes that I felt as though I could read the thoughts of these men. One beamed, prideful at his inclusion at the feast. Another smirked, perhaps contemptuous of the ostentatious display. A third gazed awestruck at his prince. A fourth grimaced slightly, as though his new sash pinched him.

"You see, now, what makes a master?" Hooman said at last.

I nodded, unable to take my eyes from the image. "I feel . . . that is, it seems . . ." I gulped a nervous breath and tried to collect my thoughts. "That which he paints has mass to it, as in life. It is as if any of these men could walk off the page and live."

Hooman drew his own breath sharply. "Exactly," he said. "And now I will show you why I have this book, and why it is not any longer the treasured property of the prince for whom it was made."

He reached down then and turned the page. The next picture was just as dazzling, just as vivid. It depicted the procession bringing the bridegroom to the house of the bride. But this time my gasp of appreciation turned to one of dismay. The difference between this image and the last was that every one of the revelers had a rough red line slashed across his neck.

"Those who did this call themselves iconoclasts—smashers of idols—and they believe they do the work of God." He closed the book, unable to bear looking at the desecration. "They paint the red line to symbolize the cutting of the throat, you see. The images, thus robbed of life, no longer compete with God's living creation. Five years ago, a band of these fanatics sacked the pavilion of the book and destroyed many notable works. It is for that reason that you see no portraits produced here. But now a request has come that may not be refused. I want you to try your hand again at this." He dropped his voice then. "I seek a *likeness*. Do you understand?"

Determined not to fail this second test, I scanned the faces in the studio. In the end, I chose the old man at work with the butterfly wings. There was an intensity to his expression that I thought I might be able to capture. As well, his composure, and the economy of his movements, would be a help to me.

It took me three days. I had stared at the old man, trying to see him as I had learned to see an unfamiliar plant, emptying my mind not just of all other plants I had painted before, but of all my assumptions about what a plant is—that it has a stem, that leaves come off at such and so an angle, that leaves, in fact, are green. Just so, I looked at the face of the butterfly man. I tried to see it as a pattern of light and dark, void and solid. I made a grid on the page in my mind and divided up his face as if each square of the grid was a separate thing, containing its unique information.

I had to ask for several more pages before I found the way to something that looked alive. My hand shook as I passed my work to Hooman. He said nothing, and his expression did not change, but he did not cast the work aside. When he looked up at me, he scanned my face, and then ran his hand across my chin, as he had at our first meeting.

"An unexpected opportunity has presented itself, and I believe you may be suitable. The emir wishes to appoint a *mussawir* to the harem. Since such a person must, of course, be cut, it is better if he is a youth not yet come to manhood, just such as yourself."

I felt the blood run out of my face. I had been too nervous to eat more than a bite or two since my return to the pavilion. Now there was a sound like surf in my head. From far away I could hear

Hooman's voice: ". . . a life of utmost ease and who knows what ultimate influence . . . a small price, in the long run . . . future uncertain otherwise . . . many others here who paint at least as well as you will ever do . . . ."

I must have tried to stand; perhaps I got to my feet. In any case, just before I fell, I saw my own arm sweeping across Hooman's table, bowls tipping, and a tide of lapis blue flowing across the floor.

When I awoke, they had laid me on the brocaded divan in Hooman's private quarters. Hooman stood over me, the lines around his eyes crinkled like crushed vellum. "It seems we will not have to trouble the eunuch maker after all," he said. "How fortunate, how very fortunate we are, to have been so deceived by you."

My mouth was dry. When I tried to speak, no words came out of it. Hooman handed me a goblet. There was wine in it. I drained the cup.

"Steady, child. Surely the Muslim daughters of Ifriqiya do not quaff their wine so thirstily. Or are you deceiving us as to your faith, also?"

"There is no God but God and Muhammad is his messenger," I whispered. "I have not tasted wine until this day. I drink it now because I have read that it gives courage."

"I do not think that you are lacking in this thing. It has taken courage enough, surely, to live this lie among us as you have done. How came you here, in the *jellaba* of a boy?"

Hooman knew well enough that I had been sold into his service by the Banu Marin, who kidnapped me from the hajj caravan. "It was my father's wish that I disguise myself after we left our city," I said. "He believed I would be more comfortable making the desert crossing if I could ride beside him, rather than stay confined all day to an airless litter. He said also that I would be safer in the guise of a boy, and events proved him right. . . ." At that, the memories pressed on me, and the wine, on my empty stomach, made my head spin. Hooman placed a hand on my shoulder and pressed me gently back against the cushions on his divan. He stared at me and shook his head. "I have always thought myself the most observant of men. Now that I know the truth, it seems impossible to have not known it. I must be getting old, indeed."

He reached out and ran his hand once again over my face, but this time, he used a touch light as mist. He sank down onto the divan beside me. My clothing had already been loosened, and his hand easily found my breast.

Much later, when I could think about it clearly, I consoled myself that there were many worse ways in which I might have been raped. I had been waiting for it, in truth, from the moment the Berber raiders appeared at the top of the dunes. Hooman's famous hands did not leave a mark on me. When I struggled and thrashed and tried to get free of him, he subdued me with a skillful grip that pinned me helpless without hurt. Even when he came into me, there was no roughness in it. The shock of it was greater than the pain. I believe I suffered less, in truth, than many brides upon their wedding bed. And yet, when he finally let me rise, and I felt the wetness dribble down my thigh, my legs folded up under me and I knelt by his divan and vomited sour wine on his fine carpet until there was nothing more in me. He gave a great sigh then, adjusted his robes, and went out.

Alone in his quarters, I wept for a long time, composing the list of my life's losses, from my mother's death to my father's murder to my own enslavement. And now, the new, darker place in which I found myself, robbed of my body in the most fundamental way. For an instant, there was a consoling thought; that my father, dead, could not know of this dishonor. But then I realized he must have died imagining just this. I retched again, but there was nothing left.

The eunuch Hooman sent to me was very young. The sight of him reminded me that there were others who suffered losses worse even than mine. The floodtide of my self-pity began to abate. He was a Persian boy who spoke no Arabic. I expect Hooman had considered that, in choosing whom to send. He removed the fouled carpet with an efficient discretion, and then returned with a silver ewer and basin of warmed rosewater. He gestured that he would help me bathe, but I dismissed him. The thought of another's touch was repulsive to me. He had brought a robe for me to wear, and he took my old garments, holding them far in front of him as if they smelled. Which I suppose they may have done.

I did not sleep for most of that night. But as the sky lightened toward dawn, I realized with relief that Hooman would not return, and fell into an exhausted, dream-racked doze, in which I sat again on the straw mats, listening as my mother hummed at her loom. But when I tugged on her robe to seek her attention, the face that turned to me wasn't her smiling, patient one, but the ravaged face of a corpse, whose pitiless gaze passed right through me.

The boy woke me, arriving with a new set of clothes. I had not known what to expect. Was I to be got up as an odalisque, since I was destined for the harem? But the clothes he brought were noblewoman's dress: a simple gown of rose-pink silk, which looked very well against the color of my skin. There were some lengths of Tunisian chiffon in a darker rose, the fabric so fine that I had to double it to wind a veil that would cover my hair. Last of all, there was a blue-black haik in the lightest merino that fell from the crown of my head to the tip of my toes.

When I had dressed, I sat on the divan, feeling despair welling once again inside me. The voice of Hooman interrupted my weeping. He stood outside, asking my permission to enter. Astonished by this, I did not answer. He asked again, in a louder tone. I could not school my voice, so I said nothing.

"Prepare yourself," he said, and pushed aside the curtain. I felt panic rise in me, and I backed away from him.

"Be at peace. After this meeting, it is unlikely that we will ever see each other again. If you have questions regarding your work, matters of material or technique, you are to write to me of these things—I am right, I think, to recall that you are lettered? Most strange, in a girl—another reason we were deceived—and you are to send me, from time to time, samples of your work for review. I will reply and instruct you as best I can, and if I see areas that require improvement, I shall write of them to you. Although you are far from attaining the rank of master, you are to assume a position that normally would fall to one of such a standing. No matter your feelings toward me, do not discredit my skills, or your own. The work that we do here will live longer than any of us. Remember that. It is of far greater importance than any . . . personal sentiments."

A sob escaped me. He winced, and spoke to me coldly.

"Do you think you are the only one brought here bound and humbled? The emira herself walked through the gates of this city in chains, driven at spear point before the warhorse of the man who became her husband."

He did not need to tell me this: the scandal of the emir's beautiful captive had been the subject of salacious gossip among the preparers of the ground. Listless as I had been during those months, this story had captured my interest, for it touched on certain aspects of my own history. Everyone, it seemed, had an opinion on the matter.

Early in his rule, the emir had famously refused to pay the city's customary tribute to the Castilians. From now on, he said, "the royal mint makes nothing but sword blades." Constant skirmishes had been the result. In one of these engagements, the emir had ridden into a Christian hamlet and carried off the daughter of its tax collector. No one had thought anything about the emir taking spoils of war; the Prophet Muhammad himself had taken wives from among both Jews and Christians when his forces had defeated them. It was understood that captives joined the harem from time to time, and rape was briefly legalized as marriage. What had shocked the city was the emir's elevation of this captive over the emira, a Sevillian noblewoman, the emir's cousin and the mother of his heir. She had been banished from the palace to her own house outside the walls from where, it was said, she schemed constantly, eliciting support from the Abu Siraj, whose ferocity in matters of faith was notorious. The rift had passed far beyond the walls of the harem, and even beyond the city, and rumors now said that the crown of Castile was looking for a way to exploit it.

The Persian eunuch entered then, with goblets of sherbet. Hooman signaled me to take one. "The emir has charged me with his orders in this, and I tell these to you now so that there will be no misunderstanding. The emir is, as you know, very often gone from the city on campaign. He has confided that at such times he misses the sight of the emira, and desires likenesses to which he can turn at such times.

"You will be painting, therefore, for an audience of one. The images will be seen only by the emir, only when he is alone. Your work will be safe, therefore, from the iconoclasts, and you need not fear charges of heresy."

I had been looking at my hands, wrapped around the goblet, for most of his speech, unable to bear the sight of his face. But now I looked up sharply. He stared back at me, as if challenging me to speak. When I said nothing, he lifted the haik and handed it to me.

"Put this on now. It is time for me to take you to the palace."

My mother had taught me to walk in my veil as if I had no feet, gliding over the ground as gracefully as a waterbird slides upon liquid. But after so many months living as a boy, I had lost the art. I stumbled several times as we made our way through the crowded alleys of the medina. In their summer attire, the merchants in the courtyard of the caravansary looked as colorful as a field of flowers: there were men in striped Persian linens, Ifriqiyans in *jellabas* of saffron and indigo, and here and there, moving circumspectly, yellow-breeched Jews, their heads bare of turbans as the law required, even under the punishing sun of noonday.

The sun was blinding as we finally reached the approach to the palace. The walls had been white once, a hundred years ago, but the iron-rich earth had bled through the stucco and warmed them to a rosy madder. With my one uncovered eye, I looked up and saw the inscriptions carved on the great arched doorway, countless numbers of them, as if the voices of a thousand believers had been caught in

the swirling stonework, trapped on their way up to the heavens:
There is no victor but God.

I entered the huge wooden doors of that place knowing that I
might never leave it. An old woman, her face cracked like a dry wadi,
received me into the women's quarters.

"So this is al-Mora?" said the crone. *The Moorish woman.* In this
new life, I was not even to have a name.

"Yes," Hooman replied. "May she give good service." And so I
was passed off with no more thought than a hand tool. I parted from
Hooman without returning his farewell. Yet as the old woman drew
the door closed beside me, I had a sudden urge to turn and run
through it, to clutch even his despised arm and beg him to deliver me
from the palace, whose walls loomed suddenly like a prison.

Since my capture, my mind had fed on every kind of fear. I had
pictured myself performing crushing toil in the foulest places—
beaten, exhausted, abused. Now, the old woman held out a hand for
the haik, which she passed to a beautiful boy, I judged not more than
seven or eight years old, who hovered behind her. She signed for me
to take off my sandals. A pair of embroidered slippers lay ready for
me inside the door. She beckoned me to follow her, and we passed
from the portico into rooms whose magnificence has stolen the
words from the mouths of the poets.

At first, it seemed as if the walls themselves were in motion, the
ceiling swooping down toward me. I raised a hand as if to steady
myself, and closed my eyes against the dazzle. When I opened them,
I forced myself to look at one small area of the room only, at tiles
glazed and colored in blue-green and brown, black and lilac, so cun-
ningly laid that they seemed to be spinning in pinwheels around the
lower third of the wall. When I could look up, I saw that the swooping ceiling was in fact a lofty dome, from which descended an upside-
down forest of plaster, each shape an echo and a harmony of its
neighbor.

We walked, it seemed, through an endless series of chambers as lovely as they were various. Once or twice, a serving girl slid by, nodding deferentially to the older woman and shooting a swift, curious glance at me. In the soft slippers we passed silently through mazes of slender pillars and beside long pools, still as mirrors, reflecting the numberless entwined inscriptions above.

Eventually, we began to climb stone steps into an elevated section of the palace that narrowed as it rose. When we reached the top, the old woman, breathing hard, leaned against the wall and groped in the folds of her garments for a large brass key. She fitted it into the lock and opened the door. The room was round, its white walls bare of decoration except for some remarkable carved and painted stone spandrels around a pair of arched windows set high into the far wall. There was little furniture: a small silk prayer rug, Persian and very fine; a slim divan covered in bright cushions; a low table inlaid with mother-of-pearl; a book stand; and a carved sandalwood chest. I walked to the windows, stood on tiptoe, put my hands to the sill, and hoisted myself up so I could glimpse the outside. The view was of gardens thick with fruit-bearing trees. I recognized fig, peach, almond, quince, and sour cherry, their boughs so laden with fruit that you could not glimpse the ground below them.

"It will do for you?" The old woman spoke for the first time, her voice cracked with age, but cultured. I dropped down from the sill and turned, embarrassed. "They told me of your task, and it seemed good to find you a room alone for the peace and privacy of your work. This one has not been used since the last emira left the palace."

"It will do very well," I said.

"A girl will bring refreshment. You must tell her if you require anything particular. You will find that most needs can be met here."

The old woman turned to go, signaling for the page to follow her. "Please," I said swiftly, my head full of questions. "Please, if it is permitted to ask, why are there so few people in the women's quarters?"

The old woman sighed and pressed the heel of her hand to her temple. "May I sit?" she said, already easing her frail body down onto the divan. "I do not think you have been long in the city."

It was a statement more than a question.

"You come here at a troubled time. The emir presently has but two thoughts in his mind: the war with Castile and his appetite for the girl he now calls Nura." Her eyes, buried in that lined face like a pair of bright pebbles, scrutinized me closely. "In his folly, he has sent away his cousin Sahar and all her household. The emir trusts no one. He knows his cousin and her taste for conspiracy. He also has sent away the concubines—handed them off hastily to his favorite officers, lest any one of them became a tool of vengeance for Sahar and her son, Abu Abd Allah, who keenly feels his mother's insult.

"Nura, of course, came here with nothing but the torn robe she stood up in. She has a small retinue to serve her; myself and a handful of half-trained tribal girls who have no allegiances in the city."

I was too astonished by her frankness to say anything. I glanced with concern at the turbaned boy standing by the wall. "Do not worry about him," she said. "He is Nura's brother. He was to be taken for a catamite but, as a favor to his sister, the emir forbears for now from having him used so. I am to train him for a page." She sighed again, but a hint of a smile lit her eyes.

"You think me irreverent? It is natural to lose your reverence of princes when you've seen them limp-membered and panting like dogs. I was concubine to this emir's grandfather. The old goat's flesh already stank of death when he took me to his bed. This one," she said, inclining her head in the direction of the throne room, "I suckled, and I've watched him ever since. A brat born and a bloody tyrant grown. He had the head struck off every high-bred youth in the city who might have challenged for the throne. And now he has it, and he throws it all away and puts the very city at risk, simply to scratch an itch in his crotch."

She tossed her head then and cackled. "I have shocked you! Do not mind my rough old tongue. I have grown too bent with age for any further bowing." She stood, rising with an ease that belied all her talk of infirmity. "You will see how it is, soon enough. You are to attend the emira tomorrow. I will send a girl to fetch you."

I wanted to thank her for her openness, but as I began to speak, I realized that I had no idea how to address her. "Please, what is your name?"

She smiled then, and gave another cackle. "My name? I have had so many names I hardly know which one to give you. Muna, I was called when the old man wished his withered cock was hard enough to have me every night. 'If wishes were horses, beggars would ride,' eh?" The cackle died, and her face folded in on itself. "Then I was Umm Harb for the strong son I bore—just one of the brave youths who died at the point of his half brother's sword. It seems that name sticks in throats now. So they call me just Kebira."

The old one. So she was the old one, and I was the Moorish woman, and neither of us a person beyond the withering of our flesh or the blackness of our skin. I had a sudden glimpse of my own future here in this gorgeous prison, bitter and nameless and worn out in the service of the contemptible. The pain of the thought must have shown in my face, for she took a sudden step toward me and wrapped me in a swift, bony embrace. "Be careful, my daughter," she whispered, and then she slipped away, the boy following like a shadow.

I woke the next morning to a scent of roses that thickened as a sun whose heat I could not feel beat down on the massive outer walls. It is a perfume that even today brings back a memory of despair. I dragged myself from the divan, washed, dressed, performed my prayers, and waited. A girl came with warm water for my toilet and another with a tray containing apricot juice, steaming rounds of flat bread, a dish of creamy yogurt, and a half dozen ripe figs. I ate what I could, then waited again. I feared to leave the room lest the summons to the emira come while I was absent.

But the noon prayer came and went, then the evening prayer, and finally the night, and I rose from my prostrations and went to bed.

No summons came that day, or the one after. Finally, on the afternoon of the third day, it was Kebira and the page who came to fetch me, and Kebira's old face was drawn and grave. She closed the door and leaned against it. "The emir has taken leave of his reason," she said, speaking quickly and in a cracked whisper, even though in that empty palace it was hard to know whom she thought could overhear. "He rode in last night, late, and was with the emira until after dawn prayers, when he had a meeting with the nobles. Well, he conducted his business with them and then demanded that they stay and join him in the courtyard for some entertainment. This," she said, and her lips thinned as she hissed the words, "turned out to be watching his wife take her bath."

"Implore the pardon of God!" I could not credit her words. For a man to glimpse another's wife unveiled was a matter for blows. To deliberately display a wife's body to others was an unthinkable dishonor. "What manner of Muslim could do such a thing?"

"What manner of *man* could do such a thing? A man grown coarse and arrogant," Kebira said. "The nobles are appalled—most of them suspected it was some pretext of the emir's to have them executed; they left here fingering their necks. And as for the emira, well . . . You will see for yourself how she is. The emir has heard that you are here, and he demands an image to take with him when he rides out again tomorrow after dawn prayer."

"But that is impossible!" I cried.

"Impossible or not, you are commanded to do it. He was furious that none had yet been made. So come quickly with me now." Outside the door, the beautiful page waited, carrying the box of pigments that Hooman had sent to me.

When we reached the salon, Kebira knocked upon the door and said, "I have brought her."

A serving girl opened the door and slid out, so swift to exit that she almost knocked me over. One side of her face was red, as if from a recent blow. Kebira pushed me forward with a hand to the small of my back. The boy glided in behind me, set down the box, and slid

back out again. I realized that Kebira herself had not entered the
room, and I felt a moment of panic when I realized that she did not
plan to present me, or to in any manner ease this first encounter. I
heard the door gently pulled closed behind me.

The emira stood with her back to me, a tall woman in an embroidered gown that fell heavily from her shoulders and spilled across the
tiles at her feet. Her hair, still slightly damp, hung freely down her
back. Its colors were remarkable, for it was not one hue only, but
many: dull gold entwined with warm, gleaming umber, lit from beneath with streaks as red as sudden tongues of flame. Despite my
nerves, I was already thinking how to render it. Then she turned, and
the look on her face drove all such thought from my mind.

Her eyes, too, were a remarkable color: a dark gold like honey.
She had been weeping, the redness around her eyes and the uneven
mottle of her pale skin testified to that. However, she wept no longer. The look upon her face was not grief, but rage. She held herself
rigid, as if she were braced with an iron flagstaff. Even so, or perhaps
because of the effort her regal posture was costing her, she shook all
over with a barely discernible tremor.

I made my salaam, wondering whether she expected some kind
of bow or prostration. She said nothing in reply, but stared at me,
and then she raised a long hand with a disdainful gesture. "You have
your commands. Get to work."

"But perhaps you would like to sit, *ya emira*? For this will take
some time. . . ."

"I will stand!" she said, and the eyes brimmed suddenly. And stand
she did, for the rest of that entire, interminable afternoon. My hands
shook under her fierce, wounded gaze as I opened my box and arranged the materials. It took all my will to empty my mind of noisy
thought, and even more to raise my gaze to her, and study her as I
had to do.

I do not need to tell of her beauty, for it has been celebrated in
many famous poems and songs. I worked without a break, and she
did not move or take her eyes from me. When the *muezzin's* call for

salat sounded, faint and plaintive through the thick walls, I asked her if she wished to stop and pray, but she just shook that heavy mane of hair and glared at me. Finally, when it was about to become neces- sary to call for the lamps, I realized I had a likeness. The decorations I could complete in my own chamber. These would be, perforce, simple, but if what the emir craved was an image of his wife—her beautiful face and her queenly bearing, then he had it here.

I rose to show her my work, and she regarded it with that same unfliching, angry stare. If her expression changed at all, it was in the brief flicker of a fleeting triumph. She stood there still, even as I packed my implements. Only when the young page entered did she stir. "Pedro," she said, calling him to her. She leaned to him, caressing his brow with a swift, tender kiss. Then, she turned her back on us and did not acknowledge our going.

After making my delayed prayers, and taking some food and drink, I looked again at the parchment with fresher eyes and mind. Then I saw clearly what she had accomplished. She had stood to show that she was unbowed by whatever mad acts of violation the emir had committed. The image he would carry away with him was of a queen unconquered, a rock he could not break. And I realized something else, as I studied the portrait. There was no hint in it of the tears or the trembling that revealed the struggle behind her show of strength. I knew that she did not want to display these to him, and in their concealment I had become her accomplice.

I worked through the night to complete that first work for my new lord. Just before the dawn prayer, Kebira scraped on my door, and I handed it to her, too exhausted to care what her reaction might be. But I might have known that she would let me have her view, whether sought or not.

"'The angels enter not into a house where there is a dog or a like- ness'—are those not the words of our Prophet? If the emir seeks to displease God, he has found the right instrument in you. But I won- der if even the emir wished for so faithful a rendering." She smiled, a bitter little smile of satisfaction, and left me. Too tired to fathom whether I had been insulted or complimented, I made my prayers without waiting for the call, then fell onto my divan and into a long, deep sleep.

In the weeks that followed, it sometimes seemed as if I never fully awakened. I had thought that there would be other calls to the emira's chamber, chances to make portraits more carefully composed and thoroughly realized than that first fevered effort. But no summons came, day following day.

The emir had ridden out not to some skirmish, but on a long besiegement of a Christian hilltown that commanded some of the city's key supply roads. For the first weeks of his absence, I dedicated myself to learning what lay within my new world, exploring the precincts of the women's palace and making drawings of its tiles, fountains, and carved inscriptions. But even with this pleasant distraction, many hours remained unfilled by either occupation or companionship.

As I wandered aimlessly from one beautiful, silent chamber to another, I longed for meaningful tasks such as I had done for my father, and pined for the bustle of our mud-walled house. There were times I sighed even for the abrasive banter of the preparers of the ground. In those months, at least, I had had too much toil to taste the poison of idleness. Some days, I kept entirely to my room, breathing the stultifying scent of the roses until the light failed and I fell upon my divan in an exhaustion that I had not even earned.

After many weeks of this, I sent a sherbet girl to seek out Kebira. I begged her to ask the emira to let me paint her, but the request met with curt rejection.

"Well, can I not paint you, or the young page?" I asked the old woman. The boy, Pedro, had followed one day and stood behind me as I drew an inscribed spandrel, watching my hand for hours with his strange, unchildlike stillness. But Kebira would neither sit for me nor allow the boy to do so.

"It is one thing for the emir to condone the sin of image making, but I will not willingly further such work," she said. She was not harsh about this, merely resolute. I wondered at the strength of her faith, that had withstood so many years of battering. I wondered how she felt now, in the service of a *rayah*.

She laughed at me gently when I asked this. "As far as the world is concerned, she is not any longer a *rayah*. The emir put it out that she had embraced Islam, praise be to the Almighty. But I know it is not so. I hear her pray her infidel prayers, call on her Jesus and her Santiago. . . . Neither of them seem to hear her, though. . . ." And she cackled again, and left me.

That night, I lay on my pallet thinking how little I knew of infidels' religions and wondering why Christians and Jews were too stiff-necked to recognize the Seal of the Prophets. I wondered from what manner of home the emira had been snatched, and if she missed the familiar rites of her childhood.

The scent of the roses had waned, and their petals had fallen when the emir returned to the palace, riding to the gate by night so that the people would not see him, bloodied from a battle injury. When Kebira came to fetch me in the morning, she told me that he had taken a cut to the brow from an arrowhead that must have been dipped in foulness, for the wound, which had gashed his eyelid, stank and festered. Nevertheless, he had gone straight to Nura without troubling to have the cut seen to, or even removing his rank battle dress. Kebira's wrinkled face folded as she told me this, as if the stench of him lingered in her nostrils.

Like a fool, I welcomed the summons to the emira's rooms, so hungry was I for something to do. I hurried through the salons and up the stone stairs, eager for the challenge of work. The minute I saw her I realized my folly. The woman I faced seemed lit from within by a rage that burned her like a torch. Her hair was elaborately dressed with strings of pearls and bright jewels that seemed to catch the glow of its red strands, but she wore only a plain haik draped loosely around her. The servant who had brought my box slipped out silently, and I looked down, trying to escape the dreadful wrath of her gaze. She shrugged the haik from her shoulders. It fell to her feet, and when I looked up, she stood there before me, naked.

I looked away again, deeply shamed.

"This"—the word was a hiss such as a snake might make—"is what my lord wills you to paint today. Get to your work!"

I knelt and reached for my pen. But it was no use. The tremor in my hand and the grief in my heart would not allow me to grasp it. The words of the Koran were seared in my mind. *Tell the believing women to lower their gaze and be modest, and to show of their adornment only that which is apparent, and to throw their veils over their bosoms.* How then could I make an image of a naked woman? To do so was to defile her.

"I said get to your work!" Her voice was louder now.

"No," I whispered.

"No?" she hissed.

"No."

"What do you mean, you insolent black slut?" Her voice was a high, thin whine, such a cry as a cornered fox makes.

"No," I said again, my own voice breaking. "I can't do this. I know what it is to be raped. You can't ask me to assist your rapist."

She advanced on me, picking up the heavy lid of my box. I felt a wind whistle past my ear as she raised it. I did not even lift a hand to defend myself, but waited for the crack of it against my skull. She threw the lid, and it splintered against the stone floor. Then she picked up a jar of pigment and hurled that. The worm scarlet splattered against the tile and oozed down the wall. She was crazed, looking around for the next object to fling. I stood, and grasped her by the wrists. She was far taller than I was, and stronger, but as I touched her, she sagged against me. I bent for her haik and covered her. I folded my arms around her, and we fell together onto her divan and lay there, soaking the cushions with our grief.

. . . . .

From that morning, we spent our days and nights together, and I made many beautiful images of her. I made them for her, and for myself, for the pleasure of doing it. Oh, I made the emir a picture to take back with him to his failing siege, but it was not a picture of his wife. I painted a figure reclining so that the face was not recognizable; a lewd arrangement of thighs and breasts that were nothing like Nura's. They say the fool was pleased with it.

Her voice, in the darkness. "You were crying out in your sleep." She laid a long hand gently on my breast. "Your heart is pounding so."

"I dreamed of my father—the vulture tearing at— No, I cannot speak of it. . . ."

She held me close and sang to me softly in a low hum that recalled the soft voice of my mother.

Another night. I woke and turned to her. The moonlight glinted on her eyes, which were open, staring into the darkness. I touched her hand gently, and she turned to me. Her eyes caught the light. They were wet with unspilled tears. Slowly, she began to speak.

They had impaled her father on the iron gatepost of his home. They killed her mother in front of him as he writhed in his helpless agony. She had to listen to his screams of pain and grief as she hid with her sister and brother in a space under the floorboards of the house. Then they set the house on fire. She had run out, clutching her brother by the hand, and slipped in her mother's blood. Her sister had kept running; her brother stayed to help her. She saw a knight snatch up her sister and drag her up onto his horse. What became of her, she was never able to discover.

She tried to run with her brother, but in her confusion they fled right into the path of a great war stallion. "I thought the hoofs would mash us to pieces," she said. But the rider wheeled his mount. "I looked up and saw his eyes, peering down at me through the slits in his visor. He unhooked his mantle and threw it down to cover me."

The other knights recognized that their lord had made his claim. When someone tried to drag away her brother, she had clung to the boy and pleaded with the emir to save him.

"He granted me that, and in return, God forgive me, I feigned desire for him. To this day, he has no idea how my gorge rises and my inner parts shrivel when he comes near me. When he is inside me, all I can feel is the agony of my father, skewered like a beast. . . ."

I placed my hand on her lips then. "No more," I whispered. I stroked her skin as gently as I could. In the dark, I could not see my own dark hand, just the shadow of it as it passed across her pale flesh. I tried to make my touch as soft as a shadow. After a very long while, she reached for my hand and kissed it. "After he . . . after I lay with him, I never thought I would be able to take pleasure in another human's touch," she said. She turned, and raised herself on one elbow, gazing at me. I think it was at that moment that I let myself forget I was a slave. It was a mistake to do so; I recognize that now.

Within the month, rumors began to reach us from elsewhere in the palace of urgent meetings and bitter debates. The enemy had broken the emir's siege and retaken control of the hill. Our forces had been pushed back to the surrounding plain, where they were scrambling to retain control of the main supply road. It was crucial that they not fall back any farther, especially at this time, for if they lost the road before the fruits of the harvest were brought in, it would be a hungry winter for the city.

The swollen rose hips were ripening around the high window, and the emira reclined on a divan beneath it as I painted her, trying to match the glow of the reddening fruits to the lights in her hair. Her face was serene, although still heavy with sadness. She fingered the pearl at her throat.

"Your craft, it makes you fortunate, I think. You at least will have something to offer to a conquerer, if the city should fall."

I dropped my brush. It fell on the tile, smearing the pale glaze with a saffron slash.

"Do not look so astonished," she chided me. "These walls are thick, but even the thickest walls can be breached by treachery."

"Do you have reason to fear it?" I could barely speak.

She tossed her head and gave a small laugh. "Oh yes, I have reason. The emir's son, Abu Abd Allah, comes and goes from the palace, his faction growing with his father's waning fortunes."

She was tall, as I have said, and could easily reach up to the high windowsill. She stood up then and grasped the spray of rose hips resting there. As she reached out, the roundness of her belly revealed itself. She, too, was ripening. But of this, she had not spoken. And so therefore neither had I. Was the child as repulsive to her as the act by which she had gotten it? Until I could fathom her feelings on the matter I thought it best to keep my peace.

She turned the rose hips in her hands. "I do not rely upon seeing these roses budding here again in the springtime," she said. Her voice was neither sad nor frightened, simply matter-of-fact. But the expression on my face must have been dreadful, for she came to me then and folded me in her arms. "We cannot know the future, nor can we change it," she whispered gently. "It is best to be realistic about such things. But we have the time we have been given. So let us treasure it while we can."

And so I tried to do so. And there were hours, sometimes even days, when I pushed aside my fear. I had dreaded growing old in this palace. Now, that was all I hoped for.

The nights grew cold. I woke, shivering, at dawn. I was alone on the bed. She was kneeling by the window, praying in a language that was not Arabic. She had a small book in her hands.

"Nura?"

She twitched in surprise and motioned as if to hide the book. Her face as she turned to me was severe.

"Do not call me that!" Her tone was harsh, and I flinched. She softened. "It recalls to me the stink of the emir."

"What name should I call you?"

"Before, I was Isabella. It is my Christian name."

"Isabella . . ." I said, tasting the unfamiliar sounds on my tongue. I held out my arms. She came to me. I asked if I might see the book, having glimpsed a flash of color as she closed the pages. Together, we looked at it, a beautiful little volume, filled with luminous illustrations. The paintings were neither aiming to exactly copy nature nor were they an idealized, formal representation, but some interesting melding of the two. The saint or the angel in one picture might be indistinguishable from that in the next, but there would be details, such as a little dog, or a wooden table, or a sheaf of grain, that the artist had represented just as if from life.

"It is called a Book of Hours," she said. "Just as you have prayers such as *fajr* at dawn and *maghrib* at sunset, and so on, Christians, too, have prayers for morning, which are called matins, and vespers, for evening, and others, so that the day may be marked by devotion."

"This artist is very skilled," I said. "Can you read the words?"

"No," she said. "I cannot read Latin. But I know most of the prayers by heart, and the pictures help me in my devotions. The doctor brought me this book. It was very kind of him."

"But the doctor . . . surely he is a Jew?"

"Yes, of course. Netanel ha-Levi is a devout Jew. But he respects all faiths, and people of all faiths seek his care. Otherwise how would he work for the emir? This book was given to him by the family of a Christian patient who had died."

"But isn't it dangerous, that he knows you pray to the Christians' God?"

"I trust him," she said. "He is the only one I really can trust. Except for you."

The golden eyes looked into mine. Her hand touched me lightly on the side of my face. She smiled one of her rare, bright smiles. I turned my head against her shoulder, hoping to catch some of her warmth, while it lasted.

·   ·   ·   ·

There were horsemen. They had breached the outer walls and now they trampled the myrtle court. Their hooves rang on the stone. There was the clang of metal, and shouting.

Her hand was cool on my hot shoulder. "You were crying out in your sleep," she whispered. "Were you dreaming of your father again?"

"No," I said. "Not this time."

We lay silent for a while in the dark.

"I think I know what was in your dream," she said at last. "I, too, am consumed by thoughts of it. The time for silence is past. We must make plans. I have been thinking about what would be best."

"Allahu akbar," I murmured. "'What is, is. What will be, will be.'"

She turned to me then and took my hands in hers.

"No!" she said, her tone firm and urgent. "I cannot trust my life to God's will as you do. I must make provision for my survival, and my brother's, and that which I carry." She placed a hand on her swollen belly. At last, she had acknowledged it. "I stand in need of protection. If it seems as if we will lose the city, Abu Abd Allah will have me killed, I am certain of it. He will use the chaos of battle to cover his deed. He does not want to see this child born."

She rose, restless, and paced the chamber. "If it were not for Pedro . . . There was a convent near our house. The nuns there were very kind to me. I used to think how fortunate they were, those women, shut away together. Safe. Not married off in girlhood, facing childbed after childbed till fever or bleeding claimed them. I always wanted to join them." Her lovely head drooped then. "I was going to be a bride of Christ, and instead—" She cradled her belly protectively. "I think the nuns would still take us, in spite of everything. We would be safe there; the sisters have the ear of the Castilian monarchs."

I sat up and looked at her in disbelief. I could not bear to spend my life locked up in the prison of an infidel convent. How could she propose it?

"They would not let us be together. Not as we are now," I said.

"No. I know that," she said. "But we would see each other. And we would be alive."

But what kind of life? Lying about a faith I did not profess. Forced to worship idols. Living without true prayer, without my art, without human touch. But all I said was, "Your brother could not come."

"No," she said. "Pedro could not come."

When the emir learned of his wife's pregnancy, he sent the doctor directly to her. Even in Ifriqiya, I had heard of this man, Netanel ha-Levi. His healing skills were as renowned as his poetry, which he wrote in a most beautiful Arabic. I had not thought a Jew could master our poetry, the language of the Holy Koran. But it seemed that in al-Andalus, where Jews and Arabs worked side by side, such a thing was not unheard of. I had picked up some verses of his and scanned them with a skeptical eye, and at the end of it, that same eye brimmed with tears from the beauty of his words and the emotion he conveyed through them. Ha-Levi's counsels to the court went well beyond medical matters, and Kebira said that if it were not for the doctor's wisdom and his ability to sometimes temper the emir's crueler impulses, our ruler might have slipped off his throne long since.

I was working on the last touches to a likeness of Pedro when the doctor came. The emira had asked me, of late, to give her a rest from posing. I thought it because she was uneasy at the change in her appearance as the child grew within her. To me, her rounder face, her heavy breasts were very beautiful. But she insisted that I give her a respite. One day, she swept the dates off the large polished silver serving dish and propped it up against the wall. She made me stand before it and stare at my reflection. "Make a portrait of yourself. I want you to see what it is like, this relentless business of being looked at." She laughed. But she was serious, and kept at me, despite my hesitation. She disliked my first attempt. "You must look more kindly at yourself. Look with tenderness," she said. "I want the portrait I would paint of you, had I your skills." So I stared at my face and tried not to see the lines that had been etched there by loss and anxiety. I painted the girl I had been in Ifriqiya, the protected, cherished daughter who had not known fear and exile, who had never been a slave. That portrait, she approved of. "I like this girl. I shall name her Muna al-Emira, the emira's desire. What do you think?"

I gave a strained smile and tried to look flattered. Just at that moment a flock of swallows swooped past the high window, blocking the sun. I felt a sudden coldness. At the time, I did not know why. But later I realized. Kebira had told me, that first day, which seemed so very distant, but really was not so, that Muna had once been her name. The wishes and desires of the powerful can be fickle things. I knew this. But I knew it in that deep place where one hides knowledge that is inconvenient, or too painful to admit, even to oneself.

Usually, I withdrew when the doctor came, but this day he motioned me to stay as I made to take my work away. He walked over to look at the portrait of Pedro, and complimented it, and asked a question about my training. I told him I had been in the service of Hooman, and he looked astonished at that, considering my gender. Without going into detail I explained that I had passed myself off as a youth for a time, because it had seemed safer. He did not press this, but neither did he let me be. "No," he said. "It is not court training. I see something more in your work. Something . . . less practiced. Less sophisticated, perhaps. Or perhaps I should say, more honest?" So I told him then of my father, and the pride I had taken in learning to illustrate his medical texts.

"Then I know your work," he said, his voice full of surprise. "I admire it. The herbals of Ibrahim al-Tarek have no peer." I flushed with pride. "But what befell your father? How came you here?"

I related to him the story, in brief. He bowed his head when I told him of my father's ignominious end, unburied and abandoned. He cast a hand over his eyes and murmured a prayer. "He was a very great man. His work saved many lives. I mourn his untimely death."

He looked at me then, a physician's evaluating look. There was great compassion in his gaze, and I understood why his patients admired him so. "He was lucky, to raise a child such as you, who could assist him so ably. I have only one child, and he . . ." He did not finish that sentence. "Well, I wish I had someone as skilled as you to work with me."

The emira spoke then, and her words almost stopped the blood in my veins.

"Then you must take her, *ya doktur*. Al-Mora will be my gift to you for the great care you have bestowed on me. Kebira will see to it. You may take her today, if you like."

I looked at Nura, my eyes imploring, but her face was very calm. Only a slight pulse in the vein at her temple revealed that she felt anything at all, even as she threw me off like a used robe.

"Go now and gather your things," she said. "You may take your box of pigments, and the books of gold and silver leaf. I want the doctor to have the very best." And then, as if it were an afterthought, "*Ya doktur*, I will send my brother, Pedro, with al-Mora, if you will take him. He can serve as her apprentice, as she is, as you say, very skilled." She turned to me then, and there was just the slightest catch in her voice. "Teach him well for me."

So that was it. Once again, I was just a tool, a thing to be used and then passed along into other hands. This time, it seemed, I was a shield for the protection of her brother. She had turned away, listening to the doctor, who was expressing his thanks most effusively. I was, in his words, "a most generous gift." The great doctor, so noted for his compassion. Where was his compassion for the feelings of a slave?

I was standing there, shaking, as they discussed me. The emira did not even turn to look at me directly. She waved her hand at me, as if I were a blowfly to be shooed away.

"Go," she said. "Go now. I have dismissed you."

Still I stood there.

"Go *now*. If you want to live."

She thought she was saving my life. My life, and the life of her beloved brother. She had calculated it, lying there in the dark. Worked it all out—When? How long ago?—without consulting me. She knew that with the Jew, we would survive whatever befell the city, because Abd Allah and his faction also leaned heavily on ha-Levi's skills, and would seek his counsel. My hands shook as I gathered up my things. I had the portrait I had been working on in my hand when she strode across the room and snatched it from me. "This, I will keep. And take care to leave behind the other also—the portrait of Muna." Her eyes, as she said this, glistened.

I wanted to say, Not this way. I wanted to say, Give me more days, more nights with you. But she had turned away from me, and I knew the strength of her will. She would not turn back.

So, that was how I came here, and here I have been, living and working, for almost two years. Perhaps she was right to send me away like that, but I will never feel so in my heart. What she feared came to pass: when the emir's wound turned poison, Abd Allah took the chance to overthrow him. Nura had made her provisions by then, and went straight to the protection of the nuns. In due season, the doctor delivered her there of a healthy girl, whose existence causes Abd Allah no anxiety. Not that he will likely reign long enough to need a successor: the breath of the Castilians blows ever hotter. And of what will come to any of us then, who knows. The doctor does not speak of it, and there are no signs of any preparations under way if we need to quit this place. I think that he has come to believe himself indispensable, whoever is in power. But I am not sure the Castilians will have the wit to value his skills.

For myself, for now, I have little of which to complain. Here, I am called al-Mora no longer. When I came to live in the doctor's palace, he asked me my name, so that he might present me to his wife. When I said al-Mora, he shook his head. "No. The name given to you by your father."

"Zahra," I said, and realized that the last time I heard my own name was from the lips of my father, as he cried out to warn me that the raiders were upon us. "Zahra bint Ibrahim al-Tarek."

The doctor has restored much to me, in addition to my name. The work I do for him is important work, and I feel connected by it to my father. Every plant, every diagram I make, I offer to the glory of Allah in my father's memory. The doctor, although a very devout Jew, respects my faith and allows for the prayers and the fasts. When he saw me making prostrations on the bare floor of his library, he sent me a prayer rug even finer than the one I left behind at the palace. His wife, too, is very kindly and commands her large staff with gentle discipline that breeds a calm and peaceful house.

In the spring, on the full moon, she invited me to join the family at table for one of their feasts. Although the invitation surprised me, I did so, out of respect, although I did not drink the wine that has a very large part in their ritual. The rite was performed in Hebrew, which I did not, of course, understand. But the doctor took great pains to explain to me what was meant by the various things that were said and done. It is a very moving feast, celebrating the delivery of the Hebrews from slavery in a land called Mizraim.

He confided in me, at one point, that he felt great sadness, because tradition commands that a father must teach his son this ritual, in all its particulars, and the doctor's only son, Benjamin, is a deaf-mute and cannot understand. He is a sweet boy, not at all simple. He likes to spend time with Pedro, who has become Benjamin's body servant, in fact, and my apprentice in little but name. It has been good for Pedro, taking care of this needy youngster. It has given him purpose more than he was able to find in his work with me, for which he had, in truth, little aptitude. I think he has grown to love the boy, and that helps him when he misses his sister. I try to fill her place with him as best I can, but we, each of us, know that nothing can make up for such a loss as ours.

I have taken it upon myself to make, in secret, a set of drawings for Benjamin that together will tell the story of the world as the Jews believe it to have come to be. The doctor has many books about his faith, but they have words only, not pictures such as the Christians use to help them understand their prayers. The Jews, it seems, are as reluctant to make images as we Muslims are. But as I considered Benjamin, in his silence, shut out of understanding the beautiful and moving ceremonies of his faith, I remembered Isabella's prayer book, and the figures in it, and how she said it helped her to pray. The idea came to me that such drawings would be of like help to Benjamin. I cannot think the doctor or his God will be offended by my pictures.

I ask the doctor or his wife from time to time, and they are always pleased to explain to me, how Jews conceive of this or that. I reflect on what they say, and try to devise a way to illustrate it so that a young boy can understand. What struck me is how much of it I already know, for the Jews' account of God's creation differs only slightly from the correct version given in our Holy Koran.

I have made images that show God's separation of light from dark, the making of land and water. I have drawn the earth he created as if it were a sphere. My father held this to be so, and I lately had a conversation with the doctor on this subject. While difficult to grasp such a thing, he said, it was a fact that the calculations of our Muslim astronomers are far more advanced than any others. He said if he had to choose between the opinion of a Muslim astronomer and the dogma of a Catholic priest, he would not choose the priest. And anyway, I prefer compositions using circles and curves. They are harmonious, and interesting to draw. I want these drawings to be pleasing, so the boy will want to look at them. To that end, I have filled the garden of paradise with the animals of my childhood, spotted pards and fierce-jawed lions. I hope he will enjoy them.

I am using the last of Hooman's fine pigments to make this present for the Jew, and I wonder what he would think of that. Soon, I will have to send to the market for more pigments, but the works the doctor needs, for his texts, require only simple inks, not lapis or saffron and surely not gold. So I am taking pleasure in the use of these for what may be the last time in my life. I still have one or two of the brushes made from the fine white hair of Hooman's cat, but these, too, are wearing out and beginning to shed.

Sometimes, when I ask the doctor about his faith, I find myself swept up in the narrative of his stiff-necked people, so often punished by their disappointed God. I have painted the story of Nuh's flood, and Lut's city of fire, and his woman turned to a hill of salt. I have struggled hard to devise pictures that make clear all the elements of the spring festival story, which is, at times, quite terrible. How to show, for example, why the king of Mizraim yielded at last to Musa? How to show the horror in the tale, the terror of the plagues, or the deaths of the firstborn? I want Benjamin to understand that the children in my picture all are dead, but in my first attempt they might just as well have been asleep. Yesterday, an idea came to me. I thought of the iconoclasts and how they had slashed red lines across the throats of the human likenesses in the books they had defaced. So I painted dark shapes over each sleeping child's mouth, to represent the dark force of the angel of death, stealing away the breath of life. The image I have made is exceedingly disturbing. I wonder if Benjamin will understand it?

My plan is to present these pictures to the doctor at the next occasion of this feast, which is soon. I am working now on a picture of the feast itself. I have set the doctor at the head of the table with Benjamin beside him, and his wife, finely dressed, and her sisters, who share this house. Then it came into my head to add myself to the gathering. I have given myself a gown of saffron, ever my favorite color, and in doing so have used the very last I have of that pigment. I am pleased with this picture, above all those that I have done. It seemed good to me to sign it with my name, which the doctor has returned to me. I used the last of my fine brushes to do it, the last of those with but a single hair.

I have set my head at an attentive angle, and imagine myself listening as the doctor tells of Musa, who defied the king of Mizraim, and used his enchanted staff to win his people's freedom from their bondage.

If only there could be another such staff, to free me from my bondage. Freedom, indeed, is the main part of what I lack now in this place where I have honorable work, and comfort enough. Yet it is not my own country. Freedom and a country. The two things the Jews craved, and which their God delivered to them through the staff of Musa.

I set down the cat-hair brush and imagine how it might be to have such a staff. I see myself, walking to the coast. The great sea would part, and I would cross it, and make my way, in slow stages, down all the dusty roads that lead toward home.

Hanna

Sarajevo, Spring 1996

THERE WAS NO United Nations escort waiting for me at the Sarajevo airport, for the simple reason that I hadn't told anyone I was coming.

It was late when I arrived; the connection through Vienna had been delayed two and a half hours. It was jarring, going from the Vienna airport, which is basically a big, shiny shopping mall, and arriving not quite half an hour later at the spare, empty, still-militarized terminal in Sarajevo. Outside, the cab pulled away from the airport entrance into streets still unnaturally dark—they'd repaired very few streetlights, which was a blessing, I suppose, given the blasted and depopulated appearance of the neighborhoods surrounding the airport. Although I wasn't in quite the same state of dread as on my first visit, I was still pretty relieved when I got into my hotel room and locked the door behind me.

In the morning I called Hamish Sajjan at the UN office and asked him if I could sneak a look at the new display room at the museum. The official ceremony was still twenty-four hours away, but he said he was sure the museum director wouldn't mind if I had a look before the crowds of invited dignitaries descended.

The wide boulevard, formerly known as Sniper Alley, on which the museum was located, had been given a Potemkin village spruce-up in the two weeks I'd been gone. The rubble piles had been moved, and some of the worst shell holes in the road had been filled in. A tram was running again, which somehow gave the street a sense of normalcy. I walked up the familiar stairs of the museum and was escorted to the director's office for the compulsory Turkish coffee. Hamish Sajjan was there, beaming. For once, the UN was getting a bit of credit for doing something right in Bosnia. After sufficient pleasantries, he and the director escorted me down the hall to the new room, which was guarded by two security men. The director punched in the code. You could hear the slick new bolts retracting.

The room was lovely. The light was perfect: even and not too bright. State-of-the-art sensors scribbled out lines that tracked temperature and humidity. I checked the graphs: 18 degrees Celsius, perfect, plus or minus 1 degree. Humidity, 53 percent. Right where it should be. The walls gave off the clean, sharp scent of fresh plaster. I thought that just being in this space would be a morale boost for most Sarajevans, a big contrast with their broken city outside.

A specially made case occupied the center of the room. The haggadah rested inside, under a pyramid of glass that would protect it from dust and pollution as well as from people. On the walls were the related exhibits—Orthodox icons, Islamic calligraphy, Catholic psalter pages. I walked past each one of these, slowly. The selection was excellent, thoughtful. I sensed Ozren's intelligence at work. Each piece had something in common with the haggadah—similar materials or a related artistic style. The point—that diverse cultures influence and enrich one another—was made with silent eloquence.

Finally, I turned to the haggadah. The case had been crafted by a master cabinetmaker from a handsome burled walnut. The book was open at the Creation illuminations—the pages would be turned on a schedule so as not to expose any one page to too much light.

I looked down through the glass, thinking about the artist, about the brush dipping into saffron pigment. The cat hair that Clarissa Montague-Morgan had identified—cut cleanly on both ends, stained with traces of yellow pigment—had come from the artist's paintbrush. Spanish brushes were more commonly squirrel or miniver fur. Fur from the throat area of two-month-old Persian longhairs, specially bred for the purpose, was the brush material of choice for Iranian miniaturists. *Irani qalam.* Iranian pen. It was the name for the style, rather than the implement. And yet these miniatures were not at all Iranian in style or technique. So why had an illuminator working in Spain, for a Jewish client, in the manner of a European Christian, have used an Iranian paintbrush? Clarissa's identification of this anomaly had been great for my essay. It had given me an excuse to riff on the way knowledge had traveled amazing distances during the *Convivencia,* over well-established routes linking the artists and intellectuals of Spain with their counterparts in Baghdad, Cairo, and Isphahan.

I stood there, gazing, wondering which had done the traveling—the brush or the artisan who assembled it. I imagined the stir in the Spanish atelier the first time someone used one of these superior brushes, felt the soft swish of the fine white hair across the carefully prepared parchment.

The parchment.

I blinked, and then leaned closer to the vitrine, doubting the evidence of my own eyes. The floor seemed to drop away from under my feet.

I straightened and turned to Sajjan. His broad smile faltered when he saw my face, which must have been as white as the fresh plaster. I tried to control my voice.

"Where is Dr. Karaman? I need to see him."

"Is something the matter—the vitrine, the temperature?"

"No, no. There's nothing wrong . . . nothing wrong with the room." I didn't want to start a fuss in public. There would be more chance of dealing with this if we acted quietly. "I need to see Dr. Karaman—about my essay. I just realized I forgot to make a necessary correction."

"My dear Dr. Heath, the catalogs are printed already. Any corrections—"

"Never mind. I just need to tell him. . . ."

"I believe he is in the library; shall I send for him?"

"No, I know the way."

We went out, the new door closing and locking with a soft click behind us. Sajjan started translating the director's very formal leave-taking, which I abbreviated rudely by walking backward away from them down the corridor. It was all I could do to avoid breaking into a run. I burst through the library's large oak doors and hurried down the narrow alley between the stacks, almost knocking over an assistant librarian busy reshelving volumes. Ozren was in his office, seated at his desk, talking to someone whose back was turned to me.

I plunged through the door without knocking. Ozren stood up, surprised at the intrusion. His face was gray and haggard. His eyes were smudged with dark circles. For a moment I'd forgotten that his son had been in the ground for just a little more than forty-eight hours. My anxiety retreated for a moment behind a wave of feeling for him. I moved forward and put my arms around him.

His body was absolutely rigid. He stepped backward, out of my embrace.

"Ozren, I'm so sorry about Alia, and I'm really sorry to burst in on you like this, but I—"

"Hello, Dr. Heath." His voice, cutting me off, was flat, formal.

"Hallo, Hanna!" The man in the chair was rising, slowly, as I turned.

"Werner! I didn't know—thank goodness you're here." Werner Heinrich, my teacher, the best forgery-spotter in the business, would be able to see it instantly; he'd be able to back me up.

"Of course I'm here, Hanna, *Liebchen*. I wouldn't miss tomorrow's ceremony. But you didn't tell me that you were coming. I imagined you were back home by now. It is wonderful you will be here for the ceremony."

"Well, if we don't move fast, there won't be a ceremony tomorrow. Somebody's stolen the haggadah. I think it must have been Amitai, he's the only one who—"

"Hanna, my dear, slow down. . . ." Werner reached for my hands, with which I'd been wildly gesticulating. "Tell us calmly. . . ."

"It's nonsense." Ozren spoke over Werner. "The haggadah is locked in the vitrine. I secured it there myself."

"Ozren, it's a fake, the thing in the vitrine. It's a fantastic fake—the oxidized silver, the stains, the smeared pigments. I mean, we've all seen fakes, but this is outstanding. It's a perfect replica. Perfect, except for one thing. The one thing that can't be replicated because it hasn't existed for three centuries." I had to stop. I could hardly breathe. Werner was patting my hand as if I were a hysterical child. His hands, his hard, craftsman's hands, had the usual perfectly manicured fingernails. I pulled away my ugly untended mitt and raked it through my hair.

Ozren was pale now. He stood.

"What are you talking about?"

"The parchment. The sheep they made it from, that breed—*Ovis aries Aragonosa ornata*—it's been extinct in Spain since the fifteenth century. What they've used, the pore holes, they're all wrong . . . the size, the scatter . . . it's parchment made from a different breed. . . ."

"You could hardly tell that, surely, from inspecting one page." Ozren spoke with a tense, thin-lipped terseness.

"Yes, I can." I took a deep breath, trying not to hyperventilate. "It's a subtle thing, unless you've spent hours comparing old parchments. I mean, to me it's bloody obvious. Werner, you'll see it right away, I know you will." Werner's face was creased now with concern. "Where is Amitai?" I demanded. "Has he already left the country? If he has, we're in deep shit. . . ."

"Hanna. Stop this." Werner's soft voice had a stern edge. I realized that the look I'd taken for concern was actually irritation. He wasn't taking me seriously. To him, I was still the pupil from the antipodes, the girl who had so much to learn. I turned to Ozren. He, surely, would listen to me.

"Dr. Yomtov is right here in Sarajevo," Ozren said. "He is the guest of the Jewish community for the ceremony tomorrow. He hasn't been near the haggadah. The book has been locked in the vault at the central bank from the day you left here last month, until we moved it, under heavy guard, yesterday. It was in the box designed to your specifications, which you yourself watched me seal, until I personally broke the wax and the strings and deposited it in the vitrine. It was not out of my hand for one moment of that time. The vitrine is armed with state-of-the-art equipment, and the room is crisscrossed with sensors. There is a twenty-four-hour surveillance camera and a guard. You are making a fool of yourself with these accusations."

"Me? Ozren, matey. Can't you see? The Israelis—they must have wanted this book for ages . . . you must've heard all those rumors, during the war. . . . And Amitai, he's an ex-commando, did you know that?"

Werner shook his silvery mane. "I had no idea." Ozren just looked at me, blankly. I couldn't understand why he was so passive. I wanted to shake him. Maybe he was still in shock over Alia. And then I thought of the weird phone call I'd made to his apartment.

"What was Amitai doing at your place, anyway, the other night?"

"Hanna." His voice had been cold. Now it was icy. "I risked my life to save that book. If you are suggesting . . ."

Werner raised his hand. "I am sure Dr. Heath is not suggesting anything. But I think we'd best make an examination." His brow was furrowed. His hands were trembling. What I'd said about Amitai clearly concerned him. "Come, my dear, and show us what it is that troubles you so."

Werner, unsteady, took my arm. I was suddenly worried about him. He would be so shocked when he saw the fake.

Ozren rose from his desk and led the way back down the interminable corridor, through the exhibition halls where glaziers were at work, replacing the plastic sheeting that still covered many of the museum's shattered windows. Ozren nodded to the guards and punched his code into the keypad.

"Can we take it out?"

"Not without disarming the entire system," Ozren said. "Show us what it is that you think you are seeing."

I pointed.

Werner bent over and peered into the vitrine. He examined the place I'd indicated for several minutes. Then he straightened.

"I'm relieved to say I can't agree with you, my dear. The scatter is entirely in keeping with many examples I've examined from that type of parchment. We can, in any case, compare the page with the documentation photographs you took at the time of the stabilization, to set your mind at rest."

"But I sent those negatives to Amitai! He used them to make this fake, don't you see? And then he'll have replaced my photos with pictures of this . . . thing. You've got to call the police, now, and alert the border authorities, and the UN. . . ."

"Hanna, my dear, I am sure you are mistaken. And I think you must be a little more circumspect about throwing around such wild accusations against an esteemed colleague."

Werner's voice was low and soothing, still treating me like an overexcited child. He laid a hand on my arm. "I've known and worked with Amitai Yomtov for more than thirty years. His reputation is impeccable. You know that." He turned to Ozren then. "But perhaps, Dr. Karaman, to reassure Dr. Heath, we'd best disarm the system and do a full inspection of the codex?"

Ozren nodded. "Yes, of course. We can do that. We must do that. But I will have to inform the director. The system is designed so that it requires both of us to input the codes that authorize a shutdown."

The next hour was the strangest and most uncomfortable of my professional life. Werner, Ozren, and I went through the codex page by page. Everywhere I pointed out an anomaly, they both professed to see nothing irregular. Of course they sent for the facsimile photos, which were in perfect accordance with the book, as I knew they would be. But Werner's conviction was unshakable, and my opinion wasn't worth much, compared with his. Ozren, who, as he said, had risked his life for the book, was adamant that any security breach was impossible. In the end, a rat's tooth of self-doubt began to gnaw at me. Little hot beads of sweat broke out all over my skin. Maybe it was all the stress of the last few days: Mum's accident, the shock of finding out about my father, the news about Alia. And something else. When I'd seen Ozren, his forlorn eyes, his exhausted face, I'd felt something. Something unfamiliar to me, but I knew what it was. I knew then that I'd come back to Sarajevo because of him, not just for the book. I'd been missing him, desperately. They say love is blind. I started to believe that I was seeing things.

At the end of the inspection, Ozren and Werner turned to me.

"Well, what do you want to do?" Ozren said.

"Do? Me? I want you to get a search warrant and check out every last jockstrap and handkerchief in Amitai's suitcase. I want you to close the borders in case he's already given the codex to an accomplice."

"Hanna." Ozren's voice was low. "If we do these things, we will be creating an international incident over an allegation that both Dr. Heinrich, whose expertise is without question, and I, myself, believe to be false and without foundation. Because of the special tensions here, once such an allegation is made, certain people will chose to believe it, even if it proves groundless. You will be sowing intercommunal dissent over the very artifact that was meant to stand for the survival of our multiethnic ideal. And you will be making a fool of yourself, ruining your professional reputation. If you are completely and utterly convinced that you know better than Werner Heinrich, then go ahead, inform the UN. But the museum will not support you." He paused, then delivered the hammer blow. "And I will not support you."

I couldn't talk anymore. I just looked from one to the other of them, and then at the book. I let my hand rest on the binding. The tips of my fingers sought the small area where I'd repaired the worn leather. I could just feel the minute ridge where the new fibers melded with the old.

I turned away then and walked out of the room.

Lola

Jerusalem, 2002

And to them I will give in my house and within
my walls a memorial and a name.

—Isaiah

I AM AN OLD WOMAN NOW, and mornings are hard for me. I wake early these days. I think it's the cold that wakes me, stirring up the ache in my bones. People don't realize how cold it is here in winter. Not like the cold in the mountains of Sarajevo, but cold enough. This apartment was part of an Arab's house, before '48, and the old stones suck the chill into their crevices. I can't afford much heat. But maybe I just wake early because I am afraid to sleep too long. I know that one day, not so very many days from now, the cold will creep out of the stones and into my body where it lies in this narrow bed. And then I'll never get up again.

And what of it? I have had enough. More than my measure. Anyone who was born when I was, where I was, what I was, cannot complain of a death that will come, as mine will, in its due season.

I get a pension, but it is small, so I still go to work for a few hours each week, mostly on Shabbat. It's the easiest day to find work if you're not religious. The Orthodox won't work that day, and people with families want to enjoy the day off. Years ago, I used to have to compete with the Arabs for Shabbat work, but since the intifada, there are always too many curfews, too many checkpoints, so they're late or absent half the time, and nobody wants to hire them. I feel sorry for them, I do. I feel sorry that they have to suffer so.

In any case, the job I have now, they wouldn't want it. Not many people would. For myself, I have made my peace with the dead. The photographs of the women standing on the edge of the pit that will be their grave, the lamp shade made of human skin, these things don't bother me anymore.

I clean the display cases and I dust the frames and I think about the women. It is good to think about them. To remember them. Not naked and terrified, as they are in the photos, but as they were: at home, beloved, doing ordinary things in ordinary lives.

I think, also, about the person whose skin is stretched across the lamp shade. It's the first thing you see when you walk into the museum. I've watched some visitors, when they realize what it is, just turn around and walk out. They are too upset to go on. Me, when I look at it, I feel almost a kind of tenderness. It could be my mother's skin, for all I know. If things had been just a little different, it could have been mine.

Cleaning those rooms is, for me, a privilege. I can say that, old and slow as I am, I clean them perfectly. When I am done, there is not a speck of dust or scuff on the floor or a smear of a fingerprint. It's what I can do for them.

I used to come here, even before I got this job. Not to the museum, but to the garden, because Serif and Stela Kamal have a plaque there, in the Garden of the Righteous, their names among those of the other Gentiles who risked so much to save people like me.

I never saw them again, after that late-summer evening in the mountains outside Sarajevo. I was so afraid, that night, that I didn't even say a proper good-bye. Didn't even thank them.

The man they took me to that night was a Ustashe officer, of all things. He was secretly married to a Jewish woman, and so he helped people like me, when he could. It was simple for him to arrange everything for me. I went south with proper papers and spent the rest of the war safely, in the Italian zone. After, when Tito came to power, I was an important person for the first and last time in my life. For a few months, we were big socialist heroes, the young ones who had been Partisans with him in the mountains. The fact that he'd betrayed us, abandoned us to die out there, all that was forgotten and not mentioned, even by us. I got a job in the new army, assigned to work as an aide in a home for wounded Partisans in an old building by the sea in Split. That was where I found Branko, who had been our leader and then left us to die. He'd been shot, in the hip and the gut. He looked awful. He could barely walk and he was constantly falling ill with infections.

I married him. Don't ask me why. I was a stupid girl. But when you have no one left, no one at all who remembers you, anyone who has a shared past with you becomes special. Even someone like Branko.

I knew I had made a mistake well before we reached our first wedding anniversary. His wound had left him damaged, as a man, and it was as if he blamed me somehow for that. He wanted me to do all kinds of strange things to satisfy him. I'm not a prude. I really tried, but I was so young and innocent, in that way, at least. . . . Well, it was hard on me, to do some of the things he wanted. If he had been the least bit tender, it might have felt different. But he was a bully, even from his sickbed, and most of the time I just felt used.

When I read in the newspaper that Serif Kamal was to go on trial as a Nazi collaborator, I told Branko I was going to Sarajevo to testify on his behalf. I remember how he looked at me. He was propped up in an armchair by the window. We had a room of our own in the married barracks because of my job, and because of his status as an injured hero. He leaned forward, and tapped his cane on the floorboards. It was summer, very hot. The light poured in through the narrow window that looked out over the port.

"No," he said. There was glare off the dark blue water, and I had to raise my hand to shade my eyes.

"What do you mean, 'no'?"

"You are not going to Sarajevo. You are a soldier in the Yugoslav army, as am I. You will not jeopardize our position by standing against the will of the party. If they have seen fit to bring charges against this man, then they have their reasons. It is not for the likes of you to question them."

"But Effendi Kamal was no collaborator! He hated the Nazis! He saved me, Branko, after you had turned your back on me. I wouldn't be alive today if he hadn't risked so much—"

He cut me off. He had a loud voice and he used it, anytime I disagreed with him, even about something as small as whether his boots needed blacking or not. The walls were thin in the barracks, and he knew how I hated our neighbors hearing his abuse.

He was used to me giving in, the moment he raised his voice. But that one time, I stood my ground. I said he could bellow at me all he liked, I would do what was right. He swore and he cursed, and when I still would not yield, he flung his cane at me. Weak as he was, his aim was good, and the metal tip caught me just below my jaw and stung.

In the end, he arranged to have me put under surveillance while the trial was on. I could go to my work and come home, but always guarded. It was demeaning. I had no idea what he'd told them, what excuse he'd given to have me watched. But he succeeded in keeping me in Split. There was no way I could get to Sarajevo.

I didn't think I had any tears left in those days. I'd spent so many during the war. So many more just after, when I learned the fates of my mother and father, my little sister, my auntie. Auntie's weak heart gave out in the truck taking them to the Kruscia transit camp. Dora died there, starved and weak, two months later. My mother kept herself alive through all that grief almost to the end of the war. But then they sent her to Auschwitz. I thought I had spent all the tears I had. But I cried that week, for Serif, who would surely be hanged or face a firing squad. For Stela, left all alone with her beautiful baby son. And for myself. For my humiliation at the hands of the brute I'd married, who had turned me into a betrayer.

Branko died of complications from a gastric infection in 1951. I did not mourn him. I had heard that Tito was allowing Jews to go to Israel, and so I decided to leave my country—I had nothing left there—and start again here. I suppose, in the back of my mind, I thought I might find Mordecai, my old teacher from the Young

Guardians all those years ago. I was still young, you see. Still a stupid girl.

I did find Mordecai, eventually, in the military cemetery on Mount Hertzl. He fell in the '48 war. He was a leader in a Nahal unit, with the other boys and girls from the kibbutzim, and he died on the Jerusalem road.

So I have had to make my own life here, and it has not been a bad life. Hard, yes; much work, little money. But not bad. I never married again, but I had a lover for a time. A big, laughing truck driver who'd come here from Poland and belonged to a kibbutz in the Negev. It started with him making fun of me when I bought from his stall in the market. I was shy because of my bad Hebrew, so he would tease me until he could make me laugh. Soon, every time he drove the kibbutz produce to the city he would come to me. He would feed me the dates he'd helped to grow, and oranges, and we'd lie together in the afternoons, with the sun streaming in the window. Our skin smelled of citrus oil, and our kisses were sweetened by the plump, sticky dates.

I would have married him, if he'd asked. But he'd had a wife in Poland who'd been taken from the ghetto in Warsaw. He said he had never been able to find out what had happened to her. He could not be sure if she was alive or dead. Maybe it was just a line, a way to keep his distance. But I don't know. I think he felt guilty that he had lived. I liked him better because he honored her memory with his hope. Anyway, eventually some other kibbutznik got the truck-driving job, and he came to the city less and less, and finally not at all. I missed him. I still think about those afternoons.

I don't have a lot of friends. My Hebrew isn't so great, even today. Oh, I can get by: people here are used to making sense of foreign accents and mistaken grammar because almost everyone here came from somewhere else. But to tell the things of my heart to someone, I don't have the words in Hebrew for that.

Over time, I've grown used to the hot, dry summers, the fields of ripe cotton, the white glare, and the bare, rock-ribbed rises of land where no trees grow. And while the hills of Jerusalem are not the mountains of home, it sometimes snows here in winter and if I close my eyes tight, I can imagine I'm in Sarajevo. Even though many of my friends think I am a crazy old woman to do it, sometimes I still go to the Arab quarter in the Old City and sit in a café where the coffee smells like home.

During the war in Yugoslavia, there were some Bosnians here. Israel took in quite a few refugees. Some Jews, but mostly Muslims. So I was able to speak my own language for a while, and it was lovely, such a relief. I volunteered at the resettlement center to help them fill out simple forms—this country loves forms—or read the bus timetable, or make appointments for their kids to see a dentist. It was just by chance, reading an old magazine someone had left behind there, that I saw Effendi Kamal's obituary and learned that he had recently died.

It was like a stone fell from my heart. I had lived for years believing he'd been executed, because that was the sentence passed on all Nazi collaborators. But the obituary said he'd died after a long illness, and that he was *kustos* of the library at the National Museum, just as he had been when I knew him.

I felt like a sentence had been lifted from me, as well as him. I had been given another chance to do what was right, to testify for him. It took me two nights to carefully write down the story of what he had done for me. I sent it to the Holocaust museum, to Yad Vashem. After some little time, I had a letter from Stela, who had gone to stay in Paris with her son after her apartment in Sarajevo was destroyed by a Serb mortar. She said there had been a very nice ceremony in their honor at the Israeli embassy in Paris, that she understood why I had not been able to help them after the war, and that she was very glad I was alive and doing well. She said, Thank you for telling the world that my husband was a great friend to the Jews at a time when they had few true friends.

After they put the plaque for the Kamals in the museum garden,

I started to go there quite often. It made me feel better. I would pull some weeds from under the cypress trees, and pinch the dead blooms from the flowers. One day, a custodian from the museum saw me doing that and asked if I would like to work there as a janitor.

It is very quiet on Shabbat. Some people might say ghostly quiet. It doesn't bother. In fact, I hate the noise my polisher makes when I do the floors. I prefer the hours when I walk from chamber to chamber with my dust cloths, working in silence. The library takes the longest. I asked once, and the library assistant told me there were more than a hundred thousand books there, and more than sixty million pages of documents. It's a good number, I think: ten pages for every person who died. A kind of monument in paper for people who have no gravestones.

When you think about it, one small book among so many, it seems like a miracle, what happened. Maybe it *was* a miracle. I think it was. I had, of course, dusted those shelves for more than a year. Every week, I made a habit to take all the books down from one section of shelf, to dust beneath and behind them, then to dust the tops of the pages. Stela had taught me to do that when I cleaned the many bookshelves in the Kamals' apartment. So I suppose the memory of them, and that time, was always there in a small measure whenever I did that work. It might have been what made it possible for me to see.

I came into the library that day, and I found the section of shelves I'd cleaned the week before, and started taking down the books on the next section. They were older books, mostly, so I was especially careful when I set them to one side. And then I had it in my hand. I looked at it. I opened it. And I was back in Sarajevo, in Effendi Kamal's study, with Stela trembling beside me, realizing, in a way I only half understood at the time, that Effendi Kamal must have done something that made her very afraid. And then it was as if I could hear Effendi Kamal's voice: "The best place to hide a book might be in a library."

I wasn't sure what to do. For all I knew the book was supposed to be here. But it seemed strange, that such a famous old manuscript would be just shoved on a shelf like that.

That's what I said to them, when they questioned me, the head librarian, and the museum director, and another man I didn't know, who looked like a soldier but seemed to know all about the book, and about Serif Kamal as well. I was nervous, because they didn't seem to believe me, to believe that such a coincidence could really happen, and when I am anxious, the Hebrew words fly away from me. I couldn't think of the word *peleh,* for "miracle," and said *siman,* which is more like a sign.

But in the end, the one who looked like a soldier understood me. He smiled at me, very kindly. Then he turned to the others and said, Well, why not, *kinderlach?* The entire story of this book, its survival until today, has been a series of miracles. So why not just one more?

Hanna

Arnhem Land, Gunumeleng, 2002

I WAS IN A CAVE six hundred meters up a rock escarpment and a hundred clicks from the nearest landline when they finally got ahold of me.

The message, brought by one of the Aboriginal kids, was odd, and I didn't know what to make of it. He was a bright kid, and a bit of a prankster, so at first I thought it was some kind of joke.

"No, missus. No gammon this time. Fella from that Canberra mob, he bin call all day. We bin tell 'im, you mob's bush all week, but 'im call and 'im call, even after Butcher growled 'im."

Butcher was the boy's uncle and the manager of Jabiru Station, the cattle property where we stayed when we weren't doing field-work.

"Did he say what he wanted?"

The boy tilted his head to the side, the ambiguous gesture that might mean "no," or "I don't know," or maybe "I don't have the right to tell you."

"You better come, missus, or Butcher'll growl me, too."

I stepped out of the cave and blinked in the bright daylight. The sun was a big disk of brilliant madder, reddening the stripes of ore that ran through the sheer black-and-ocher rock face. Down below, the first shoots of new spear grass washed the plain in vivid green. Light silvered the sheets of water left behind by the previous night's downpour. We'd moved into Gunumeleng—one of six seasons the Aborigines identified in a year that whites divided simply into Wet and Dry. Gunumeleng brought the first storms. In another month, the entire plain would be flooded. The so-called road, which was actually a really marginal dirt track, would be impassable. I was hoping to get this section of caves documented and at least minimally conserved before another big Wet set in. The last thing I needed was a two-and-a-half-hour, bone-jarring drive back to the station to talk to some clown in Canberra. But in the distance, where the track ended, I could just make out the glint on the windshield of Butcher's beloved Toyota. Butcher wouldn't have let the boy drive it unless the message really was important.

"OK, then, Lofty. You go on ahead and tell Uncle that Jim and I'll be along by teatime. I'll just finish up a few silicone lines here, then we'll follow you."

The boy turned and scrambled down the escarpment. He was a skinny kid, and small for a sixteen-year-old (which was why everyone called him Lofty). But he could get up and down a rock face about twenty times more quickly than I could. I returned to the cave where Jim Bardayal, the archeologist I worked with, was waiting for me.

"At least we'll get to sleep in a bed tonight, then," he said, handing me the silicone cartridge.

"Ah, listen to you. What a softie. Back in Sydney you were always banging on about your country, how you missed it. Now, we get one night's drizzle, and someone dangles a hot and a cot in front of you, you can't get there quick enough."

Jim grinned. "Bloody balanda," he said. The storm the night before had actually been a lashing. Strobes of lightning had lit up the twisted white gum trees, and gusts of wind had just about blown the tarps right off our shelter.

"It's not the rain," Jim said. "It's the bloody mozzies."

I couldn't argue with that. There was no such thing as peacefully contemplating the gorgeous sunsets out here. Dusk was a dinner bell for millions of mosquitoes, and we were the catch of the day. Just thinking about them made me itch all over. I shot a line of silicone, like a ridge of sticky chewing gum, across the rock face where we'd determined the rainwater would be likely to flow. The idea was to divert the water away from the soluble ochers of the paintings. This part of the escarpment was rich with art: Mimi paintings, the wonderful, energetic pictures of lithe figures hunting. Jim's people, the Mirarr, believed they'd been painted by spirits. His other people, the archeological community, had established that the earliest of the paintings had been done thirty thousand years ago. All through those ages, certain knowledgeable elders had been charged with ceremonially restoring them when necessary. But after Europeans came, the Mirarr had gradually stopped inhabiting the caves of the stone country. They'd moved off to work for the balanda—the white settlers—on cattle stations, or gone to live in the towns. Our job now was to protect what they had left behind.

It wasn't work I'd ever imagined myself doing. But Sarajevo had destroyed my confidence. While part of me continued to believe that it was Ozren and Heinrich who were wrong, the larger part—the coward in me—had swamped that conviction in a toxic sea of self-doubt. I'd come home feeling humiliated and unworthy and suddenly unsure of my own expertise. For a month, I moped around my Sydney lab, turning down any assignment that sounded the least bit challenging. If I'd made such an embarrassing mistake in Sarajevo, who was I to be passing judgment on anything?

Then I got a call from Jonah Sharansky. He had two things to tell me. One was that Delilah had left me a substantial inheritance. The other was that the family wanted me to take over my mother's role in Aaron's foundation. The other board members had already voted on it, apparently. I felt like I needed to get away from the lab for a while, so I decided to use the inheritance money and take some time to go and see what the foundation's work was all about, and if there was something I might be able to contribute to it.

My mother went spare when she found out she'd been given the shove. At first, I felt bad. I assumed she saw the foundation as a last link with Aaron, and I could imagine how painful it would be, to have his family reject her like that.

She'd returned to Sydney a few weeks after I had. After she got out of the hospital, she'd taken herself off to some fancy spa in California to recuperate. "I've got to be in good shape when I get back to Sydney," she told me on the phone. "Those vultures at the hospital will be circling." When I met her at the airport, she looked amazing, fit for anything. But when I got her home, I noticed there were lines of strain around her mouth and shadows under her eyes and that she really was holding it together by force of will.

"You could take some more time off, Mum. Make sure you're really, you know, ready to go back to work."

She was sitting on the bed, letting me unpack for her. She kicked off her Manolos or Jimmy Choos or whatever they were—why she subjected herself to such torturing shoes I have no idea—and leaned back against the pillows. "I've got an eighth-nerve tumor on the schedule the day after tomorrow. Do you know what that's like? No, how would you. Well, it's like picking bits of wet Kleenex out of a bowl of tofu. . . ."

"Mum, please . . ." I felt nauseated. "I'll never be able to eat tofu again."

"Oh, for goodness' sake, Hanna. Can you stop being solipsistic for five minutes? I'm just trying to explain it to you in a way you can grasp." (Dear old Mum. Never let a chance go by to make me feel like the dimmest bulb in the chandelier.) "It's difficult surgery, takes hours. And I skedded it on purpose, to show those vultures that I'm not a corpse yet." She closed her eyes. "I'll just take a nap now; pass me that throw, will you? Leave the rest of the unpacking. And you needn't stay. . . . I can manage quite well with the housekeeper."

It was just a few days later that she heard from the Sharanskys that they wanted me to replace her on the board. She summoned me to Bellevue Hill. She was sitting on the veranda when I arrived, with a bottle of Hill of Grace open and breathing on the table. With Mum, the quality of the wine was an indicator of the gravity of the talk. This one, I could tell, was going to be mega.

She had already told me, from her hospital bed in Boston, that she wanted me to keep my paternity a secret. I thought she was nuts. I mean, who cared who she'd slept with all those years ago. But she asked me to think about her position, and I considered it. I considered her position. I really did. I was still considering it when the foundation thing came up.

"If you join that board, Hanna, it will raise all kinds of questions." The sun filtered through blooming tibouchinas and gave the light a violet shimmer. Fallen frangipani blossoms littered the manicured lawn, releasing a spicy scent. I sipped the glorious wine and didn't say anything. "Awkward questions. For me. The accident has already put me in a precarious position at the hospital. Davis and Harrington couldn't *wait* to raise the infection issue, and there are others who've never reconciled themselves to my appointment as chair. I've had to work twice as hard as usual to make it clear to them that I'm not going anywhere. It would be unfortunate timing if the other matter . . ." She left the sentence hanging.

"Well, but I might actually have some skills that would be useful, you know, to the Sharansky Foundation."

"Skills? What skills could you possibly have, darling? I mean, you know nothing about the management of nonprofits, and I hadn't noticed that you are a particular wizard in the investment field."

I gripped the stem of my glass and stared into the shiraz. I sipped the wine and let the flavors billow in my mouth. I was determined not to let her set me off.

"Art skills, Mum. I thought I might possibly be able to help in the field, with the conservation program."

She put her wineglass down on the marble table so hard I was surprised it didn't shatter.

"It's bad enough, Hanna, that you've spent all these years playing with paste and scraps of paper. But at least books have something to do with culture. Now you are proposing to go out to the middle of absolutely nowhere, to save meaningless, muddy daubs of primitives?"

I looked at her. I imagine my jaw might've actually dropped.

"How is it," I blurted, "that a man like Aaron Sharansky could have loved someone like you?"

It went on from there. One last, god-awful, no-holds-barred blue; one of those fights where you pour out every poisonous thought you've ever had, the dregs of every grievance, and you set the cup in front of the other person and force them to drink it. I had to hear again what a disappointment I'd always been; a self-pitying pygmy of a personality who'd thought my scraped knees were more worthy of attention than her critically ill patients. I'd been an insufferable brat as a kid, and a delinquent slut as an adolescent. I'd glommed on to the Sharanskys in desperation because I was so busy nursing childish resentments that I couldn't form adult attachments of my own. And then the familiar kicker: I'd squandered my opportunity to enter a real profession and wasted my life as "a tradeswoman."

When you've fought with someone all your life, you know where the weaknesses are. By this point I was casting around for a weapon I could use to retaliate, so I went for her where I knew it would wound. "So, what good was it, all your precious medical expertise, when you couldn't even save the bloke you loved?"

She suddenly looked stricken. I felt exultant, and pressed my advantage. "That's what this is all about, isn't it? I have to pay, all my life. No father, not even a name, all because you feel you fucked up your most important case."

"Hanna, you don't know what you are talking about."

"That's it, isn't it? You referred him to the great almighty Andersen, and Andersen blew it. You would have done better. That's what you think, isn't it? You're so arrogant, and then the one time when you should have trusted your own expertise—"

"Hanna. Shut up. You have no idea—"

"You could have saved him, that's what you think, right? You would have picked up the bleed, if he'd been your patient."

"I did pick up the bleed."

Because I was still ranting, right over the top of her, it took me a second to process what she'd said.

"You . . . what?"

"Of course I picked it up. I monitored him all that night. I knew he was hemorrhaging. I let it happen. I knew he wouldn't want to wake up blind."

For several minutes, I was too stunned to say anything. A flock of rainbow lorikeets swooped and screeched through the garden then, on their way to their nighttime roost. I let my eyes follow them, until their colors—the royal blue, the emerald green, the scarlet—became suddenly blurred by my tears. I'm not going to go into what I said to her. I'm not sure I recall it all that accurately. But at the end of it, I told her I was going to change my name to Sharansky.

I don't see her anymore. We don't even go through the motions. Ozren had been right about one thing: some stories just don't have happy endings.

I expected to feel more adrift than I did, being entirely on my own. But if there was an empty place in my life, it wasn't very much bigger than it always had been. She had never understood me, or why what I did mattered, and why I loved it. And those were the important things. Without that, our conversations had just been noise.

Leaving Sydney helped. Clean break and all that. The Sharansky Foundation's projects were in places I'd barely heard of, like Oenepelli and Burrup, where mining companies wanted to turn incredible natural landscapes and ancient cultural sites into giant holes in the ground. The foundation funded research and then, if there was enough to sustain a case, they'd assist the traditional Aboriginal owners of the land to bring a lawsuit against the companies.

It didn't take me long out there, in the landscapes my father had painted, to realize that as much as I loved my country, I barely knew it. I'd spent so many years studying the art of our immigrant cultures, and barely any time at all on the one that had been here all along. I'd gone cross-eyed swotting classical Arabic and biblical Hebrew but could barely name even five out of the five hundred Aboriginal languages spoken here. So I set myself a crash course and became a pioneer in a new field: desperation conservation. My job became the documentation and preservation of ancient Aboriginal rock art, before the uranium or bauxite companies had a chance to blast it into rubble.

It was hard physical work, getting to remote sites, often on foot, usually in tremendous heat, backpacking kilos of equipment. Sometimes, the best thing you could do to conserve a piece of rock art was to take a mattock and hack away invading tree roots. Not exactly fine-motor-skill stuff. To my surprise, I found I loved it. For the first time in my life, I was tanned and sinewy. I traded in my cashmeres and silks for serviceable khakis, and one day, because I was hot and sweaty and my French twist kept falling down, I hacked off my long hair. New name, new look, new life. And a very long way from anything that reminded me of extinct Spanish sheep and pore-scatter patterns on parchment.

I fell asleep in the truck on the way to Jabiru Station. That's how exhausted I was. It's not what you'd call a relaxing drive. The track is a hundred clicks of washboard, when it isn't one big sandpit. Plus there are big mobs of roos that appear from nowhere at dusk, and if you swerve to avoid them, you can wind up bogged to your manifold.

But Jim had driven on tracks like this since he could see over the top of a steering wheel, so we got there. Butcher had roasted a whole barramundi he'd caught that day, and flavored it with dried jupie, little sweet-tart berries that were a Mirarr staple. The station phone rang right as I was licking the last succulent morsel of fish off my fork.

"Yeah, she here," Butcher said, handing me the phone.

"Dr. Sharansky? It's Keith Lowery calling, from DFAT."

"From where, sorry?"

"DFAT. Department of Foreign Affairs and Trade. You're a hard woman to get ahold of."

"Yeah. I know."

"Dr. Sharansky, we were hoping we might be able to get you back here, to Canberra, or Sydney if that's easier. We've got a bit of a situation, and your name came up as someone who might be in a position to help."

"Well, I'm going to be back in Sydney in two or three weeks, when Gudjewg—I mean, when the wet season really sets in. . . ."

"Ah, right. The thing is, we were hoping you might fly down here tomorrow."

"Mr. Lowery, I'm in the middle of a project. The mining company is breathing down these people's neck here and the escarpment's going to be inaccessible in about two weeks. So I'm not real keen on junketing anywhere just at the minute. Do you mind telling me what this is all about?"

"I can't discuss it on the phone, sorry."

"Is this something the bloody mining companies have cooked up? I mean, that'd be pretty desperate. I know that some of those characters are lower than a snake's armpit. . . . But involving your mob to do their dirty work . . ."

"It's nothing like that. Much as my colleagues over in Trade might lament the Sharansky Foundation's occasionally negative impact on mining export revenues, that is not our concern here on the Near East desk. I'm not calling about your present work. It's about a rather, ah, high-profile job you undertook six years ago. In Europe."

Suddenly, the barramundi wasn't sitting too well.

"Do you mean the Sara—"

"It would be better to discuss this in person."

Near East desk. I started to feel the onset of heartburn. "You deal with Israel, right?"

"As I said, Dr. Sharansky, better in person. Now, would you like me to arrange your flight out of Darwin tomorrow to Canberra, or to Sydney?"

The view from the DFAT office in Sydney is enough to make a diplomat turn down a foreign posting. As I waited in the tenth-floor lobby for Keith Lowery, I watched the yachts skittering across the sun-spangled harbor, heeling in the breeze as if in homage to the soaring white sails of the Opera House.

The interior decor was pretty nice, too. Foreign Affairs had its pick of art from the national collection, so the reception area had a Sidney Nolan *Ned Kelly* canvas on one wall and a fabulous Rover Thomas *Roads Crossing* on the opposite.

I was admiring the rich ochers in Rover's painting when Lowery came up behind me.

"Sorry we don't have one of your dad's here—brilliant painter. We've got an absolute beauty down in Canberra."

Lowery was a tall, broad, sandy-haired bloke with the easy swagger and the slightly stove-in features of a serious rugby player. Made sense. Rugby was a big sport at the elite private schools, and most Aussie dips still tended to have that background, despite all our egalitarian myths.

"Thanks for coming down here, Dr. Sharansky. I know it's a big ask."

"Yeah, well. Odd, isn't it, that you can get to Sydney from London or New York in twenty-four hours, but it still takes almost twice that from some parts of the Top End."

"Does it? Never been up there, myself."

Typical, I thought. Probably been to every museum in Florence and yet never seen the Lightning Man at Nourlangie Rock.

"I usually work in Canberra, so I've borrowed an office here for our meeting. Margaret . . . it is Margaret, isn't it?" He'd turned to the receptionist. "We're in Mr. Kensington's office. Will you make sure that we're not disturbed?"

We walked through a metal detector and down a corridor to a large corner office. Lowery punched a code that opened the door. My eyes went straight to the windows, which offered a panorama even more spectacular than the one in the lobby, because it took in the whole sweep from the Botanic Gardens to the bridge.

"Your mate Mr. Kensington must be a big muckety muck," I said, turning to Lowery. Because I'd been distracted by the view, I hadn't noticed that there was someone else already in the room. He'd been sitting on the couch, but he was on his feet now, moving toward me with his hand outstretched.

"Shalom, Channa."

His hair had thinned a bit, but he still had the tanned, muscular look that had always set him apart from everyone else in our line of work.

I took a step away from him and put my hands behind my back.

"No 'G'day, mate'? You are still angry with me? Even after six years?"

I glanced at Lowery, wondering how much he knew about all this.

"Six years?" My voice was as cold as I could make it. "Six years is nothing, compared with five hundred years. What did you do with it?"

"Nothing. I did nothing with it." He paused a beat, and then walked across the room to a handsome desk made of Huon pine. An archival box was sitting there. He eased the catches.

"See for yourself."

I crossed the room, blinking hard. My hands hovered over the box. I lifted the lid, and there it was. I hesitated a moment. I didn't have gloves, forms. I had no business touching it. But I had to be sure. As carefully as I could, I removed it from the box and set it on the desk. I turned to the Creation illuminations. And there it was. The difference between being right, and being wrong. Of knowing my craft, and not knowing it.

I blinked away tears that were partly relief, and partly self-pity for the misery I'd lived with, thinking I'd been wrong, for six long years. When I looked up at Amitai, all the uncertainty, all the self-doubt dissolved and reformed into the purest rage I think I have ever felt. "How could you?"

To my intense irritation, he smiled at me. "I didn't."

I slammed my hand down so hard on the desk that it hurt.

"Stop it!" I yelled. "You're a thief and a crook and a bloody liar."

He just kept smiling slightly, a calm, infuriating, shit-eating grin. I wanted to slap him. "You're a disgrace to the profession."

"Dr. Sharansky." It was Lowery, trying, I suppose, to be diplomatic. He took a step toward me and laid his hand on my shoulder. I shrugged it off and stepped away from him.

"Why is this man here? He's guilty of grand larceny. He should be in the slammer. Don't tell me this bloody government is mixed up in this . . . in this . . . heist . . . this conspiracy. . . . ."

"Dr. Sharansky, you'd better sit down."

"Don't tell me to sit down! I don't want anything to do with this. And why is that book here? How on *earth* can you justify bringing a five-hundred-year-old codex halfway across the world? It's beyond unethical, it's criminal. I'm walking out of here and I'm calling Interpol. I suppose you think you can hide this behind diplomatic immunity or some crap like that."

I was at the door. There was no knob, no handle. Just a keypad, for which I didn't know the combination.

"You better let me out of here or I'll—"

"Dr. Sharansky!" Lowrey had raised his voice. He suddenly looked a lot more like a front-row forward than a smooth diplomat. "Shut up for a second, will you, and let Dr. Yomtov get a word in."

Amitai had stopped grinning. He spread his hands as if in supplication. "It wasn't me. If you had come to me when you spotted the forgery, together we might have stopped them."

"Stopped who?"

His voice was very soft. Almost a whisper. "It was Dr. Heinrich."

"Werner?" I felt all the air go out of my body. I sank down onto the couch. "Werner Heinrich?" I repeated stupidly. "Who else? You just said, 'Stopped *them*.'"

"Ozren Karaman, I am most sorry to tell you. It would not have been possible otherwise." My teacher and my lover. They had both of them stood there, together, and told me I didn't know what I was talking about. I felt absolutely betrayed.

"But why? And how come you've got it now. Here."

"It is a bit of a long story." Amitai sat down on the couch beside me and poured a glass of water from a decanter on the coffee table. He handed it to me and poured another for Lowery, who waved no thanks. Amitai took a sip and then he began to speak.

"A long story that starts in the winter of 1944, when Werner was just fourteen years old. He was conscripted, as all the boys and the old men were, at that time. Most of them ended up manning antiaircraft guns, things of that nature. But he was required for a different service. Werner went to work for the Einsatzstab Reichsleiter Rosenberg—you know what that is?"

Of course I knew about the infamous arm of the Third Reich, the most efficient and methodical looters in the history of art. It had been headed by Hitler's confidant Alfred Rosenberg, who had written a book before the war calling German abstract expressionism "syphilitic." He'd formed the Combat League for German Culture, aimed at eradicating anything "degenerate," which, of course, included anything written or painted by Jews.

"As the Reich was speeding up the Final Solution, so Rosenberg's unit was rushing to finish the destruction of all the Jewish materials they had confiscated from the synagogues, from the great collections of Europe. Werner's job was to transport the Torah scrolls and the incunabula to the incinerators and burn them. One of the collections he burned was the Sarajevo *pincus*—" He looked up at Lowery. "That's the complete records of a Jewish community. Irreplaceable. Sarajevo's *pincus* was very old. It contained documents that went back as far as 1565."

"So," I said. "That's why he specialized in Hebrew manuscripts."

Amitai nodded. "Exactly. It was his passion that not another book should be lost. During the early months of the Bosnian war, he approached me because the Serbs' bombing of the Oriental Institute and the National and University Library mirrored what had happened in his own past. In particular, he wanted the Israeli government to mount a rescue mission for the haggadah. I told him we didn't have any intelligence about where it was, whether, in fact, it still existed. He thought I was hiding the truth from him. And then, after the war, when the United Nations determined to conserve the haggadah and put it on display, he still believed it was in danger. He didn't have faith in the peace. He told me he thought there was a very strong chance that when NATO and the UN lost interest, Bosnia could be hijacked by fanatical Islamists. He feared the influence of the Saudis, who, of course, have a terrible record of destroying ancient Jewish sites on the Arabian Peninsula. He was tormented by the idea that the haggadah would once again be at risk."

Amitai took another sip of water. "I should have listened more carefully to what he was saying. I had no idea that his past had made him into such an extremist. You would think, an Israeli my age, I would know from extremists. But still, I missed it."

"But what about Ozren? Surely he didn't believe those things about Bosnia?"

"Why not? Bosnia hadn't protected his wife. It hadn't saved his little son. Ozren had seen too much. He had seen people shot by snipers as they tried to carry books from the burning library. He had risked his own life to save the haggadah, and he knew what a close call that had been. I think it would have been easy, at a certain time, for Werner to find Ozren most receptive to his views."

I couldn't bring myself to believe that Ozren would think that way. He loved his city. Loved what it stood for. I couldn't believe he had given up on it.

The unsparing Sydney light was pouring through the huge windows, falling onto the open pages of the haggadah. I went over to the desk and picked up the book. I placed the haggadah carefully back into the protection of the archive box. I was about to close the lid, but then I paused. I felt the edges of the binding, and found the ridge where the fibers of leather—the new ones I'd placed—merged with the older work of Florien Mittl. I turned back to Amitai.

"You were the one who had the negatives."

"Werner convinced me that he could get the German government to sponsor a better facsimile edition than the one we were planning. He was very persuasive. They were prepared to spend six times our budget, they were going to print on vellum . . . it was going to be a gesture of goodwill from the new Germany. What can I say? I believed him. I gave your documentation to him. Of course he used it to mimic every possible detail—even your conservation work. And since he was your teacher, he knew very well how to do that."

"But why were you there, that night, at Ozren's place?"

Amitai sighed. "I was there, Channa, because I, too, lost a child. My daughter. She was three."

"Amitai." I had no idea. I knew he was divorced. I hadn't realized there was a child. "I'm so sorry. Was it a suicide bombing?"

He shook his head and gave a slight smile. "Everyone thinks Israelis always die in wars or bombings. Some few of us do manage to die in our beds. For her, it was a heart defect. A child lost—it is the same emptiness, I think, however it happens. I was there to bring materials donated by Israel as part of the library restoration project, and I heard the news about Ozren's son. As a father, I felt for him."

There was an awkward silence for a few moments. "I don't blame you, Channa, for suspecting me. You shouldn't think I do."

He went on then to tell me how the book had been found and how he'd immediately suspected Werner, because of the quality of the fake that was on display in Sarajevo.

"But why did Werner choose Yad Vashem?"

"He knew it well. He'd worked there as a visiting scholar many times over the years. It was the simplest thing for him to place the haggadah there. He did not care, you see, that no one would know, that no one would study it, or celebrate it. He was only concerned that it would be safeguarded, and he told me he had decided that Yad Vashem was the safest place in the world. That even if the worst happened, and Israel was in an existential conflict, we would defend that place above all others." Amitai looked down. "And about that, at least, he is correct."

"You've seen him? Is he under arrest?"

"Yes, I have seen him. And no, he is not under arrest."

"But why not?"

"He is in a hospice in Vienna. He is an old man, Channa. He is very frail, not too lucid. It took me many hours to learn what I have told you."

"Well, what about Ozren? Has *he* been arrested?"

"No. In fact he has been promoted. He is director of the National Museum now."

"But why are you letting him get away with this? Why hasn't he been charged?"

Amitai glanced at Lowery.

"The Israelis are of the opinion that it is better if this doesn't become a public matter," Lowery said. "The fact that the book was discovered in Israel would be enough to . . . well . . . With Heinrich too out of it to be a credible witness, nobody sees any point in stirring up negative sentiment. I think the technical diplomatic term is *shit storm*."

"I still don't get it. You are saying that the Israeli government supports giving this back, right? Surely you could just do it, quiet diplomacy, diplomatic pouch, something like that. . . ."

Amitai looked down at his hands. "You know the old saying, Channa? Two Jews, three opinions? There are certain factions in my country's government who would insist to keep this book in Israel. It would be like all their Hanukkahs had come at once." He coughed and reached for his water glass. "When Mr. Lowery said 'the Israelis,' he was not speaking of the actual government."

I turned to Lowery. "So what on earth is the Department of Foreign Affairs doing, involving itself in this mess? What's the possible Australian interest?"

Lowery cleared his throat. "The prime minister's a close personal friend of the president of Israel, and the president's an old army mate of Amitai here. So we're giving them a crack at you as a sort of, well, favor." He grinned sheepishly. "Even though I'm guessing that you're not a big fan of this particular PM, we're hoping you might see your way clear to pitch in and give a hand on this one."

Amitai chimed in. "I could smuggle the book to Sarajevo. Yes, no question. But then what? Believe me, I did not do this lightly—bringing the codex all this way. We took the decision and the risk of bringing the haggadah here because of you, Channa. Because we think you have the best chance to convince Ozren to restore it to its rightful place." Amitai paused. I was pretty stunned, and trying to process this. I must've had a blank look on my face.

"Because of the nature of your past relationship with him," Lowery added.

That was too much. "How the *hell* do you know about my 'past relationship'? How dare you all pry into my personal life? What ever happened to civil liberties around here?"

Amitai raised a hand. "It wasn't just you, Channa. You were in Sarajevo at a delicate time. The CIA, the Mossad, the DGSE . . ."

"Even ASIO," Lowery interjected. "At that time, just about any person with a pulse in the former Yugoslavia was either a spy, or being spied on. Or both. Don't take it so personally."

I got up, agitated. Easy for him to say. How would he like it if I turned around and told him who he'd slept with six years ago? Well, maybe in his line of work you expect that sort of thing. But it creeped me out. I'm a bookworm; not a diplomat, not a spook. And certainly not some kind of commando Ms. Fix-It for Israel. Or any other country for that matter.

I walked over to the desk and looked down at the haggadah. It had already survived so many risky journeys. Now it sat on a desk in a land that hadn't even been part of its makers' known world. And it was here because of me.

Years ago, when I came home from Sarajevo, I'd gone to the archives of the Australian National Gallery and listened to hours of taped interviews with my father. I knew the sound of his voice now. It was a voice with many layers. The top layer, the dominant one, was the spare, laconic cadence of the outback. The voice he'd found as a young man, when he was discovering what he loved and what he was meant to do. But there were other layers underneath. Hints of a

Boston boyhood. A tiny trace of Russian accent. An occasional Yiddish inflection.

What I do is me, for that I came.

I knew now how he would sound, saying that line from the Hopkins poem. I could hear him saying it in my head.

What I do is me.

He made art. I saved it. That was my life's work. *What I do.* But taking a risk. A big one. That, most definitely, is *not* what I do. Not me at all.

I turned around and leaned against the desk. I was feeling a bit shaky. They were both staring at me.

"And if I get caught? In possession of—I'll take a wild stab here—fifty, sixty million dollars' worth of stolen goods. What then?"

Amitai suddenly seemed really interested in his hands again. Lowery, meanwhile, became transfixed by the lunching office workers, sunning themselves on the grass in the Botanic Gardens. Nobody said anything.

"I asked you both a question. What if I get caught with this, and accused of boosting an incredibly important piece of the world's cultural heritage?"

Amitai glanced up at Lowery, who couldn't seem to tear his gaze away from the view.

"Well?"

Amitai and Lowery both started talking at once.

"The Australian government . . ."

"The Israeli government . . ."

They both stopped and looked at each other, making polite "after you" gestures. It was almost comical, really. Lowery cracked first.

"See that place over there, under those Moreton Bay fig trees?" He was pointing at a grassy rise of harbor-hugging foreshore. "Bit of a coincidence, really. That's exactly where they shot the final scene in *Mission: Impossible II.*"

.　　.　　.　　.　　.

They'd built a new airport in Sarajevo. It was all spiffy and totally ci-vilian, with nice bars and gift shops. Normal.

Me, I wasn't feeling too normal. As I stood in the immigration line, I was very glad of the beta-blockers Amitai had given me an hour earlier, before I left him in Vienna. "These will stop the appear-ance of nervousness," he'd said. "The sweaty hands, the breathless-ness. Ninety-nine percent of what customs officers look for is nervous demeanor. Of course, you will still *feel* nervous. The pills won't stop that."

He was right. I felt horrible. I'd had to take the beta-blockers twice. I'd thrown up the first lot.

He had also given me the case he'd used to transport the haggadah from Israel to Australia. It was a black nylon wheelie bag and it looked just like every other wheelie bag—the kind that just barely fit in the overhead lockers—but it had a false back panel made with some supersecret, X-ray-filtering fiber. "Undetectable by any current screening technology," he assured me.

"Do I really need that?" I'd asked. "I mean, so what if the X-ray machine shows a book in my bag? Nobody but a specialist is going to know what it is. But if I get caught with some kind of smug-gler's kit . . . "

"Why take a chance? You are going to Sarajevo. There are people in that city, not even Jews, who bought facsimile copies of the haggadah even when they couldn't afford food for their table. It is a most beloved object there. Anyone—a customs officer, a person in the queue behind you—might recognize it. The bag, it really is the best we can do. No one is going to catch you."

There were a half dozen Iranian nationals on my flight, and that, as it turned out, was a stroke of luck for me. Those poor blokes sucked up all the attention in the arrivals hall. Sarajevo had become a favorite entry port for people trying to sneak into Europe, because Bosnia's borders were still pretty porous, and the EU had been on the Bosnians to do something about the influx. The Iranian ahead of me got his cases opened, his documents scrutinized. I could tell he hadn't had the benefit of a beta-blocker. He was sweating like crazy.

When I reached the front of the line, all I got was a smile and a "Welcome in Bosnia," and suddenly I was out of the airport, in a taxi, driving past a mammoth new mosque built by the Gulfies and then past a sex shop and an Irish pub offering "20 brands of world beer." The much-shelled Holiday Inn had been revamped, bright as a child's Lego tower in blocks of vibrant yellow. Sycamore saplings, planted to replace the trees cut for fuel during the siege, lined the main thoroughfares. When we entered the narrow ways of the Baščaršija, the alleys were filled with brightly dressed women and men in their best suits, braving subzero weather to promenade among balloon sellers and flower vendors.

I wanted to ask the taxi driver what was going on. I pointed to a group of little girls in velvet party frocks.

"Biram!" he replied, smiling broadly. So that was it; I hadn't realized. Ramadan had just ended, and the town was celebrating one of the biggest feasts of the Muslim calendar.

The pastry shop at Sweet Corner was absolutely packed. I could barely get through to the counter with my wheelie bag in tow. The pastry chef didn't recognize me, and why would he, after six years? I pointed to the stairs that ran up to the attic.

"Ozren Karaman?" I said.

He nodded, and then pointed to his watch and then the door, which I took to indicate that Ozren would be back soon. I waited for a stool in the bustling, noisy shop to become vacant. Then I sat down in a warm corner, nibbling the crisp edge of a too-sugary confection, watching the door.

I waited an hour, then two. The pastry chef began to look at me oddly, so I ordered another honey-drenched sweet, even though I hadn't eaten the first one.

Finally, at around eleven o'clock, Ozren pushed open the steam-misted door. If I hadn't been staring at every face intently, if I'd just passed him on the street, I'm not sure I would have recognized him.

His hair was still long and tousled, but it had turned completely silver. His face had not softened into jowls—he was still lean, still without a gram of spare fat—but there were hard lines scoured into his cheeks and brow. As he shrugged off his overcoat—the same threadbare one I remembered from six years earlier—I could see that he was actually wearing a suit. Must be a requirement of the museum director's job—no way he'd do that voluntarily. It was a nice suit, good fabric, well tailored, but it looked as if he'd slept in it.

By the time I excused my way around the chairs and stools, he was already halfway up the stairs to the attic.

"Ozren." He turned and looked at me, blinking. He didn't recognize me. Tense as I was, a whisper of vanity told me it must be the poor light, or the short haircut. I didn't like to think that I'd aged that much.

"It's me. Hanna Shar— Hanna Heath."

"Good God." He didn't say anything else. Just stood there, blinking.

"Can I, you know, come up?" I said. "I need to talk with you."

"Uh, my apartment, it's not . . . It's very late. What about tomorrow, at the museum? It is a holiday, but I will be there in the morning." He had recovered from his surprise and schooled his voice. His tone was very correct, cool and professional.

"I need to talk to you now, Ozren. I think you know what it is about."

"I really don't think I—"

"Ozren. I have something. Here. In this bag." I inclined my head toward the wheelie. "Something that belongs to your museum."

"Good God," he said again. He was sweating, and not from the warmth of the pastry shop. He extended an arm. "After you, by all means." I pushed past him on the narrow stairway, wrestling with the bag. He made to take it from me, but I gripped it so hard my knuckles whitened. Some people in the shop, including the chef, had turned to look at us, sensing a tiff of some kind. I headed up the stairs, the bag thumping noisily on the treads behind me. Ozren followed. I heard the noise level rise again as the patrons, realizing there wasn't going to be any spectacle, turned back to their coffee and their cheerful holiday conversations.

Ozren ushered me into the attic. He closed the door, shot the old wrought-iron bolt, and leaned his back against it. His silver hair, brushing the rafters, brought back memories. Distracting memories.

There was kindling laid ready in the small grate. Wood had still been scarce in Sarajevo when I'd been there before, and we'd never had the luxury of a fire. Ozren bent to the grate. As the flame caught, he laid a single log upon the kindling. He took a bottle of *rakijah* from a shelf and poured two glasses. He handed me one, unsmiling.

"To a happy reunion," he said dourly, and downed his drink in a swallow. I sipped mine.

"I imagine you have come to put me behind bars," he said.

"Don't be ridiculous."

"Well, why not? I deserve it. I have been expecting it, every day for six years. Better it should be you. You have more right than anyone."

"I don't know what you mean."

"It was terrible, what we did to you. Making you doubt your own expertise like that, lying to you." He poured himself another shot of *rakijah.* "When you saw it, that should have been enough. We should have ended it right there. But I was not myself, and Werner—you must know it was Werner, yes?"

I nodded.

"Werner was obsessed." His face crumpled suddenly, the hard lines softening. "Hanna, there is not a day since that book left this country that I have not regretted it. I tried, just a few months afterward, to convince Werner to return it. I told him I was going to confess. He said if I did, he would deny everything. And that he would move the haggadah to some place where no one would ever find it. By that time, my vision had cleared. I could see that he was mad enough to do it. Hanna . . ."

He moved toward me then and took my glass from me, set it down, and grasped my hands. "I missed you so much. I wanted so much to find you, to tell you . . . to ask for your pardon. . . . "

I felt my throat tighten as all the feelings I had for him—for him, and no one since—started to overwhelm me in that room, with its memories. But then the anger at what he'd put me through got the upper hand. I pulled away.

He raised his own hands, palms toward me, as if to show that he understood that he had stepped over a line.

"You know I've barely touched a book in six years, because of you? Because of your lies. I gave it up, because you told me I was wrong."

He walked over to where the dormer window looked out on a patch of sky and city. There were lights twinkling outside. The lights of a living city. Six years ago, there hadn't been any.

"There is no excuse for what I did. But when Alia died, I was so angry with my country. I gave way to despair. And Werner was there, whispering in my ear, telling me it was the right thing that this book be returned to the Jews in recompense for all that had been stolen from them. That it was theirs, and that they could protect it. Protect it in a way that this fledgling state—in this region whose very name is a synonym for murderous hostility and ineffectuality—would not be able to."

"How could you think that way, Ozren? When you, a Sarajevan and a Muslim, saved it. When that other librarian, Serif Kamal, risked his life for it?" He didn't say anything. "Do you think that way, still?"

"No," he said. "Not now. You know I am not a religious man. But Hanna, I have spent many nights, lying awake here in this room, thinking that the haggadah came to Sarajevo for a reason. It was here to test us, to see if there were people who could see that what united us was more than what divided us. That to be a human being matters more than to be a Jew or a Muslim, Catholic or Orthodox."

Downstairs, in the pastry shop, someone gave a raucous laugh. The log shifted and fell in the fireplace.

"So," I said. "How do we put it back?"

Later, when I met up with Amitai and told him how we did it, he smiled.

"It's almost always that way. Ninety-nine percent of what I did in the unit was that way. But people who go to the movies or read spy novels don't want to believe it. They like to think there are agents in ninja suits dropping on wires out of air-conditioning ducts, plastic explosives, disguised as . . . as *pineapples* or something, going off everywhere. But so much more often it is exactly like what you did: a combination of luck, timing, and a bit of common sense. And that we have a Muslim feast day to thank for it—even better."

Because it was Biram, there was only a single guard on duty at the museum that night. We waited till just after 4:00 a.m., knowing that the morning guards' shift began at 5:00. Ozren simply told the guard that he couldn't sleep after too much revelry, and had decided to do some work. Since it was Biram, he sent the guard home to get some rest so he could celebrate with his family later in the day. Ozren assured him he would make the necessary security checks.

I waited outside, shivering, until I saw the guard leave. Ozren let me in. We went first to the basement, where the panel that controlled the sensors in the haggadah gallery was located. As director, Ozren had the override codes, so the crisscross of motion sensors could be temporarily blinded. The video monitor was another thing: that couldn't be disconnected without triggering an alarm. But Ozren said he'd thought of that. We walked down the halls, past the prehistoric boat and the antiquities collections, until we stood at the door of the haggadah gallery.

Ozren's hand was shaking a little as he entered his code, and he mispunched one of the numbers.

"I can do that only once. A second error, the alarm goes off." He took a deep breath and punched his numbers again. The pad blinked back at him: ENTERED. But the door did not open. "It's on after-hours setting, so it takes two of us. The chief librarian's code also is necessary. You do it, will you? My hand won't stop shaking."

"But I don't know it!"

"Twenty-five, five, eighteen, ninety-two," he said without hesitation. I looked at him questioningly, but he just nodded to go ahead. I did. The door swished open.

"But how did you know it?"

He smiled. "She was my assistant for nine years. She's a great librarian, but she has no head for figures. The only number she can remember is Tito's birthday. She uses it for everything."

We entered the room, which was kept very dim, with just enough light to allow the security camera to function. The lens stared down at us, recording our every move. Ozren had brought a flashlight so that we wouldn't have to turn lights on. He'd tied a red dishcloth over it to mute the brightness. The beam danced around the walls for a second as he reached into his pocket for the digital key that opened the vitrine.

He swiped the key, then folded back the glass pane. Werner's fake was open to the illumination of the Spanish seder, the prosperous family, and the mysterious African woman in her Jewish dress. It was the page where I'd found the white hair in the original. Ozren closed Werner's copy, lifted it from the vitrine, and set it on the floor.

In the reverse of the moment that had passed between us six years before, I handed him the Sarajevo Haggadah.

He held it in both hands, and then he pressed it to his forehead for a moment. "Welcome back," he said.

He set it carefully on the forms and gingerly turned the parchments until he reached the seder illumination.

I had been holding my breath without even knowing it. Ozren reached to close the vitrine.

"Wait," I said. "Just let me look at it for one more second." I wanted another instant with the book before I had to let go of it forever.

It wasn't until later that I realized why I could see it, there, in that dim light, when I hadn't ever seen it before. The color temperature of the red light emitted by the torch made it possible. There were faint markings following the line of the hem of the African woman's gown. The artist had used a tone just one value darker than the saffron of the robe. The lines of script were so fine, impossibly fine—made by a brush of just a single hair. When I had studied the image in daylight, or in the cool light of fluorescent bulbs, the tiny lines had looked like shading, merely; a clever artist's suggestion of fabric folds.

But in the warmer light of Ozren's muted torch, I could see that the hairlike lines were script. Arabic script.

"Quick! Quick, Ozren, give me a magnifying glass."

"What? Are you mad? We don't have time for this. What the—"

I reached up and pulled his glasses off his face. I lowered the left lens to the tiny line of script and squinted. Then I read aloud:

" '*I fashioned*'—or the word could be translated as 'made' or 'painted'—" My voice was breaking. I put out a hand to steady myself against the vitrine. " '*I fashioned these pictures for Binyamin ben Netanel ha-Levi.*' And then there's a name. Ozren, there's a name! Zana—no, not Zana, it's Zahra—'*Zahra bint Ibrahim al-Tarek, known in Seville as al-Mora.*' Al-Mora—it means 'the Moorish woman.' Ozren, it must be her—the woman in saffron. She's the artist."

Ozren snatched back his glasses and peered closely at the script as I held the flashlight steady. "An African Muslim. Woman. The mysterious illuminator of the Sarajevo Haggadah. And we've been staring at her self-portrait for five hundred years."

I was so thrilled by the discovery that I'd forgotten we were in the middle of a reverse heist. The low whir of the video camera, doing an automatic pan of the room, reminded me. Ozren lifted the side of the vitrine and locked it with a definitive click.

"What do we do about that?" I said, pointing up at the video camera.

He signaled me to follow him. From a locked cabinet in his office, he selected a tape from a shelf of videos arranged by date. He set the chosen one on his desk. He had a sticky label prepared, marked with that day's date. He simply placed that label over the existing one, from the same hour a week earlier.

"Now we have to get you out of here before the guards arrive." On the way out, we stopped at the security desk. Ozren filled in the log, showing that the 4:30 rounds had been completed without incident. Then he pressed the Eject button on the video monitor and switched the videos.

With a few quick tugs, he pulled the incriminating tape from its plastic container.

"Dump it on the way back to Sweet Corner, would you? Somewhere inconspicuous, where there is a lot of garbage already. I just have to reset the motion sensors and wait to brief the morning guards. Then I'll meet you there. We still have to dispose of the fake haggad—"

We both realized at the same moment. The fake—the incriminating, perfect fake—was still where we had left it, on the gallery floor.

It was ten minutes to five. If one of the morning guards arrived early, we would be, as they say in the classics, totally stuffed. The next few minutes of my life might be the segment I would be most inclined to edit out. To say my heart was pounding would be a gross understatement. I fully expected to have an aneurysm. I sprinted to Ozren's office, fumbled with keys, opened the case, grabbed another substitute tape, and then rifled through his assistant's desk, looking for a sticky label. I couldn't find one.

"Shit! Shit!" I couldn't believe we were going to be caught redhanded for the lack of a damn sticky label.

"They're in here," said Ozren, opening a small wooden box. He had raced back to the haggadah gallery, repunched the codes, and grabbed the fake. Together, we ran to the security desk. I slipped on the marble floor and cracked my knee, hard. The tape skidded across the floor. Ozren turned and swept it up, then pulled me to my feet so roughly he almost dislocated my shoulder. My eyes were tearing. "I'm *so* not cut out for this kind of thing," I whimpered.

"Never mind that now, OK? Just go, quick. Take this." He thrust Werner's fake at me. "I'll see you at Sweet Corner." He pushed me out the door.

I was one block from the museum when I saw a man in a gray museum guard's uniform ambling toward me, yawning. As I passed him, I had to force myself to keep walking normally—as normally as I could with my aching knee. When I got to Sweet Corner, the pastry chef was already at work, firing up his ovens. He gave me a very strange look as I hobbled up the steps to the attic, alone. Inside, I rekindled the fire and thought about Zahra al-Tarek, artist. How she had learned how to paint, how to write. No mean achievements for a woman of her day. There were so many anonymous women artists who had been cheated of the acclaim that was their due. Now, at last, this one would be known. Famous. I could do that for her.

And it was just a beginning. The other name, ha-Levi. The mention of Seville—if she was in Seville, and the ha-Levi family was, too, then that meant the illuminations probably predated the text. . . . The number of lines of inquiry radiating from these few words would lead to so many more discoveries, so much more knowledge. I propped a couple of Ozren's pillows against the wall. It would be wet season in the Top End for two, three months. I leaned back and started planning a trip to Spain.

A few minutes later, I heard Ozren coming. He was calling out my name as he bounded up the stairs, two at a time. I could hear the ancient treads and risers creaking in complaint. He was as excited about this as I was. He understood. He would help me. Together, we would seek out the truth about Zahra al-Tarek. Together, we would bring her back to life.

But first, there was a chore to do.

Ozren stood in front of the fire, Werner's facsimile in his hand. He didn't move.

"What are you thinking about?"

"I'm thinking that if I could have one wish, this would be the last book ever to be burned in my city."

It was the cold hour, just before sunrise. I stared at the flames, thinking of blackening parchments in a medieval auto-da-fé; of youthful Nazi faces, lit by bonfires of burning books; of the shelled and gutted ruin, just a few blocks away, of Sarajevo's library. Book burnings. Always the forerunners. Heralds of the stake, the ovens, the mass graves.

" 'Burn but his books,' " I said. Caliban, plotting against Prospero. I couldn't remember the rest. But Ozren knew.

> "Remember first to possess his books; for without them
> He's but a sot, as I am, nor hath not
> One spirit to command. . . ."

Through the frosty panes of the dormer window, I watched the stars fade as the sky slowly brightened to a rich ultramarine. *Ultra*, "the far side." *Marine*, "of the sea." The color named for the journey of lapis lazuli, from the far side of the sea to the palette of Zahra al-Tarek. The same stone that Werner had ground to make the rich blues that would soon blacken to carbon.

Ozren stared at the book in his hand, then at the fire. "I don't think I can," he said.

I looked at the fake. As a facsimile, it was a masterpiece. My master's piece. The epitome of everything Werner had learned in his long life, everything he'd taught me about the importance of mastering the old crafts until you could do what the craftsmen had known how to do. Perhaps, I thought, I could put it in the wheelie cart. Take it to Amitai. After a decent interval, he could announce that it was a gift, made as a labor of love by the great Werner Heinrich for the people of Israel. It was, after all, now a part of the history of the true haggadah. Even though it was a part of the history that would need to stay secret for a while. But one day, maybe, somebody would puzzle it out. Just as a conservator in the next century, or the one after, would find the seed I dropped into the binding of the genuine haggadah, between the first and second quires. A Moreton Bay fig seed, from the fruit of the big twisty trees that line the shores of Sydney Harbour. I had done it on a whim, my last day in Sydney. My mark. A clue, for someone like me in the far future, who would find it, and wonder. . . .

"It's incriminating," I said. "Dangerous for you."

"I know. But there have been too many books burned in this city."

"Too many books burned in the world."

Even though we were by the fire, I shivered. Ozren put the book down, on the mantel above the hearth. He reached for me. This time, I didn't pull away.

Afterword

People of the Book is a work of fiction inspired by the true story of the Hebrew codex known as the Sarajevo Haggadah. While some of the facts are true to the haggadah's known history, most of the plot and all of the characters are imaginary.

I first heard of the haggadah when I was a newspaper reporter, in Sarajevo to cover the Bosnian war for *The Wall Street Journal*. At that time, the city's fire-gutted library reeked of burned pages after the barrage of Serbian phosphorous shells. The Oriental Institute and its marvelous manuscripts were in ashes, and the National Museum of Bosnia was splattered with the shrapnel of frequent shelling. The fate of the Sarajevo Haggadah—priceless jewel of the Bosnian collections—was unknown, and the subject of much journalistic speculation.

Only after the war was it revealed that a Muslim librarian, Enver Imamovic, had rescued the codex during the shelling and hidden it for safekeeping in a bank vault. It was not the first time this Jewish book had been saved by Muslim hands. In 1941, Dervis Korkut, a renowned Islamic scholar, smuggled the manuscript out of the museum under the very nose of a Nazi general, Johann Hans Fortner (later hanged for war crimes), and spirited it away to a mosque in the mountains, where it remained safely hidden till after World War II. While these heroic rescues were my initial inspirations, the characters to whom I have ascribed these actions in the novel are entirely fictional.

The haggadah first came to the attention of scholars in Sarajevo in 1894, when an indigent Jewish family offered it for sale. Art historians were excited by its discovery because it was one of the earliest illuminated medieval Hebrew books to come to light. Its discovery called into question the belief that figurative art had been suppressed among medieval Jews for religious reasons. Unfortunately, scholars were not able to learn much of the book's creation other than that it was made in Spain, possibly as early as the mid-fourteenth century, toward the close of the period known as *Convivencia*, when Jews, Christians, and Muslims coexisted in relative peace.

Of the haggadah's history during the tumultuous years of the Spanish Inquisition and the 1492 expulsion of the Jews nothing is known. The novel's chapters "A White Hair" and "Saltwater" are entirely fictional. However, there is a saffron-robed, black-skinned woman at the seder table in one of the haggadah's illuminations, and the mystery of her identity inspired my inventions.

By 1609, the haggadah had found its way to Venice, where the handwritten inscription by a Catholic priest named Vistorini apparently saved it from the book burnings of the pope's Inquisition. Nothing is known of Vistorini beyond the books that have survived because they bear his signature. But many of the Catholic Hebraists of the period were converted Jews, and I used that fact in "Wine Stains." In that chapter, also, the character of Judah Aryeh is inspired by the life of Leon Modena as described in *The Autobiography of a Seventeenth Century Rabbi*, translated and edited by Mark R. Cohen. Richard Zacks provided an invaluable collection of materials on gambling in seventeenth-century Venice.

Because Bosnia was under occupation by the Austro-Hungarian empire when the haggadah came to light there in 1894, it was natural that it should be sent to Vienna, hub of culture and scholarship, for study and restoration. For the atmosphere in the city at that time, and especially for details such as the unctuous manners of telephone operators, I am in debt to the remarkable narrative history *A Nervous Splendour* by Frederic Morton. Similarly, Brian Hall's *The Dreamers* and *The Impossible Country* provided indispensable insights. While it is true that, by modern standards, the rebinding of the haggadah was mishandled in Vienna, the matter of the missing clasps is a novelist's invention.

Before writing "An Insect's Wing" I had many long conversations

with members of the family of Dervis Korkut, and am in especial debt
to Servet Korkut, who was by her husband's side and supported his many
heroic acts of resistance during the fascist occupation of Sarajevo. I hope
that the Korkut family will find my invented family, the Kamals, in sympathy with their humanistic ideals. For details of the experiences of
young Jewish Partisans, I relied on the harrowing account by Mira Papo,
which is in the collection of Yad Vashem, where the librarians were most
helpful.

The librarians of Sarajevo are a very special breed. At least one of
them, Aida Buturovic, gave her life as she saved books from Sarajevo's
burning library. Others, such as Kemal Bakarsic, took immense risks,
night after night, to evacuate collections under dangerous conditions.
Enver Imamovic, as previously noted, saved the haggadah during a period of intense shelling. I am grateful to both men for speaking to me
about their experiences, and also to Sanja Baranac, Jacob Finci, Mirsada
Muskic, Denana Buturovic, Bernard Septimus, Bezalel Narkiss, and B.
Nezirovic for their help and insight.

For assistance with research and translation, I would like to thank
Andrew Crocker, Naida Alic, Halima Korkut, and Pamela J. Matz. For
introducing me to the *Parnassius* butterfly at the Harvard Museum of
Natural History, I'm grateful to Naomi Pierce.

Pamela J. Spitzmueller and Thea Burns of Harvard College Library
were generous with their stories of the sleuthing aspect of book conservation. In December 2001, Andrea Pataki very kindly allowed me to be
one more presence in a very crowded room while she worked on the real
Sarajevo Haggadah under heavy guard at the European Union Bank. I
would not have been able to observe her meticulous work without the
intercession of Fred Eckhard and Jacques Klein of the United Nations.

For letting me spill kosher wine on bits of old parchment, for explaining the fine points of video spectral comparators, and for being an Aussie
when I wasn't sure that the career I'd invented for Hanna was all that
plausible, I am thankful to my *paysan* Narayan Khandekar at the Straus
Center for Conservation. While I learned a great deal about the career
and the technical aspects of conservation from both Andrea Pataki and

Narayan Khandekar, the fictional characters Hanna Heath and Razmus Kanaha bear absolutely no resemblance to either one of these real-life professionals.

I would not have had access to all the riches of Harvard's libraries and museums were it not for a fellowship at the Radcliffe Institute for Advanced Study, for which I am most grateful to Drew Gilpin Faust. Judy Vichniac led an amazingly supportive staff at the institute. The Radcliffe fellows, especially the members of the Tuesday writers' table, helped shape my thinking and writing in myriad ways.

I also relied heavily on the insights of my early readers, especially Graham Thorburn, the Horwitz team of Joshua, Elinor, Norman, and Tony, Rabbi Caryn Broitman of the Martha's Vineyard Hebrew Center, *sofer stam* Jay Greenspan, Christine Farmer, Linda Funnel, Clare Reihill, Marie Anderson, and Gail Morgan.

Thanks hardly seem adequate for my editor Molly Stern and my agent Kris Dahl, who are, as ever, my indispensable supports and two of the most formidable professionals in publishing.

Lastly and most of all, I have to thank Tony and Nathaniel, inspirations and welcome distractions, without whom nothing is possible.

**Geraldine Brooks's newest novel
is available from Viking.**

Read on for the opening pages of . . .

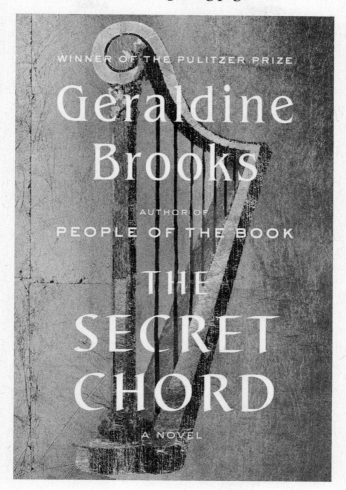

WINNER OF THE PULITZER PRIZE

Geraldine
Brooks

AUTHOR OF
PEOPLE OF THE BOOK

THE
SECRET
CHORD

A NOVEL

*T*here was an almond blossom, yesterday. It had opened its pale petals on a twig of the bough that curls and twists up to my windowsill. This morning, the blossom is gone; the paleness upon the twig is snow. It does one no good, in these hills, to set store by the earth's steady warming.

My body is as bent as that bough. The cold is an ache in my bones. I am sure that this year's reaping will be the last that I see. I hope only for one more season of summer fruit, for the ease of the hot sun on my back, for ripe figs, warm from the tree, spilling their sweet nectar through these splayed fingers. I have come to love this plain house, here among the groves. I have laid my head down in many places—on greasy sheepskins at the edge of battlefields, under the black expanse of goat hair tents, on the cold stone of caves and on the scented linens of palaces. But this is the only home that has been my own.

They are at work, already, on Har Moriah. From across the wadi, I can hear the thin squeal of the planes scraping upon the logs. Hard work to get these trees here; felled in the forests of the Lebanon, lashed together into rafts, floated south on the sea, dragged up from the coast by oxen. Now the tang of cut cedar perfumes the air. Soon, the king will come, as he does every morning, to inspect the progress of the work. I know when he arrives by the cheers of the men. Even conscripted workers and slaves call out in praise of him, because he treats them fairly and honors their skill.

I close my eyes, and imagine how it will be, when the walls have risen from the foundations of dressed stone: the vast pillars carved with lilies and pomegranates, sunlight glinting on cladding of gold . . .

It is the only way I will ever see it: these pictures in my mind's eye. I will not live to make the ascent up the broad stairs, to stand within the gilded precincts as the scent *of burning fat and incense rises to the sky. It is well. I would not wish to go without him. I thought, at one time, that we would go together. I can still see his eyes, bright with the joy of creation, as he chose and planned what materials, what embellishments, pacing the floor, throwing his arms up and shaping the pillars as he envisioned them, his long fingers carving the air. But that was before I had to tell him that he would never build the temple. Before I had to tell him that all his killing——the very blood that, one might say, slakes the mortar of those foundation stones——had stained him too deeply. Strange words, you might think, to come from the selfsame source that had required these killings of him.*

Hard words, like blows. The blast from heaven, issuing from my mouth. Words born of thoughts I had not had, delivered with anger I did not feel, spilling out in a voice I did not even know for my own. Words whose reason no human heart could fathom. Civilization is built upon the backs of men like him, whose blood and sweat make it possible. But comes the peace, and the civil world has scant place for such men. It fell to me to tell him so.

And like all such words that have formed upon my lips, these have become true in fact. It has come to be just as the voice said it would: this one dear ambition denied him. A bequest, instead, to his heir.

In this, I am more fortunate than he. I have lived to complete my life's great work. I have rolled and tied the scrolls with my own hands, sealed them with wax, secured them in clay vessels, and seen to their placement in the high, dry caves where I played as a child. In the nights, which have become so long for me, I think of those scrolls, and I feel a measure of peace. I remember it all so clearly, that day, at the turn of the year, the month when kings go out to battle. How warily I broached the matter. It might seem odd to say so, as my whole life in his service had been bent to this purpose: the speaking of truth, welcome or no. But it is one thing to transmit the divine through a blasting storm of holy noise, another thing entirely to write a history forged from human voices, imperfect memories, self-interested accounts.

I have set it all down, first and last, the light and the dark. Because of my work, he will live. And not just as a legend lives, a safe tale for the fireside, fit for the ears of the young. Nothing about him ever was safe. Because of me, he will live in death as he did in life: a man who dwelt in the searing glance of the divine, but who sweated and stank, rutted without restraint, butchered the innocent, betrayed those most loyal to him.

Who loved hugely, and was kind; who listened to brutal truth and honored the truth teller; who flayed himself for his wrongdoing; who built a nation, made music that pleased heaven and left poems in our mouths that will be spoken by people yet unborn.

I have had a great length of days, and been many things. A reluctant warrior. A servant, a counselor. Sometimes, perhaps, his friend. And this, also, have I been: a hollow reed through which the breath of truth sounded its discordant notes.

Words. Words upon the wind. What will endure, perhaps, is what I have written. If so, it is enough.

I

A man alone in a room. Not such an extraordinary thing. Yet as I stepped into the chamber I had a sense of something out of place. My eye traveled around the space, the woven pillows, the low tables set with sweating ewers of cool water . . . all was in order, yet something was not right. Then I grasped it. It had been a while since I had found him in a room by himself. For a long time, it seemed, he had moved in a press of people: members of his household, the men of his army, his sons, servants, sycophants.

He stood by the open window, his back to me. From my place by the door I could not see what he saw, but the sounds made plain enough what held his gaze: the snap of banners in the breeze, the stamp of hooves, the wince and grind of iron on stone. And woven among these, like a bright thread through homespun, the sudden excited shouts of little boys. For them, born in the years of victory, muster for war was cause for uncomplicated joy. I knew that giddy thrill. I had been such a boy myself, once. When he, little more than a youth, led the band that sacked my village.

His fists, balled tight, were planted on the wide sill of the window embrasure, his arms encircled by polished copper cuffs. His hair, the same color as the copper, was undressed, and fell in a dense mane against the fine black wool of his mantle. The cuffs glinted in the low slant of early light as his arm muscles flexed. He was clenched from head to foot.

I am not a coward. Being in his service does not allow for it. My life, at certain times, has required me to draw upon deep wells of courage, and I am glad to say that I have never yet come up dry. But as I have resolved to set down a full account here, so I must begin with an honest accounting of myself. That morning, I was afraid. I had been summoned from my bed when it was still full dark, and though my slave, when he called me, had thought to bring a tray of warm bread fresh from the ovens, I had not touched it. Now, my empty stomach churned. Sound carries, at that hour, and as I waited in the anteroom, even the heavy cedar door could not muffle the angry voices within.

When Yoav exited the room, he burst through the door so abruptly that the young guard barely had time to come to attention, the butt of his spear striking the stone floor a few seconds after his general had already swept past him. Yoav's lips were drawn thin as a sheet of linen, his skin as pallid. He paused for a moment, fiddling with a strap on his greaves. His hand, which I saw was trembling slightly, could not manage the buckle. I have known Yoav since I was a child and he a youth thinking to kill me. I have seen him outnumbered on the battlefield and watched him run a man through at close quarters. I have seen him stand accused of murder, awaiting a death sentence. But never before had I seen his hand shake. He saw that I noticed, and he scowled. "Go in," he said tersely. "He wants you." Then, as I edged past him: "Take care. He is in a rage. His mood is foul."

The guard opened the door for me, looking to neither right nor left as I passed from the anteroom to the inner chamber. I stood, just inside, waiting for acknowledgment. After a time, unsure if he knew that I was there, I cleared my throat. Still he did not turn. I held myself motionless, my gaze on the yellow shaft of sunlight widening upon the flagstones. Although it was early, the room was warming. Soon enough, it would be hot. I felt a bead of sweat forming on my brow.

Suddenly, he opened his fists, reached for the shutters, and slammed them shut. He turned, his light mantle swinging. I, who had served him for years, was used to that face, its grave beauty, the bright glance that could kindle love or fear. But the expression was not the one I had expected. Yoav was son of the king's older sister; they had become men together. He knew David as well as anyone alive. Yoav had said anger, and anger was there, but I could tell he had not read his uncle in full. Anger was there, but not anger only. The tense set of David's body showed will at work, containing wrath, but also grief. The glint in his eye was, I believe, a tear.

"What is the profit of being an anointed king, Natan, if I am to be confined here like a prisoner?"

"Your generals act only out of love for you—"

His hand spliced the air. "They act out of fear." He had never been a man for platitude. "Love?" He spat the word. "There is no love in this. This is fear and mistrust. And for what? The lapse of a moment, merely. How many wars have we made together? You have been at my side, time and again, when we fought the Plishtim. You were with me in the south when we crushed the Moavites, and in the north against the Arameans. And you know well—who better?—I was a warrior for years before that. In all those battles, when did I ever flinch? Tell me. Tell me a time I faltered." The voice had steadied now, and was rising.

That voice. So familiar to me. So familiar to all of us. *The sweet singer of Israel.* So the people called him, long before he was king. I had heard that singer's voice fill a hall, and bring tears to the cheeks of seasoned warriors. But I had heard it also on the battlefield, fierce and wild, carrying over the clash of arms and the cries of the dying.

"Never," I answered him. This was not flattery, but unburnished truth. In my mind, the visions crowded, one layered upon the other, each of them with the unnatural vividness of memories forged at moments when one's life is at risk. I could see bright hair flying from beneath the iron helmet as he sprinted before us into a clatter of arrows, the faceted muscles of his calves as he led the swarm up a siege ladder, the sinews of his back, taut with the strain of the pulled bow as he braced himself in the *merkava*. Every memory I had of him was a view from behind. Simply because, at the deadly moment, he was always in the forefront.

I had been trailing after him, as ever, at the end of that most recent campaign, of which he now spoke. We had been fighting for more than a week, the advantage now theirs, now ours. The day was hot, windless. The air was thick with lingering smoke from the night's death pyres, still smoldering. The stench of charred bone met the stink of rot and vomit, shit and sweat. I have never loved war, as some men love it. I have fought of necessity, as has every man my age with two legs, two arms and wit enough to follow a simple order. It is what the times, and the Land, have required of us.

It was nearing sunset on the eighth day. We'd fought since dawn. I had reached that point beyond exhaustion, where every muscle quivers and my mind could not hold a thought beyond the next step, and the one after, the next breath, and the one after. We went forward through sheer will—his will, that force that could goad a man to do what was beyond him. Finally, in the long shadows of the late afternoon, the Plishtim began to fall back from the plain. Their retreat was toward the foothills. Another general would have let them go and been glad of it. But he saw that if they secured that high ground they might regroup and come at us again, this time with their archers positioned to advantage. So he called us to ranks with a curdling cry. I glimpsed his face through the crowd of men. It was bloodied, dirt-streaked, avid. Then he turned, fist to the sky, and sprinted. He set the pace for the fleetest of his runners, youths who could give him a decade. Even uphill, he seemed to fly over the loose stones that slid out from underfoot and left me skidding and swearing.

I fell behind, and lost sight of him. Others—younger men, better fighters—overtook me, swarming to him, compelled by his courage. When I finally glimpsed him again, he was above me on a long, slender ridge, in the thick of fierce fighting. Trying to narrow the distance between us, I lost my footing entirely on the uncertain ground. I slipped. Metal, leather and flesh scraped against rough limestone that bit like snaggleteeth. I could not control my fall until I planted my foot into something that gave softly under my weight. The man had been attempting to crawl away, dragging himself with his remaining hand while a slime of blood pulsed from the stump of his sword arm. My boot, mashing his neck flat into stone, had put an end to that. When I lifted my foot, the man gave a wet gargle, and was still. I scraped the mess off my boot onto the nearest rock and went on.

When I reached the ridge, the king was making an end of another fighter. He was up close, eye to eye. His sword had entered just above the man's groin. He drew it upward, in a long, slow, arcing slash. As he pulled the blade back—slick, dripping—long tubes of bowel came tumbling after. I could see the dying man's eyes, wide with horror, his hands gripping for his guts, trying to push them back into the gaping hole in his belly. The king's own eyes were blank—all the warmth swallowed by the black stain of widening pupils. David reached out an arm and pushed the man hard in the chest. He fell backward off the narrow ledge and rolled down the slope, his entrails unfurling after him like a glossy ribband.

I was engaged myself then, by a bullnecked spearman who required all my flagging strength. He was bigger than me, but clumsy, and I used his size against him, so that as I feinted one way, he lunged with his spear, overbalanced and fell right onto the dagger that I held close and short at my side. I felt the metal grating against the bone of his rib, and then I mustered enough force to thrust the tip sharply upward, the blade's full length inside him, in the direction of his heart. I felt the warm wetness of his insides closing about my fist. It was intimate as a rape.

When I made an end of it and could look up, the king had advanced again, to a higher ledge, and stood atop another fleeing adversary. Legs astride the body, he raised his dagger arm. The air throbbed then, the skirl of wings. A carrion bird. Reflexively, my eye followed it. That is how I saw the spearman. The setting sun had been hidden in a purple flounce of cloud, but just then a throbbing yellow crescent of fire broke the edge, and in the beam of sudden light, I caught a glint from behind the cover of an outcrop—a spear, poised for the cast. The spear thrower was above and to the right of the king. His legs were well braced, his line perfect. The bronze shaft sailed out of his hand. It would have been a lethal throw, if Yoav's younger brother Avishai had not risked his own life to deflect it.

Avishai leaped between the king and the spear, his head back, howling. He expected to die. Every man on that ridge turned to witness it. At the deadly second, some warrior instinct caused him to adjust his stance by a hairbreadth and raise his bow. The spear tip caught on the edge of it, splintering the wood, skittering harmlessly across the rocky ledge. It was the kind of thing we'd seen David do. Now a younger man had done it for him.

We all cheered, of course. Someone slew the spearman, and then the fighting resumed in the exhilarated frenzy that comes from catastrophe averted.

But the king did not wish to hear of this from me. Not today. So I buried the image of his near death and said: "Every man who has served with you knows how you have prevailed. Every one of us knows what you are."

"'Are'? Say, rather, 'were.' That is what Yoav means: 'You *were* a mighty soldier, but now we must fight your battles for you. I tell you, when Avishai leaped before that spear, I knew how it would be seen. I had to laud Avishai before the men. It was his due. But the words were gall in my mouth. And even though he is my sister's son and the brother of my general, I tell you this, Natan: I wanted to strike him dead. I wanted to grasp the end of that shattered shaft and plunge it through his side. I have lived most of my life in soldiers' camps. I know what they saw. I know how they think. Their confidence sours as sudden as curdled milk."

"Not so. You may think you know the mind of the common soldier, but with respect—you are not one, and have not been for some time. The men know this, even if you do not. Times have changed, and you, King, have changed them. You are not that petty chieftain who led scattered bands of outlaws to skirmishes in the hills. Why do we not cower in the wastes, hiding amid thorns and rocks as we used to do every time a sortie out of Mitzrayim marched across our land? Why do we not huddle trapped in the highlands while the Plishtim garrison the passes to the fertile plains? It is not so long since we had to grovel to them for enough iron even to make farm tools, much less weapons. Now we push them to the coast and pursue them to the very gates of their towns. Now the very best of their fighters come and offer their sword hilts in your service. You know they would not bend the knee to any other man. Not they, nor the Hittites, nor the Yebusites, nor any other of the strangers who serve you. Do not tell me you would put all this at risk—after all it cost to bring it about—for some warrior-pride. You, who have nothing to prove to anyone about valor or skill at arms. You have taught our enemies to fear us. You are the lamp of Israel. Would you chance to quench it?"

I had thought what I said would stoke his vanity. Instead, he glared at me. His eyes, that amber gaze that I was used to feel warm with affection, had turned cold. "Spare me, Natan. I have had an earful of this womanly keening, these empty pieties. From you, at least, I expect to hear the truth. The truth is, I have made this army. It's I who drove them, I who gave them confidence. Too much, it seems. They think they can do without me, set me aside like some heathen's war-god idol, set up in a temple to bring good luck." He turned away, back to the window. He flung open one of the shutters. A few minutes, and Yoav's voice rose, giving the order to move out.

"Will you not go down? It would put heart into the troops."

"'Go down'?" He mimicked my solicitous tone in a voice oily with contempt. "To remind my men that I stay behind? That for the first time in memory I do not lead them? Are you mad? Of course I will not go down."

A great cheer rose as the runners set off. The foot soldiers first—spears, archers, slings. This was followed by a clatter of hoof-beats and the squeal of metal wheels as fifty merkavot—a full half of all we had then—pulled out behind them. Dust motes rose from the street and drifted into the room, sparkling. He turned from the window, crossed the room and laid his fingers lightly upon the neck of his harp. There was always one near to hand; every servant knew to see to that. A small one hung by the window in his bedchamber. He said that when a night wind stirred the strings, it was a welcome awakening. He would rise from his bed and pray to the Name, who had blessed him so greatly. The instrument he reached for now was one of his favorites, a fine tall harp from Mitzrayim, the slender curve of its soundboard a smooth and perfect arc such as that land's craftsmen know how to fashion. But, like all his harps, this one had been adapted to his use, the number of its strings doubled to allow for strange tunings, with half and quarter tones that gave his music its unique, complex sound.

"You know, I suppose, why Yoav sent you." I was unsure how to answer this. I did not want him to think that Yoav and I had been discussing ways to handle him, even though this was the truth. But it seemed he did not expect an answer. He snorted, and gave a smile that had no joy in it. "I know what Yoav has in his mind: he sees me sitting here with you, picking at the skein of my deeds like a woman at her weaving basket. He wants to give me occupation while he usurps my place and marches my men to war. You, I suppose, support him in this."

"No, I do not."

"No?" He looked up. "What's this? You are at odds with Yoav?"

"I do not think a recitation of your victories is worthy of your time." I took a breath and dived deep. "Nor mine."

"Is that so? My victories are an unworthy subject for your talents?"

Have a care, Natan, I told myself. It is one thing to speak hard truths to a king in that strange voice that rises up unbidden from the earth and echoes with the power of the heavens. It is another thing entirely to speak frankly to him as one man to another, especially as I am a man in his service. *Eved hamalek*. The servant of the king. But, then, what service could I offer, if not this: speaking, where other men held a prudent peace. Whatever the risk, I had him now. His anger was shifting, away from Yoav and toward me. I had drawn the boar. Now I had to stick him.

"Any half-skilled graver can etch a stela that says in this or that place the king did vanquish this or that people. I am sure the great king of the Two Rivers and your neighbor the pharaoh, each of them, has a legion of gravers at work this very moment, making fine monuments."

"And why should they not?"

"Because the rubble of a hundred such stelae lines the walls of our sheep folds. And the dust of a thousand more blows about the Land, ground down to sand."

He gave me a glance that, if not warm, was no longer a shard of cold stone. He returned his gaze to the harp, running a finger up and down the silken grain of the wood. "Go on."

"In our wine store at home, there was a graved stone, holding up the lintel. Basalt, I think, finely dressed. It stood out among the common limestone, so that was why I noticed it, I suppose, when I was a boy. There were just a few words of an inscription, very worn. I was excited when I found it—it is the kind of thing that fires the mind of a child—and I showed my father." I remembered the cool dark cavern carved deep into the rock, the tall, sweating rows of pithoi, the biscuit scent of the clay, the rich aroma of fermentation. My father's large hand, stained from many pressings, fingering the hollows etched into the stone. I remember that he turned to me, and smiled, and commended me for noticing it. "He was an unlettered man, but he guessed the writing might be in the style of the Hittites. No doubt it lauded the victory of some important leader. I would look at those words and wonder, Who was he? What manner of man? What sort of boy? Which people helped him to power? Which hindered him . . ." I paused, uncertain whether to continue. But David's gaze was on me now, arrested. So I plowed on.

"Whoever he was, he was gone. His story, however glorious, lost, and so thoroughly forgotten that his monument had been broken up into building stones and set to use in a humble vintner's storeroom." Here we came to the nub of it. My own voice had risen as I spoke. I took a breath, and lowered it. "You know my first prophecy." Even as I said the words, I felt sickness rise at my own memory of it. When one becomes a sounding brass for the voice of the unseen, there is a price to be paid: the throbbing head, the darkening vision, the rasping breath, the falling fits and spasms. And when it happens to you on a day when you have lost everything, a wicked day of death and butchery, it is hard, indeed, to revisit the moment. I had begun to breathe unevenly, just bringing it to mind.

"Of course I know. I have built all this"—he swept his arm in a wide, expansive gesture meant to encompass more than a fine room in a well-built palace—"on the foundation of those words. Every man alive knows what you said that day."

"It was not I who said it," I murmured, but he shrugged off my correction.

"What has that to do with this matter?"

"Your line will not fail. You know this. Yet memory surely will. Your sons—what will they remember? Or their sons, after? When all who knew you in life are but bleached bone and dust, your descendants, your people, will crave to understand what manner of man you were when you did these deeds, first and last. Not just the deeds. The man."

He gazed at me for a long moment. His face was unreadable. He picked up a low carved stool then, and when I moved to take it from him, he waved me off. He carried it to the harp and settled himself to play. As an afterthought, he motioned me to sit, so I sank gratefully upon the pillows and let out the breath I had not even realized I was holding. He tilted the tall harp, settling it against his shoulder gently, as a woman settles her infant. His fingers rolled a few idle triplets, but his gaze was fixed on the distant view of hills, the olive trees silver in the sunlight.

"It is true, what you say." All the anger was gone from his voice. "When I was a youth, learning war, I often thought of it. We hear of men like Shalmanezer or Sargon, who won great battles. Of Ramses, who built the mighty temples on the backs of our ancestors, or of Hammurabi, who, they say, ruled with wise laws. But these are names only. It would be something, to know their nature. To know them as men." He paused, his eyes still distant. "To be known as a man." His fingertips pressed harder against the strings. His hands were strong, but the fingers were slender, moving swiftly through the tall strings, weaving sound from the filaments.

It was as if the harp were a loom, the notes he drew from it a bright thread forming a splendid pattern. He played this way often, even interrupting meetings with his generals. He said that the music—its order and precision—helped him find the patterns in things—the way through the confusion of events and opinions to direction, to order, and beyond, to inspiration.

He played for some time. I do not know if he was improvising or playing from memory. The melody was sweet, intricate and soothing. You could read his mind through his music, always. I felt the tension in my body easing. I had been braced against his anger and his grief, but the music revealed a mellowing of his mood. Finally, he brought it to an end, in a graceful run of notes, and set the harp back upright. He turned his eyes on me. They were not cold now, but the expression remained opaque. "Catch a true likeness, see a plain reflection in the water of the well, you will not like the flaws revealed in the face that stares back at you."

I struggled to suppress a smile. I could not imagine that his own reflection had ever given him much grief. The golden shimmer of his youth had been tempered like worked metal in his adult years so that even now, in middle age, he gleamed. Years had brought only distinction to a beauty that had proved irresistible to men and women alike. But he was serious, deep in consideration of what I had said. I thought it best to add nothing further, to let the line of his thought lead him to his own conclusions. He commenced to play again, but after a time, his fingers paused and hovered above the strings. He turned his face to me.

"Perhaps I can prove myself brave in this, at least. I will consider it. Now go."

As the young guards' spears hit the floor and the door closed behind me, he started to play in earnest. His large, strong hands could draw forth a breadth of sound that one did not generally associate with the gentle harp. He could make it speak with a thousand voices, soft or stormy. He did so now. And then, that other instrument over which he had full mastery—his voice. It was an old song; I recognized it. He had sung it at his coronation.

> . . . in the day of thy power,
> in the beauties of holiness
> from the womb of the morning:
> thou hast the dew of thy youth. . . .

Good, I thought. Already he has turned his mind from the gnarled present to the shimmering past.

The next day, he sent word that I might make the history if I wished to do so. I assumed he would call for me when he was ready to begin. Awaiting his summons, I busied myself with the pumice, scraping calfskin. This work I would not trust to fragile clay. I have yet to train a servant who can bring a hide to my standard, and the scrolls to record the life of a king had to be free of all blemish.

But instead of the call to audience, what came from him instead that afternoon was a clay tablet with a list of three names upon it. Seraiah, his scribe, had graven it, apparently in some haste. I had to carry the tablet to the light to make sense of his hand. At first, I did not understand what David meant by it, but then I grasped his purpose. It was very like him. He was sending me to talk to those who had known him in childhood and as a youth, before I came into his service. At the end of the short list of names, Seraiah had added a note: *The king says: after these, you know the story as well as any and may set down what you see fit.* I smiled when I saw what he intended. It seemed he did not plan to give his own account at all. The work here would fall all to me, to gather and record these testimonies, to write my own account. I ran a finger over the names. *Mikhal.* That one name, alone, showed that he did not depend upon the emergence of a flattering portrait. Mikhal, for whom his very name was bile. Well, I thought. *That* will be a challenging encounter. She had been his first wife and, in name, a wife she remained, although to my knowledge she and David had not seen each other nor exchanged words in years. But as she remained part of his household, if the king bade her speak to me she would be obliged, at least, to receive me.

For a seer, I was remarkably obtuse. I know this now; I did not know it then. Yoav and I had conspired to find some occupation that, while worthwhile in itself, would serve to distract a restless and unhappy king. Instead, he had found a way to distract *me*, to get me out of his way. A man will silence the voice of his conscience when it suits him to commit sin. But if your "conscience" walks and breathes as a living man in your service, you might have to go to some additional lengths. I did not see this. I did not see that a proud and vital man who feared his manhood waning might take any reckless step to prove to himself it wasn't so. In the service of my gift, I have had to forgo much that makes a man in full. I know now that this sacrifice has left me blind to certain things. I can see what others cannot see, but sometimes I miss what is apparent to the dimmest simpleton.

At the time, I was caught up in the project, and interested in the names upon the list. One was unknown to me, and yet it was the very first he had set down. Seraiah the scribe had underscored it heavily, and written a note: *The king says, This one, before all others.* The next name, *Shammah,* I knew well enough. Shammah was one of David's older brothers. There had been seven of them, but Shammah was the last still living. He had been with us in the outlaw years, when Shaul the king turned on David and sought his death. There had been little love lost between David and his brothers. But Shaul's hatred of David had spread like a stain upon his close kin. They had been obliged to go into hiding with him in those years, because the alternative was imprisonment or execution. Now Shammah kept a household on the outskirts of Beit Lehem and administered that settlement in the king's name. According to the tablet, the unfamiliar name, *Nizevet bat Adael*, was a woman who was part of Shammah's household.

It was too late that day to set out, so I sent word to the stable to bespeak a mule for the following morning, and to the kitchens for provision. I left at first light.

A PENGUIN READERS GUIDE TO

PEOPLE OF THE BOOK

Geraldine Brooks

An Introduction to
People of the Book

Hanna Heath has cultivated a life of exquisite detachment. Raised by an aloof and often absent mother, she has eschewed any kind of deep emotional involvement. But—as an expert on rare books and an Australian whose nationality makes her the least controversial political choice to inspect a priceless Hebrew codex—Hanna is about to be plunged into a dangerous drama that will force her to confront both her past and the passions she has worked so hard to conceal.

It is 1996 when Hanna first flies to Sarajevo. The city's peace is new and still tenuous, but the opportunity to inspect the famous Sarajevo Haggadah is a career maker that she cannot pass up. A lavishly illuminated medieval Hebrew text, this haggadah is an anomaly that has fascinated scholars for generations and its survival in war-torn Bosnia is hailed as "a symbol of the survival of Sarajevo's multiethnic ideal."

Initially put off by her armed UN escort and the intense scrutiny of the National Museum where she is forced to perform her delicate work, Hanna is nonetheless mesmerized by the book's astonishing beauty. She studies its inks and parchment and recovers a fragment of an insect wing, salt crystals, wine stains, and a single white hair from between the delicate pages. She also notes that the clumsily rebound book is missing its original clasps. Each discovery is a clue that offers to unlock a chapter of the haggadah's mysterious history.

But Hanna becomes involved with more than the book during her time in Sarajevo. After she completes her initial documentation and repair work and leaves the city, she remains haunted by the few nights of intimacy she shared with Ozren Karaman, the Muslim librarian who braved enemy shelling to rescue the hagaddah. As she travels from Vienna to Boston and then to London in the hope of deciphering her scant evidence, Hanna fleshes out shadows of the book's past. Simultaneously, Brooks reveals the gripping tale of survival behind each miniscule artifact.

During World War II, a young partisan is saved by the same Muslim who risks his life to protect the haggadah from the Nazis. In fin-de-siècle Vienna, a Jewish doctor unwittingly plays a role in the theft of the book's clasps. In Inquisition-era Venice, a Catholic priest's most damning secret spares the book from burning. In Tarragona in 1492, a poor scribe completes the text just days before the expulsion of Spain's entire Jewish community. And in Seville in 1480, the unlikely artist paints a self-portrait into the Seder illustration.

Hanna is thrilled by her discoveries, little suspecting that her professional and personal worlds are about to come crashing down around her. When she returns to Sarajevo under very different circumstances, Hanna can no longer remain a dispassionate observer and finds that she has become one of the "people of the book" whose passions and sufferings, nobility and frailty, contribute to the hagaddah's continuing history.

The author of *Year of Wonders* and the Pulitzer Prize–winning *March*, Geraldine Brooks has made a name for herself as one of the foremost novelists of our era. In *People of the Book*—inspired by the true story of the Sarajevo Haggadah—she brilliantly interweaves an epic historical saga of persecution and survival with a powerful modern-day tale of private betrayals and international intrigue.

ABOUT GERALDINE BROOKS

Australian-born Geraldine Brooks is an author and journalist who grew up in the western suburbs of Sydney and attended Bethlehem College Ashfield and the University of Sydney. She worked as a reporter for *The Sydney Morning Herald* for three years as a feature writer with a special interest in environmental issues.

In 1982 she won the Greg Shackleton Australian News Correspondents scholarship to the journalism master's program at Columbia University in New York City. Later she worked for *The Wall Street Journal,* where she covered crises in the the the Middle East, Africa, and the Balkans.

She was awarded the Pulitzer Prize in fiction in 2006 for her novel *March* and her novel *Year of Wonders* is an international bestseller. She is also the author of the nonfiction works *Nine Parts of Desire* and *Foreign Correspondence.*

Brooks married author Tony Horwitz in Tourette-sur-loup, France, in 1984. They have one child and three dogs, and divide their time between homes in Martha's Vineyard, Massachusetts, and Sydney, Australia.

A Conversation with Geraldine Brooks

Your previous two novels are set during Europe's plague years and the American Civil War. Now, you've created an epic story about art and religious persecution. What is it that draws you to a particular subject or a particular historical era?

I love to find stories from the past where we can know something, but not everything; where there is enough of a historical record to have left us with an intriguing factual scaffolding, but where there are also enough unknowable voids in that record to allow room for imagination to work.

What do you think it is about the real Sarajevo Haggadah that has allowed it to survive the centuries?

It's a fascinating question: Why did this little book always find its protectors when so many others did not? It is interesting to me that the book was created in a period—*convivencia* Spain—when diversity was tolerated, even somewhat celebrated, and that it found its way centuries later to a similar place, Sarajevo. So even when hateful forces arose in those societies and crushed the spirit of multiethnic, interfaith acceptance, there were those individuals who saw what was happening and acted to stop it in any way they could.

Were you already working on People of the Book *when* March *won the Pulitzer Prize? How does winning such a prestigious award affect your writing?*

I was working on *People of the Book* even before I started to write *March*. I'd been struggling quite a bit with the World War II story: It's such a picked-over period and I was looking for a backwater of the war that wouldn't perhaps feel so familiar to readers. That search was leading to a lot of dead ends when I suddenly got the idea for *March* and it was so clear to me how to write that book that I just did it.

The "Pulitzer Surprise," as my then-nine-year-old son so accurately dubbed it, affected my writing only in that it interrupted it for a while by drawing renewed attention to *March*. But after a few weeks of pleasant distraction I was back at my desk, alone in a room, simply doing what I've always done, which is trying to write as best I can, day after day.

Book conservation is hardly a glamorous job, but Hanna's framing narrative is every bit as action-packed and compelling as the stories in the hagaddah's history. What inspired her creation?

Because I like to write with a first-person narrator, getting the voice of the book is everything to me. I'd struggled a lot with my first idea, which was to have the conservator be Bosnian. I love the way Sarajevans express themselves; it's a kind of world-weary, mordant wit overlying an amazing ability to absorb and survive great suffering. But I wasn't getting the voice and the book was stalled as a result. Then I suddenly thought, Well, why shouldn't she be Australian? That's a voice I *can* hear clearly. Hanna came alive in my head and as a result the contemporary story, which I'd originally thought of as merely a framing device for the stories from the past, became much more important.

The scientific resources that Hanna employs to find out more about the book's artifacts are really fascinating. How much of that is drawn from actual research and how much springs from your imagination?

I went to labs. I interviewed scientists and conservators and observed their work. But the book is fiction, not a technical treatise, so experts will be able to spot a place or two where I took some small liberties.

The Jewish people have endured extraordinary trials. How much about this history did you know before writing the book?

Most of it. The whipsaw of Jewish history has fascinated me since I was in junior high.

Who is your favorite character and why?

That's like asking a parent to name a favorite child. Hanna became like a good mate, and I actually miss hanging out with her. But I feel a certain tenderness toward all of the characters, perhaps especially the most flawed ones.

People of the Book *is set in so many different eras. Was it a more difficult book to research and write than your previous novels?*

There was definitely more to research, but it wasn't difficult. I loved the various journeys—actual and intellectual—that it took me on. Seeing the domes and spires of Venice shimmering in the watery morning light; having the great privilege of meeting Servet Korkut, who supported her husband in resisting fascism; watching Andrea Pataki painstakingly take apart the real Sarajevo Haggadah—these are experiences of a lifetime.

Will the book be published in Bosnia and, if so, what kind of reception do you anticipate?

I hope it will. I have no idea about the reception. It's very presumptuous, what I do—meddling around in other people's history. When I went back to Eyam, the plague village, I fully expected a faction of the townsfolk to want to have me clapped in the stocks. (They still have them there.) To my intense relief, the people I met had really embraced the book. I had the same feelings of trepidation when I went to read *March* in Concord, Massachusetts. I was delighted to be met at the reading by Louisa May Alcott (Jan Turnquist, director of the remarkable Orchard House Museum, in costume), who thanked me for being one of the very few who had tried to understand and appreciate her father. So I hope the people of Bosnia will forgive me for taking liberties with their history and see the book as a tribute from someone who was inspired by the remarkable spirit of Sarajevo.

What are you working on now?

I'm just at the earliest stages of exploring an intriguing story set very close to home, on Martha's Vineyard. It concerns people who lived on this island in 1666, one of my favorite years, and seems to have just the right mix of knowns and unknowables— a lovely incomplete scaffold to build on.

QUESTIONS FOR DISCUSSION

1. When Hanna implores Ozren to solicit a second opinion on Alia's condition, he becomes angry and tells her, "Not every story has a happy ending" (p. 37). To what extent do you believe that their perspectives on tragedy and death are cultural? To what extent are they personal?

2. Isak tells Mordechai, "At least the pigeon does no harm. The hawk lives at the expense of the other creatures that dwell in the desert" (p. 50). If you were Lola, would you have left the safety of your known life and gone to Palestine? Is it better to live as a pigeon or a hawk? Is there an alternative?

3. When Father Vistorni asks Rabbi Judah Ayreh to warn the printer that the Church disapproves of one of their recently published texts, Ayreh tells him, "Better you do it than to have us so intellectually enslaved that we do it for you" (p. 156). Do you agree or disagree with his argument? With the way he handled Vistorni's request?

4. What was it, ultimately, that made Father Vistorini approve the haggadah? Since Brooks leaves this part of the story unclear, how do you imagine it made its way from his rooms to Sarajevo?

5. Several of the novel's female characters lived in the prefeminist era and certainly fared poorly at the hands of men. Does the fact that she was pushing for gender equality—not to mention saving lives—justify Sarah Heath's poor parenting skills? Would women's rights be where they are today if it weren't for women like her?

6. Have you ever been in a position where your professional judgment has been called into question? How did you react?

7. Was Hanna being fair to suspect only Amitai of the theft? Do you think charges should have been pressed against the culprits?

8. How did Hanna change after discovering the truth about her father? Would the person she was before her mother's accident have realized that she loved Ozren? Or risked the dangers involved in returning the codex?

9. There is an amazing array of "people of the book"—both base and noble—whose lifetimes span some remarkable periods in human history. Who is your favorite and why?

For more information about or to order other Penguin Readers Guides, please e-mail the Penguin Marketing Department at reading@us.penguingroup.com or write to us at:

Penguin Books Marketing Dept.
Readers Guides
375 Hudson Street
New York, NY 10014-3657

Please allow 4–6 weeks for delivery.
To access Penguin Readers Guides online, visit the Penguin Group (USA) Inc. Web site at www.penguin.com and www.vpbookclub.com.

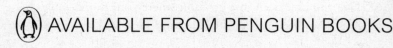

A *New York Times* Bestseller

Caleb's Crossing

Once again, Geraldine Brooks takes a remarkable shard of history and brings it to vivid life. In this luminous tale of passion and belief, magic and adventure, Brooks transports readers to 1660s Martha's Vineyard and Cambridge to tell the story of the intertwined fortunes of the first Native American to graduate from Harvard College and a restless and curious young woman struggling to find her place in the world. What triumphs and turmoil will each have to endure in embracing their new destinies?

———

Winner of the Pulitzer Prize for Fiction

March

From the beloved classic *Little Women*, Geraldine Brooks has animated the character of the absent father, Mr. March, and crafted a story "filled with the ache of love and marriage and with the power of war upon the mind and heart of one unforgettable man" (Sue Monk Kidd). Brooks follows Mr. March as he leaves his family behind to aid the Union cause in the Civil War. His experiences will utterly change his marriage and challenge his most ardently held beliefs. A lushly written, wholly original tale steeped in the details of another time, *March* secures Geraldine Brooks's place as a renowned author of historical fiction.

———

National Bestseller

Year of Wonders

In 1666, an infected bolt of cloth carries plague from London to an isolated village, where a housemaid named Anna Frith emerges as an unlikely heroine and healer. Despite making the extraordinary choice to quarantine themselves within the village boundaries to arrest the spread of the disease, death reaches into every household. As the villagers turn from prayers to murderous witch-hunting, Anna must confront the deaths in her family, the disintegration of her community, and the lure of illicit love. As she struggles to survive, a year of plague becomes instead *annus mirabilis*, a "year of wonders."